ALONE IN THE DARK

Jenna tried to tell herself that a man like Nick, a man who'd been on his own and had traveled the world couldn't have been lonely when he'd been doing what he'd loved.

But what about now?

Now Jenna understood too much about loneliness not to recognize it in another person's posture and in his voice. "Don't go, Nick."

He turned slowly, first his head and shoulders, and finally the rest of him. Neither of them moved. It only seemed that way.

"I don't think it would be a good idea for me to stay."

"And why is that?" she asked quietly.

"Because it's dark and we're the only two people awake." His voice dipped lower. "And you're right there, close enough to . . ."

Nick's sensuality level was every bit as deep as his voice, and every bit as unsettling. She couldn't see his eyes plainly. Instinctively she knew his gaze had settled on her mouth.

"Close enough to what, Nick?"

"Close enough," he said, still not moving, "to kiss you . . ."

"It wouldn't be the first time." She closed her mouth and held her breath as she waited for his response.

After a long, nearly tangible silence, he said, "So you remember that kiss."

"A woman never forgets a kiss like that . . ."

Books by Sandra Steffen

THE COTTAGE

DAY BY DAY

317 BEULAH STREET

Published by Zebra Books

317 BEULAH STREET

Sandra Steffen

ZEBRA BOOKS
KENSINGTON PUBLISHING CORP.
http://www.kensingtonbooks.com

For my five greatest blessings, my husband and our four sons, the basis, in one way or another for the heroes in each of my books.

Chapter One

God Almighty, it was hot.

Only hell could be hotter. Maybe he'd died and gone there.

Nicholas Proffit considered the possibility. Perhaps the fever and the weakness in his muscles were products of hell, but the ruts in the mountain road and the heavy, humid air streaming through the Jeep's windows were part of ordinary life in Central America.

He forced his eyes to remain open, his body in an upright position, his hands gripping the steering wheel. He'd set out to find a hospital hours ago. The farther he went, the hotter and worse things got. The heat came from everywhere. It beat down from a cloudless, merciless sky, radiated upward from the moist earth, and outward from the rusty Jeep's engine.

Heat. Dirt. Fever. Those three stark realities mixed like muddy water inside his skull every time the Jeep bounced through a pothole. He'd had some close brushes with death before. Nick wasn't sure he was going to pull through this time.

His hand shook as he removed it from the steering wheel. Slowly, he groped the seat next to him. He felt his duffel bag, his gear, his camera. Finally, a tattered envelope crinkled beneath his fingers.

He had the letter.

He breathed. He kept his eyes straight ahead. And he held on.

The weakness had started ten days ago. At first, he thought it was something he ate or drank. Strange, because he'd always had an iron stomach. He'd spent most of the winter photographing the people and animals of Central America. It was possible it was his best work. Or it might stink. By the time he'd finished, he'd been too delirious to know the difference. Delirious or not, the photo spread had taken a long time.

Nick Proffit didn't care about time. He lived by his own rules, set his own pace. The fever had a pace all its own. Every day, his condition worsened. And then, the day before yesterday, the letter from the States had arrived via a fellow photographer. Nick smoothed his hand over the envelope that had taken two years to catch up with him. Two years.

The Jeep bounced through another rut. On his left was a Salvadoran farmhouse, called a wattle hut, its walls made of interwoven branches covered with mud. The late afternoon light was perfect. If he'd been well, he would have stopped to take pictures. The poor farmer who lived in the hut with his family would have tried to help, but Nick needed a hospital. He wasn't afraid to die. In a way, he was even prepared for it. But he wasn't in any hurry.

He crested a hill. There, in the distance, was a village. He stopped in the middle of the road on the outskirts of town where chickens pecked the ground and an old man selling cornmeal cakes was resting in the shade of a roadside stand.

"Hospital?" Nick's voice was nothing more than a dry rasp.

The man pointed a gnarled finger toward a building a blessed few hundred feet away. Nick grasped the steering wheel, pushed in the clutch, and coasted the rest of the way. Stopping near the building, he slung the strap of his camera over one shoulder, tucked the letter in his pocket, and staggered inside.

The strong smell of disinfectant let him know he was in the right place, but he was only vaguely aware of the shadowy interior of a large room containing beds, and an overhead fan that made him dizzy. A middle-aged nurse gasped when she saw him. Nick didn't blame her. He'd been told he had the face of an outlaw. Five days' worth of whisker stubble didn't help. Neither did a raging fever.

She called for assistance, then helped him to a bed. He willingly handed over his watch, his wallet and whatever loose change was left in his pockets, but held fast to his camera and the letter from home. Clutching his two most prized possessions, he fell onto the narrow cot, and closed his eyes.

"Señor, wake up. You hear me?"

Rosita? Nick tried to open his eyes. They wouldn't budge. If his father caught him lazing in bed, there would be hell to pay. It seemed there was always hell to pay where his father was concerned.

"Señor. Wake up. You must try."

Nick was trying. How many times had the beloved family housekeeper saved him from his father's wrath? Poor Rosita. He didn't make it easy for her.

The sheets were sweat-soaked and scratchy. Rosita laundered the bedding every Wednesday and Saturday, come hell or high water. He tried to remember if this was her week off.

A moan echoed in his ears. It must have come from him.

"Señor? You want for me to send for priest?"

Nick surfaced enough to realize that he wasn't lazing in his bed in Georgia. And it wasn't Rosita bathing his face with cool water, but the nurse who had been caring for him at the small hospital in El Salvador. Out of respect for her, he didn't swear out loud, but a dozen expletives found their way inside his head. Whether he came face-to-face with his maker soon, as this woman seemed to expect, or fifty years from now, he wouldn't be using anyone as a buffer.

He opened his eyes a crack. "No . . . priest."

In broken English, the nurse asked if there was anyone else he wanted her to call. He gave his head the barest shake. His energy sapped, oblivion claimed him once again.

The next time he surfaced, there was an IV in his arm, and the woman was reading to him. Nick could speak Spanish, but the words she was reciting were in English. He forced his eyes open, and tried to wet his lips. His tongue was too dry. Two other patients were talking in hushed whispers on the other side of the room as he felt for the pocket of his pants. His jeans were missing. He panicked. "My . . . letter?"

"Do not worry. Your letter, it is here." The nurse brought the tattered envelope from a small stand next to his cot.

"How long . . . have I been . . . here?"

"Two days."

Two days, and he remembered nothing. His eyes closed again. "Read it . . . to me . . . *por favor?*"

Paper crinkled. Slowly, the nurse began to read the words Nick already knew by heart.

Dear Nick,
    The letters Craig wrote to you over the years always came back, address unknown. Perhaps it's futile to try again, but I don't know what else to do. I have bad news, sad news. Craig died, Nick.

Although the kind nurse reading the letter spoke with a heavy Spanish accent, Nick was imagining the soft southern lilt of Jenna's voice telling him of his only brother's shocking aneurysm and death.

We're doing okay, all things considered. We know you're out there, somewhere, because we see your photographs. The piece you did on life on the Amazon was wonderful. There are no large animals there, really? Craig and Brandon liked the wombats and koalas from the spread you did in Australia last year. Benji loved the crocodiles. You have no idea how much this concerns me. My favorites are still the early photographs you took of the moss-laden oaks and wisteria growing in every garden, and along nearly every road right here in Georgia.

The words conjured up memories and sensations of gentle breezes, the sway of a wooden swing on a wide verandah, the strong taste of sour mash whiskey, and ah, yes, the heady scent of wisteria that hung on the air every spring.

The letter ended with, *I'm sorry, Nick. God bless, Jenna.*

He wondered why she was apologizing. Was she sorry for being the one to tell him his brother was dead? Or was she sorry for choosing the better man all those years ago?

No. She wasn't sorry about that. She'd loved Craig. There had never been any doubt about that. So of course she was truly sorry he had died. Nick was sorry, too, the biggest shock of all.

His stomach was on fire; his body, too. He was so weak it hurt to think. Every muscle ached. And yet his mind was on regrets.

He went perfectly still.

"Señor? You want me to bring priest now?"

He shook his head weakly. "Bring me . . . water . . . broth . . . medicine. Must get . . . well. Have to go home."

* * *

No other place in the world smelled like southern Georgia in May. Nick should know. He'd been just about everywhere else. He'd ridden camels across deserts and had photographed goats on the sides of mountains. He'd been chased by polar bears in the Arctic and had slept in trees in the rain forest.

No other place in the world looked exactly like southern Georgia, either. If houses had a gender, surely it was female. New York had its voluptuous brownstones, San Francisco its painted Victorian duchesses. The antebellum-style houses sitting back from the roads leading to Harmony Hills, Georgia, were boxy, buxom ladies with wide verandahs, huge lawns, and fences, miles and miles of fences.

Nick knew he was nearing town when he passed one of the largest houses in the county. Amy Jo Miller had lived there when they'd been kids. She and her brother, Aaron, were direct descendants of Colonel Daniel Miller, who founded the town in 1835. Like most "nice" girls, Amy Jo had been forbidden to talk to Nick. Her older brother, Aaron, had been friends with Craig, and once, Nick had let Craig talk him into tagging along. Aaron hadn't been any too happy about it. "What's *he* doing here?" he'd sneered.

"Come on, Aaron," Craig had said. "Nick's okay. You'll see."

Aaron Miller had looked down at Nick. With a smirk, he'd said, "Shouldn't you be in Special Ed?"

As usual back then, Nick had reacted first and thought later. Much later.

He wondered if Aaron's nose still bore the slight bump where Nick had busted it with his bare fist. It had been the talk of Harmony Hills for weeks.

Harmony Hills. Nick shook his head. In all his travels, he'd never come across a town more poorly suited to its name. There were stinking few hills in Harmony

Hills, and damned little harmony. Most people dropped the Hills, and called it simply, Harmony. Nick could think of a lot of names a hell of a lot more fitting. Sniveling Flats. Snobsville. Two-Face Place.

It had been more than a month since he'd stumbled into the hospital in El Salvador. He'd been back in the States nearly a week, in Georgia since yesterday. The trip had exhausted him, so he'd holed up at a friend's beach house near Savannah last night and most of today.

He rolled down his window and took a deep breath. The scents of long-needled pines and moist, red-brown earth combined on the humid evening air. It smelled like . . .

Georgia.

It smelled like home. Homesickness washed over him. Didn't that beat all.

He'd left town when he was eighteen. In the years since, he'd come back only twice. Once, for Craig and Jenna's wedding. The second time had been nearly four years ago, for his mother's funeral. His father hadn't spoken a word to him. But Craig had been genuinely glad to see Nick. And Jenna had been kind. So kind, it had made him ache all over again.

The kids had been little then, and not terribly concerned about losing a grandmother who'd given up on life long before they'd even been born. He wondered how Brandon and Benji had taken their father's death two years later. How much did six and seven-year-olds understand?

Nick had understood a shitload by the time he was their age. He'd known he'd been born second, and for reasons beyond his control, he'd been a disappointment to his father. Because of that, he'd made certain he was an embarrassment, as well.

The new sign at the edge of town read, WELCOME TO HARMONY HILLS. POPULATION: 15,000, just as the old one had. He used to say there were two ways out of Harmony. The first was to escape. The second was to die.

Nick slowed as he passed the cemetery. The heaviness in his chest came out of nowhere, cutting off his breathing. It turned out the Proffit brothers had each taken a different route out of town.

He drew to a stop at the main four-corners, and sat waiting for a woman to cross the street. "Nick Proffit, is that you?"

Nick came to with a start. Squinting against the long rays of the evening sun, he studied the woman hurrying around to the sidewalk six feet away. Although she looked familiar, it took him a second to place her face. When he did, he smiled. "Well, Cherie Marie Bradley. You're lookin' as good as ever!"

She sashayed closer. "Sure I do. Last I recall, you told me I looked like I'd been played with hard and put away wet."

It reminded Nick that he hadn't always been kind. "And I remember getting my foot stomped on for saying it."

Her pout turned into a broad grin at the memory. Cherie was one of those girls who'd developed early, and had made the most of it. She wasn't the kind of girl whose father ever forbade her to talk to Nick, or any other boy, for that matter. In seventh grade, the guys had made up a limerick. "Cherie Marie, come climb my tree." They'd thought the hand gestures that had accompanied it had been brilliant.

Adolescent boys could be such asses.

Today, Cherie looked softer of body and harder of face. She wore her dark hair short, her makeup heavy, and her clothes tight. She wasn't wearing a ring. "I figured you'd have a husband and a house full of kids by now, Cherie."

"Three kids, two dogs, a trailer and one ex-husband." She moved her shoulders in a way that called attention to her breasts in that universal language certain women used to let a man know what was on her mind. "What are y'all doing back in town? We figured if Craig's funeral didn't bring you back, nothin' would."

Nick was aware of a sudden, harsh stillness. Birds were chirping and the wind was blowing. So it wasn't coming from outside. Craig was dead. Nick had known it for a month. And yet the knowledge twisted and turned inside him. Closing the door on his mind, he said, "I'm on my way over to Magnolia Drive to see Jenna and the boys."

"Magnolia Drive?" Looking at him more closely, she said, "Didn't you know?"

"Know what?"

"They don't live there anymore, Nick."

Jenna and the kids moved?

"Jenna lives over on Beulah Street." She gave him simple directions, then said, "You planning to stay in Harmony long?"

He shrugged. "I doubt it."

Drawing herself up and away, Cherie wet her lips. "My last name's Martin now. I'm in the book."

Nick knew exactly what she was offering. She smiled wistfully, and he thought, *She's not ugly.* If life had been kinder to her, she might have been pretty in her own way. Her eyes were even blue. It wasn't her fault they weren't the right shade.

He told her good-bye. A matter of minutes later, he pulled his SUV to a stop in front of a big house on Beulah Street. Staring at the structure, Nick thought there had to be some mistake. By fate or design, the class system in Harmony had been firmly in place long before he'd been born thirty-four years ago. Anybody who was anybody lived on streets named after trees or generals. The "other" people lived on streets named for old ladies. What in the world would Jenna and the kids be doing in this big old house on Beulah Street?

Like a lot of houses that had been made into apartments thirty years ago with little regard to form, this house was a hodgepodge. The roof showed where it had been patched. Half of the front porch had been painted. The can of paint sat on the top step as if waiting for someone to finish the job. There was a weedy flower garden to the right of the steps. A path had been trampled in the overgrown grass all the way from the moving van parked in the driveway, to the front door. The house may have been historic, but it was more ramshackle than antebellum. A hell of a lot more.

He couldn't imagine Jenna living here. Cherie must have been mistaken.

He shut off the Land Rover's engine, and climbed out. He would knock on the door, and ask whoever answered if they knew where Jenna Proffit and her sons lived now. Halfway to the porch, he noticed pansies spilling out of a row of enamel tea kettles on a bench in the yard. Too bad he'd left his camera in the car.

His foot was on the bottom step when another splotch of color caught his eye. Hunkering down, he peered into the azalea bushes where a sandy-haired urchin of seven or eight was hiding.

There was a smudge of dirt on the boy's face, but it was the expression in the round brown eyes studying Nick unhurriedly, feature by feature, that kept Nick from speaking first. The boy tipped his head slightly and in a tone of voice that called 'em like he saw 'em, said, "You'all look like my daddy."

A lump came and went in Nick's throat. "So do you. What are you doing under there, Benji?"

A change came over the boy. "Nothin'."

Which of course meant something. "Does this nothing you're doing involve hiding from somebody?"

"What's it to ya?"

Another Proffit with an attitude. Nick almost smiled. "It's no skin off my nose. Is your mom around?"

"She's in the house, dancin' around the kitchen with

a check from the new tenants. Go 'round back. But don't tell her you saw me."

Nick didn't remember the last time he'd been bossed around by an eight-year-old. "Sorry, but I'm not making any promises I can't keep."

Suddenly, a voice, sultry and cultured and very southern carried to the front yard. "Benjamin James Brannigan Proffit!"

The boy's eyes grew round, and his bravado evaporated.

Nick straightened. Giving his head time to stop swimming, a by-product of a lingering weakness that was improving far too slowly to suit him, he said, "Come on, sport. Might as well go face the music."

Craig's younger son crawled out of his hiding place with agility, strength, and great reluctance. With a sigh that was bigger than he was, Benji set off toward the backyard. Looking over his shoulder to make sure Nick was following, he said, "Just let me do the talkin'."

Nick surprised himself by laughing.

Benji was quiet as he led the way through the side yard. Coming to an abrupt stop just around the back corner of the house, the child called, "Mom, Brandon! Look who's here."

Nick was vaguely aware of more moss-draped trees, of long stretches of dappled shade and a flagstone patio. Most of his attention was on the boy and the woman who looked up from the textbook on a glass-topped table. Nick couldn't help staring. Tall for a nine-year-old, Brandon had dark hair, like Jenna's. Both boys had brown eyes, like their father. Jenna's were an extraordinary Nordic blue. It was Nick's favorite color.

"It's Uncle Nick!" Benji exclaimed. "Remember him?"

Jenna Brannigan Proffit drew her hand from the pocket of her flowered skirt. From there, her fingers somehow fluttered to her neck. Realizing how silly she must look, she smoothed her collar. And then, drawing herself up to her full height, she sauntered toward her brother-in-law.

He stood looking at her, his weight, what there was of it, on his right leg, his thumbs hitched in the front pockets of low-slung pants. She had never known anyone who could stand so still.

She waited to speak until she was close enough to do so quietly. Her gaze on his, she said, "Hello, Nick."

Chapter Two

Jenna went up on tiptoe, brushing her lips across her brother-in-law's lean cheek. In the front yard, a cart rattled and a ramp clanked; the movers were making a lot of racket. All was quiet in the backyard. Nick was the quietest of all. He remained completely motionless, too, until she'd glided back to the low heels of her shoes and had moved an appropriate distance away.

There was a spark of an indefinable emotion in his eyes as he said, "I'll bet you're surprised to see me."

Over the years, his voice had lost all but the faintest southern inflection. Like the rest of him, it contained a tinge of awkwardness, as if he didn't know what to say next. His gaze was steady though and, as always, didn't miss a thing.

"A surprise, yes," she said, "but a nice sort of surprise." She was certain he'd noticed her simple skirt, her chipped nail polish, the fact that it had been hours since she'd combed her hair. Nicholas Proffit always made a woman aware of how she looked. Raising her chin just enough to meet his gaze more directly, she said, "It's been a long time."

He stilled, and grew even more serious. "Your letter went halfway around the world and back before it reached me in Central America. It took almost two years. I came as soon as I could."

She wanted him to know that he didn't need to defend himself, not with her. "I always wondered if that letter ever reached you. The others came back to us, eventually, but that one never did. When you didn't reply, I assumed you had a good reason. Welcome home."

His smile was slow and stark and white, and called to mind simpler times, a long, long time ago. She was aware of her sons, watching. She was equally aware that there was an aura about Nick, a haughtiness mixed with a hint of danger. Somewhere in the configuration was an endearing kindness. He wore loose-fitting khakis and a white cotton shirt, the sleeves rolled up. His medium-brown hair was thick and windblown and appeared freshly cut. Craig's had been nearly the same color. Nick had the wide Proffit mouth and angular jaw, too, but his green eyes were a throwback from who knows where.

"I see you've already been reacquainted with Benji." Her younger son suddenly showed a keen interest in the dirty toe of his new Nikes. She'd left the boys on the patio with strict instructions to do their homework while she did the supper dishes. Brandon's math was nearly done. Benji hadn't even opened his spelling book.

It was uncanny the way Brandon chose that moment to nudge his way into the circle. "Hi, Uncle Nick. I told Mom 'n Benji you were probably in the jungle somewhere, or else the desert. Right, Benj?"

Benji eased on around to his brother's side as if he thought that as long as his mother couldn't see him, she would forget that he hadn't done what he'd been told. Brandon often ran interference for his younger brother. Craig used to do that for Nick.

She glanced at Nick, and caught him looking at her. His expression was severe, causing her to wonder if he'd been thinking the same thing. He was the first to look away.

She'd never completely understood Nick. Perhaps no one had. But she'd always liked him, even when it seemed as though she and Craig were the only ones who did.

Off the hook for now, Benji said, "Did you take pictures of any pythons, Uncle Nick?"

Lowering carefully to his haunches, Nick looked deep into Benji's eyes, and then into Brandon's. Once again, Jenna witnessed an almost immortal patience inside Nick. She'd read the newspaper and magazine articles about the world-renowned photographer Nicholas Proffit and his artistic talent. Talent like his *was* rare, but she believed the gentling of his gaze, and the way he could beam it at a creature, be it completely helpless or utterly dangerous, was the real power behind his success.

"Not pythons," he said, "but I got some great pictures and films of a mother boa constrictor and all fifty of her babies."

"Fifty-one snakes in one place." Brandon shuddered.

Not Benji. He was completely impressed and totally enthralled. "You counted 'em? Cool."

The smudge of dirt on his face added to his wide-eyed wonder. It reminded Jenna just what a handful he'd been lately. She and Nick both smiled, though. This time, Nick waited a little longer to look away.

"How long are you staying, Uncle Nick?"

Nick started at Brandon's question, then ran a hand through his hair. Jenna thought he looked pale for a man who'd recently returned from a tropical climate.

"A few days, maybe," he finally said.

"Only a few days?" the boys complained in unison.

Nick's throat convulsed, but he eased into a small smile. "Maybe longer. It depends."

Jenna saw the way he looked around her yard, taking everything in. He was going to want to know what had happened, why she'd moved, why she was wearing a skirt off the sale rack at Wal-Mart. Craig had been his brother. Nick deserved answers. Later, after the boys were in bed, she would do her best to tell him.

She gestured to the table behind them. "If you three would like to have a seat, I'll go see to some snacks."

Behind her, iron chairs were dragged out across hundred-year-old flagstones. Her hand on the door-knob, Jenna imagined the three of them looking at one another. Brandon was the first to speak. "Our dad died."

Eyes straight ahead, she opened the door quietly.

"Yeah," she heard Nick say. "I got a letter from your mom a little more than a month ago. I bet you guys miss him, but it looks like you're doing okay."

She swallowed the lump in her throat. He was right. They were doing okay. In fact, she and the boys were going to be just fine. For a while there, she hadn't been so sure.

"Isn't this the best house?" Benji asked. "The back-yard's way better than our old one."

Since there was no return on the screen door, Jenna reached around to close it by hand. She glanced at the three Proffits seated a dozen feet away. Somehow she'd known Nick would be the only one looking at her. He was probably thinking that, no matter what Benji said, this house was a far cry from the estate on Magnolia Drive. Taking charge with quiet assurance, she raised her chin slightly, then hurried toward the kitchen.

The longer the shadows in the backyard grew, the more the insects buzzed. Swatting at the most bother-some of them all, the mosquitoes, Benji and Brandon asked their uncle Nick all about his travels.

Nick knew what they wanted, and he gave it to them, regaling them with stories of some of the funnier mishaps he'd encountered in the wild. From time to time, the boys launched into their own daring tales. Nick noticed that Jenna didn't prod them to hurry, to be quiet, or to sit up straight, as Nick's mother had. She reminded them to chew with their mouths closed but gave them free reign to the conversation. In fact, other than pouring more drinks and joining in the laughter now and then, she kept a low profile, letting him and the kids have center stage. She was quiet, but not awkward, as warm, welcoming and accepting as she'd always been.

The boys appeared to be happy and well-adjusted. They mentioned their father in passing but didn't say enough to give Nick even an inkling as to what had happened to Craig and Jenna's money and prestige. Taking a sip of the purple liquid in the glass in front of him, Nick wondered if it was possible that Craig might have developed a gambling problem and lost everything. What else could it have been?

Every human being harbored at least one irrational impulse, right? Nick swirled the Kool-Aid in his glass.

Every human being except his brother.

What then? What the hell had happened? And where was Nick's father, the imperial, the imposing, the impenetrable Reginald Proffit?

Benji was the spitting image of the old man, with one huge difference. Benji's laughter reached his eyes. The boy had been a towhead as a toddler. At eight years old, his hair was the color of straw. It would probably darken more, as Craig's and Nick's had, by the time he was grown. Although Brandon's hair was already nearly as dark as his mother's, he looked more like the Proffits than the Brannigans, too. Nick's father always said Proffit genes were dominant, as if that were a good thing, and he was directly responsible. What an ego.

"Does your beverage need more sugar?"

It took Nick a second or two to comprehend Jenna's meaning. He'd been scowling.

She winked. For a moment, he let his guard down and relaxed. Suddenly, it was as if they were kids again. Sometimes, it was still hard for him to believe that she'd chosen him as her friend. She'd been the best part of his childhood, right up until the day she fell in love with his only brother. Who could blame her? Craig had been damn close to perfect.

They'd been sitting out here for nearly an hour, eating store-bought cookies served from a silver platter and drinking grape Kool-Aid from Waterford crystal. He'd always thought of Jenna as softly southern, and always, always a lady. Only Jenna could manage to look more beautiful at thirty-four. She also looked tired, as if she'd put in a long day. She was still a lady, despite the wink, the inexpensive clothes, the disarray of her wavy hair.

She made him feel anything but gentlemanly.

He wasn't a well man, and it had nothing to do with exotic illnesses and mind-numbing fevers. There was no excuse for it, really. There had been little between them. Little, other than friendship, and a few minutes when he'd stepped over the line. It shouldn't have happened, but had, and in happening it had seared its way into his memory.

"Hear that, Uncle Nick?" Benji asked, calling Nick's attention back to him. "The spring peepers are startin' to sing. I know what tree they're in. You wanna see, and maybe take their picture?"

Benji's eyebrows shot up a split-second before Brandon nudged him. It was comical, really, the way those two commiserated. They both held their breath, right up until the moment Jenna said, "Those spring peepers only sing when it's getting late. It's bedtime, you two."

Brandon and Benji groaned.

"How much of your homework did you boys get done?"

"All but the last problem," Brandon answered.

"How about you?" she asked Benji.

He said something that sounded like "none" into his hand.

"It's too late to do it tonight."

The boy brightened.

"You can do it in the morning."

His face fell.

"Now," she said firmly, "you two had better hit the shower."

They left the table, grumbling under their breath. Jenna rose, too, automatically gathering the dishes onto the tray. She finally looked at Nick, the silver tray held loosely in her hands between them. "As soon as they're settled down for the night, we can talk."

He nodded, and she disappeared inside the house.

She was straightening the kitchen when Nick joined her. Somewhere, pipes rattled and two boys squawked and laughed. Nick leaned a hip against the counter and said, "Those two could give lessons in the three *C*s."

"Cajoling, coercing and covert maneuvers." Jenna spoke without looking up from the glass she was drying. "Craig used to say that. I'd forgotten."

Nick looked away from the fleeting sadness that crossed her face. For the span of one heartbeat, jealousy burned inside him. For the duration of that same heartbeat, he wished he could at least hate his dead brother.

He had to say something. Unsure where to start, he looked around. "How long have you lived here?"

"More than a year and a half now."

He digested the information. Something didn't add up. He'd expected Jenna to be rolling in clover, financially at least. Why was she living in an apartment house in need of repair? Where was the paid help?

"Don't you want to ask about Craig?"

He studied her, and finally said, "Did he suffer, Jenna?"

She put the last glass in the cupboard, folded the towel and then hung it over the handle on the oven door. "The doctors don't think so. I like to believe they're right. He complained of a headache that morning. You knew Craig. He didn't get headaches. And he rarely complained. But he went to the office, and I assumed it went away. They called me later that afternoon. Craig had collapsed at his desk and was being rushed to the hospital. He was in a coma by the time I arrived. He had an aneurysm in his brain, and slipped away the following morning."

Nick didn't have to ask if she'd been there. It didn't take a great imagination to picture the hospital, the tubes and machines, Jenna holding Craig's limp hand while he took his last breath. It had been two years, and Nick hadn't so much as sensed his brother's passing.

"I was bereft, in shock, beyond words," she said.

Nick could picture that, too. His father would have been even more devastated, for Reginald Proffit had placed all his hopes, dreams and aspirations on his firstborn son's shoulders.

He didn't want to think about his father. Instead, Nick studied the way the waning evening light filtered through the kitchen window. The cabinets looked original. That wasn't necessarily a good thing. The counters were worn, the sink was cast-iron, the refrigerator a noisy old number that had seen better days.

Maybe Craig and Jenna lost their other house and life savings in the stock market. He couldn't imagine Craig taking that kind of gamble, but it was possible, Nick supposed.

"What does my father have to say about you and the kids moving here?"

She opened her mouth to speak.

Nick rushed on. "Don't get me wrong. I don't have a problem with apartment houses. Hell, I live out of a duffel bag half the time. And in caves, huts, hovels the other ha—"

"Reginald is dead, too, Nick."

Suddenly, Nick's gaze was on Jenna, boring into hers. He felt a lot of things. The greatest was shock. Remorse and sorrow didn't even enter into the spectrum.

His father was dead. That only brought more questions. If the ornery, condescending old bastard had died, Jenna and the boys should have inherited a small fortune. Unless he'd died before Craig, and all his money was gone, too.

"When?" Nick asked.

She took a deep breath before answering. "He had a heart attack four weeks after Craig's funeral." She was quiet for a moment, as if letting the information soak in. "It was a shock to everyone."

"That he had a heart, you mean?" He knew it was a nasty thing to say. As far as Nick was concerned, Reginald Proffit deserved worse.

"That, too," Jenna said.

And it occurred to Nick that he wasn't the only one who was harboring grudges.

Bare feet, what sounded like a dozen of them, slapped the floor. Suddenly, Brandon and Benji bounded into the kitchen in lightweight summer pajamas, their hair wet, their faces clean-scrubbed.

"Teeth brushed?" Jenna asked.

"Yes, ma'am," Brandon said.

"Ears clean?"

"Check," Benji declared.

Their mother smiled. "All right, then. Tell Uncle Nick good night."

"Good night, Uncle Nick," Brandon said.

"Are you sleeping over?" Benji asked.

While Nick was fumbling for an answer or at least an excuse, Jenna said, "Of course, he is." She turned to Nick before he could argue. "You're family, Nick. Why don't you have a seat in the living room?"

She gestured to a room as she passed it, then strolled with the kids into a shadowy hall. Nick meandered to the living room. It looked more like a den and contained furniture from Jenna's other house. Uncertain what to do with himself next, he wandered around the room, then settled in an overstuffed chair the color of butter. He leaned back, listening to the sounds of his brother's family, a boyish voice, a woman's quiet reply. He closed his eyes for a moment, thinking about what might have been.

* * *

"Nick?"

The voice had come from far away. It was soft and Southern, sultry and sexy; he'd heard it often in his dreams, and in his fantasies.

"Ni-i-i-ck? Can you hear me?"

Oh, he could hear her. He could feel her, too, her breath on his cheek, her soft hand nudging his shoulder. He opened his eyes to a mirage. No, not a mirage. Jenna was a flesh-and-blood woman.

A woman who happened to be his brother's widow.

"You're exhausted," she said.

"Evidently."

Jenna had never been put off by Nick's flip replies. Straightening, she placed linens on the arm of another chair and then looked closely at him. Awake now, he was sitting up straight in the chair, knees spread out, hands on his thighs. If she would have stopped there, she might have believed he was completely at ease. It only took one look at his lean face, slightly pale, his lips firmly together, his eyes hooded, and she knew the ease was secondary.

Nick Proffit took nothing for granted. He never had.

"You look done in," she said. "And frankly, so am I. It might be best if this waited until after we've both had a good night's sleep." She strode to the sofa, removed the cushions, and began opening it into a bed.

A few months ago, Nick would have argued. He damned the fever that had sapped his strength. There was nothing he could do about how slowly he was regaining his stamina, except give in to the need to sleep, and give it time.

"What about your reputation, Jenna?"

"What about it?"

Her answer was much more abrupt than he'd expected. "The battle-axes of the society might look askance if they find out I'm sleeping here."

"They can take a flying leap off a short pier."

He chuckled. "Damn, Jenna, I couldn't have said it better myself."

He went to the sofa to help her. Their shoulders brushed. They paused, sharing an awkward moment. He swore to himself. He wanted her, always had, probably always would. He didn't know why she would feel awkward, unless she was wishing he were Craig, which rankled the hell out of him, and brought him to ask, "Did you think I was Craig?"

She looked up at him, her pupils dilated in the semi-darkness, so that only a thin ring of blue surround them. "What?" And then, a moment later, "When?"

"During that first millisecond when I rounded the corner of your yard and you saw me standing there with Benji. Did you think I was Craig?"

He knew better than to ask if she'd wished he were.

"I was struck by the resemblance, but I've always known the difference."

Nick didn't know what to make of her reply. But he wouldn't ask any more questions tonight. They folded out the bed, and together made it up with the linens she'd stacked nearby. When they were done, all that was left was a pair of pajamas Nick assumed had been Craig's. "I sleep in the nude."

He didn't know whether he expected her to turn huffy or blush. Her face was averted as she smoothed a wrinkle from the sheet. "Do me a favor," she said. Was there a smile in her voice? "And don't let Benji know that, or I'll never get him into a pair of pajamas again. He already informed me at supper tonight that having two forks on the table was dumb."

Nick had been a lot of places, had heard a lot of accents. None could compare to the southern cadence in Jenna's speech, *ah* for *I, suppah* for supper.

She straightened, heading for the door. "If there's anything else you need, holler, or make yourself at home and go searching for it yourself, whichever you prefer. Good night, Nick."

"Jenna?"

She looked over her shoulder, one hand flattened along

the old door, her dark hair in tumbled disarray down her back. "Yes?"

"I'm sorry about Craig."

He would have walked across hot coals for the smile she gave him for free. "I know, Nick." She cast one last glance at the pajamas, then quietly left the room.

The following morning, Jenna tucked her blouse into the waistband of her navy slacks. Hurrying, she slipped into her shoes.

She'd gotten the boys up half an hour early so they could finish their homework, and they were all still running late. It didn't help that every five minutes Benji tiptoed to the living room to see if Nick was awake. A glance at her watch told her he was about due. Sure enough, she found him standing in the living room doorway, looking at his uncle. Nick was sound asleep, sprawled on his stomach, arms akimbo, one pillow on the floor. He was covered to his waist, weak morning sunlight spilling across one shoulder. Benji gazed longingly at him, reminding Jenna of a plant on a windowsill, straining toward the sun.

Gently, she took Benji's hand and led him back to the table where his spelling book was open. She thought about the questions Nick was surely going to ask, and the answers that even he wasn't going to like. She considered that notion for a moment, that "even he," and decided that wasn't fair. None of this was Nick's fault. Still, his arrival was another situation she had to deal with.

Brandon wanted more juice. Benji couldn't find his left shoe. Relegating her worries to the back of her mind, Jenna packed lunches with one hand, poured juice with the other, and kept her eyes peeled for the missing shoe.

Mornings were always hectic. Tossing a sleeping

man into the jumble was bound to add to the chaos. Not that Benji didn't come up with plenty other reasons to keep from doing his schoolwork. He'd been a decent student until this year. She hoped it was just a phase, spring fever, something easily remedied. Summer vacation would be starting soon. She told herself to hold on until then.

An out-of-tune screech rent the air. "Merciful heavens . . . I do declare!"

Jenna, Brandon and Benji looked at one another. "Nearly scared me half to death . . ."

"I wonder what Twyla Mae's yellin' about now," Brandon said calmly.

"Probably saw another spider," Benji said, his mouth full of cold cereal.

Nick bounded into the room, living proof that a man could go from deep sleep to wide awake in under three seconds. He was out the door before anyone could say another word.

Benji and Brandon raced after him. By the time Jenna reached the back stoop, Twyla Mae Johnson, the seventy-two-year-old tenant who'd come with the building, was clutching a springy, snake-like contraption with one hand, her throat with the other.

Hat askew, she sputtered. "This just came shooting out of the dryer when I opened it. I do declare, a woman my age is liable to have a heart attack. If I die, it'll be on Suzanne's conscience."

The minute she noticed Nick, her entire countenance changed. Her eyelashes fluttered, color brightened her cheeks, and a soft gasp escaped her. Jenna smiled to herself, wondering if Nick was aware of the effect he had on women. It was hard to tell with him. He was full of a lot of things, but he wasn't full of himself.

Taking a moment to straighten her hat, Twyla Mae said, "Why, you're Reginald Proffit's other boy, aren't you?"

Jenna closed her eyes for a moment, wishing Twyla Mae hadn't used that terminology. Next, she looked at Nick. He hadn't moved, not even to blink.

Holding her breath, she waited for the explosion.

Chapter Three

Jenna waited. A car drove by on the street out front. The only sounds in the backyard were the birds, busy this Friday morning. If there had been an explosion, Nick had turned it inward.

He stood motionless at the bottom of the steps that led to the service porch, his bare feet wet from the dew. His eyes were hooded, his lips pressed into a thin, straight line. His chest was covered by a fine mat of light brown hair that disappeared under the low-slung waistband of wrinkled, lightweight pajamas.

Her heart ached suddenly. It hurt, kindness.

Benji ran to the base of the verandah where he fished his missing shoe out of a low shrub. He put it on, painstakingly tying the laces.

Meanwhile, Twyla Mae was still staring Nick down. "Well, young man," she said. "Cat got your tongue?"

Cold sweat broke out on Nick's chest. Inside, he was a boy again, looking up at a principal, a neighbor, a policeman, even his own father. When Nick's baseball went crashing through old lady Oberlitner's window, the first thing out of the woman's mouth had been, "What do you have to say for yourself, young man? Well? Cat got your tongue?"

Nick had looked up at her, mute.

"Humph," she'd sneered. "You know, Craig would never do anything like this."

As a child, Nick had hated school. Reading gave him the most trouble. He'd had no trouble reading the teachers' measure of him, from the thinning of their lips, to the narrowed, mustard-seed eyes. "You're Craig Proffit's brother," they all said the first day of school every year. By the second day, they were saying, "Why can't you be more like Craig?"

When it came to his father, it wouldn't have mattered if Nick had been Craig's clone. Nick had heard of one-man dogs. Reginald Proffit was a one-son man.

Craig hadn't been a bad brother. Three years older, he'd often covered for Nick. In his own way, he'd tried to shield Nick from their father. Their mother had tried, too. Maybe it would have been enough, if Nick hadn't been so headstrong, so hell-bent on proving to everyone in Harmony that there were two Proffit boys, and the second couldn't be broken, not with his father's belt, not with taunts, not detentions and "or elses." Only one person had come close. To this day, he doubted she'd even known.

He caught a movement from the corner of his eye. A woman with short, dark hair sauntered onto a verandah on the second floor.

Shielding his eyes with one hand, Nick recognized the woman about the same time it occurred to him that he was standing in a backyard in Harmony, Georgia, in the bottoms of his brother's pajamas and nothing else.

"Nick Proffit. You look like hell."

"Suzanne!" Jenna exclaimed.

"Well, he does!"

Nick could see the sass in the other woman's brown eyes all the way from here.

"Don't get me wrong," she said. "I don't have anything against looking at a half-naked man now and then. It's truly a nice change of scenery around here, but I usually prefer men with a little more meat on their bones."

Suzie Hartman had been one of those girls a guy was never quite sure about. She hadn't been forbidden to talk to him, and she'd definitely had a reputation. Nick had never been certain she'd earned it, for she hadn't given just any guy the time of day.

"What happened to you?" she asked. "Malaria? Cancer? The Chinese flu?"

He cocked one eyebrow. "I'm not familiar with the Chinese flu."

She stuck her hands into the pockets of what appeared to be some sort of waitress uniform. "The symptoms include tiredness and draggin' ass."

Brandon giggled, and of course Benji said, "Dragon ass. Get it, Mom?"

Nick tried not to grin. Jenna closed her eyes and shook her head in futility. Nick figured it was a bad joke, but at least it broke the ice. "That about sums it up," he answered.

Jenna looked closely at Nick. Last night, she'd noticed he was pale and thin. A blind woman could see that there was more to his loss of weight than a bad joke or a common germ. And Jenna had never been blind when it came to the Proffit brothers.

Suzanne called, "Has anybody seen Kenzie?"

"She sulkin' again?" Twyla Mae asked. "That girl's harder to keep track of than a hen in a foxhouse these days."

Brandon and Benji ran off to look for their friend. Watching them go, Jenna faced the fact that her younger son wouldn't get to his homework again this morning. She was going to have to speak to his teacher.

"When is the new tenant supposed to arrive?" Suzanne asked.

"Tomorrow." Twyla Mae, who had a sixth sense about someone else's business, momentarily forgot her raised hackles regarding the prank, and added, "That's some mighty fine-looking furniture to be moving into a house on Beulah Street."

Jenna felt Nick's eyes on her. Her newest tenant, Faith Silvers, wasn't the only person whose furniture had been chosen for another kind of house, and another kind of life.

"So, Nick," Suzanne called. "How long are you staying?"

Nick glanced at her. "A week. Maybe a little longer."

"What do you think of the carriage house?" she asked.

"The what?"

"The carriage house. Isn't that where you'll be staying?"

"I don't . . ."

"That's a marvelous idea," Jenna exclaimed. "I don't know why I didn't think of it myself." She spun around. "Don't move," she said to Nick. "I'll be right back."

For once, Nick did as he was told. Suzanne sauntered back into her apartment. The boys had disappeared around the front of the house to search for their friend, the old lady Jenna had called Twyla Mae went back to the service porch and her laundry, leaving what resembled a snake fashioned from a fabric-covered spring dangling over the railing. Apparently, she'd been on the receiving end of a practical joke.

Alone in the backyard, Nick kneaded a sore spot in his shoulder, a by-product of sleeping on the thin mattress. When he'd gotten Jenna's letter, and decided to come home, he hadn't expected her life to include tenants, shared laundry facilities and practical jokes. With a practiced eye, he looked at the backyard in need of cutting, the bushes in need of a good trim. The house itself was tall, like the other houses in the neighborhood, but some of its porches had been eliminated, others made smaller, making the house appear to be in a perpetual crouch.

"I've been fixing up the carriage house."

He turned at the sound of that smooth voice.

Jenna glanced at him on her way by, talking as she went. "I'm sure you'll agree that you'll be a lot more comfortable there than on the foldout couch."

She seemed to expect him to follow.

"The carriage house apartment isn't the Regent, but it's no hovel." She turned the key in the lock.

"Then you're planning to rent this, too?"

"I wouldn't dream of charging you, Nick."

That wasn't what he'd meant, but as long as they were on the subject, he said, "I'm not a charity case, dammit."

The door swung open. "I'll have you know there's a big difference between charity and hospitality."

He surprised himself when he laughed. Jenna was one of the few people on the planet who knew how to deal with his attitude.

"What do you think?" She strode directly to a window, opening it as she talked.

Quietly, Nick followed her. What did he think? He thought the place was small but adequately furnished with more of the furniture that had come out of Craig and Jenna's other house. He was more intrigued by the woman than the apartment. Jenna was peering out the window. She'd been beautiful when they were kids. Back then, she'd been all cream and ivory and gold. Except for the plain wedding band she still wore, the ivory and gold were gone now, replaced by navy slacks and a simple white blouse. Yet there was still something about her that was golden, and soft, like the sunlight spilling across the windowsill.

Beyond her, he could see a portion of the backyard. It looked as if the boys had found Suzanne's daughter. Brandon and the girl were talking under a maple tree. Benji was swinging on an old tire swing, kicking up dirt with one foot.

"Benji reminds me of myself at that age."

She jumped, and Nick realized she hadn't heard him approach. He wondered if he was making her nervous.

"Sometimes," she said quietly, "that scares the breath out of me."

Nick's hands squeezed into fists at his sides.

"And other times it makes me smile."

Just like that, the tension drained out of him.

She turned, letting the thin curtain fall back into place over the window. Somewhere, a branch brushed against the wooden siding. Otherwise, the carriage house was quiet.

How many times had he wished for a quiet room, just him and Jenna? He thought of all the things he'd wanted to tell her but never had. For some reason, he still couldn't. Maybe some things never changed. He didn't tell her how sick he'd been, just how close to death he'd slipped. He didn't tell her how pretty she looked in the morning light, or how he'd gauged every woman he'd ever met against her.

She looked at her watch. "I wish . . ."

He waited for her to finish.

She sighed. "I wish I had time to stay and talk, but if I don't leave in the next two minutes, all three of us will be late."

Nick understood how the kids might be late for school. "What will you be late for?"

"I teach kindergarten at Benji and Brandon's school." She was already at the door. "Will you be all right?"

"I'm a big boy."

"Still, I feel like a terrible hostess."

"I thought you said we're family." Nick rather enjoyed being the one doing the surprising for a change. "Well?"

"You're right."

"Then stop apologizing already."

Humor softened the corners of her blue, blue eyes. "Are you all right, Nick? I mean, all joking aside, you're not sick or dying?"

"I look that good, do I?"

She didn't let him off the hook that easily. Folding

her arms, she waited, and he thought she was probably a very good teacher. He cringed a little at the thought.

"I've had a little brush with a serious fever, but I'm better now. What about you, Jenna?"

"What about me?"

"Are you okay?"

She seemed to be considering the question. "We've fallen on hard times, but we're coming out of them. I'll be home at a little after three. Meanwhile, help yourself to anything you want in the refrigerator. I left the house open. Lock it if you leave, okay?" She left a key on a low table near the door. "I'll see you'all later, Nick."

The *you'all* was nearly his undoing.

He waited to move until she'd gone. In many places here in the South, *you'all* was plural, but here in Harmony, folks said you'all when referring to one person, *all you'all* when speaking of more than one. Strolling to the window, he scoffed. He'd been standing in a quiet house, half-naked, as Suzanne had put it, alone with the woman he'd been fantasizing about most of his life, and all he'd done was remind her that they were family.

He really wasn't well.

He thought about that as he checked out the small apartment. Minutes later, he heard a car drive out of the driveway. Jenna and the kids were on their way to school.

They'd fallen on hard times, she'd said.

And the sky was blue. Film at eleven.

He finished the tour of the carriage house. Closing the door behind him, he returned to the big house. He still didn't know what had happened to Craig and Jenna's money, or his father's either, for that matter. He didn't care about the money. But he did care about Jenna and her sons, and some unfinished business that was long overdue.

She'd said she would be home around three. With time

on his hands, he gathered up his clothes and headed for the shower. By eight-thirty, he was showered, shaved and dressed, and had restored order to the room where he'd slept. Trying to decide what to do next took a little longer. He brought the gear he'd stashed in the Land Rover to the carriage house, but didn't bother putting anything away.

He went outside next. If a person overlooked the slight lean in the back porch and the peeling paint, it wasn't a bad-looking house. In its day it had probably been beautiful. He thought about taking pictures. Instead, he climbed into his SUV, then drove through the quiet streets of town, one arm resting on the lowered window, the radio tuned to a station playing old rock and roll. Dozens of people saw him. Some stared openly. Others were more discreet.

Either way, word was out. Nick Proffit was back in Harmony.

It didn't take Nick long to discover that not much had changed in Harmony, not the businesses, not the houses, not the industrial-strength coffee he bought at the convenience store on the edge of town.

The brochure he'd picked up with his coffee described Harmony Hills as a small city of pre–Civil War grace and timeless dignity. The founding fathers had wanted to name the town Rome, but a group of men up in northwestern Georgia beat them to it a year earlier. According to the brochure, Savannah, located fifty-five miles east of Harmony, had its seaport, Vidalia, a small town to the west, its famous crop of onions, but no southern town had Harmony's soul.

Nick crumpled the brochure and tossed it out the window.

The post office, library and newspaper offices looked exactly as they always had. The fronts of the clothing stores and insurance agencies had been upgraded a little but bore the same names as before. The courthouse was still perched eight steps up on the town square; the law office where Craig had worked was a stone's throw away. Nick wondered if Craig made full partner before he died.

Before he died . . . before he died . . .

Nick had been driving around for the better part of an hour, the taste of bitter coffee on his tongue, a bad feeling in the pit of his stomach, a low-grade headache on the back burner. There wasn't much he could do about the headache or bitter-tasting coffee, but eating might help his stomach.

He considered his options. Anyone who was anyone had breakfast at Chelsea's Café. It had been his father's favorite restaurant, and Nick's least favorite. He'd eaten there the last time he was home, four years ago. Never had he been more aware of the eyes on him. The moment he'd walked in, the volume had lowered as if someone had turned a knob, the patrons' censure thick enough to slice. Nothing new there.

The food had been fair. All right, it had been good, although in all honesty, he hadn't chosen to eat at Chelsea's to get the best food in town. He'd done it to stir things up.

His stomach rumbled. If he ate at Chelsea's today, he would have to saunter past tables where lawyers, doctors, developers and bankers sat. He would have to bear their censure in silence while his body language told them to stick their condescending attitudes where the sun doesn't shine.

Nick put the lever in drive and headed for the truck stop on the outskirts of town. He just wasn't up to stirring things up today. Maybe some things had changed in Harmony, after all.

The truck stop wasn't busy. He sat at a relatively clean booth across from a truck driver named Ed. The eggs were salty, the conversation decent. When he was finished, the pit of his stomach was no longer on fire.

He paid for his meal, left an adequate tip and then sauntered out the way he'd come. Next, Nick headed toward the oldest, most prestigious, and historic district in Harmony. He knew the area called the Heights well. Located between a U-curve in the Canoochee River, it was where he and Craig had grown up.

He parked his SUV at the curb in front of a large, white house sitting far back from the street. The tall columns were as pristine white as ever, the grounds impeccably tended, the shrubs pruned into perfect cones and matching spheres. Nick had seen snake pits that were more inviting.

Several expensive cars were parked in the cement driveway beyond the wrought-iron gate. He didn't know why he got out of the Land Rover and sauntered closer.

A man in a white uniform was putting a sign up near the front courtyard. Nick was in the process of saying hello when someone spoke behind him. "May we help you?"

He turned. And two of the biggest snobs in Harmony gasped.

"I'm afraid this is private property," Lenore Jones stated.

"Is it *your* private property?" he asked.

Nick knew they would have ignored him if they could. "Not ours, per se, but the society's."

No kidding? His father left the estate to the Garden Club, called "the society" by its members? Digesting the information, Nick moved to go around them. "I won't disturb anything."

Abigail Prichart blocked his path. "I'm afraid the house isn't open to the public yet."

She wanted to play dirty? Fine, they could do this her way. Nick rocked back on his heels and crossed his arms, as if settling in for a good, long conversation. "Mrs. Prichart. Mrs. Jones. Nice day."

Silence.

"How's Mr. Prichart?" he asked.

As if not at all confident Nick wouldn't ask how Mr. Prichart's mistress was these days unless she responded, and soon, Abigail Prichart said, "He's fine. We heard you were visiting."

"I'm taking a vacation."

"How nice."

"Isn't it? You've probably seen the spread I did for *National Geographic* in last month's issue."

Abigail was heavyset, Lenore Jones, reed thin. Abigail's hair was white, Lenore's gray. Their expressions were identical. His notoriety was a thorn in the sides of the snobs of Harmony. No one had been more surprised, shocked, and disgusted when Nicholas Proffit, a troublemaker who hadn't even bothered to graduate from high school, had made such a name for himself.

"*National Geographic?* Ah, well, that is," Lenore stammered.

"Actually," Abigail said, "We don't subscribe to the magazine, you see. Therefore, we . . ."

Nick knew damn well they took it as a personal affront every time he failed to mention his roots in interview after interview, magazine after magazine, newspaper after newspaper. To them, it was a slap on the faces of Harmony's finest. Figuratively, of course.

"I have extra copies in the Land Rover."

Lenore and Abigail exchanged a look.

Now *this* was fun. "I'd be happy to get one for each of you. I'll tell you what. I'll even autograph them for you."

"That's very kind of you."

"Isn't it, though?" Nick was pretty sure he saw a small grin on the face of the man who was putting up the large sign. Before it got him in trouble, the groundskeeper moved a discreet distance away.

"But totally unnecessary."

"Abigail's right, of course."

Nick wondered how Lenore and Abigail managed to get the words through the stiff, narrow opening of their lips. "I'll tell you what," he said, flashing them a smile as manufactured as the bright spots of rouge on their cheeks. "I'll send a few copies with Jenna to the next Garden Club meeting."

An even bigger chill settled over the women. "As you can imagine, Jenna no longer attends our meetings."

Nick kept his expression exactly as it had been. The way Lenore had said it sounded as if Jenna was no longer welcome at their meetings. Why the hell not?

Nick's mother had been a member of the Garden Club. Jenna had been a member, too. What had she done to fall out of their social graces? It wasn't as if everyone in the society was wealthy. Although money never hurt, the society was more concerned with lineage and status. Nick called it "the pedigree." Jenna's father had been the bank president, her mother at the helm of several charities. Craig and Jenna had certainly been among the Who's Who in Harmony. He thought about that for a moment, wondering if this had something to do with Craig. "Jenna and the boys took Craig's death very hard. She may have fallen on hard times, but she's . . ."

"Is that what she's calling it?" Abigail's voice shook, her double chin wobbling as she said, "Your poor father! The historic society is dedicating the new library to him. You know what a generous man he was."

It required considerable effort to keep all emotion out of his voice as he said, "I know exactly what kind of man my father was."

His meaning hit its mark, smack-dab between the women's penciled-on eyebrows. *"Hmmff,"* Abigail said.

Lenore mimicked the sentiment. No one looked down their noses better than the self-appointed and self-proclaimed leaders of the society.

"Look, Abigail," Lenore said. "Genevieve Sorenson is motioning for us. We really must hurry."

They rushed away, thick heels clunking across the sidewalk, their purses clutched tightly in their white-knuckled hands. Nick stared after them, lost in thought. Jenna was no longer welcome in the society. He didn't see it as a great loss. Still, something had happened. Whatever it was, it didn't add up. Squinting against the late morning sun, he knew where he had to go next.

A lot of people liked cemeteries. They left Nick cold. Especially this one.

Deep Dell—Christ, who named these places anyway—was well kept and surrounded by an ornate wrought-iron fence that dated back to the turn of the last century. Some of the graves had been here since before the Civil War, still referred to as The Rebellion by the staunchest history buffs and war reenactment people in town. Every Halloween, stories were resurrected of the ghost of an unnamed Union soldier who was said to roam the grounds at night. Every year, the guys from school had tried to get Nick to come here with them at the stroke of midnight to see if the legends were true. There was no way in hell he had ever let anyone talk him into that. The place spooked him enough during the day.

He parked his car on the street near the open gate. Birds twittered, two chipmunks scuttled across the path, and a breeze stirred the leaves on the trees as he walked to the area where they'd buried his mother. There were three headstones now. His father's, the largest of course, was in the middle, his mother's on the left, Craig's on the right.

There was no room for Nick. Not that there ever was.

He stared at the names and dates on the elaborate stones. His mother had been sixty-two. Pauline Proffit had loved Nick. She'd loved both her sons. She might have been a better mother, if she'd been stronger, or if she'd married someone else. Her fate had pretty much been sealed the day she said "I do" to Reginald Proffit, just as Nick's had been sealed the day he'd been born second. In a sense, Craig's had been sealed, too.

Nick had known for a month that his brother had died. It was still hard to fathom. Craig William Proffit would be thirty-seven now. He'd already been gone two years. Looking at the grass covering his brother's grave, he said, "What the hell happened?"

"It was scand'lous, it was."

Nick jumped straight up, then spun around. A stoop-shouldered old man in overalls, a rake in one hand, grinned at Nick.

"Simon. You spooked me."

Seventy if he was a day, Simon Smith had been the caretaker of Deep Dell for as long as Nick could remember. The man had been born with a slightly deformed leg and a low IQ. He grinned most of the time, and answered to Simple Simon.

"Didn't mean to spook ya. Just doin' my job. You won't tell no one, will ya?"

"Who would I tell? Your cemetery looks neat as a pin, Simon."

The old man hooked a thumb through one suspender and grinned some more before pointing to the headstones. "Those there are the Proffits' graves."

Despite the family resemblance, the man obviously didn't recognize Nick, who had left town a long time ago.

"Them people were rich. Rich. The missus was nice. Used to give me candy. Who woulda thought the oldest boy would turn out to be a liar and a cheat."

Nick held perfectly still, holding Simon's gaze the way he would if he were photographing a wary mountain goat. "Craig Proffit cheated?"

Simon rested the handle of his rake in the crook of one arm. "All that money he stole. Can't trust nobody. "Specially not lawyers. That's why I keep my money under my mattress."

Craig stole money?

"It was a scandal, *oo-ee*. Blew up in his face, it did." Simon made an explosion sound with his mouth, then pantomimed it with both hands.

"What do you mean by scandal?" Nick asked.

The sound of a passing car drew Simon's attention.

"Simon?"

"Huh?"

"You said Craig Proffit was involved in a scandal."

"Huh?" Simon's eyes were now on the neat rows of headstones. "I hafta get on over to the next section." Whatever had been on his mind forgotten, Simon shuffled off to do his life's work.

Nick turned back to Craig's grave. Simon had said Craig had been involved in a scandal. That didn't make sense to Nick. He looked at his watch. It was eleven-thirty. Jenna wouldn't be home until three. Nick couldn't wait until three.

He strode to his Land Rover, questions already forming in his mind. He was going to apply the old tried-and-true journalism rule of thumb. He would ask who, when, where, what and how. There would be no theatrics, no high drama.

He drove straight to the elementary school on Elm Street and parked in the lot across from the playground where kids were playing. Ignoring the lead in the pit of his stomach, he told himself he was going to keep this simple. He would stay calm.

The scents of crayons, chalk and floor polish assailed him the instant he went through the front door. By the time he reached the main hall, he smelled the remnants of hot lunches wafting on the air from the cafeteria. Focusing on the questions he would ask, he walked up several steps before turning right into a long corridor.

He stopped at the very last classroom where he could see Jenna through the glass. Her back to him, she was pinning artwork on a bulletin board across the room.

Remember, he told himself. "Ask who, what, where, when and how. Keep it simple. Keep it calm. Keep it to the point."

Cool, calm and collected, Nick opened the door and went in.

Chapter Four

"What did Craig do? Rob the goddamn bank?"

Jenna straightened with such precision Nick could practically hear each vertebra click into place. He cringed. So much for going by the book. He didn't know why he'd ever thought he could keep this simple.

The kids were at recess, and Jenna had been doing whatever teachers did on their lunch hour. She faced him in the empty room, the usual smile of welcoming recognition she doled out to everyone missing, as expected. The majority of her dark hair was secured high on the back of her head, only the most tenacious tendrils curling around her face and collar. It was no use trying to stare her down. His calming, gentling gaze didn't work on Jenna. If she'd been a tiger, and this was the wilds of Africa, he would have been torn limb from limb by now. The idea was only slightly less appealing than waiting for Jenna to say something.

No other woman in the world had ever wrung so many emotions out of him in such a short span of time: dread, yearning, and dammit, shyness. And underlying everything, always, desire.

"Go ahead," he said, eyeing the untucked portion of

her blouse, the perfect little watercolor handprint on one sleeve. "Give me hell and get it over with."

Jenna stared wordlessly at Nick, her breath stuck in her throat. She had never given anyone hell in her life. Her mother had raised her to the old adage *A lady is as a lady does*. Widowed for five years, Roseline Brannigan lived in Florida now. She'd always liked Nick. Even when he was a kid, she'd thought he needed feeding. Right now, Jenna would rather toss him out on his ear.

She felt as if she'd been walking on eggshells since his arrival last night. She'd known she would have to get into difficult explanations. She'd been preparing for his questions all morning. Leave it to him to catch her unaware. "Perhaps you should close the door."

It took him but a moment to reach behind him and shut the door. She used the time to gather her wits. He stood perfectly still again, his feet apart, his back ramrod straight, something fierce glittering far back in his eyes. He'd always been rugged looking, but the weight he'd lost made his features appear stark, as if cut from stone. She had a feeling that somewhere in the deepest, darkest recesses of his mind, he knew exactly what he was doing. She envied him that; in the past two years, she'd second-guessed every decision she'd made.

Replacing the lid on the tin of stick pins, she said, "I can see you're upset."

"Yeah, well, nothing can drain the pleasure out of a day like a morning spent in Harmony."

He'd never liked Harmony. He had good reason to dislike some of the people here, but not everyone here was nasty. In fact, Jenna said, most of the people she came into contact with on a daily basis were decent; many were kind. Nick hadn't come to her classroom to be set straight about the town. He'd come for answers. She would have preferred to do this in the privacy of her own home, but some things couldn't be put off any longer.

"Would you care to sit down?"

He released her from his piercing stare long enough

to glance at the small chairs. "Those contraptions were damned uncomfortable when I was six."

She took a deep breath, letting it all out along with her next question. "Why don't you tell me what you've heard today, and we can go from there."

He stared at her longer than she considered polite, and then he stared a little more. Finally, he went to the sturdy bookshelves that lined the entire wall beneath the windows. Testing the one closest to her desk for strength, he shoved a stack of papers aside then sat down. "You're right. This probably isn't something that should be done standing. What do you say we both take a load off?"

She wasn't surprised he'd noticed her weariness, but she was surprised by the way her throat tightened. What was there about Nick that always made her feel so unsettled?

She lowered to the edge of her desk and perched there, looking at him. He crossed his arms. He didn't smile. And yet, even though his mouth was set in a firm line, it was still the softest thing about him. Maybe the only soft thing about him. Everything else seemed hard and more than a little jaded, just as it had always been. In some perverse and completely unexplainable way, there was something comforting in that.

"Tell me what you've discovered."

His expression held a note of mockery. "I don't know a hell of a lot. I know my old man donated the house to the Garden Club instead of leaving it to you and the boys. What I don't know is where Simon Smith got the idea that Craig was a cheat, or why the old biddies in the society seem to think you have leprosy."

"My, you *have* had a busy morning."

A stare-down ensued.

"You know, Nick, you can intimidate a lot of people with those green eyes of yours, but you don't intimidate me. I know you had a rough time of it as a child. Believe me, I've never understood what you went through better than I have these past two years. If you expect me to feel sorry for you, think again."

He sat up. Then he sat back. Finally, he uncrossed his arms. Settling his hands on his knees, he said, "Go on."

"You're right about your father's house. He put enough money for a college education in trust funds for Brandon and Benji, and donated everything else to charity. The house went to the Garden Club. The rest of his money was split between the college and the Harmony Hills Historic Society. The college is building an addition to the library, and naming it after him."

"I know the old bastard liked to think of himself as a big man in a small town, but why didn't he leave half, hell, all of his money to you and Brandon and Benji?"

Jenna noticed that Nick wasn't the least bit surprised that his father hadn't left anything to him. Whatever tenacious ties they'd once had, had been severed years ago. She didn't want to get into that now. "Why do you think?"

"I think a lot of things. I'd prefer to hear what is."

"All right. Your father didn't want some other man to get part of his fortune in the event I remarry."

He went perfectly still again. She always wondered what he was thinking when he did that.

"Why does Lenore Jones act as if you're white trash?"

Jenna couldn't help cringing at his terminology. She took a steadying breath, the events leading to the ruin of Craig Proffit's good name running through her mind. "Craig had only been gone a week when Maxwell Walker called me, personally, and asked me to come to the office. I was reeling from the funeral, and grappling with the realization that Craig wasn't coming back. In a daze, I drove to the law firm. My mind was so sluggish, I didn't pay much attention to the fact that Maxwell's assistant, Diana Barclay, seemed to have trouble looking me in the eye, but I knew something was gravely wrong when she escorted me into Maxwell's private office. When Craig first went to work there, he called it the lion pit, remember? Anyway, Maxwell wasn't the only one there. Stuart Whitman, who'd been less active in the firm for several years due to health problems, was there, too, along with Oliver Sinclair. As I looked from one to the other, I took a backward step. Before I could take another, Diana left the office, quietly closing the door behind her. I was trapped. I didn't have any idea why I'd been summoned to the firm, but I knew something very bad was about to happen."

The windows were open in Jenna's classroom, the sounds of children's voices raised in play carrying faintly from the playground on the other side of the school. The only other sound in the room was the *tick-tick-tick* of the big clock over the door, and her own slowly drawn breath.

A thousand times she'd relived the scene that had taken place in that austere office that morning. To this day, she could hear the quiet rustle of the leather chair as she lowered to its edge, could smell the beeswax the cleaning service applied to the mahogany paneling every weekend. Maxwell's throat had tensed as he swallowed, his hands shaking slightly as he placed them on his desk.

She would never forget the words that changed her life.

Looking into the distance, Jenna said, "Maxwell Walker put it best when he said there was no easy way to say it. Nothing could have prepared me for the questions he asked next."

"What did he ask?" Nick said.

"First, he wanted to know if I was aware that Craig had been handling a trust fund for Nathaniel Sherman." Jenna turned her head slightly, looking at Nick. "I told him of course I was aware of that. Craig often talked about his clients. Not the details, mind you. He kept those confidential. He liked Mr. Sherman, and had taken over the account when Mr. Whitman went into semire-tirement. Which was what I was telling them when out of the blue, Stuart Whitman said, 'Four hundred thousand dollars is missing from Mr. Sherman's trust fund.'"

Jenna swallowed. "I swear no one said another word for a full minute. I still didn't see what that had to do with me or with Craig until Sinclair mentioned how expensive it must be to renovate the old mansion—turned–apartment house Craig and I had recently purchased. Craig had talked about how we were going to restore it to its original glory."

Jenna was quiet for a moment, recalling how staggered she'd been by the insinuation. Her stomach knotted and twisted at the memory alone. She'd nearly retched that day. She didn't know how she'd refrained, but somehow she'd staved off being ill and insisted that Craig was innocent.

"I could tell Whitman and Sinclair didn't believe me, but Maxwell Walker's expression was less severe. I clung to it, babbling about Craig's innocence. I even went so far as to exclaim that I could prove that every dollar in our bank accounts could be accounted for."

She grew silent.

Finally, Nick said, "And then what happened, Jenna?"

Jenna wrung her hands. Realizing what she was doing, she clasped them tightly in her lap. "Maxwell and I walked across the street. Diana must have called ahead, because the bank president was waiting for us when we arrived. George Benson escorted us into his private office. Our records, Craig's and mine, were brought up on the computer.

"I remember watching Mr. Benson's face as he reviewed the printout. The room was eerily silent. If I could have read auras, Benson's would have been the same muddy brown as his suit. He slid one copy of our statement across the desk to me, and another to Maxwell. A deposit of a hundred thousand dollars had been made to our savings account the day before Craig died."

She saw Nick's eyes narrow, heard his sharply drawn breath. "Then Craig took the money."

It hadn't been a question. She jerked to her feet, torn between being disappointed and being angry. "Of course he didn't take the money."

"But you just said . . ."

Anger won over disappointment. She knew what she'd said, darn it all. She knew what Nick was thinking. "You know what's really sad, Nick, is that if the situation had been reversed, Craig would have believed in you." There was a slight quiver in her voice and in her chin as she whispered, "He would have believed in you, sight unseen, no questions asked." Her voice trailed away, and the room was silent.

Nick held still as stone.

Even in her anger, Jenna regretted her outburst. A slap would have stung Nick less. It had been the equivalent of "Craig would never do such a thing," and "Why can't you be more like Craig?" Nick had heard it all his life. This was the first time he'd heard it from her.

If she could call back the words, she would. She was sorry, but darn it all, Craig hadn't taken that money. He hadn't.

She and Nick stared at each other through the ringing stillness. It might have lasted minutes, or mere seconds. The bell sounded, indicating that recess was over. Nick got up, and quietly left the room.

"Pocket Protector came to Marcel's again today."

Jenna looked up from the towels she was folding and watched Suzanne pour laundry soap into the washer without measuring. It was dark outside; the kids were all asleep. One by one, the stars had appeared, but the three-quarter silver moon was stealing the nightly show.

The windows of the carriage house were dark, and had been all evening. Earlier, Brandon and Benji had asked where their uncle Nick was. Jenna just didn't know. She hadn't seen him since he'd walked out of her classroom at noon.

The barest hint of a breeze fluttered the curtains at the windows. Other than a large moth sweeping its wings across the screen in futile pursuit of the light on the ceiling, and the night peepers serenading them from the dark yard, Suzanne and Jenna were the only residents awake at 317 Beulah Street.

"It's a nice night."

"If I've told you once, I've told you a thousand times," Suzanne grumbled. "There's no such thing as a nice night to do laundry."

Dressed in sandals, shorts and an orange baseball cap, Suzanne looked about nineteen. Brassy and sassy, she could swear with the best of them and got along well with the college kids who frequented her coffee shop. It was difficult to tell that she was really thirty-three, unless you took the time to look deep into her eyes.

Her eyes told a different story.

A lot of people said that the two of them were unlikely friends, but in reality, Jenna was closer to Suzanne than she was to her younger sister, who lived in California. For weeks now, Suzanne had been talking about this man who came into her coffee shop on a regular basis.

"Does your visitor have a real name?"

Suzanne wrinkled up her nose. "He isn't a visitor. He's a customer. And he must have a real name. I doubt any mother would name her child Pocket Protector, although in this case it would explain a lot."

Jenna chuckled as she reached for another towel. Suzanne had been a grade behind her in school, but they'd only known each other well for two years, since shortly after the gossip mill had chewed Craig's good name up and spit it out.

They'd met up again at the principal's office, of all places, the day Jenna was summoned there because

Brandon had gotten into trouble for hitting an older girl. Jenna hadn't known how that could be. Brandon wasn't an aggressive child, and she and Craig had taught him the importance of behaving like a gentleman and treating girls with respect. And yet, the first person she'd seen upon her arrival in the small outer office was a little girl two years older than Brandon, with short, brown hair, an ice pack on an eye that was already turning black and blue.

The girl's mother, Suzanne Hartman Nash, was there, too. Jenna was bereft, and had done everything in her power to keep in check the tears that ran so freely down her face those days.

"Oh, Brandon, did you tell Kenzie you're sorry?"

For a split second, Brandon's little chin had wobbled, but he'd recovered, and shook his head three times. Belligerence was so unlike him. She knew the past several weeks since their father's death had been hard on the boys. It broke her heart to see them hurting, but Brandon's behavior mystified her.

Gliding down to her knees, she'd reached a hand to Kenzie Nash. "Does it hurt much?"

The child, a spitting image of Suzanne, shook her head.

And Jenna said, "Oh, honey, it's so unlike Brandon to hit anybody, let alone a girl who didn't so much as provoke him."

Kenzie had blurted, "What's provoke mean?"

Behind her daughter, Suzanne said, "It means you didn't start it."

"Oh."

There must have been something about the way that one little word had been issued, because Suzanne had said, "You didn't call him names or do anything that might provoke him to hit you, did you?"

"Of course she didn't," Brandon sputtered.

"I hit you first and you know it!"

Silence.

"Kenzie!" Suzanne was the first to speak.

The principal had stepped out of the room earlier. Seeing Mr. Buchanan striding toward them from down the hall, Brandon said, "Shut up, Kenzie."

"You shut up!"

"Kenzie!" Suzanne said again.

"Brandon!" Jenna issued his name like a warning.

"I mean it," he said quickly. "I don't want the guys to say I got beat up by a girl."

"Somebody else must have seen what happened," Jenna said.

Both children shook their heads.

"Where did she hit you?" Jenna asked quietly.

Slowly, his hand went to his stomach.

Suzanne said, "Brandon, if Kenzie hit you first, she's the one who needs to be punished."

"So punish her when you get home," Brandon stated evenly. "Just promise you won't tell."

He turned brown eyes so like his father's to Jenna. Swallowing tears, Jenna had said, "We have to tell the truth, Brandon."

"Zack Miller is already telling everyone my dad was a crook, and Andy Callahan said I'm a sissy 'cuz I didn't beat Zack up for it. If they find out a girl hit me first, I'll get teased even worse, and nobody's gonna want me on their team to play kickball."

"Oh, dear," Suzanne had said. "His manhood is in jeopardy. It's that vast murky area that makes no sense to a woman but means life or death to every guy on the planet."

Jenna didn't know what to do. Mr. Buchanan was nearly at the door. Her son had already lost his father, and had suffered taunts about his father's reputation. How much more humiliation should he have to endure?

She and Suzanne shared a look. Suzanne nodded, and Jenna said, "All right. We'll deal with this ourselves at home."

Brandon sighed.

Kenzie lowered the ice pack from her eye. "You mean it?"

"It'll be our secret," Jenna said.

"The four of ours," Suzanne added. Turning to her darling daughter, she added, "That doesn't mean you're getting off the hook, missy."

Brandon grinned, more like his old self. At that moment, Jenna knew he was going to be all right. Maybe, just maybe, they would all be all right.

The principal returned, asked if everything was in order, and if anybody had anything else to say. Two mothers and two children stood mute. Brandon had to stay after school, but what was left of his reputation was salvaged. It was the strange beginning of a true friendship, for all of them.

"What did this man with the pocket protector do today?" Jenna asked.

Suzanne closed the lid on the washer then reached for the jumbo-size tankard of mint julep she'd retrieved from her freezer upstairs. "Same thing he always does. Strolled to the counter, ordered his tea and a bagel, a plain bagel. Jesus. What kind of a dweeb comes to a *coffee* shop and orders a plain bagel and *tea?* He paid for them, then sauntered on over to the farthest table and waited for me to bring them to him."

"Maybe he likes you."

"He's a man. He likes watching me walk toward him and away."

"What if he lost the pocket protector?" Jenna asked, picturing those plastic devices some men placed inside their shirt pockets to protect their clothing from ink stains. "Would you be interested in him then?"

"He'd still be a man. The Rat cured me of the opposite sex. I talked to him today."

Jenna folded another towel then started in on the boys' shirts. Finally, they were getting to what was really bothering Suzanne. Eddie Nash, a charming man when he wanted to be, was originally from North Carolina. He and Suzanne had opened a restaurant in Savannah, where they'd met twelve years ago. While Suzanne was working two jobs and juggling motherhood, Eddie was having an affair with his prettiest waitress. He was habitually late with his child support payments, and generally ignored his eleven year-old daughter, Kenzie. Suzanne and Kenzie had moved back to Harmony after the divorce. The first few years, Kenzie had been happy and well adjusted, but lately she'd become sullen one minute, irritable the next. Recently, Eddie had expressed an interest in seeing his daughter occasionally. Suzanne was hoping that spending time with her father would help. So far, it hadn't.

"Did Eddie call you?" Jenna asked.

"He left a message on my machine at the coffee shop before it opened so I would have to call him back."

Jenna inspected a tear in Benji's newest shirt. "What did he say?"

"He wants to get out of taking Kenzie this weekend. He said something important came up. And it's like I told him, I know what came up, and it's not that big a deal. I guess the new little bleached blonde he's ditching Kenzie for is just going to have to discover that on her own. Which is what I was telling Cherie when Pocket Protector strolled in as if he owns the place. Of course, all Cherie could talk about all morning was Nick."

Cherie had talked to Nick?

The washer chugged and the dryer whirred. All was quiet outside. Jenna looked at the dark windows in the building at the very back of the yard, wondering . . .

Suzanne topped off her glass. "You sure you don't want any mint julep? It's my mother's secret family recipe. I guarantee it's good for what ails you."

The idea of something ice cold was appealing, but Jenna didn't see how bourbon, no matter how it was dressed up, would help what was ailing her. She'd hurt Nick. She didn't know how to undo it. She didn't even know if it was possible. Maybe her anger was understandable. God knows she was weary of how easy it was for people to believe the worst. That still didn't make what she'd said right. Where in the world was he?

"Know what our problem is?" Suzanne flipped her bright orange baseball cap backward, causing her short brown hair to stick out around her ears. "Sex. Or should I say the lack of it."

Jenna laughed out loud.

"It's not funny."

"What about your whole Y chromosome embargo?" Jenna asked.

"I didn't call it that, you did. I called it a penis boycott. It's only a word, you know. Just don't say that to any man, because they think it's the beginning and end of everything meaningful and wonderful. Anyway, I think I'm going to end the boycott. I think we both should."

Jenna leaned one hip against the trim around the windows. She could see an owl sitting on a dead branch in the oak tree. He looked so lonely. She understood loneliness. Unlike Suzanne, Jenna wasn't alone due to some embargo or boycott. She was alone because Craig had died. Sometimes she didn't know how she'd gotten through that first year without him. During the day she'd had the boys to fill her time and her thoughts, but at night, when they slept, the loneliness had crept in, sucking all the air right out of her. In time, she'd grown accustomed to her nightly solitude. She tried not to think about what she was missing.

"What does sex have to do with Eddie trying to get out of taking Kenzie on his weekend?"

"Oh, that. Nothing really. Talking to Eddie always gets me stirred up, is all." She took a long drink from her glass. "Maybe women under thirty-five aren't meant to go month after month without being touched.

It's making me have weird dreams, and it's making you fidgety."

Her? Fidgety? Jenna stopped toying with the top button on the dress she'd donned after her shower earlier. She *had* been fidgeting. It was totally unlike her.

Pulling a face, she walked to the cooler and lifted the lid. Maybe she was a little thirsty after all.

An hour later, two large tankards were nearly empty. Their laundry had been done for a while. Jenna and Suzanne weren't in a hurry to go back to their quiet apartments.

"What do you think?" Suzanne asked.

Jenna looked at her friend over the neat piles of clean laundry she was loading into the basket. "About what?"

Suzanne blinked as if in slow motion. "Hello! What have we been talking about all night?"

Jenna didn't readily recall, but it seemed to her that Suzanne had done most of the talking, and most of the drinking. That was a good thing, because it didn't take a lot to get Jenna tipsy.

It was midnight, and Suzanne was sitting on top of the dryer, painting her toe nails fuchsia. "I read somewhere that midwestern boys fantasize about marrying a woman with D-cups. And men out East long to settle down with a woman who earned herself a Phi Beta Kappa key. Dixie boys don't give a rip about either of those things. Know what Dixie boys dream of? They dream of marrying a girl who's worn a crown, any crown."

Now that Jenna thought about it, the topic did ring a bell.

Dipping the brush into the little bottle of nail polish, Suzanne said, "The average southern boy would trade his favorite hunting dog for a chance to date a former

Miss South Carolina, or a Memphis State Homecoming Queen, or even a Miss Stock Car nineteen eighty-nine."

Jenna stashed the laundry basket near the door. She knew what was coming next.

"I gave up the Miss Cotton Crown for Eddie."

"I know, Suzie." The fact was, Suzanne had never actually won the Miss Cotton Crown, but she'd gotten in the finals of the first round up in Glascook County, and would have headed for the regionals in Augusta, if she hadn't gotten herself disqualified for falling head over heals in love with Eddie Nash. Technically, falling in love hadn't gotten her disqualified. Getting pregnant the first time she let him in her bed was what did that. Unwed mothers weren't eligible to be Miss Cotton anything.

"You think Eddie would have treated me like a queen for life if I'd won that crown, Jenna?"

What Jenna thought was that Suzanne was still in love with her low-down, no-good, lying cheat of an ex-husband. But she didn't say it. Instead, she said, "I think you can do a lot better than Eddie." And she meant it.

Somehow, through the course of the evening, Suzanne's hat had gotten turned even farther and was perched at a precarious angle on her head. "Forget it." She tipped her glass all the way back, draining the last drop of lukewarm mint julep onto her tongue. Her orange hat landed on the floor. Smacking her lips, she said, "I'm through with men. Finished. They aren't worth the trouble."

Jenna laughed, because the conversation had come full circle, just as it always did. The faint ripple of a breeze blew through the quiet night, slipping through the door that opened and closed with barely a sound.

"Hey, Nick," Suzanne said.

Jenna nearly dropped the orange baseball cap she'd leaned over to get, her mind and body failing to operate fully together. She must have turned, because suddenly, she was facing the door. And that was where Nick was standing.

"Suzanne." His gaze went to Jenna, and then to the tankards sitting nearby. "You two having fun?"

Suzanne slid off the dryer and almost fell down. "I'm giving Jenna lessons on the male anatomy."

Jenna choked on thin air.

"How's it going?"

"She can say *dick* and *cock* just fine, but the *P* word is still giving her some trouble. Cherie was right. You are a sore for sight eyes."

He flashed Suzanne a grin. Jenna couldn't tell if it reached his eyes. "What are you two drinking?"

"Jint Muleps." Suzanne looked at Nick and then at Jenna. "There's a little left. Help yourself. I'm bedding to go."

Leaving the baseball cap, tankards and nail polish until morning, she hoisted her plastic clothes basket into her arms and, staggering slightly, headed for the door. Nick held it for her, closing it quietly behind her.

Once again, Jenna and Nick were alone. They faced each other. "I thought you'd gone," she said softly.

"I saw your light on," he said at the same time.

They shared another awkward moment. The dim bulb cast shadows beneath his eyes, making the smudges surrounding them appear darker, his eyes themselves, hooded. He'd told her he'd had a little brush with a fever. A minor fever couldn't have been responsible for his weight loss and gaunt appearance.

"You've been ill."

"You're the second woman to accuse me of that tonight."

So, she thought, he'd been with a woman tonight. "How ill?" she asked.

He ambled a little closer, stopping near the table where Suzanne had left what was remaining of her mother's secret family recipe. Holding the icy drink to his nose, he sniffed. "Sicker than I've ever been in my life. I picked up a mean virus when I was in Central America earlier this spring. Ended up with a secondary infection that got into my blood and just about wiped me out. It got ugly, but here I am, like they say, the same only different."

She studied him. He'd never been one to talk about himself. On the surface, he was all bluster and swagger. But if a woman paid attention, she noticed that he never really bragged about who he was on the inside. And if she looked long enough, she got a glimpse of a deep appreciation and understanding of the world around him. Perhaps that was why he'd gone into photography. His photographs certainly expressed something different to every person who looked at them. They were more than just surface, but they still couldn't take the place of conversation.

So, as he'd said, here he was. The same, only different.

"Then you're going to be all right? This fever and secondary infection are just a bad memory?"

"The doctors here in the States said it'll take me a while to build up my stamina, but yeah, I'm pretty sure I'll live."

An owl called through the silence. Jenna gestured to the old oak tree on the other side of the screen. "Two owls lived in that tree when Craig and I first bought this house. They raised their three babies every summer. Something must have happened to one of the adults over the winter, because earlier this spring, only one of them returned."

Nick didn't know why she was telling him this. He doubted she knew, either. Not that he minded listening. It was like Rosita, the family housekeeper who'd always been so much more than that, used to say. "If God hadn't wanted people to listen twice as much as they spoke, He wouldn't have given us two ears and only one mouth."

Sauntering closer, Nick could see that Jenna's eyes

were dilated. Her dress was loose fitting, flowered, the background light blue. A southern dress for a southern lady. Her curly hair was down around her shoulders, as if she'd left it to air dry after her shower. She smelled of talcum powder, too. And bourbon. It was an interesting combination, although not one he would have associated with her.

The owl hooted again. "Hear her?" she asked.

A second, deeper call sounded a few seconds later. "I hear two owls."

"They've been going through this every night this spring, flying to the same tree, sitting on separate branches. The boys and I checked out books and rented a video about owls so we could learn about them and see if there was anything we could do to help. One is a male, the other a female. Benji climbed the tree the other day, and the hollow portion where the nest always was is empty this year."

"Are you telling me she doesn't want a new mate?"

His voice sounded worn and thin, and yet the tone was more stern than she'd expected. "What? Oh. The female is the new owl on the block, so I guess it's the other way around. Evidently, he's the one who isn't ready." They were silent for a while. Finally, Jenna said, "About this afternoon, Nick."

"Forget about this afternoon. Tensions were high. A lot of things get said when tensions are high. Believe me, I know."

He *did* seem much less tense to Jenna. But then, he'd spent the evening with a woman, and was probably less frustrated on several levels. Closing her mind to that line of thinking, she said, "Still, I'm sorry about what I said. At school today, I mean. It's a sore subject, and I was angry. Craig didn't take the money. I knew him, and I know he didn't do it. His aneurysm and sudden death made him an easy scapegoat. Not that I've ever been able to prove it. You have every right to believe whatever you want to believe. I shouldn't have belittled you simply because you don't share my conviction on this particular matter."

Jenna stood there in the semidarkness, holding her breath. Nick was close, his eyes, those mesmerizing green eyes, staring into hers.

"You really won't hold my doubts regarding Craig against me?"

"Have I ever?" She waited for her question to hit its mark. With a sigh, she added, "Will you accept my apology?"

After a time, he nodded.

"Then we're friends again?"

He nodded again.

And she stuck out her hand.

He took it, wrapping his warm fingers around hers. They shook the way they had when they were kids. Except Nick didn't release her hand. And there was nothing childish in his expression or in his voice as he said, "You should tell me to go."

She knew what he wanted. A woman always knew what a man wanted when he had that look in his eyes.

Something went a little soft around her heart, and suddenly, she was aware of how alone she'd been, of how long it had been since she'd been kissed or held. She and Suzanne had just been talking about this. It was all Suzanne's fault.

Whose fault was it that Jenna wasn't at all certain she didn't want him to kiss her? She resisted. Not that it was easy. Nick Proffit wasn't an easy man to say no to. He wasn't an easy man, period. She'd had a little too much to drink, that was all. He could have any woman he wanted, and most likely had had earlier that very evening. She was just getting back on her feet and in waltzes Nick, ready and willing to sweep her off them again.

Reminding herself that she'd worked too hard to get

to this place in her life where she'd found a degree of peace, she shuffled backward a few steps. Slowly, he released her hand, their arms falling to their sides.

"I'll just get my stuff out of the carriage house and clear out."

She stared at him, trying to make sense of his statement. "Now why would you'all go and do that?"

He started for the door, stopped. "I thought . . ."

"You thought what? That just because you believe it's possible that Craig might have taken that money, and I know it's impossible, you're not welcome here?"

"I . . ."

"That's the problem with you, Nick. You always clear out of Harmony at the first sign of discord."

She walked around him while his mouth was still gaping; then she slipped quietly through her back door, leaving Nick standing there, alone, condensation dripping off his tankard of mint julep, splashing on his shoe. He stared at the southern drink, at Jenna's back door, then at the branches where two owls hooted, their calls lonely.

He raked his fingers through his hair, then swallowed the watered-down liquid. Next, he turned out the light and pushed out of the service porch, uncaring that the door bounced closed behind him. The owls were quiet as he passed beneath their tree.

Looking up, Nick could make out one of them in the moonlight. "Owls are supposed to be wise. She's right there, you fool. All you have to do is go to her. You're alone. She's alone. What are you waiting for?"

Nick glanced back at the big house, then stopped. A hand on the carriage house door, he wondered why he didn't take his own advice.

He could chart Jenna's path through her home by watching the lights that went on and then off. A lamp in the corner room remained lit. He saw movement through the gauzy curtains, but could make out only shadows. He imagined her getting ready for bed.

The owl hooted.

Nick jumped.

Swearing under his breath, he unlocked his door and tromped inside, thinking there was more than one fool in the backyard tonight. He crawled into bed, and in those few brief moments before he sank into the oblivion of sleep, he relived that instant when he'd thought about kissing her. He'd wanted to. And she'd known it. All it would have taken was the slightest lift of her face, or a gentle sway in his direction.

She hadn't issued so much as a hint of an invitation.

But she'd thought about it. In those seconds when their hands had been clasped, their gazes connected, she'd thought about it plenty. Okay, she'd fought it, but she'd thought about it first.

That was progress. Maybe, just maybe, he wasn't such a fool after all.

Chapter Five

Jenna was a little surprised to hear a knock on her door at eight o'clock on a Saturday morning. Leaving the sink half full of dishes, she dried her hands and hurried past the living room where the boys, still in their pajamas, were watching cartoons.

A slender woman impeccably dressed right down to her Gucci shoes and purse stood on the verandah, her sullen-faced daughter, a younger version of her mother, several feet behind her.

"I know it's early," Faith Silvers said.

Jenna smiled warmly at her newest tenants. "It isn't too early. Hello, Faith. And you must be Rachel."

Despite the makeup and classic hair style, Faith Silvers's smile was tired. Her daughter's was nonexistent.

"Won't you come in?" Jenna asked.

"Perhaps another time." Faith's voice was soft, cultured. "I drove most of the night. Rachel hasn't quite woke up yet. If I could just bother you for the key?"

Jenna retrieved the key for Apartment 2-C. After telling the boys she would be right back, she returned to the foyer where she spoke to her new neighbors. "This entry is common to three of the four units. You probably remember the way, but this first time, I'll take you up."

For a second, Faith looked lost. Regaining her composure, she cast an indecipherable look at her daughter, then followed Jenna to the stairs.

Other than the fact that the Silverses were moving here from the Boston area, Jenna knew little about them. Faith Silvers and her thirteen-year-old daughter dressed as if they had money. Jenna supposed that if it came right down to it, some people could say that, at times, she did, too. She knew better than anybody that what one had and what one has are two very different things. Faith had already paid the first and last months' rent as well as a security deposit. As long as they were considerate tenants, they were welcome here.

Trying to fill the tense silence, Jenna said, "When my husband and I bought this house three years ago, we'd planned to remove the apartments and return the house to a single-family home. After he died, I was glad we hadn't. Your new apartment has the room with the best view."

She unlocked the door, and held it while Faith and Rachel went inside. Like the rest of the house, this upstairs apartment had transom windows, ten foot ceilings and hundred-year-old hard rock-maple floors. It also had noisy pipes, wobbly ceiling fans and windows that were hard to open, the largest of which overlooked Beulah Street.

"You can see to the river from here," Jenna said.

Faith joined Jenna at the window. Rachel hung back as if determined to remain bored and aloof.

Jenna pointed to the dozen ornate brick chimneys intersecting the cloudless sky. "See there? That's the Canoochee River. The entire eight block stretch on the river between Buchanan Street and Miller Street is in the Historic District." It was where Craig's father had lived, and where Craig and Nick grew up. "And that's the old City Clock. It has stood in the center of Harmony atop the town's first water reservoir since it was shipped here in 1874. It's a good thing it wasn't here before The Rebellion, because Sherman's soldiers would have desecrated it for sure."

In a momentary lapse, Rachel Silvers traipsed to the window and peered out. She was tall for thirteen. Reed-thin and blue-eyed, the girl was downright pretty when she wasn't scowling.

Rather than mention it, Jenna continued to weave bits and pieces of local folklore and history around the landmarks she pointed out. "Georgia sent nearly one-hundred-twenty-five thousand men and boys into that war. Some people claim the ghost of one of the poor young soldiers who died in a fierce battle fought on the banks of the Canoochee River walks the cemetery every autumn."

"A real ghost?" Rachel asked.

Jenna shrugged. "It's just local folklore."

A quick knock sounded on the open door behind them. Suzanne entered without waiting to be invited in.

"May I help you?" Faith asked.

Already dressed for work in her French maid uniform, Suzanne stepped around a stack of boxes, then said, "I live across the hall. Guess you could say I'm the welcoming committee." She extended both hands in a comedic, dramatic gesture. "I'm Suzanne Nash. Welcome to Harmony Hills."

"Harmony Hicks, you mean!" Rachel spun around and dashed to her room.

The door slammed so hard the apartment echoed and the windows rattled. Faith stood, rooted.

In comparison, Suzanne appeared completely nonplused. "How old is your daughter?"

Faith's eyes were round twin splotches of color on her otherwise pale face. "She's thirteen. I'm so sorry. I'll speak to her about her manners."

Suzanne waved it aside. Pushing a strand of her unruly dark hair out of her eyes, she said, "My mother claims I never closed a door properly from the moment I hit puberty until the day I turned eighteen. My Kenzie's eleven. You're two years ahead of me in the game."

"She isn't normally like this," Faith said, moving slowly toward the door. "She didn't want to move."

"Yeah, well," Suzanne said, easing backward around a mauve-colored camel-back sofa. "Kids that age don't like anything unless it's their idea. Where are you from?"

"From the Boston area, most recently, The Hamptons." Faith glided toward them, around boxes and furniture. "Rachel's father just passed away. She took it very hard." With shaking fingers, Faith tucked a strand of pale blond hair behind her ear. "It's been a difficult week for both of us. Now, if you'll excuse me."

Jenna and Suzanne weren't sure how they came to be standing in the hall, staring at the 2-C on the door. Slowly they looked at each other.

Jenna said, "I'd say that went pretty well, wouldn't you?"

"Well, hell. She closed the door in our faces. I never even saw it coming."

Neither had Jenna. "Do you blame her? Rachel's father died recently, and I mention ghosts."

Suzanne said, "It looks as if Pinkie's daughter comes by her attitude naturally."

Pinkie? *Oh, oh,* Jenna thought. She really didn't like the sound of that. "Give them a chance, Suzanne. They're going through a rough time."

Suzanne and Jenna headed in the same direction, Jenna for the stairs, Suzanne for her apartment.

"Did you see that furniture?" Suzanne asked. "You don't buy that kind of furniture around here. Who'd want to? It's pink."

"It's mauve," Jenna insisted.

"The same shade as her pink shirt," Suzanne said.

That hadn't been just any pink, er, mauve shirt. Jenna knew a Donna Karan when she saw one.

"Pink clothes. Pink furniture. Pink daughter. What do you suppose they're doing in Harmony?"

Jenna reached the top of the stairs. Looking back at Suzanne, who stood at her apartment door, she said, "You heard Faith. She said Rachel took her father's death hard. She probably needed a change of scenery."

"If you need a change of scenery, you go to Disney World, or if you're rich, to Europe or the Orient. Nobody comes to Harmony for a change of scenery."

She mumbled something else Jenna couldn't make out as she disappeared inside her apartment. Jenna continued down the stairs thinking that when it came to Harmony, Suzanne was almost as bad as Nick.

She could hear the boys arguing before she opened her door.

"Give me that remote."

"Try and make me. *Ow!*"

The boys were at it again.

"Turn it back."

"No."

"Get off me!"

"Boys!" Jenna closed the door. "What's going on?"

"He started it!"

"Did not."

"Did so."

Finding the remote, she aimed it at the television, which prompted both boys to complain, Brandon about Benji, and Benji that there was nothing to do. Jenna had a porch to paint, groceries to buy, lessons to plan, children to referee, a brother-in-law to deal with. Twyla Mae and Suzanne weren't speaking. Faith and Suzanne hadn't gotten off to a good start, either.

"You're an idiot," Benji said.

"Not as big an idiot as you."

"Are so."

"You just admitted that you're an idiot!" Brandon gloated.

"Did not."

"Did so. Didn't he, Mom?"

And so it went, another peaceful morning in Harmony.

Nick dreamed he heard voices. And laughter.

Wait. He couldn't be dreaming. He never dreamed. Therefore, the voices and laughter carrying through his open window had to be real.

It was Benji and Brandon. They were playing.

Eyes closed, Nick lay in the drowsy warmth of a warm May morning, listening to the sounds outside his window. Over the years, he'd awakened to the mating calls of exotic birds, to the baying of wild animals, and the screech and chatter of chimpanzees. He couldn't recall the last time he'd awakened to the sounds of kids playing, if you could classify one calling the other stupid, and vice versa, as playing.

Nick rolled over. A forearm covering his eyes, he drifted back into the oblivion of sleep. The next time he stirred, the backyard was quiet. He surfaced more quickly this time, took one look at his watch, and sprang to a sitting position. It was almost eleven o'clock. At this rate, he was going to stinking sleep his life away. He swung his feet over the side of the bed and headed for the shower.

By the time he wandered out to the kitchen ten minutes later, he was dressed in a pair of clean faded jeans and a white T-shirt. His feet bare and his hair still damp, he discovered a box of kids' cereal on the counter, a quart of milk in the refrigerator, and a note on the table.

"In case you're hungry. Brandon, your nephew."

Nick read it three times, shaking his head because the kid had felt the need to specify which Brandon, as if there were ten kids by that name who might have left Nick breakfast. He ate three heaping bowls' full, standing at the counter. He figured if he didn't go into a sugar coma, it might tide him over long enough to get to the grocery store to pick up some real food.

That was the plan as he left the apartment. The sounds of more voices halted his footsteps. Shading his eyes, he turned in a half circle and surveyed the backyard. It was one of those green-and-yellow May mornings here in Georgia when the sun was high above the trees and the air was thick with humidity. There was a bicycle tipped over in the driveway. Jenna's car and his Land Rover, and a midsize sedan that hadn't been there last night were parked closer to the street. All he could see of the houses on either side were the second stories. Shrubs and bushes that had probably never been pruned blocked out everything else, making the property feel secluded. Secluded or not, the overgrown yard appeared empty. And yet those voices had to be coming from somewhere.

Following the quiet murmur, he made his way to the very edge of the shade of a red maple tree growing close to the house. At first, the muddy tennis shoe dangling at eye level looked out of place amongst the green foliage. Upon closer inspection, he discovered that the shoe was attached to a leg, which was part of the small boy straddling one of the lowest branches.

"Hold on to your stomachs," Benji commanded, pushing a pair of old, oversized flight goggles back over his eyes.

"Better do as he says," Brandon exclaimed.

"Where are you taking us, Ace?"

That was Jenna's voice. It had come from the tree. Since when did she climb trees? Nick eased a little closer and craned his neck. Jenna was up there, all right, perched on another branch. Benji sat in the center, and Nick could see the back of Brandon's head and a splotch of his green T-shirt on the far right.

"Where do you think?" Benji quipped. "Straight up! Higher than the clouds!"

"You sure this Vega will make it?" Brandon asked.

Benji made a series of engine noises. "Positive. Here we go!"

Brandon held onto his branch real tight. Doing the same, Jenna said, "You let us know the next time you're going to do a barrel roll so we can get a tighter grip. The last time I almost fell off this wing."

"Roger."

Jenna laughed. "There goes my stomach!"

"Don't worry," Benji said, "we'll pick it up on the way down."

"Please do."

They were playing make-believe, and Nick was entranced. He couldn't see Jenna's face from his position on the ground, but he heard the wonder in her voice as she said, "Look at that sky! Have you ever seen anything so blue?"

"It's the sky. Of course it's blue."

Evidently ignoring Brandon's spurt of realism, she said, "Benji, Brandon, look. We're higher than the clouds."

"Told ya! Hold onto your hats, ladies and gentlemen. We're cutting back through." Benji worked some invisible levers, adjusted the pitch of his engine noises, then said, "All right. Here goes that barrel roll."

Brandon guffawed, playing along. Jenna shrieked and laughed with glee, as if she'd actually done a somersault in the air.

Nick forgot about the sugar cereal that was making him see spots, and simply stood in the dappled shade while Benji flew an invisible World War One airplane and Brandon and Jenna rode on the wings.

"Hey, Uncle Nick. Wanna come aboard?"

Nick didn't know how on earth Brandon could have noticed him; he hadn't so much as moved. Not much got past that kid, that was for sure. Benji's engine noises ceased, and Jenna parted some foliage and peered through. "Better watch that landing gear, Benji. You don't want to clip it on the tops of the trees."

The boy pulled hard on the pretend instrument in both hands. "Look," he said, "Suzanne and Kenzie are back."

Instantly, Brandon started to climb down.

And Benji sputtered, "Will you give me a minute to land?"

"I'm parachuting out." He swung down. Lowering himself until he was hanging from his hands, he dropped the remaining few feet to the ground.

"Your parachute just got tangled up in the propeller," Benji grumbled, scampering down after his older brother.

"Did not."

"Did so."

"Did not. Hey, Kenzie, wait up!"

A dark-haired girl twirled around. "You don't hafta yell. I'm not deaf, you know."

"Who's yelling? I thought you were going to your dad's this weekend!" Brandon said.

She went quiet, her gaze suddenly down-turned.

"Whatcha got there?" Benji asked.

Holding up what appeared to be a videogame, she said, "Check this out!"

All three children disappeared inside the house along with Suzanne, who was dressed in a black waitress uniform like the one she'd worn last night. The backyard was quiet, all of a sudden. Too quiet.

Nick peered up.

Jenna peered down.

She was the first to speak. "You look better this morning."

"Meaning I looked bad before?"

The breeze ruffled the leaves in the tree, blowing her hair into her face. Brushing the strands away with one hand, she said, "Meaning you look rested today."

Nick knew a compliment when he heard one, even

when it was issued in a take it or leave it manner. He didn't know where she'd learned to handle people, least of all him. Perhaps she'd been born to it, the way she'd been born to behaving like a lady. A lady who happened to be sitting in a tree.

"You climb trees often?"

Jenna tucked her hair behind her ears. It had been hours since she'd shown Faith Silvers and her daughter to their apartment. Jenna had the usual Saturday morning chores to do, but Brandon and Benji were bored, and when they were bored, they bickered. She'd enlisted their help for a while, and then she'd tried to interest them in board games, but Benji had a better idea. He was struggling in school this year, but his imagination was top-notch. When he'd asked her to take a flight with him, she couldn't say no, even if it meant climbing trees.

"Actually," she said to Nick. "I haven't done this since I was a child." And hardly even then.

Another silence ensued.

Finally, he said, "You coming down?"

She eyed the route she'd taken getting up. The boys called this the climbing tree. It had low, wide spreading branches and a split trunk, perfect for getting a toehold. Easy or not, if she climbed down now, Nick would undoubtedly try to help her. And in order to help her, he would have to touch her. She didn't think that was such a good idea, especially after last night, when she'd thought he might kiss her.

During the ten years she'd been married to Craig, and then for the two years he'd been gone, she'd hadn't so much as thought about kissing another man. Sometimes, throughout the years, when she let herself, she recalled one kiss and a few moments that never should have happened, but that had been a long time ago. Alone in her bed last night, she'd thought a lot about intimacy. Perhaps some day, when the boys were older, and Craig's memory wasn't so vivid and her loss so acute, perhaps then she would meet a quiet man to spend the rest of her life with.

But not Nick. It wasn't that he wasn't quiet. Storm clouds could be quiet at times, too. Nick was like that. A person never knew whether his bluster was going to blow out with a few sprinkles, or turn into a solid wall cloud filled with great masses of churning air currents and rumbling thunder and jagged lightning. Nick had issues. Beneath his surface bluster and bad boy charm, he harbored a deep resentment toward his only brother. Maybe part of that was her fault, although for the life of her, she didn't know what she could have done to prevent it. Instead of blaming her, Nick blamed Craig.

If nothing else, these past two years had proved that she was stronger than she'd realized. She wasn't stupid, either. She certainly wasn't naïve enough to stand out in the open when a storm was brewing.

Nick wasn't here to stay. He'd said so himself a hundred times over the years, and a handful more since he'd been back. He would leave Harmony, just as he always did.

She cared about him. She always had. He'd been a wonderfully funny and true friend when they were children. She still valued his friendship. She probably always would, so, instead of climbing down, she said, "Care to join me?"

He stared up at her in silence.

"Well? Are you going to stand there all day?"

A line formed between his eyebrows. After a time, he said, "Some things a man likes to think about first."

Her stomach did a flip as surely as if this had been a real airplane. Why did everything sound so erotic when he said it? "Maybe you're thinking," she said, unable to keep from smiling. "Or maybe you're scared."

His expression harked back to one he wore a lot in his youth. "Anybody ever tell you you're a brat?"

"You. The first day we met."

Nick's thoughts filtered back to that day. A few

months into the school year, the teacher had informed the fourth-grade class that a new student would be joining them. Evidently, the new girl's father had taken over as bank president after the last guy kicked the bucket. Nick hadn't given the new student's arrival much thought. First of all, she was a girl. In his defense, he'd been only ten. And second, if her father was the new bank president, she was bound to be one of those girls who sat around *talking* during recess, or even worse, reading. Girls like that were such a waste.

The door had opened, and a girl with dark, wavy hair and blue eyes entered, as regal as royalty. Nick sat up a little straighter.

The teacher instructed Jenna Brannigan to take the empty seat next to him. For the first time that year, he almost liked Mrs. Payton.

With a sweep of one hand, he'd emptied the top of the spare desk of his practically unused books. Mrs. Payton had glared at him, but the guys had laughed, just as Nick had planned.

Jenna, however, didn't react in either of the ways he'd expected. She didn't laugh or scoff. She'd simply looked at him, quietly taking measure of him. Later, when no one was looking, she'd whispered, "You had better pick up those books."

"Make me."

A standoff of sorts had ensued.

He thought he'd won when she'd leaned down. All she did was stack them neatly near his feet. Straightening, she whispered, "Jerk."

To which he'd replied, "Brat."

He'd surprised her, and for his trouble, she'd smiled. He'd forgotten how to breathe. They became friends. For him, it had been more than that, even then. It might have become more for her, too, if he hadn't gotten held back that year. They'd remained friends, though, right up until she'd started dating Craig in her junior year. And the rest, as they said, was history.

Who would have thought that twenty-some odd years after that first meeting, he would find her sitting in a tree? He circled the trunk, spit in his hands, then grasped a low branch. He made it up. Okay, it wasn't his most graceful climb, but it was progress, proof that he was getting his strength back.

Lowering to the branch Brandon had vacated, he looked around, but ended up looking at her. She wore tennis shoes, yellow shorts and a white shirt with a daisy on one shoulder.

"What?" she asked.

He reached over and plucked a twig from her hair. "I was just imagining what the women of the society would say if they could see you right now."

Arranging her face into what happened to be a pretty good impersonation of the pinched expression Abigail Prichart wore most of the time, she said, "Really, Jenna. Neither Lenore nor I feel it is proper for a woman of your social status to climb trees. Consequently, we're going to shun you and spread hurtful, hateful rumors about you and your family for the next fifty or sixty years. We'll resurrect the rumors every time you dare show your face in our fair city."

"Fair city, my ass."

She shrugged, but didn't reply. She knew how he felt about Harmony. Evidently, she also knew it would have been futile to try to point out the town's good qualities. As if it had any.

Nick had been thinking about this, about her and Craig and this situation. He knew firsthand how it felt to be on the receiving end of the society's censure. It was no skin off his nose what they thought of him, but what about her? "Why did you stay in Harmony, Jenna?"

She leaned back against a higher branch. Bringing one foot up, she tightened her shoelace. "What do you mean?"

"Why didn't you take Brandon and Benji and start over some place else?"

She lowered her foot just as the screen door slammed. "Mom!" Brandon called. "Telephone's for you."

Jenna looked over her shoulder. "Who is it, honey?"

"Benji's teacher. Sounds important."

She looked at Nick and then at Brandon. "Ask her to hold on. I'll be right there." Jenna made her way carefully along the branch to the V in the tree trunk, talking as she went. "I stayed in Harmony because this is our home," she said. "And if I had left, people would have thought I believed Craig took that money." She hopped to the ground. Brushing tree bark from her hands, she added, "And I know he didn't."

She looked up at Nick, as if daring him to make something of it, then started toward the house. Nick swung down the way Brandon and Benji had. "Rosita doesn't believe Craig did it, either."

Jenna stopped suddenly. Rosita Garcia had worked for the Proffitts for years. Craig had loved the old housekeeper. So had Nick. "You've spoken to Rosita?"

"I went to see her last night."

"She was the woman you went to see last night?"

"Who'd you think?"

"Mom, are you coming?"

Jenna glanced sideways. "Yes, Brandon, I'm coming." She headed off across the backyard toward the door.

"Jenna?"

She looked over her shoulder at Nick. He stood perfectly still, his shoulders back, his thumbs hooked in the front pockets of faded jeans. "Yes?"

"You said four hundred thousand dollars was missing from that trust fund."

"Yes."

It never ceased to amaze Nick how different the same word could sound. It was all in the inflection and delivery. "And a hundred grand turned up in your savings."

Her throat convulsed, but she managed to reply. "That's right."

"What about the other three hundred thousand dollars?"

"What about it?"

And people said he had a bad attitude. "It never turned up?"

"No," she said with quiet dignity. "It never did."

Without another word, she went inside. When she pulled the screen door shut this time, she didn't look at him. Nick knew, because he watched until she was out of sight.

It was a long time before he moved.

Chapter Six

"Bye, guys. Behave yourselves for your uncle Nick." Jenna brushed a quick kiss on Brandon's forehead. Benji turned his back on her before she could do the same to his. Drawing him around, she bent down until they were eye-level. "Benji, I told you that Miss Mason and I are just going to talk."

Benji hadn't fallen for that ploy the first time she'd said it, and he didn't fall for it now. *Atta boy,* Nick thought. Jenna glanced at him before he had time to erase his sardonic expression.

"Are you sure you don't mind watching Brandon and Benji for an hour or two?"

"Mind hanging out with the guys. Are you kidding?" He winked at the boys. Brandon smiled feebly. Benji couldn't manage even that. Jenna was going to see his teacher. On a Saturday. Christ. Nick didn't blame the kid.

"I thought I'd pick up groceries afterward. Does anyone want anything special?"

Brandon shrugged. Benji kicked a pebble with the toe of his shoe.

And Jenna sighed. "I'll surprise you."

All three Proffit men watched her get in the family

van. She'd changed her clothes. And put her hair up. There was obviously going to be nothing casual about the meeting. Benji had every right to worry.

The sun was blistering, yet they stood, idle and silent after she drove away. Finally, Nick glanced around the yard. "What do you guys want to do?"

Brandon and Benji only shrugged, for once fresh out of ideas.

Spying the bike laying on its side near the driveway, Nick said, "Feel like going for a bike ride?"

"You have a bike?" Brandon asked.

"No."

"Oh."

He thought about how quickly he tired these days. "We could take a walk."

"You're kidding, right?" Brandon asked.

Nick conceded the point. To eight- and nine-year-old boys, taking a walk had about as much appeal as making their bed.

"Do you have any Roller Blades?" Brandon asked.

"I'm afraid not."

His reply was met with more silence.

Nick had an idea. "I need to get back in shape, increase my endurance, build my stamina. You know, beef up a little. I could use a couple of trainers. Know anybody who might want the job?"

"What's a trainer hafta do?"

Momentarily, at least, he'd taken Benji's mind off Jenna's upcoming meeting with his teacher. "A trainer would make sure I exercise. Ride my—er, not let me stop. That sort of thing. What do you think?"

The boys looked at each other. "We could do that, right, Benj?"

Brandon's hair was clipped short all around. Benji's was longer, the front brushing his eyebrows as he peered up, giving Nick a thorough once-over. "We'd better get started right away."

For the sake of principle, Nick struck a pose and said, "Watch it." It earned him a couple of small smiles.

Brandon commiserated with his brother. When they were through, he took charge with quiet authority. "Okay, here's what we're going to do. You don't have a bike or skates, but you have two legs, so you can run. Running's good for you."

"What will you two do?"

This time Benji replied. "We'll ride on the sidewalk and make sure you don't slack off."

Slack off? Nick wondered how many times Benji had heard that expression lately. "All right."

The kids made a beeline for their bikes. Nick closed the doors in their apartment and in his. Pocketing the keys, he got a drink of water from the garden hose, then jogged to the sidewalk.

Off they went, Brandon in the lead, Nick in the middle, and Benji bringing up the rear. Nick was winded by the time he reached the corner. Looking both ways, all three of them crossed the street. By the end of the third block, his lungs burned and the muscles in his thighs were screaming for a break.

"Remember when Dad used to do this with us?" Brandon called to his younger brother.

"Yeah. He could run forever."

It didn't surprise Nick. Craig had been an athlete in school. A star quarterback, champion runner, prize pitcher, he'd lettered in all three sports. Although Nick had loved sports, especially baseball, he'd never tried out for a team. Even if his grades hadn't been too poor, he'd have sooner had his fingernails ripped out than be in Craig's shadow.

"I still had my little bike then. We were too small to cross the street." Benji could be a real chatterbox when he wanted to be. "So Dad ran around and around and around the block. Remember Brand?"

"Yeah. He was the best, wasn't he?"

That was Craig, Nick thought. The best.

"Hey, Uncle Nick, wait up."

Nick stopped at the next intersection. Hands on his thighs, he took deep breaths, waiting for traffic to clear. A shiny black Camaro, driven by a young woman Nick didn't recognize, coasted to the corner where he, Brandon and Benji stood. She stared at Nick, her eyes huge, her mouth gaping. Her short, auburn hair and small glasses gave her a bookwormish quality. She was pretty, though. If she wasn't careful, she was going to get her pretty little self killed.

Tensing, Nick stepped in front of the boys.

She continued past the stop sign, and into the intersection. Tires screeched. A horn honked. She jerked to attention a split second before another car slammed on the brakes, missing her by mere inches. Flustered, she braked, too. Since she was blocking traffic, she finally drove on through the intersection and out of the way.

Something about the way she'd looked at Nick made him ask, "Do you guys know who that was?"

Benji didn't know, but Brandon said, "Her name is Shaye. She used to work at the firm with Dad."

Nick's gaze followed the brake lights, now a block away. "Used to?"

"I don't know if she still does. We don't go there anymore," Brandon said.

"You wanna talk all day?" Benji asked. "Or do you want to get in shape?"

Nick surprised himself by laughing. Benji cracked a mean whip, but no matter how fast Nick ran, he couldn't get the image of that woman out of his mind. He prided himself on his ability to read facial expressions and body language. It didn't matter whether he was staring into the eyes of a panther or a man. Or a woman.

Shaye had been plenty surprised to see him. In fact, she'd looked as if she'd seen a ghost.

Shaye. He didn't remember any girls named Shaye. The woman in the black Camaro had worked with Craig.

Nick looked a lot like Craig. Was that why she'd gaped? Or was it something else?

"Where are you going, Uncle Nick?" Brandon asked when Nick turned around, heading back the way they'd come.

"To your house."

"Already?" Benji quipped.

"Hey, Uncle Nick! Wait for us!"

Nick's lungs were on fire by the time he reached 317 Beulah Street. His jeans chafed, and there were blisters on the bottoms of his feet from his worn-out Nikes.

"You made it eight blocks," Benji stated.

"Eight and a half," Brandon amended, not the least bit winded.

Eight and a half stinking blocks. He was pathetic. But it was a start. He peeled off his sweat-dampened shirt. Turning on the garden hose, he let the cool water run down his throat. The next time he ran, he was going to wear the right clothes and shoes. And maybe, just maybe, before too long, he'd make it more than eight and a half blocks.

"What are we going to do now?" Brandon asked.

Benji stared at the place Jenna's van had been parked, his sigh bigger than he was. Nick felt for the kid. Hell, the only thing worse than knowing something bad was going to happen, was watching the clock while you waited for it to come to pass.

"Are you guys hungry?" Nick asked.

"Yeah," Benji declared.

They went inside the big house where they ate whole peanut butter–and–jelly sandwiches straight off the counter. When they were finished, they washed them down with milk, then meandered to the verandah out back.

Other than the sounds of an old movie filtering through the open window in Twyla Mae's apartment, the afternoon was quiet. Nick had heard that new tenants had moved in upstairs, but he saw no sign of them.

According to Brandon, Suzanne and Kenzie had gone to someplace called Marcel's. The boys needed something to do, and so did he. His glance around the yard was automatic. Just as automatic was the way he categorized light and shadow, texture and color, size and shape. "Do you feel like taking pictures?"

"We don't have a camera," Brandon said.

"You can use one of mine."

"You mean it?" Benji asked.

"I never say anything I don't mean. Come on. I'll show you both how to set up a good shot."

An hour, and several arguments later, Brandon and Benji were taking turns taking pictures. They'd gone through a roll of film each, and were working on another. Nick opened the paint can he'd seen sitting on the front porch, and got busy.

He'd finished half the railing by the time a van pulled into the driveway, and Brandon yelled, "Mom's back!"

Benji swung around so fast he snapped several pictures in quick succession before he remembered to take his finger off the shutter button. While Brandon ran to greet their mother, Benji slunk to a porch step near Nick.

A minute or two later, Brandon was headed for the back door, a sack of groceries in his arms. "Mom wants you to help, too, Benj."

Benji looked at his brother, at his mother, and finally up at his uncle Nick. "The sooner you face the music, the sooner you'll get it over with," Nick said.

Benji rose to his feet. Without another word, he walked stiffly toward the driveway. Storing his own questions in the back of his mind, Nick dipped the brush into the paint, and bade his time.

"Is Benji grounded forever?"

Jenna handed Benji a brown paper bag and answered Brandon's question. "Of course not."

"For how long, then?"

She looked at her sons. As usual in situations like these, Brandon was doing most of the talking. And Benji was letting him.

"He's not grounded at all."

"I'm not?"

Finally, another country heard from. "No, you're not."

"What did that dumb Miss Mason say about me?"

"First of all, Miss Mason isn't dumb." Jenna retrieved another bag from the back of the van. "And secondly, I'm not going to give you the conversation verbatim."

"What's that mean?"

"It means," Brandon said, taking the heavy bag into his thin arms, "it's for her to know and you'all to find out."

"Brandon, it does not mean that."

"What does it mean, then?" Benji asked.

Jenna reached for the last two remaining bags. Benji's problems in school didn't make sense to her. Okay, of the two, Brandon seemed to be more book smart, but her younger son was extremely intelligent in his own right, and incredibly inquisitive. How on earth could he be failing three subjects? "Verbatim means word for word."

"Was what she said that bad?" Benji asked.

"No."

"Then she didn't say anything bad?"

"Well, yes."

A frown set into Benji's features. Jenna was more concerned about the belligerence that followed it as he said, "I knew it. She hates me. I don't care. I hate her, too."

"That isn't going to help, Benji. She doesn't hate you, and I really hope you don't hate her, either. I'd like to think you don't hate anyone."

Neither Benji nor Brandon replied.

After her meeting with Benji's teacher, Jenna had

wandered aimlessly through the park where she'd often taken the boys to play, trying to decide how to handle this. She always missed Craig, but she missed him the most at times like these. The weight of responsibility was heavy on her shoulders and on her mind. She remembered when her mother used to say there were two sure-fire cures for a bad day. A hearty laugh, and a good night's sleep. Jenna couldn't have laughed heartily if her life depended on it, but she thought she could curl into a ball and sleep for a week.

Marla Mason was a good teacher. She was young and exuberant and new enough at her profession to be blindly passionate about making a difference. Most of the little girls in her class wanted to be just like her when they grew up, and most of the boys were experiencing their first crush. Jenna did not understand her son. He was like his uncle Nick that way.

She happened to glance at Nick. She didn't know where his shirt was, or why he was painting the verandah. When she'd first pulled into the driveway, Twyla Mae had been handing him something cool to drink. The seventy-two-year-old had never married and didn't like many people. Jenna had no idea what Nick had said to her, but when Twyla Mae had returned to her apartment, she'd been twittering like a schoolgirl. It seemed Nick could charm anyone. Presently, he was talking to Suzanne.

"This ice cream's melting," Brandon stated.

Closing the back of the van, Jenna decided it might be best to take the ice cream, and this conversation, out of the sweltering sun.

"I hear you've met the new neighbors," Suzanne said, being careful not to lean against the railing Nick had just painted.

"How did you hear that?"

Suzanne glanced up from the bright red thumbnail

she was studying. "You expect me to reveal my sources?" She supposed the little smirk on his mouth was the closest thing she was going to see to a grin. "If you must know, Twyla Mae mentioned it."

She could practically hear the gears turning as Nick stored the information in his brain. Twyla Mae puttered around in the garden for an hour or two every morning. After that, she spent most of her day sitting in the rocking chair in front of the window overlooking the street. That way, she was able to see most of what went on around here. Twyla Mae knew a great deal about a lot of things. She wasn't an easy woman to pull anything over on, which was what made it so much fun to try.

"So what did you think of the Silverses?" Suzanne asked.

"I told them not to touch the wet paint as they passed and they didn't. It wasn't exactly a formal introduction."

They were both quiet for a few moments. Suzanne didn't know what was on Nick's mind, but she was thinking about her daughter. Kenzie had gotten bored at the coffee shop, so Suzanne had brought her home. She'd already asked Jenna to watch her for the rest of the day. If Eddie hadn't shirked his responsibilities, again, Kenzie would be with him this weekend.

Suzanne sighed. Life was a juggling act.

"Do you still know most of the people in Harmony, Suzanne?"

She'd waitressed up north for a while after high school, but she'd missed the scents down here, the way the air was so thick in the summer you could taste it when you breathed it in. People who'd never lived in the South couldn't imagine the humidity. It was the reason she wore her hair short. A lot of places were air-conditioned nowadays. Her coffee shop downtown had ceiling fans, but no central air. She preferred it that way.

She watched Nick for a moment. He was working

on an area above his head, one hand raised high, exposing a triangle of dark hair under his arm. His chest glistened with sweat. His fever might have stripped his body of some of its former bulk, but his shoulders were still muscular, the ridges in his stomach disappearing beneath the low-slung waistband of his jeans. She tried to recall what he'd asked her. Something about Harmony. Ah. "I suppose I know most of the people in town. Why?"

He bent at the waist, inadvertently presenting her with a view of his backside. He was a sight to behold, no doubt about that. She waited for a reaction, a telltale softening, a gentle warming, something, anything. And . . .

Nothing. What was wrong with her? Maybe there was truth in the old adage, Use it or lose it.

"Do you know anybody named Shaye?"

"Shaye Townsend?"

"Does she have short hair and glasses?"

"As a matter of fact, she does. Why?" Suzanne noticed Jenna and the boys carting groceries into the house. Jenna, her kids, and Twyla Mae were like family. Which was why Suzanne had opted not to move into the apartment above the coffee shop, even though it would have saved money. She studied her jagged thumbnail. Money, now there was a real problem. Problems or not, this atmosphere was better for Kenzie, and Kenzie was her top priority. Which was why she was going to give Eddie a piece of her mind the next time he called.

"How well do you know her?" Nick asked.

"Who?"

Nick moved a few steps to the right. "Shaye Townsend. Isn't that who we were talking about?"

"Oh. She comes to the coffee shop once in a while. Why?"

"Is she married?"

Okay. That was three *whys* he hadn't answered.

Suzanne stopped chewing on her thumbnail and turned her full attention to Nick. "Not that I know of. *Why?*" she emphasized the word. "Are you in the market for a wife?"

"If I were, would she be my type?"

"Nick, I don't know what's going on with you, but to tell you the truth, I always figured that a lot of women were your type." Glancing at Jenna and the boys as they passed, she said, "Even Jenna, you know?"

He stopped painting and slowly faced her. Whoa. She certainly had his goat. Someone with less spunk and grit would have been tempted to take a step back. Sashaying a little closer, she said, "That didn't come out right. Come on, Nick. You know what I meant. Look at you. You could have any woman you want. I can't think of anything you could say that would convince me that you don't know that."

Nick took a deep breath and shook his head. He came close to blurting the truth, and the truth was, there was one woman he couldn't have. And it wasn't a simple case of wanting something he couldn't have. There was nothing simple about this.

Suzanne had insinuated that Jenna was above him. He reminded himself that this was Suzanne. She had a smart mouth and an honest soul. And she honestly didn't mean anything derogatory. He was being sensitive. That only happened when it came to Craig. And Jenna.

Nick rarely judged. He prided himself on his ability to live and let live. Sure, he cheered along with everyone else when he heard that some drug lord or terrorist was killed, and he hated it when someone good died young.

Craig had died young. Had he been as good as everyone said?

Trying a different tact, Nick said, "A lot of things have changed in Jenna's life these past two years. She seems to have handled them pretty well."

"You ask me, the woman's a saint. I would have egged those old biddies of the society and let the air out of the tires of the curmudgeons in Craig's firm."

Nick picked up the paint can by the handle. "What about Craig? Was he a saint, too?"

"He was *your* brother."

Nick bristled. "What the hell is that supposed to mean?"

He found himself staring into Suzanne's brown eyes.

She said, "God, Nick. What's going on with you? I mean, you knew Craig better than I did. He was your brother, all right?"

Of course that was all she'd meant. He'd overreacted. "Yeah, well," he said. "I didn't come home much over the years."

She seemed to accept his statement at face value. Why wouldn't she? He'd never kept his feelings concerning Harmony a secret.

"I'd better get back to my coffee shop."

"You own a coffee shop?"

She pulled a face. "Marcel's. Next to Kenzie, it's my greatest pride and joy. Maybe I'll get lucky one of these days and I'll actually show a decent profit."

"You know what they say," Nick replied. "It's better to be lucky than good."

She slid her hands into the pockets of her black waitress uniform. "Just once, I'd like be good and lucky." Kenzie and Brandon came tearing onto the porch, nearly upsetting the can of paint Nick had just moved. "You'll be wearing that paint if you two aren't careful!" Suzanne taunted.

The kids raced off the porch, unaffected.

Suzanne's eyebrows lifted slightly, and the ghost of an unholy grin lurked around the edges of her mouth that was a little too wide for her face. "I'm thirty-three years old, and I'm already turning into my mother. Heaven help us all."

Then and there, Nick understood why he liked her. At the same time, he wondered how long Jenna would stay inside, and how long he was going to have to wait to ask her a few questions.

"Stop by Marcel's sometime," Suzanne said. "I'll prepare you the best latte you ever tasted."

"I'll do that."

She started down the steps, only to turn at the bottom. "And Nick? If you want to know about Craig, ask Jenna. When she talks about him, it's the second-best thing to being there."

That "second best" was nearly Nick's undoing. This time he kept his emotions and his expression under firm control.

Jenna had her garden gloves in hand when she went into the front foyer. Of all the things she had to do, weeding promised to be the most calming. Her father had been a gardener long before it came into vogue. He used to say that no matter what else was going wrong in your life, you could always make sense out of pulling weeds. Losing him to a heart attack five years ago hadn't made any more sense than losing Craig three years later.

Jenna wished she'd paid closer attention when her father had talked about his plants. Twyla Mae tended to most of the flowers here. Bit by bit, she was rejuvenating Jenna's interest in the pastime. Reaching the verandah, she decided she didn't want to think about yesterday's losses, today's doubts, or tomorrow's worries. She didn't want to have to think about anything except the warmth of the sun and the beauty of the day.

"Hello, Nick," she said on her way by. "Did Brandon and Benji give you much trouble?"

"Nope." He paused for a second, but only a second, the brush hovering in midair as he looked at Jenna.

"Thanks for looking after them. By the way," she said. "What are you doing?"

"I'm painting the porch. What does it look like I'm doing?"

Had his tone been snide? Or was she imagining things? She studied the haughty angle of his chin and the way his mouth was set in a straight line. "Elsewhere it's called a porch. In Georgia, it's called a verandah. You don't have to paint it. You're a guest."

"I know what I am, Jenna."

She wasn't imagining anything. His tone *had* been snide. Reminding herself that she had plenty of backbone, she regarded Nick more closely. His medium-brown hair was tousled, his jaw set stubbornly.

"You know what, Nick? If you have a problem, just spell it out, because I've already had a long day and it's only three o'clock."

He balanced his paintbrush on the rim of the can. Wiping his hands on what had probably been a decent shirt this morning, he asked, "What's going on with Benji?"

"He didn't tell you?"

Well, of course, he told me, Nick thought, tucking a corner of the shirt into his back pocket But he was trying to pick a fight. Just once, he'd like her to make it easy for him. "Benji said he's going to have to work harder, or else he'll have to go to summer school."

"That's right."

"Teachers should come up with new tortures. That one's been done to death."

"I'll take it under advisement. Anything else?"

Nick blinked. He hadn't expected that caustic tone. He'd almost gotten a rise out of her. That hadn't happened in years. She'd changed back into her yellow shorts and the white T-shirt with the daisy on one shoulder. The outfit looked a lot sunnier than her expression.

"There is one other thing," he said.

"Yes?" This time, she sounded more tired than angry.

Something went soft inside him just like it always did when he tried to be angry with her for loving Craig more than him. "I'm going to stick around a while. In Harmony, I mean."

He couldn't tell if she was glad about that or not. And he'd be damned if he would be disappointed. Going back to work, he said, "While I'm here, I'm going to do some digging into those rumors about Craig."

"No."

He swung around. "What do you mean *no?*"

She folded her arms, the garden gloves clutched tight in one hand. "You know what *no* means."

He squared off opposite her. "Craig was my brother." He groaned out loud. He didn't even have fresh material.

"Why, Nick?"

He knew what she was asking. He didn't have an answer.

When he remained mute, she said, "Do you want to prove that Craig didn't take that money?"

He didn't reply.

"Or prove that he did?"

The way she'd said it made him feel like something he'd stepped in.

"Let it go, Nick. I tried to prove his innocence two years ago. No matter what they say, a person isn't innocent until proven guilty. It's pretty difficult to disprove guilt when it's based on nothing but hearsay and circumstance."

"And a hundred thousand dollars you didn't know you had."

Twin splotches of pink, like slap marks, appeared on her cheeks. She clamped her mouth shut, dropped the gloves near the door, then leaned over, picking up the paintbrush he'd put down. Insinuating herself directly in front of the portion left to do, she dipped the brush into the white paint, taking up where he'd left off.

Regret flooded through Nick. He'd never been worth

a damn at apologizing. He wasn't even sure what to apologize for. He only knew he was sorry as hell about something. Maybe about a lot of things.

Without a clear destination in mind, he walked quietly down the steps. When he climbed in his Land Rover five minutes later, he was wearing a clean shirt and an old scowl.

The wheels spun as he backed out of the driveway, churning up loose gravel. He didn't squeal the tires when he drove away. What was the use?

The porch, hell, the verandah, was empty.

It was nearing dusk when Nick returned. Five kids were playing hide and seek in the backyard. Three of them lived here. Nick didn't recognize the other two.

Brandon placed a finger to his lips in a silent plea not to give away his hiding place behind the azalea bush. Looking neither right nor left, Nick let himself into his apartment. Even then, he didn't see the stack of letters on the low table in the living room until after he put away the groceries he'd picked up on his way home.

He stopped in his tracks halfway between the kitchen area and the coffee table. He stared at those envelopes, a dozen at least, sitting squarely in the center of the table. Held together with a thick rubber band, all were yellowed with age.

They hadn't been there earlier.

He glanced around the apartment. The windows were still open, one of his shirts draped over the back of a chair, his beat-up Nikes near the door. The only thing different was the addition of those letters.

His throat was dry as he leaned over and picked them up. The top envelope was addressed to him. He fanned through the others. They were all addressed to him. All were sealed, too. Stamped across the front of every one was RETURN TO SENDER. ADDRESS UNKNOWN.

His heart took turns speeding up and slowing down

as he stared at his brother's handwriting. These were the letters Jenna had told him about in the note she'd written to him shortly after Craig died. These were the letters his brother had written to him over the course of the years he'd been married to Jenna, the years Nick had rarely come home.

He eased around to the other side of the coffee table and dropped onto the couch. An exaggerated noise filled the air.

Nick sprang to his feet and felt beneath the sofa cushion about the same time childish laughter carried through the screen in the front window. He stood for interminable seconds, the letters in one hand, a whoopee cushion in the other.

He'd been had. From the sounds of the chortles and guffaws coming from the yard, the boys had been the culprits. Craig's boys. Devilish, beguiling, amazing. Could a man like him, a man with everything, have taken that money? If so, where was the rest of it?

Nick lowered to the sofa more carefully this time. The prank had been the boys' doing. He wondered if Jenna knew about it, for the letters could have only been put here by her. Turning the stack over, he opened the first one, written nearly ten years ago in Craig's meticulous hand.

Chapter Seven

Nick read each letter slowly, many twice. Sometimes he sat; oftentimes he wandered through the three rooms that comprised the carriage house apartment. The floors creaked in places, the wood planks smooth beneath the soles of his shoes. When darkness crept through the windows, he switched on a lamp in each room, reading as he went.

He read for a long time. A long, long time.

Articulate and sometimes funny, the brother Nick remembered was evident in the words he'd chosen. The letters portrayed a cross section of Craig's life. Nick had always wondered if Craig had been aware of his feelings for Jenna. After reading every word on every page, he still didn't know. Craig's love for Jenna and the kids, however, came through loud and clear. He rarely mentioned their old man, the formidable Reginald Elliot Proffit, and never so much as hinted that there might have been tensions at home. Nor did he write anything that might have made Nick think that Craig had ever looked at another woman. Did that mean he never had? Could a man like him have stolen four hundred thousand dollars?

The expensive, monogram stationery crinkled as Nick folded the last letter and replaced it in its envelope. It had been written nearly two and a half years ago. Shortly thereafter, time had stopped for Craig Proffit.

Nick could count on one hand the number of times he'd picked up the phone and called his brother. And although he'd included a brief hello to Craig and Jenna on the postcards he'd sent to the boys over the years, none had been exclusively for Craig.

Nick didn't know why he hauled his duffel bag from the closet. After rummaging through its contents, he retrieved the letter from Jenna that had finally caught up with him in Central America. Even though he'd memorized the words, he read that one again, too. Placing the torn, worn envelope on top of the others, he stared at the stack: The entire set.

There would be no others.

The thin envelopes in Nick's hand felt as heavy as a guilty conscience. An owl hooted. Nick stood perfectly still, waiting for the answering call. When it came, his hand was on the doorknob before his subconscious bothered informing the rest of him of its plan.

Although the back light wasn't on, a lamp was lit in two of the windows in Jenna's apartment. That meant she was probably still up.

He made his way quietly through the tall grass of the backyard. It wasn't until his foot, wet from the dew, was on the bottom step that he saw the silhouette of the woman sitting perfectly still on the porch swing.

It was almost as if she'd known he would come.

The first stirring of desire started deep inside him. Calling himself every kind of fool, he walked up the remaining steps. The owls were quiet. Even the night peepers had stopped their chorus in midsong. For what seemed like a long time, he and Jenna were the quietest of all.

Jenna felt the tension in the late-night air, and although she couldn't see Nick's face clearly, she had a feeling that somewhere in the darkest recesses of his mind, he knew it.

"I saw your lights," he finally said, "and I thought you were inside. Have you been sitting out here long?"

"I've been here for a while, I guess." Actually, she'd been wandering between the house and the back verandah for nearly two hours. Waiting. She'd almost given up and gone to bed. Some thread of intuition mixed with stubbornness had convinced her to wait a little longer. "I saw a shooting star a while ago. It would have been a shame to waste the production, wouldn't it?" She gestured with one hand. "Or all the rest, for that matter."

He shifted his weight to the other foot. "All the rest?"

"You know, the creak of the swing, the songs of the night peepers, the hoot of the owls. Brandon's been trying to convince me it's more relaxing than Mozart."

"That sounds like Brandon. He's right, by the way."

Perhaps, Jenna thought, but she wasn't relaxed, and it had nothing to do with Mozart or the hoot of owls. It had to do with Nick.

His voice was a lot like the wind after midnight, a low hum that became a vibration that spread outward through the warm night. He stood on the top step, probably waiting for an invitation. For a rogue, he was terribly gentlemanly. She should be angry with him. She *was* angry with him. Or at least she had been. Nicholas Proffit was a lot of things, but he wasn't an easy man to stay mad at.

"Thanks to your sons, I can say I've officially been the butt of a practical joke. Or were you in on that, too?"

"I thought they were up to something. What did they do?"

"Never mind. What are you really doing out here, Jenna?"

She set the swing in motion once again. "I've been

waiting for you." He stood in a wan shaft of moonlight, most of his face hidden in shadow. Again, she thought she'd never known a man who could stand so still. She found herself speaking in whispers. "Did you read the letters?"

His answer was a slow nod.

She wanted to sputter, "And?" She'd spent much of the evening picturing Craig sitting at the desk at their other house, sometimes writing his letters to Nick, other times staring into space, lost in thought. The images had left her feeling achy. She wondered how Nick had felt as he'd read those words. That was only part of the reason she'd waited up for him. There was something important they needed to talk about. And the discussion was long overdue.

He started in her direction, only to stop abruptly and glance at the letters clutched tight in his hand, as if he'd forgotten about them. In one swift movement, he shoved them toward her.

She shook her head. "They're yours."

"Did you read them before he mailed them?" he asked.

Again, she shook her head.

"Craig could have spilled his guts in them."

This time, she only shrugged.

Finally, Nick said, "He didn't mention the four hundred grand."

Jenna kept her voice quiet as she said, "There's a good reason for that."

"You're saying you don't think he knew about it."

"You read his letters. What do you think?"

Nick raked his fingers through his hair. "I think," he said, heading back toward the steps, "that my brother was a lucky man."

Jenna's thoughts were in a tumult. It always came back to this. The rivalry. The competition. This unfinished business. She sighed. Nick's belief that Craig had been a lucky man was a compliment to her, and yet . . .

Sandra Steffen

And yet, what? It was confusing, exasperating, maddening, like Nick. She tried not to imagine how many times in his childhood he'd stood outside the perimeters of his parents' affection and acceptance. And later, how many times in his life had he chosen a solitary path? How many nights had he sat in dark rooms in foreign countries, alone? Okay, he probably hadn't always been alone. But he had been lonely as a child. Oh, he'd had friends, lots of them. But at home, where it mattered most, he'd been lonely. Craig had known it, but he'd been just a boy, too. She tried to tell herself that a man like Nick, a man who'd been on his own and had traveled the world couldn't have been lonely later, when he'd been doing what he'd loved.

What about now?

Now Jenna understood too much about loneliness not to recognize it in another person's posture and in his voice. "Don't go, Nick."

He turned slowly, first his head and shoulders, and finally the rest of him. Neither of them had moved closer. It only seemed that way.

"I don't think it would be a good idea for me to stay."

"And why is that?" she asked quietly.

"Because it's dark, and we're the only two people awake." His voice dipped lower. "And you're right there, close enough to . . ."

Nick's sensuality level was every bit as deep as his voice, and every bit as unsettling. She couldn't see his eyes plainly. Instinctively she knew his gaze had settled on her mouth.

"Close enough to what, Nick?"

"Close enough," he said, still not moving, "to kiss."

"It wouldn't be the first time." She closed her mouth and held her breath as she waited for his response.

After a long, nearly tangible silence, he said, "So you remember that kiss."

Searching the planes and dark hollows of his face, she said, "A woman never forgets a kiss like that. It might not be the same for a man, but that's the way it is for a woman."

He seemed to be mulling that over. "Did Craig know?"

Why did everything with him always come back to Craig? "I don't believe he ever knew."

"You never told him?" His voice was incredulous.

"No. I never did." Jenna motioned to the swing. "It's time we talked about this. Perhaps you should have a seat."

Time stood still again as he made up his mind. The swing creaked as he lowered himself onto it. The sound covered the quiet, but it didn't quiet Nick's thoughts. He didn't even have to close his eyes to picture Jenna as she'd been the night he'd kissed her. It was the night before the wedding. He'd come back to Harmony to be Craig's best man, a bitter irony if there ever was one. The rehearsal, and dinner that followed had gone off without a hitch. Everything was going to be perfect. Even the weather was cooperating. Some people were born lucky.

Some weren't.

Nick's father hadn't said more than a dozen words to him, but his disapproval was clearly evident without words. The champagne had been flowing pretty freely. Nick had pretended to enjoy the attention of Jenna's sister, who would serve as her maid of honor the following afternoon. In reality, he'd been aware of Jenna's every move. He hadn't seen her in over a year, and yet desire, hot, heavy, and as pleasurable as dread, had strummed through him the instant he'd laid eyes on her again.

At twenty-two, Jenna, fresh out of college with a teaching degree, had been nervous, elated, giddy. God, she was as beautiful and unattainable as the moonbeams in the sky tonight. And with every hour that had passed, he'd come an hour closer to never knowing how it would feel to hold her.

He had to get out of there before he did something he knew he couldn't, shouldn't, wouldn't ever be able to do. Using jet lag as an excuse to leave early, he'd said good-bye to his mother, and promised Craig he would pick him up and have him at the church plenty early the following day. Rather than have to pass his father, whose frame blocked the entrance to the foyer, Nick ducked through the kitchen. In his haste, he ran headlong into Jenna.

She'd gasped. "Oh."

His arms shot around her, steadying her.

"Nick, it's you."

And then she'd smiled, and every ounce of yearning he'd tamped down his entire life reared up inside him. "Yes, that's who it is. Me."

Their gazes met, held, her Nordic blue eyes artful and serene, her face flushed, her lips parted slightly. As if waiting. His breathing hitched, his thoughts slowed, and instead of releasing her, he drew her face up with the tip of one finger, lowering his mouth to hers.

He'd drowned in that connection.

Her eyes had closed, and for just a moment, she'd responded, softening for him, her mouth opening beneath his. But then her shoulders tensed and her spine straightened beneath his hand. A heartbeat later, she backed from his embrace, her face pale suddenly, her eyes round. Her lips moved, but no sound escaped.

He'd stood mute, too, wishing for the right words, wishing for things to be different.

"Nick, I. I'm. I mean. That is, I'm sorry."

"No," he'd finally said. "It was me. It was my fault." He took the blame. He couldn't pretend it hadn't mattered.

She backed away slowly. With shaking fingers, she

tucked her long hair behind her ears. "I love Craig, Nick."

"I know."

"Then what . . ."

"Just forget it, okay?"

"But," and then as if thinking better of saying more, she said, "Okay. I'll see you tomorrow. Right?"

"Right."

She'd swallowed audibly, then skirted him, leaving the room. That was the last they'd spoken of it. He'd assumed she'd forgotten. Maybe what she'd said was true. Maybe a woman never forgot a man who'd kissed her, which brought up an interesting concept.

"Have you kissed a lot of men, Jenna?"

"Pardon me?"

"Just how many men do you remember?" he asked.

"I don't think . . ."

"Come on. How about a ballpark figure?"

At first, he thought she wasn't going to answer. When she did, there was a smile in her voice. "A lady doesn't kiss and tell."

"Give it a whirl."

"I'm not telling."

"Fine. I'll go first."

"Nick, that isn't necessary."

"The first girl I kissed was fourteen."

She didn't say anything for a moment. And then, as if she couldn't help herself, she said, "Tell me you weren't twenty-one."

Damned if he didn't almost smile. "I was old, but not that old."

"How old?"

Aha. He'd aroused her curiosity. Suddenly, it felt the way it used to between them. "I was fourteen and a half."

"Oh, my, that old?"

"I was a late bloomer. As long as I was getting lucky,

I thought, what the hell, why not cop a feel, too? I brought my hand to the front of her sweater. So much blood drained out of my brain I said the first thing that popped into my head."

"What did you say?"

"Some lady you are, wanting to know the intimate details of my first sexual encounter."

She crossed her arms and shook her head. "What did you say?"

"Something like, wow, they're squishy."

Jenna couldn't control her burst of laughter. It had been a long time since that had happened. "What did she do?"

"She told me I was immature, put her nose in the air, then flounced away."

"Not many women can execute a really good flounce."

"Are you scoffing?"

She smiled again. "Your style improved."

They stopped pushing off with their feet. Like the swing, they were back where they'd started, back to that one kiss that neither of them had forgotten.

"Are you still planning to stay in Harmony for a while, Nick?"

"I guess that depends."

She noticed he was riffling the corners of the letters from Craig with his thumb. "On what?" she whispered.

"On you."

Jenna clasped her fingers tight in her lap to keep them still. Nick's answer had certainly been blunt. One thing she'd learned about him a long time ago was that he said a lot in very few words. Even his understatements spoke volumes.

There was more to him than met the eye, and always had been. And what met the eye was downright appealing. That always had been, too. Before, she'd had Craig as a buffer between herself and Nick's masculine allure. Except for that one kiss, there had never been anything between her and Nick, other than friendship. She'd loved Craig, and she'd honored in every way the vows she took on her wedding day.

"Tell me something, Nick."

"I'm all ears."

No, he wasn't. He was all hollows and shadows and interesting planes and deep, confusing silences. "Why did you leave Harmony the first time?"

"Why do you think?"

"I think that isn't an answer."

Quietly, Nick released a deep breath. For years, he'd told himself she was the reason he'd left Harmony. As time passed, he'd admitted that there was more to it than that. Sure, part of it had been because of Jenna. At first, he'd thought it was the biggest part, but the truth was, he'd thrived on the adventure of his chosen career. He'd loved the pursuit of the perfect photograph. Those weren't the biggest reasons, either.

"The reason I left, and the reason I stayed away, had to do with running, and with my aversion to coming in second." There, he'd said it. "In my family. In Harmony. In life."

"You realize there's no scorecard, no ribbons to run through, in life."

Now he was the one who scoffed. A lot she knew. "Second just plain wasn't good enough, especially when my older brother was perfect in every way."

"Craig wasn't perfect, Nick."

He waited, breath bated.

"He worked too much. And when he got tired, he had next to no patience."

Those weren't faults. They were Proffit traits. Frustration knotted Nick's insides. Jenna believed in Craig, and yet she'd never told him about that kiss. There had been at least one secret between them. Had there been others?

"Are you still considering looking into that missing money?"

Had she read his mind? "I honestly don't know."

"Honesty is all I ask for." She sounded tired, but she stood easily and started toward the door. "Good night, Nick."

He felt a tightening in his throat and a chugging in his chest. He wanted her. He'd always wanted her. That wanting kept crowding into his thoughts, twisting his feelings, until he didn't know what was even important anymore. She got to him. She always had.

Nick's rise to his feet wasn't nearly as agile as hers had been. Sore from his earlier run, he started down the path to the carriage house. The branch where one of the owls had been sitting was empty. He discovered the reason for that when he looked out the window a few minutes later. Two owls were perched several feet apart on the other branch. They weren't exactly acting like love birds, but it looked as if they were making progress. Turning away from the window, Nick thought that was where owls had it over on men.

Church bells were ringing in the distance when a single rap sounded on Jenna's back door. Recognizing Suzanne's distinctive knock, she continued to press lightning bolt and sunflower stickers on the tops of the math papers she'd just checked and spoke without looking up. "What are you doing using the back door?"

"Never let it be said that Suzanne Nash is predictable."

Glancing up from her schoolwork, Jenna thought that wasn't exactly an answer. Suzanne was dressed in frayed cutoff jeans, a faded T-shirt and flip-flops that paid tribute to their name with every step she took. She looked cross; her short dark hair was still damp from a recent shower.

Making a beeline for the coffeepot, she said, "Some day I'm going to run for a political office just so I can

make it illegal to be cheerful before noon on Sundays."
She studied her watch. "Four, three, two, one."

Another chorus of church bells sounded, right on
schedule.

"I think they do that so you can't sleep whether you
go to church or not." Taking a long slurp of steaming
coffee, Suzanne stared out the window overlooking the
backyard. "Cherie claims there are four great places to
meet men. The first is via the Internet; the second is in
the grocery store. Next is the laundry mat, and finally
at church. Church. Can you believe that?"

Jenna took a sip of her own lukewarm coffee and
shrugged.

It was all the encouragement Suzanne needed.

"I never would have thought of that one. There are
certainly enough churches to choose from in Harmony.
To this day, my mother attends the First Methodist
Church over on Elm Street. Ever wonder why the found-
ers felt the need to include that First in its name? Come
on. Has anybody ever heard of a second? The Presby-
terians have the best parking, the Baptists the biggest
building. The pastor of the Congregational Church is
the shortest-winded, which means his service is over a
full fifteen minutes ahead of the others."

"Are you considering joining a congregation, Suzanne?"

Suzanne shrugged, then plunked her cell phone and
cup of coffee on the table and lowered into a chair.

Eyeing the small phone, Jenna said, "Are you expecting an important call?"

"I'm waiting for a call from Eddie."

Jenna stopped stacking checked papers and looked
closely at her friend. "Is something wrong, Suzanne?"

"Kenzie cried in her sleep again last night. She was
mumbling about her father, and dammit, I want him to
know what it does to her when he lets her down."

"Did you ask Kenzie about the dream this morning?"

Suzanne sighed. "She clamps her mouth shut the way she used to when I tried to get her to take medicine." Making circle-eight patterns in the coffee she'd sloshed on the table, she said, "To make matters worse, I had that *X*-rated dream again."

"No wonder you're tired."

"I suppose you know how funny you are."

Jenna yawned.

And Suzanne said, "I hate to be the one to break this to you, but you don't look all that rested yourself. Don't tell me you're having erotic dreams, too."

Jenna shook her head. She hadn't slept well. She'd dreamed, but hers hadn't been erotic. She'd dreamed of a huge room empty of everything except Craig, and Nick, and her in the middle.

She finished stacking the folders into her schoolbag, talking as she worked. "Was your dream the same as before?"

"Pretty much."

"A naked, faceless man slowly undresses you, and does incredible, unspeakable, arousing things to you."

Suzanne fanned herself with one hand.

"What happened then?" Jenna asked.

"I woke up."

"Can you describe him?"

Suzanne looked out the window, making sure the coast was clear. Twyla Mae had gone to Mass, and Nick and his new trainers had gone running. He'd asked Kenzie to go, but she'd turned all shy and refused. Suzanne didn't get it. That was strange behavior, even for Kenzie. "I told you," Suzanne said when she was certain they were alone. "He was faceless."

"I wasn't referring to his face."

Suzanne's mouth dropped open. "Some refined southern schoolmarm you're turning out to be."

Jenna laughed. "Well?"

"If you must know, he did have an interesting . . ."

"Redeeming quality?"

"Now that's a new word for it."

The sleep-deprived friends began to laugh. They laughed until their stomachs hurt. They were still laughing when a soft knock sounded on the back door. Wiping tears, Jenna called, "The door's open!"

Faith Summers entered hesitantly. "I'm sorry to intrude." The pale blonde glanced at Suzanne. "Did you say anything to Jenna about my use of the laundry facilities?"

Her back to Faith, Suzanne rolled her eyes. She grabbed up her phone and rose to her feet, her footwear flopping as she strode to the door. "Jenna, Pinkie here wants to know if it would be all right if she used the laundry facilities today."

With a wink, she was gone, and Jenna was left staring at Faith, trying in vain to think of something appropriate to say. Faith looked back at her, her flat, unspeaking eyes prolonging the awkward moment. "Pinkie?" she finally said.

Jenna decided it wouldn't be in anyone's best interest to point out the fact that Faith *was* wearing a sleeveless pink shell. "When you get to know Suzanne, you'll discover she has quite a sense of humor."

"I'm sure she's a laugh a minute. You mentioned that my lease includes access to the laundry facilities."

Jenna smiled encouragingly. "Yes. Yes, it does. The service porch is right through here."

She led the way out the back door, down the verandah steps, across a portion of grass, then back up two more steps. Holding the door for Faith, she said, "The washer and dryer were new two years ago." Striding to a metal floor-to-ceiling cabinet, she said, "We share the facilities, but everyone has their own soap, fabric softener and what-not." She cleared off a shelf. "You can keep yours here if you'd like."

Faith looked around uncertainly before lifting the lid of the washer and peering in. Jenna had never seen anyone do that before, and wondered if she was inspecting it for cleanliness. Preferring not to be caught staring, she strolled to the other side of the room and said, "How is your daughter adjusting to her new home?"

Faith closed the lid gently. "Rachel is trying to maintain a permanent sulk, but she slipped last night and spoke to another girl her age at the restaurant."

Jenna smiled. "I'm glad. How about you? Is everything to your liking so far?"

Faith turned her head to look at Jenna. "There have been a lot of changes in our lives lately, but this one is a good one, I think. I did the right thing moving here. It's the first time we've lived in the South. Even the air feels different here."

"It's the humidity. Some days, you can almost drink the air."

"Perhaps that's why everything feels closer here. Scents are thicker, and sounds carry," Faith said, her fingers curled around the handle on the dryer. Bent over that way, she looked thin to the point of gauntness. "Especially voices late at night."

Faith didn't say more. She didn't have to. In her own reserved way, she had let Jenna know that she'd overheard the conversation on the back verandah late last night. "I'll keep that in mind," Jenna said. The women shared a tentative smile, and Jenna thought she was going to like this reticent easterner.

Turning back to the dryer, Faith tugged on the door. She lunged backward, screaming. A huge springy-snakelike contraption bounced off her and landed on the floor.

That scream brought everybody running: Nick, shirtless again, and winded from his workout; Brandon and Benji, their faces flushed, too; Twyla Mae, just home from church, her best Sunday hat secured firmly on her head; and last but not least, Suzanne, looking as innocent as the proverbial cat with a mouth full of canary feathers.

Faith looked from the coil to each of her new neighbors. Benji crept closer and picked up the lifeless, gag-store item. Handing it to Faith, he said, "I'm Benji. I'd keep this if I were you."

She accepted it with a tight smile. "I'm Faith. It's nice to meet you, Benji."

Nick and Brandon introduced themselves next. Twyla Mae said, "I got surprised by that same prank a few days ago."

The only person Faith didn't speak to was Suzanne. At least now Jenna knew why Suzanne had used the back door earlier.

Five pairs of eyes turned on Suzanne the instant Faith left, censure written all over their faces. "What?" Suzanne asked.

"The rule is," Brandon stated coolly, his orange muscle shirt precariously close to sliding off one shoulder, "you can't play a practical joke if it might hurt somebody."

"I know the rule," Suzanne replied levelly. "That spring was covered in fabric and soft as a baby's bottom. The only thing it broke was the ice."

"She looks sad," Benji said.

"Maybe she needs somebody to take her mind off her troubles."

"You think?" Brandon asked.

"Yes, I do."

The boys ambled outside. Twyla Mae followed close behind, shaking a bony finger at Suzanne as she passed. "Somebody's going to get even one of these days, Missy."

Suzanne waved it aside. "Nobody's been able to pull anything over on me since I caught The Rat in bed with our newest waitress." The phone rang in her hand. Muttering under her breath, she punched the button and marched outside. "Yes, Eddie, it's me."

Jenna and Nick were the only two people left in the service porch. Jenna was dressed in lightweight summer slacks and a sleeveless blouse. Nick wore only low-slung jeans and a stare. This was the first she'd seen of him since their talk last night. Whatever he was thinking, his thoughts were running deep. Perhaps he'd done some soul-searching regarding those letters from Craig.

He glanced at the dryer, still open after Suzanne's last prank. Finally, he said, "She really found Eddie in bed with a waitress?"

Jenna did a double-take. That was his deep thought? When would she learn that she couldn't read this man?

"Has she gotten even yet?"

"Even, how?" she asked, in spite of herself.

"You know, an eye for an eye. I heard of one woman who duct-taped her husband's Johnson to his leg while he slept."

She bit her lip to keep from smiling.

Nick continued. "Everybody knows there's a certain tolerance in the South for crabby uncles and shirttail cousins no matter how slight the connection, but I can't believe Suzanne would have let Eddie get away with that scot-free."

Jenna folded her arms and redistributed her weight to one foot. Actually, Suzanne had put pepper spray in Eddie's boxers after the little incident. It seems Eddie had howled louder than Suzanne had while giving birth. He'd even threatened to sue. Of course, she'd told him to go ahead. The media would have a field day with it. Suzanne had told Jenna in confidence, and Jenna wouldn't betray a confidence no matter how long Nick stared at her in that gentling way that made everyone else either babble or back down.

Taking a deep breath, Nick said, "I'm thinking about going on a little tour. Care to join me?"

"Where are we going?"

Nick blinked. There was a time when that *we* would have buckled his knees. He was older now, and hopefully, wiser. "The society is opening a new museum."

"The only museum the society is opening is your father's old house, Nick."

"That's what I heard, too."

"Y'all really want to revisit the place you grew up?"

He never tired of the soft southern cadence in her speech. "I thought Brandon and Benji might enjoy it. If I'm going to take a stroll down memory lane, I might as well start at the beginning."

"You realize that no one can ever really start over at the beginning." But she went to call Brandon and Benji just the same.

Chapter Eight

Suzanne's footsteps were light on the stairs leading to her apartment. She laughed, a deep, throaty rumble that sounded foreign in her own ears. She was still smiling as she opened the door and came face-to-face with her daughter.

"Who was that?" There was suspicion in Kenzie's voice.

Suzanne brought the phone from her ear. "It was your father."

Kenzie's eyes narrowed about the same time she snorted. "What did *he* want?"

Suzanne swore her daughter got more like her every-day. Suzanne's mother thought it was hilarious. Oh, yeah, it was real funny all right. A regular laugh a minute.

Kenzie had always been a handful. Born adorable, she'd been a pudgy baby with round cheeks and big brown eyes. She'd learned to pout before she learned to smile. To this day, it was her preferred expression. She had a smart mind and a mouth to match. Until about three months ago, she'd worn her hair short, like Suzanne's. Now, Kenzie's coffee colored tresses strag-gled, shocked and bewildered, down the back of her neck. She was growing it out, she said. Suzanne was thankful she hadn't died it orange or bleached it white. Yet. Hairstyle aside, she was going to be a looker, no doubt about it. With a little luck, she'd get taller than her mother. It was possible. Eddie was tall.

Now, about Eddie.

Suzanne put the phone on the hall table. "Your father said he's sorry for standing you up for the weekend. He'd like to make it up to you by taking you to a matinee this afternoon."

"You said somebody can't make something up to somebody else just like you can't ever take something back after you said it. What's done is done, you said."

How could Suzanne have known Kenzie had been listening? One of these days she would remember that Kenzie heard more than she let on. "That's true," Suzanne said. "Your dad would still like to spend time with you."

"Just Dad and me?"

"That's what he said."

Kenzie's severe expression eased a little. "What movie?"

"What movie do you want to see?"

The girl shrugged. Before she glanced away, Suzanne caught a glimpse of the excitement and spunk that used to be so apparent in her daughter.

"Hey, I know," Suzanne said. "They're having an Orson Twins movie marathon at the Plaza all weekend."

Kenzie spun around. "Just poke me in the eye with a sharp stick. You know I can't stand all that prissy bullsh—"

Suzanne cast her darling daughter a watch-it-kid look along with the entertainment section of the newspaper.

Grabbing the paper, Kenzie said, "I suppose you think you're smart."

"You didn't get it from the man in the moon, kiddo."

The girl spent the next several minutes perusing the

newspaper and chewing on her finger nail. "Think I could pass for thirteen?"

Suzanne turned on the light in the bathroom. "So you can get in to see a PG-13 movie?" She opened a drawer and rummaged through it. "Think again!"

Kenzie moved on to the next page of movie advertisements, keeping her place with the tip of her pointer finger, the nail chewed ragged, all the way to the skin. The choices for her age bracket were lame. They included an animated movie where all the characters broke out into stupid song. Another show starred talking dogs on about their fourth cross-country adventure. Her only other choice was the Orson Twins movie marathon. Being eleven was a pain in the ass.

"What did you decide on?" her mother called.

"The talking dogs, I guess. I heard the trainers put peanut butter on the dogs' gums to make them move their mouths so they look like they're talking."

"I think they only did that with Mr. Ed."

Her mother's voice sounded muffled. Kenzie peered around the corner, where she could see into the bathroom. Her mom was standing in front of the mirror. Kenzie's throat felt funny all of a sudden.

"What are you doing?" she asked.

Her mother finished outlining her lips with the new lipstick pencil they'd gotten free in the mail the other day. "I'm getting ready for work. What does it look like I'm doing?"

It looked like her mom was getting all gussied up, like she'd been doing lately since Kenzie's dad started coming over. Kenzie's stomach started to hurt again. She took deep breaths and tried to shake it off, the way her soccer coach told her to do when she got creamed at practice. "Marcel's ain't open on Sundays."

"Isn't open. That's precisely why it's the best time to clean it."

Kenzie released a deep breath and whispered to herself, "Who needs to put on lipstick to clean?"

* * *

Suzanne turned her back on the dishes stacked in the sink then promptly wandered out of her little kitchen. The state of the rest of the apartment wasn't much better. A chair was out at the table. There were clothes strewn about the living room, along with an array of shoes, some Kenzie's, others Suzanne's, all of them looking as if their occupants had been plucked right out of them by a sudden gust of wind. At that very moment, a sweating glass was leaving another water stain on an old end stand. Suzanne turned her back on that, too.

She'd switched on the radio shortly after Eddie and Kenzie had left. She'd tried cranking up the volume. Her conscience only screamed louder. Marching to the shelf, she cut the power and faced the quiet. From there, she stomped into the front entryway. Reaching for her keys and the bag of cleaning supplies she'd picked up yesterday, she headed for the door. She'd told Kenzie she was going to Marcel's to clean, and by God, that's what she would do.

Thinking about Marcel's calmed her. The coffee shop was her creation, a mix and match of soft lights and strong flavors. Everything about it was her inspiration, from the stained glass window of the Eiffel Tower, to the small, outdoor café-style tables and chairs, to the deep comfy sofas.

The menu was in French and English. Suzanne had taken two years of French in high school. Back then, she'd dreamed of going there, living there, doing something marvelous with her life there. Marcel's and Kenzie were about the closest she'd ever gotten to doing anything marvelous. Some day, she'd get to Paris. If she was lucky, she would make it before she lost all her teeth and half her marbles.

She wasn't sure she had half her marbles now. Kenzie had caught her applying lipstick before Eddie came over, and she'd called her on it. For crying out loud, Eddie was history. He was a dog, his nose always in the air for the scent of a female. Any female.

God, she'd loved him.

She gave up Paris for him. But she'd gotten Kenzie. She figured she'd come out way ahead in that deal. Still, Eddie was history. The only reason she ever saw him was that he'd taken a renewed interest in their daughter. Kenzie loved him. That girl needed something right now, something that Suzanne couldn't seem to give her. It would help if she knew what that something was. But Kenzie wasn't talking, and until she did, all Suzanne could do was guess, and try to do the right thing.

She was thinking about that as she locked the door and descended the stairs. Jenna and the boys had gone somewhere with Nick. Twyla Mae was playing bridge with Mrs. Ferguson across the street. It looked like Pinkie was doing laundry in the service porch.

Suzanne's conscience itched way back in a place she couldn't reach to scratch. Calling her new neighbor Pinkie wasn't the nicest thing she'd ever done. Okay, it wasn't the nastiest, either, but that was beside the point. She stashed the cleaning supplies on the backseat of her ten-year-old Impala, then plodded on over to the service porch.

Masses of dark clouds gathered overhead, hovering over Harmony like an upside-down Tupperware bowl. Suzanne tried to think of something to say. The weather didn't offer much in the way of conversation, the afternoon hot and airless with the coming storm.

Faith looked up when Suzanne entered, but she didn't speak. Or smile. In some perverse way, Suzanne respected her for it. Faith went to the metal cabinet and removed a jumbo-size jug of laundry soap. Despite the fact that she didn't have a lot in the curves department, hers was the walk of a woman accustomed to getting a second look. She wore the same clothes she'd had on that morning. There wasn't a wrinkle in her gray slacks and pink top. Suzanne didn't know how rich people did that, if she was indeed still rich, which Suzanne doubted. Rich people didn't live on Beulah Street, and that was that.

The blonde glanced at Suzanne, still unsmiling, still not saying a word. The lift of her pale eyebrows was a prod if Suzanne ever saw one.

Suzanne opened her mouth, and out tumbled, "I'm sorry."

It was a toss-up to say who was more surprised, and yet the apology was met with more silence. Suzanne was prepared to do an about-face and leave, when, finally, Faith spoke. "Are you referring to that silly practical joke?"

The "silly" description rankled, but Suzanne swallowed it and said, "I guess."

"All right, then. Apology accepted." She didn't add, *You can go now,* but she might as well have.

Suzanne had experienced warmer conversations with answering machines. She was mildly aware of buttons being pushed, a knob being turned, and Faith pouring blue liquid from the jug into the cap. She drizzled the detergent into the washer, poured another cupful of soap, and added that one, too. She was pouring another when Suzanne marched forward and covered the full cap with one hand. "What are you doing?"

"What do you mean?"

"I mean, if you add more soap you'll be knee-deep in suds before the wash cycle is through."

Faith peered into the washer, where suds were beginning to form. "Really?"

"Haven't you ever done laundry?"

She glanced at Suzanne, then quickly away in her ongoing flirtation with shyness. "Actually, this is my first time."

For a split second, Suzanne was sure Faith was kidding, but the twin splotches of pink on that pale face made a believer out of her. Oh, for crying out loud. She bit that back and said, "It isn't hard. In fact, once you get the basics down, it's easy."

Faith's gaze darted to Suzanne's, one part reserve, nine parts distrust. Suzanne figured she deserved that. With a roll of her eyes, she ran through the short version of Laundry 101. When Faith made no move to follow her brief instructions, Suzanne said, "If you don't believe me, there are directions on the back of that jug of Tide."

Faith turned it over and began to read.

Suzanne was at the door when the other woman said, "Thank you."

Thunder rumbled softly in the distance. Nick and Jenna and the boys had gone on a picnic. It looked as if they might end up getting wet. "Jenna and I often do our laundry together on Friday nights. You can join us next time, if you'd like."

"This Friday?"

"It's a pathetic way to spend a Friday night, I know. Do you like mint juleps?"

"I've never had one."

Suzanne grinned. "You're in for a real treat."

Faith smiled, too. Feeling strangely better, Suzanne set foot outside just as thunder rumbled again.

Brandon and Benji were quiet as Nick drove through the gate and beyond the new sign, Proffit Manor. For once, Nick wasn't quiet. He was whistling. Jenna couldn't recall having ever heard him do that.

They'd all rolled down their windows when they'd driven down Jefferson Street so they could smell the Cherokee roses and honeysuckle. Brandon and Benji were still looking out their windows, their eyes big, their expressions serious.

"You boys remember your grandparents' house, don't you?" she asked.

"We couldn't touch anything," Brandon said.

"Or play," Benji added.

"Or breathe."

The last had been muttered under Nick's breath. Jenna cast him a sidelong glance again, but he'd already gone back to whistling tunelessly. The driveway veered to the right, curving toward the house. Jenna recognized most of the cars parked in a half circle in front of the wide marble steps and tall pillars. The vehicles belonged to the members of Ladies Historic Society or the Garden Club, which might as well have been the same organization.

Proffit Manor was located in the Heights, which was only high on paper and in certain people's minds. It sat on the edge of the historic district located between a U-curve of the Canoochee River. The house was white and big and antebellum in style. It wasn't the largest or the oldest house in Harmony, but it was the most ostentatious, especially today, surrounded as it was by a dome of gray clouds.

The cement driveway was lined with moss-draped oaks and magnolias, the tangled fronds as limp and still as the air. The grass was cut short, the bushes and shrubs perfectly manicured. An ornate sign directed visitors toward the house. Instead, Nick followed a narrower, blacktop drive through a brick and wrought-iron gate, open today. He hadn't gotten far when a bone-thin woman with gray hair hurried toward the path, waving for him to stop.

"The tour is open only to the house . . . Oh, it's you," Lenore Jones said to Nick. "The grounds are not part of the tour as of yet."

The way she enunciated each word, and turned up the volume reminded Nick of the way Lenore spoke to Simon, the caretaker at the cemetery, who sometimes did odd jobs for the wealthy. A slow simmer started deep inside him, building up steam and pressure.

"How are you, Jenna?"

Beside him, Jenna said, "I'm fine, Lenore."

Lenore was halfway into a fake smile before she realized that Jenna hadn't asked after her in return. The pressure leaked out of Nick like air around a faulty valve. Lenore's smile slid away in a similar fashion.

Nick took his foot from the brake. Lenore moved as if to step in front of his vehicle.

"I wouldn't do that if I were you," he called through Jenna's open window.

Lenore's eyes narrowed into slits and anger pinched the corners of her mouth, but he noticed she took a backward, not a forward, step. "So it's true," she said, her gaze darting from Jenna to Nick and back again.

Nick wanted to ask what the hell was true, but Jenna placed a hand on his arm, silencing him. "Let's keep going, shall we?" she said, staring straight ahead.

He drove on. They were both quiet. Suddenly Brandon and Benji weren't.

"Would you have run over her, Uncle Nick? Huh? Would you?"

"Of course he wouldn't," Brandon stated. "You wouldn't, would you, Uncle Nick?"

And risk damaging the Land Rover? Nick looked at Jenna. She kept her eyes straight ahead.

"No," he said, watching the path, too. "I wouldn't have run over her. But don't tell her that."

A hundred yards ahead, the paved drive gave way to a gravel lane. He followed it to the end, then parked in the shade of an old oak tree. From there, the land rolled gently to the river, lazy between rains.

The boys pushed out of Nick's Land Rover as soon as he put it in park. Nick retrieved the picnic basket and his camera from the back, Jenna a quilt that had belonged to her grandmother. Brandon and Benji spread the blanket on the grass. Jenna set out paper plates. Nick doled out forks. The kids dug into their thick roast beef sandwiches with gusto. Nick and Jenna ate more slowly and quietly. After polishing off two sandwiches each, a juice box and two rows of brownies, the boys ran down to the river's edge to look for frogs. Reminding Brandon and Benji about safety, Jenna put away the remainder of her uneaten sandwich. Finally, she looked at Nick. He was whistling tunelessly again.

"We'd better keep an eye on the storm," she said.

He looked at the sky.

"Not that storm," she said.

His eyebrows shot up, the only indication he gave of surprise.

Stones went *kerplunk* in the river. Satisfied that the boys weren't too close to the water's edge, she said, "Do you always whistle when you're angry?"

"Was I whistling?"

"Are you angry?"

He didn't readily reply. He was looking at the boys. She wasn't sure that was what he was seeing. "I shouldn't have brought you and Brandon and Benji here."

"Why ever not?"

Nick let all his breath out through his mouth and glared at her. "You know damn well why not. I didn't think about what it would do to your reputation."

"Please don't tell me you're worried about my reputation."

"I could have sworn I just did."

"Then stop it. The society shredded my reputation two years ago, Nick."

They looked at each other, Jenna's eyes wide and blue, Nick's narrowed and green. "All right," he said. "If you mean that, why didn't you tell Lenore off a little while ago?"

"What good would it have done?"

"You would have felt better. I would have felt better."

"I doubt that. I'm trying to teach Brandon and Benji to rise above that sort of thing. Besides, I don't care what Lenore thinks." She turned her attention to the boys. It looked as if they were gathering sticks and twigs. "Is there anything else on your mind?"

"There is one thing."

Thunder rumbled, closer this time. Rising as far as her knees, she said, "Yes?"

"Why didn't you tell Craig about that kiss?"

Outwardly, Jenna didn't move. Inside, she sighed. They were back to that kiss again. On her knees in the center of the quilt, she stared at Nick in silent contemplation. She wasn't a fanciful woman, or a particularly romantic one, not anymore. She knew her strengths and her weaknesses, and she knew herself inside and out. She was a modern-day southern woman with a fair mind and an honest soul. And she honestly didn't know why Nick couldn't accept the notion, no, the fact that Craig had been a good, kind, decent man.

She was drawn to Nick, but at that moment, thunder rumbling, the boys squabbling, it occurred to her that his qualms about Craig would always be between them. It made her sad, just as it always had, but it also made her determined.

"If you must know, I didn't tell Craig because it would have hurt him." She rose to her feet and smoothed the wrinkles in her slacks.

"So you were protecting Craig."

She started toward the river's edge, a sudden gust of wind blowing her hair across her face. She continued walking, answering over her shoulder. "I was protecting both of you."

Her reply sneaked up on Nick like a smile, warming him in ways he didn't appreciate. Was he so pathetic, so in need of a gentle touch and a kind smile, that it rendered him speechless and immobile when he got it? Evidently he was.

The hell he was.

He grabbed his camera and rolled to his feet. The light was perfect for photographs and he saw no reason to waste it. He took countless pictures of Brandon and Benji skipping stones, of Brandon pretending to be a fur trader and Benji one of the Creek Indians who'd once lived and traded on the banks of this very river. Jenna talked and laughed and played with the kids, but kept a cool shoulder turned to Nick. Despite that, he snapped her picture time and again. Exasperated, she finally looked directly at the camera, and stuck out her tongue. Nick took that picture, too. He could tell she was having a hard time holding a grudge. At least he hadn't lost his touch there.

The clouds hung close to the ground all around them. Those overhead were beginning to churn. The wind was picking up, rustling the new green leaves in the old oak tree.

"We're going to have to go soon," Jenna said.

"We're building a raft," Benji called.

For the first time in a while, Nick lowered his camera and looked beyond the lens to the broader picture. He'd noticed Brandon and Benji gathering twigs and branches. Now, he saw that they'd placed them side by side on the bank of the river. A distant memory tapped along the edges of his mind, as if trying to get in.

"Your dad and I did that once," he said.

His voice had been so quiet, he was surprised anyone had heard him over the wind. But all three of them had. Jenna was on her haunches, balancing on the balls of her feet, a stick in each hand. Brandon was bent at the waist, Benji on his knees in the dirt. All of them were looking at Nick, waiting for him to continue.

"A big raft?" Brandon finally asked.

"Huge." Nick glanced past the kids to Jenna. "We pretended we were in the Okefenokee Swamp, and there were alligators all around us."

"How old were you?" Brandon asked. As often happened with these two, Brandon did most of the talking, and Benji most of the listening.

"How old? Let's see." Nick started toward them, his camera dangling from one hand. "I was probably eight or nine." He thought back, and said, "I was eight. That would have made your dad eleven. Your grandparents had gone somewhere for several days, and your dad and I had escaped Rosita's list of chores. We worked for days, cutting the branches with a rusty hatchet, and tying them together with old baling twine. We made the thing huge. The entire time we worked, we made plans to build boats together some day when we grew up."

The only sound for a long time was the water meandering over stones worn smooth over the centuries. Finally, Brandon said, "What happened?"

For a moment, Nick thought that was a good question. But then he realized his nephew was referring to the raft, and not life, itself. "When the raft was finished, we pushed and pulled until we got it into the water. We hopped on, balancing on the logs we'd secured with our own hands. I'll never forget how it felt as we floated toward the center of the river. The current caught it, and we started floating downstream."

"Just like Huckleberry Finn," Brandon said.

Nick almost smiled. "We didn't make it quite as far as Huckleberry did."

"You didn't?"

Nick shook his head. "After a matter of minutes, our raft started to take on water. It slipped under the surface of the river, slowly sinking until water covered our shoes, our ankles, our knees. It was late spring, and the river was higher, the current faster than it is today. We rode that raft until we had to tread water, and then Craig helped me to shore."

Everyone was quiet, Nick remembering, the others picturing it. "Be careful," Jenna said. "That almost sounded like a fond memory."

Nick turned his head slowly. She stood, hands on her hips, her head tilted slightly, sass written all over her face. He was going to have to come up with a new definition of a lady.

The first drop of rain landed in the center of Nick's forehead, running slowly down the bridge of his nose.

Others landed on his head, on his shoulders, on the ground around him. Any second now, the sky was going to open up. Coming to their senses, they all scrambled for cover. The boys raced to the Land Rover while Nick and Jenna grabbed up everything else.

"Did your father know about that raft, Nick?" She shook the dirt off the quilt, but she looked at him.

He had no idea why she asked, but he nodded. "He and Mom got home about the time we made it to the house."

"What did Reginald do?"

"He unbuckled his belt, removed it, and whipped Craig's bony butt with it."

Jenna's hand flew to her mouth.

They picked up the picnic basket together as he said, "It happened to me a lot, but that's the only time I remember it happening to Craig."

"Why?"

"What do you mean, why?"

"Why did he whip Craig? Was your father angry with him because he was older and should have known better?"

"Yeah, right."

"What then? Was he worried that you might have drowned?"

"Not me, Jenna." Thunder rumbled, and it was beginning to rain as if it meant it. "It was Craig he was worried about. He was terrified that Craig might have drowned. I heard him say it the first time his belt smacked against the seat of Craig's pants. 'You might have drowned,' he said. 'What would I have then?' "

Jenna was quiet as she walked to the Land Rover. Looking at Nick over the top of his vehicle, rain bouncing on the shiny surface, she said, "Your father was a piece of work. It's a miracle you boys ever turned out decent."

Something opened inside him, something he'd sealed off a long time ago. Jenna had always believed in him.

Not many people in Harmony had. There was good reason for that. The word *attitude* could have been coined after him. He'd flirted with danger, had loved a good fight, and took pleasure in rubbing the law the wrong way. Jenna knew all that. She believed in him anyway. Just as she believed in Craig. Nick was going to have to think about that, and come to terms with that, then decide what to do about it.

"Are we going to tour the house?" Brandon asked when everyone was snug and secure inside the SUV.

Nick considered that for a moment. The thought of tracking in mud was appealing. In the end, he said, "There's nothing for us in that house."

He put the Land Rover in gear, turned the windshield wipers on, and headed for someplace, anyplace, but here.

Chapter Nine

Nick exited the Proffit Manor driveway slowly. Driving north along Jefferson Street, he followed the curves and gently rolling hills along the river, the windshield wipers keeping time with a rhythmic swish. The radio was turned low, the atmosphere inside the Land Rover subdued.

Jenna couldn't help thinking about what it had been like for Craig and Nick as children. How could any man treat two sons the way Reginald Proffit had treated his? It left a lingering sadness in the back of her mind and a hollowed-out feeling in the pit of her stomach. She'd liked Craig's mother, but she'd never been close to her father-in-law. Even Craig's relationship with his father had been one of tolerance more than love. Although Craig had done his best, having to be perfect in every way hadn't been easy. Still, Nick was the one who'd suffered the most. That made his rise above his childhood all the more dignified. She wanted to tell him as much, but he was staring straight ahead, his mouth set, his emotions evidently locked up tight beneath his matching expression.

The boys grew restless in the backseat. Since there wasn't much to see out the rain-soaked windows, Jenna asked them what game they'd like to play. They conferred, and decided on the game they called the I'm-thinking-of-something game. It was a simple, heartwarming, funny game in which the person who was It thought of something from home, then proceeded to give one description of the item. The first opponent took a guess. If it was wrong, the player gave another clue, and so it went, until the item was identified.

Benji went first. He described his item as gray. Jenna noticed that Nick wasn't really into the game. His thoughts, it seemed were miles away. Still, they browbeat him into playing along, and he guessed socks after Jenna's and Brandon's guesses proved to be wrong. In the end, Brandon nailed Benji's secret item, spouting, "It's your arrowhead in the top drawer of your desk."

Next, it was Brandon's turn. His secret something was red. Again, Nick guessed socks. He did the same thing when it was Jenna's turn to be It, and she described the item she was thinking of as "something yellow."

And then it was Nick's turn to describe something in his house. He strummed his fingers on the steering wheel and said, "I'm thinking of something white."

In unison, Jenna, Brandon and Benji all shouted, "Socks."

And they were all right.

Everybody laughed, the boys' childish, Jenna's soft and sultry, and Nick's a deep, rusty rumble that sounded a little like an engine that hadn't been started in a long, long time. Tension seemed to ease out of him, and he relaxed. Nick knew Jenna's gaze was on him. He knew what her gaze was doing to him. Maybe sitting next to a blue-eyed woman while two beguiling kids laughed and bickered in the backseat was the reason he felt oddly content and strangely understood. The fact that he'd left the city limit sign behind didn't hurt, either. The truth was, Nick hadn't known a lot of contentment in his life. He'd reached a point where he was comfortable with his success, with who he was and where he was going. But comfort and contentment were two entirely different things.

They hadn't gone far when Nick saw something in the middle of the highway up ahead. It looked like either a rock or some small animal that had been hit on the road. He slowed as he passed, braking gradually in the pouring rain.

"What's wrong?" Jenna asked.

"I don't know yet," he replied.

There were only a few cars ahead of them, and a few others far behind. He pulled to the shoulder of the road. Throwing an arm over the back of Jenna's seat, he squinted through the rain-streaked back window and slowly began to back up.

Jenna looked behind her, too, the action causing her hair to fall across Nick's forearm. The muscles in his forearm flexed. He glanced at her hair briefly. It was enough to let her know he felt the electrical charge in the air, too. Suddenly, she didn't know where to look, so she looked everywhere except at Nick. He brought the vehicle to a stop, put it in park, and switched on his emergency flashers.

Brandon and Benji peered through the side window. Jenna noticed that neither of them said a word. It occurred to her that they often adopted a wait-and-see attitude when they were with Nick. He had that effect on people. It was part of his mystery. It wasn't the biggest part.

Benji said, "That's a turtle, isn't it, Uncle Nick?"

"It sure is." He unfastened his seat belt and moved to open his door.

The kids opened their doors, too.

"Whoa," Nick and Jenna said at the same time.

"We're coming with you!" Benji exclaimed.

"It's pouring," Jenna said.

"It's a painted turtle, Mom," Brandon said. "A car'll hit it for sure. It'll die without us."

Nick looked at each of the boys for a moment. As if reaching a decision, he eased toward Jenna, resting one hand on her seat near her knee. He didn't bring his fingers quite close enough to touch her, but he came close enough to make her the tiniest bit uncomfortable and a whole lot aware. Of him, as a man, and of her, as a woman.

"They can help me," he said. "I'll make sure they stay right next to me."

She looked into his moss green eyes, and couldn't look away.

A moment later, he reached with his other hand, retrieving a black umbrella from under her seat. "I'll keep them completely safe. And relatively dry," he added. "I promise."

Brandon, Benji and Nick exited the vehicle. Once outside, Nick handed the umbrella to Brandon. With a hand at each of their shoulders, he waited until a car had passed before striding to the center of the highway.

Brandon quickly opened the umbrella. Reaching up as high as he could, he held it over the three of them. Heat flooded Jenna's throat at the sight of her sons dressed in khaki shorts and colorful shirts standing on either side of Nick, dressed all in black, water streaming down all around them.

She wished she could have a picture of that. Why couldn't she? Tucking Nick's camera under her arm, she slipped into the rain, too. She studied the buttons on the expensive camera for a moment, removed the lens cover and looked through. Benji was bent at the waist, inspecting the turtle. Nick bent over, too, while Brandon held onto the large umbrella with both hands, keeping them all dry. She snapped picture after picture as the trio moved en masse to the side of the highway closest to the river.

She captured on film the solemnity of the procession as the three of them delivered the animal to safety. She was getting soaked, and was about to get back in the Land Rover when she noticed Brandon say some-thing to Nick. She couldn't hear what her son said, but a change came over Nick before her very eyes. It wasn't any one thing, but a culmination of the way Nick straight-ened, the way he turned and began to walk, the set of his shoulders and the grim angle of his chin.

He looked both ways, but not at her. Taking the um-brella from Brandon, Nick escorted the kids safely to the Land Rover.

Jenna got in, too, her arms, hair and shoulders rain soaked. "Everything okay?" she asked, eyeing Nick.

The boys' answer was a resounding, "Yes!"

"We did it!"

"We're the best!"

"Nick?" she asked.

"Everything's fine and dandy."

He barely uttered another sound all the way home.

"What does this say?" Jenna pointed to a line in the middle of the page in Benji's library book.

Benji concentrated. His face contorting with effort, he sounded out a choppy *to-see-if-the-le-gend-was-true*.

"Very good."

He sighed before glancing out the window. Brandon was tossing a ball onto the roof of the carriage house, catching it forlornly each time it rolled down again. He didn't appreciate having to play alone anymore than Benji appreciated having to read when he could have been playing.

The rain had moved on, leaving behind puddles and a sauna-like heat that had forced Jenna to finally give in and turn on the air conditioning. The atmosphere had changed. There was more to it than the appearance of the sun.

Jenna continued to listen as Benji read. The moment he'd completed the pre-agreed number of pages, he closed the book and scrambled to his feet. She put the book away then followed her son outside. A steam bath assaulted her the moment she set foot on the back verandah.

Her hair had dried into an unruly mass of curls. Tucking the tendrils behind her ears, she wandered as far as the railing. The neighbor boy she'd hired last summer to cut the grass had appeared the moment the rain had stopped. Now, the scent of damp, fresh-cut grass was strong in the air.

Like most kids, Brandon and Benji were oblivious to the heat as they raced to the climbing tree. Twyla Mae was showing Faith and Rachel her flower garden. Suzanne had returned after cleaning the coffee shop, but had gone directly up to her apartment. Kenzie hadn't yet arrived back from her afternoon with her father. The only person not accounted for at 317 Beulah Street was Nick. He'd left an hour ago. Jenna had no idea where he'd gone or when he would return. If he would return. That "if" nagged at the back of her mind.

When they'd first arrived home after rescuing that turtle, she'd invited Nick inside for something cold to drink. He'd mumbled an excuse she hadn't quite been able to hear, then ambled into his own apartment. She'd poured Kool-Aid for the boys and a tall glass of ice tea for herself. Being as nonchalant as possible, she'd asked about the rescue of the turtle.

Brandon and Benji had both looked at her, but Benji had said, "You were there."

So much for nonchalance. "Was the turtle okay?" she'd prodded.

"Yeah. Uncle Nick said he was pretty big for a painted turtle. He wasn't too heavy for Uncle Nick, though," Brandon declared. "We're getting him back in shape."

She smiled. "Did you ask him questions about the turtle?"

"What's to ask?" Benji quipped. "We know all about painted turtles."

"What did you say to him, then, if it wasn't to inquire after the animal?"

"When?" Brandon asked.

Jenna took a small sip of her cool drink. "Right after Uncle Nick carried the turtle across the road. He let him go on the other side, and then you said something, Brandon. I was just wondering what you talked about."

"I don't remember saying anything." Brandon shrugged.

Setting his beverage on the table with a loud clunk, Benji said, "You told him Dad did that, remember?"

A vibration started deep in Jenna's chest, winding upward like a fan on reverse, drawing the air out of her, causing her voice to wobble as she said, "What did your dad do?"

"He rescued a turtle just like Uncle Nick did!" Benji declared. "I don't remember, but Brandon does. Right, Brandon?"

Brandon nodded importantly. "I was five. I don't know where Benj was, but me and Dad were goin' to the park. It wasn't raining that time."

"Your father carried a turtle across the road, too?"

Brandon nodded. "He stopped on the side of the road just like Uncle Nick did. I've helped two times now. First when I was little, and the second time, today."

First and second. Better and best. At least Jenna had a pretty good idea what had caused the sudden change in Nick. She wondered where he was, and what it would take for him to finally get over feeling second best.

Jenna opened her eyes. It was late. She'd fallen asleep on the sofa in front of the television. Her neck was stiff, her right hand numb where she'd rested her head. Shaking her hand awake, she sat up and switched off the TV.

Earlier, she'd locked the doors and turned off all but a few dim lights. Now that the air conditioner was running and the windows closed tight, the only outdoor sound she could hear were the bushes scraping the siding in the wind.

When she'd first moved into this apartment house, she'd had to get used to pipes rattling and footsteps overhead. No pipes rattled tonight, and no footsteps sounded anywhere. Everything was quiet as Jenna padded out to the kitchen. She switched off the light over the sink and peered out the window. Lingering clouds obliterated all but a few stars. The sky was black, the backyard dark, the carriage house apartment the darkest of all. She couldn't see the parking area from here, so she didn't know if Nick's Land Rover was parked with the other cars.

She glanced at the clock on the stove. It was midnight. Tomorrow was Monday. It was time she went to bed.

The bath she'd taken earlier had failed to lift her melancholy mood. Unfastening her robe as she went, she tiptoed into the boys' room. Brandon was sprawled on his back, Benji on his stomach. She picked up a discarded shirt, and tugged the sheet up over Brandon's shoulders, kissing the top of his head in the process. Next, she tucked Benji's sheet under his chin and kissed his forehead, too. Turning off the lamp under the window between the two beds, she quietly left their room.

She was prepared for the coming week. Papers were graded, lesson plans complete. The pantry was stocked, all their clothes were clean, backpacks were ready and waiting on their designated pegs near the door. There was really no reason for her to feel so unsettled.

In her bedroom, she slipped out of her robe and toed out of her slippers. Dropping the robe to the foot of the bed, she straightened. Something banged hollowly in the wind. She paused, listening intently. The noise came again. After a few moments, she identified it as the screen door hitting the house. She must have forgotten to latch it.

She hurried through the dark kitchen. Feeling for the lock, she turned it and opened the back door. She reached for the screen door next. A dark form in the shape of a man beat her to it. She reeled backward, too stunned to scream.

The man started, too, and swore. "It's me, Jenna." Nick.

She couldn't release the stronghold she had on her throat. But at least she could breathe.

"The door was beating against the house in the wind," he said.

"Yes. I heard it, too."

He stood on one side of the screen, her on the other. "You okay?"

"Yes."

He let himself in. "Are you sure?"

"I'm fine." Her heart was beating fast and she was still a little breathless. "Are you just getting home?"

"Yeah."

He smelled faintly of beer, cigarette smoke and the warm Georgia wind. He'd probably driven home with his windows down after keeping a barstool warm somewhere. There was no law against having a beer. Or driving with the windows down. Or staying out late.

"It didn't occur to me to call."

Had he read her mind? "You're a big boy, Nick. You don't owe me an explanation."

He was looking at her in the near darkness, and it occurred to her that he could probably see her in her white nightgown better than she could see him in his dark clothing. Suddenly, she was aware of how little she had on.

The floor creaked as he took a step closer. The only other sound was his deeply drawn breath before he said, "You're angry."

She didn't deny it. Being angry was unusual for her. "I'm tired, that's all."

He eased a little closer. "Is that all?"

Okay, maybe he wasn't reading her mind. Maybe what he was sensing was the low vibration of awareness thrumming to life inside her. Then and there, Jenna acknowledged the reason she felt so unsettled. She'd been thinking about making love. All evening she'd been trying to conjure up Craig's image. It wasn't Craig who'd sparked this longing deep inside her. Craig wasn't here. She doubted the reality of that, the sheer enormity of it, would ever fail to make her sad. Her vows had been until death. She'd kept them two years beyond that. What she felt at this moment wasn't sadness. She felt young in a way she hadn't felt in a long time, and alive, and jittery.

She'd loved Craig. She loved him still. And yet it was Nick she wanted tonight.

No, she didn't. Yes, she did.

Yes. She did. It was confusing. It was unsettling. Hadn't Nick always confused and unsettled her?

"Jenna?"

It was as if he knew. She held out a hand in a halting gesture. He took her hand in his own, his fingers enveloping hers. She thought he might tug on her hand, toppling her into his arms. Instead, he kissed the skin above her knuckles. No one had ever kissed her there before.

Unable to see in the dark, she could only feel, and hear, and smell. His lips were dry, the kiss warm, his breathing slow and deep. He smelled very masculine and a little dangerous. Turning her hand palm-side up, he kissed her wrist, his touch a delicious sensation. And then he brought his other hand to her face, grazing her cheek. She turned into his touch.

"It's late," she whispered.

He kissed her cheek, his voice rasping close to her ear. "Is it too late?" he whispered.

Too late for what? she wondered. The air conditioner came on, the cool current of air stirring her nightgown, raising goose bumps on her arms, bringing her to her senses.

She backed out of his embrace. They needed to talk. First, she needed to put on more clothes. "I'll just be a moment." Turning on her heel, she practically ran to her bedroom. She was reaching for her robe when footsteps sounded behind her. Nick had followed her. She shouldn't have been surprised, and yet, turning slowly, she clutched the robe in her hand, but couldn't seem to move to put it on.

He'd paused a moment in the hall.

"Nick, what are you . . ."

"I'm a man who lives by instinct."

"Instinct? Nick. I . . . What do you . . ."

Desire surged through Nick, yet he moved slowly toward her. A lamp glowed behind her, the light delineating the curve of her hip and the length of her thigh through the knee-skimming white nightgown. "What do I want? Is that what you were going to ask me?"

She didn't answer.

Reaching a hand to her, he traced her lips with the blunt tip of one finger. "I want to make love to you. Very bad. Or very good, depending on your perspective."

Her lips were full, her skin smooth. Her neck was slender, the hollow at its base a delicate shadow. He touched her there, too, and felt the flutter of her pulse. Her collarbones were narrow ridges; her shoulders were pale, but not as pale as the narrow straps of her white gown.

"You want to make love to me?" she whispered. "But I don't think . . ."

"Don't think." He wanted to tell her to simply feel, to let it happen, but he didn't say it. Nick Proffit knew when to keep his mouth shut. For now, he let his hands do the convincing.

Her eyes closed part-way, and her hands came to rest lightly on his shoulders. He'd imagined this day a thousand times. His imagination hadn't done it justice. "I want to love you slow, touch you everywhere." He slid his fingers into her hair, down the side of her neck to her shoulder. His thumb skimmed her collarbone, easing the narrow strap down an inch, and then another. "I want to kiss you, taste you, savor you." He could feel her warming, responding. "I want to be the best lover you've ever had."

"The best, Nick?"

He stopped. Held perfectly still. Didn't even breathe until his lungs threatened to explode. Jenna was looking at him, her eyes open wide now. "You want to be the best. Those were your exact words."

She must have taken a backward step. Nick knew he hadn't moved. For a moment, he didn't know what the hell had happened. But Jenna was slipping the strap back up her shoulder and straightening her nightgown.

"What are you doing?" he asked.

She donned a long robe. Cinching the belt tight at her waist, she said, "I'm going to read for a while." She picked up a book. "And then I'm going to sleep."

The look she gave him said a hell of a lot more. A stare-down ensued.

Jenna refused to let the steel in Nick's gaze intimidate her. The shadow of a day-old beard darkened the lower half of his face. His jaw was squared, the bridge of his nose bore a tiny scar that gave testimony to an old injury. He wore black jeans and a faded black T-shirt. There was enough heat in his eyes to take the starch out of her knees, but not out of her spine.

"I won't be a trophy, Nick. Or a measuring stick for your issues or your ego or your success."

"I don't have issues, damn it."

Out of everything she'd said, he'd chosen *that* to argue about? Everybody had issues. But fine, they would do this his way. "Why did you really come back to Harmony, Nick?"

"You know why."

His voice was still a low rumble, a masculine sweep across her senses. "Yes, but do you?" she asked.

He looked like a man whose temper was about to go through the roof. Finally, he said, "You want me to put it in words?"

She waited, arms folded at her ribs.

"I returned to make sure you and the boys were okay."

"We're alive and well. And so are you."

Nick didn't know what Jenna was getting at. He wasn't at all sure he wanted to know. But she was right about one thing. He was alive. And so was his desire. "I suppose you think there's more to it than that."

She shrugged.

"By all means," he said. "Enlighten me."

"I think you want to be first, not second, best, not better."

Nick didn't reply one way or the other.

And she said, "I can't explain what almost happened between us a few minutes ago. I won't diminish it by trying to chalk it up to loneliness. There's something you should know. I don't give out grades for making love."

It was unnerving, the way she understood him when he didn't understand himself. It was also damned infuriating.

"I'll make a goddamn mental note." He turned on his heel and hightailed it out of Jenna's bedroom and straight to the carriage house's main door. He opened his door and slammed it hard enough to rattle the rafters.

He'd never known a woman who could irritate him faster or so thoroughly. His jeans were still a good size too small, and it was all Jenna's fault. He grabbed his duffel bag out of the closet and began stuffing it with clothes. Damned fool woman anyway. Why did women always psychoanalyze men?

He did not have issues.

He turned in a half circle, catching his reflection in the mirror attached to the dresser that now sat on the other side of the room. Earlier, he'd hauled the furniture out of the bedroom. The living room was cluttered now. Clutter didn't bother him. He'd gone to Savannah where he'd purchased photography tools and trays and solutions he would need to transform the bedroom into a darkroom where he could work.

He balled up another shirt, stuffed it in his bag. He stared at the bag. It was old and black and frayed. One of the zippers was permanently stuck shut. This bag had crisscrossed the globe with him. He thought about where he should go next. There were photographs to take, parts of the planet he hadn't explored. His options were endless. He could run, fly, drive, take a train, a boat or a bus.

He'd already done all those things many times over.

No mode of travel stood apart from the others; no destination came to mind. Still agitated, he traversed the room. What the hell did she mean she didn't give out grades? Who was asking her to?

He paused in front of his own reflection again. The answer stared him in the face.

He was asking her to.

Not with words. Okay, maybe with words.

He raked a hand through his hair. What the hell was wrong with him? Nothing.

He lied. There was something wrong with him, something innately, perhaps irrevocably wrong. Jenna didn't compare his kisses to Craig's. She accepted him exactly as he was, just as Brandon and Benji did. The problem was with him. Whatever it was, it had followed him to the far corners of the earth. And here he was, back in Harmony, where it had all started.

He strode to the nearly empty, nearly dark room

where his equipment was stacked. There was no air-conditioning in the carriage house. Even at this late hour, the rooms were hot and sticky. The windows were open, the wind whistling outside. A branch scraped against the siding, and the night insects sang noisily. The owls were as silent as the breath Nick took.

Slowly, he let the strap slip from his hand, and drop-kicked his duffel bag into the corner. A tripod and some trays toppled.

He turned his back on the heap, but couldn't seem to do the same to his conscience. Whatever it was he'd been running from all his life wasn't going to let him get away this time.

He wasn't going anywhere.

Sonofabitch.

Chapter Ten

"Sonofa-ow!" Suzanne examined her thumb. "Call nine-one-one. I just broke a nail."

On the other side of the room, Cherie Marie Martin said, "Pity. I just gave you that French manicure, too."

Suzanne went back to straightening the canisters and resetting the cappuccino machine and stacking the white coffee mugs she'd just washed. From there it was an easy reach to wipe off the ceramic tile countertops, and set out clean napkins and towels. The routine was as automatic as breathing. She'd done it so often these past three years, she swore she did it in her dreams.

Hold it right there. She pink-slipped that train of thought. She was absolutely, positively not going to think about her dreams.

Overhead fans stirred the coffee-scented air, and the sun shone through the stained-glass artwork hanging in the window above the front door, casting airy patches of red, green, yellow and blue onto the tiled floor. Cherie fluffed pillows and straightened magazines and coffee-table books. They worked in companionable silence, Suzanne occasionally clattering dishes, Cherie occasionally snapping her gum.

Suzanne liked everything about the café. It was a good thing. She spent most of her time here. The street was tree lined, the shade deep and cool and sweet smelling. Occasionally, traffic noises carried through the open windows. In a former life, the building had been a toy store. Before that, it had been part of a furniture factory. The space had spent the previous twenty years as a catch-all. Consequently, she'd had to cart away truckloads of junk and cut through years' worth of spiderwebs. The building had good bones. She'd seen it the first time she laid eyes on the place. The outside walls were the original brick, the ceiling tin, the floor a combination of wide plank boards and more ceramic tile.

Marcel's was nothing like the big chain coffee houses that had sprung up across the country, or the coffee shops featured in movies and on television sitcoms. Her café was small, quaint, one of a kind. She liked to think it was a little like her.

The who's-who businesses of the shopping district in Harmony claimed Center Avenue. Marcel's was one of a few dozen other small stores and businesses located around corners and on side streets intersecting Center Avenue. Her coffee shop was just far enough off the beaten path to give it a French cobblestone coziness, and yet close enough to lure in foot traffic, as well as commuters on their way to and from Savannah.

At shortly after eleven on this Monday morning, it was too early for the regulars who met here for their afternoon coffee klatches, and too late for the morning rush when people needed a cup of coffee more than they needed to be on time for work. Even the stragglers had gone. Any minute now, Cherie would be leaving, too. Shortly thereafter, the people who worked in the offices and stores downtown would hurry in for a coffee and a bagel or fruit salad or a croissant to go. Eventually, the college kids would wander in, open their books, study, or talk or stare into space. Soon, classes would be over for the summer, and business would be slower at Marcel's. Suzanne would worry about that later.

"Another hectic morning!" Cherie declared, removing her apron.

"You must be doing something right to draw them in." Suzanne believed in giving credit where credit was due.

Cherie put a hand on each hip and stuck out her chest. "When you've got it, you've got it."

In her own unique way, Cherie was a godsend. She was Suzanne's height. This month her hair was dark, too. And yet no one ever mistook them for sisters. Secretly, Suzanne was thankful for that. Cherie had lived a hard life, and it showed.

"I can't open in the morning," Cherie said, reaching behind the counter for her purse. "I have to meet with Josh's counselor first thing." It seemed Cherie was always meeting with one of her three kids' counselors.

"All right," Suzanne said. "Good luck."

Cherie untied her apron, changed her shoes, and left via the back door. Alone in the small café, Suzanne made a mental note to ask Jenna to drive Kenzie to school tomorrow. Tuesday promised to be a long day.

She sank into the overstuffed cushions of the sofa. Something crinkled behind her. Feeling beneath a pillow, she brought out a glossy magazine. She hadn't discovered reading material of this nature here in a long time. She didn't care what a person did in the privacy of his own home, but she was running a tasteful establishment. What if those four little old ladies with the blue hair who met here every Tuesday would have found such a magazine? What if Kenzie had?

She studied the cover. The words were in French. Well, well, well. Perhaps *oui, oui,* was more fitting.

While the cappuccino machine and coffeemaker gurgled in the background, she opened the magazine.

The first photo she came to was enough to raise her eyebrows. She turned the magazine 180 degrees in one direction, and then the other. How on earth did they get the camera there?

"Are you having fun?"

Suzanne sprang to her feet and spun around, the centerfold flapping as it fell to the floor. Nick stood in the colored light falling through the stained-glass window, shoulders back, hips forward, thumbs hooked in the front pockets of faded jeans.

"Nicholas Proffit," she sputtered, "I swear somebody should put a bell on you!"

She scooped the magazine off the floor, marched to the counter area and tossed the magazine on the coffee grounds already in the trash. "Somebody left it under the cushion. I was just . . ."

"Reading informative articles about stem cell research and astral travel?"

"Very funny."

The door opened—lo and behold, she heard it this time—and Priscilla Mason, a middle-aged woman who worked at the clothing store across the street, hurried in.

"Do you know what you want?" Suzanne asked Nick.

There was a question. Nick knew his expression was tight and grim. The woman who'd taken his order for breakfast at the truck stop had told him the set of his mouth was vicious, although coming from her, it hadn't sounded like an insult.

"I'm in no hurry, Suzanne."

"Okay. Let me get Priscilla her latte first. I'll be with you in a second."

First and second. He scowled.

He meandered to a sofa tucked in a cozy alcove, but he didn't sit down. So this was Suzanne's venture. He studied the Monet posters on the wall. Behind him,

Suzanne made small-talk with her customer. The cash register drawer dinged, and the outer door opened and closed.

"Okay, what would you like, Nick?" Suzanne called.

He didn't reply.

"I make the best coffee in Harmony."

Again, he made no comment.

"Fine. I'll surprise you." A cup rattled, and something gurgled. "You know," she said, carrying a cup of steaming liquid toward him, "you don't look any better than I feel."

First and second. Better and best. His scowl deepened.

"Might as well take a load off." She set the cup on the table at the corner booth. Sliding onto one bench, she yawned.

He faced her slowly, and quietly crossed the room. "Late night?"

She shuddered. "Bed dream."

"Do you mean bad?" Nick sat down opposite her.

"Whatever."

"Did you have a nightmare?"

"Not exactly." She slid the cup of coffee toward him, and started to talk. "I've been having strange dreams."

"Define strange."

"Promise not to laugh?"

In his frame of mind? Right. "I'll do my best."

"Erotic."

Nick studied Suzanne. Her hair was short, wispy tendrils brushing her neck and jaw and eyebrows. Now that he'd seen the coffee shop, he understood the black French maid–style waitress uniform. The fact that she'd been having strange, erotic dreams explained the dark smudges under her eyes.

He hadn't dreamed at all. He never dreamed. Last night, he'd paced the crowded apartment until the wee hours of the morning, finally falling into bed around three. He'd awakened groggy and grouchy, and still thoroughly ticked off at Jenna. He didn't even know why the hell he was mad. But they weren't talking about him. They were talking about Suzanne's erotic dream.

"Maybe," he said, slurping his coffee, "it has something to do with your reading material."

"Don't start, all right?"

Suzanne felt a headache coming on. She'd had the dream again. It had happened after Eddie brought Kenzie home last night. Eddie had been his usual charming, flirtatious, conceited self. He'd sat on the sofa as if he planned to stay forever. How many times had she fallen for forever with him? And then out of the blue, he'd gotten up and sauntered to the door. With a swagger and a devastatingly appealing grin, he'd called her and Kenzie his two best girls. Kenzie had studied her mother's face for several seconds, then retreated quietly to her bedroom. Suzanne had tried to talk to her, to no avail.

Later, Suzanne fell asleep thinking about her ex-husband. It hadn't been Eddie in her dream, of that much she was certain.

She'd never had any complaints in that department, but compared to the man in her fantasy, Eddie simply didn't stack up. She'd even go so far as to say he'd fallen terribly short. She grinned. She cracked herself up.

"Private joke?" Nick asked.

Oh. Nick. She pulled a face. "Yes. As a matter of fact, the joke's private, and so was the dream."

She noticed Nick didn't smile. He wasn't one to pry. She liked that about him. He leaned back, strumming his fingers on the table. She studied those blunt-tipped fingers. Her mind wandered. In her dream, a faceless man had undressed her once again. Normally, he was already as naked as a jaybird when her dream began. Last night, the dream started a little earlier and had lasted longer. She'd watched, stretched out on her bed, as he'd undressed himself first. She remembered the way he unfastened his belt and lowered his zipper. She didn't really recall what his clothes looked like. She'd been a little too involved with what he'd been doing to pay attention to details such as clothing color and style. But something about what he'd been wearing had bothered her long after she woke up, warm and unsettled and unsatisfied.

"Suzanne?"

"Hmm?"

"I've gotta go. You okay?"

She looked across the table at Nick. His coffee was almost gone, which meant she'd been daydreaming for a while. "It's possible I need my head examined."

He dropped a five on the table, slid to the end of the bench seat, and slowly stood. "There seems to be a lot of that going around."

"That's what Jenna said this morning."

"You talked to Jenna this morning?"

Suzanne stood up, too. Suddenly, she looked at Nick a little differently. "Is something going on between you and Jenna?"

"Me and Miss High-And-Mighty? What do you think?"

She watched him saunter out the door, thinking that Jenna hadn't been in a good mood, either. She wondered if there was a connection. She tried to picture Nick and Jenna together. He was certainly good looking. He had a long, smooth stride, enough muscle to draw a woman's eye, and enough bluster to keep her looking. My, my, my. That man could earn a living with that walk, if he ever needed the money. It was a shame it didn't do anything for her. There was just no accounting for taste.

She yawned again. Caffeine. She needed caffeine. She went to the counter, reached for a white cup and saucer. Nick was barely out the door when the door opened again. Already grinning, she said, "You just can't resist me, can you?"

She looked up. And froze.

A man had entered. Only it wasn't Nick this time. It was the accountant. He stood as quietly as Nick had. He wasn't as tall, as rugged, as glum-faced or as brooding as Nick, not by a long shot. In fact, compared to Nick, he was bland. She preferred a man with more—more whisker stubble on his chin, more muscle, more brawn, more shoulder, more sulk, more bluster, more everything. This guy looked like a thousand other guys, the kind of man you saw at airports and government offices, the kind of guy most women wouldn't give a second look. It was all that gray. Nondescript gray pants. Plain gray tie. Nondescript striped gray shirt complete with a clear plastic pocket protector containing several pens. Why, even his eyes were gray . . .

Her gaze returned to that pocket protector. An image, like a hazy, heated memory, shimmered across her mind. Her empty cup and saucer slipped out of her hands, shattering on the floor.

He was next to her in an instant, his shoes crunching over shards of earthenware. He lowered to his haunches as she lowered to hers. This close, she saw that his eyes were the same smoky shade of gray as the Eiffel Tower in the stained glass behind him. It was a trick of the light. An optical illusion.

"I can get this," she said tightly. "I don't want anybody suing me."

He studied her far longer than she considered polite. Finally, he said, "Have it your way, Suzanne." He dropped the few pieces he'd picked up, then rose quietly, effortlessly to his feet.

He knew her first name, her first thought, her only thought.

Eventually, she recovered. So what if he knew her first name? Everybody who came to the coffee shop knew her first name. She heard, "Hey, Suzanne, can we get another cappuccino over here?" and "Hey, Suzanne, how about another scone?" and "Suzanne dear, would you bring us the cream?" dozens of time every day.

This was the man in her dreams? A sexual fantasy in the making? She looked at him as he walked away.

He was skinny. But underneath that shirt was sinew and muscle and warm, solid man. Heat rose to her cheeks.

She didn't know what was underneath that shirt. She didn't know what he looked like naked. It had been a dream. Not only did she not know what he looked like naked, she would never know what he looked like naked. And that was final.

"I guess I'll skip the tea today."

She looked up at him, still unable to speak. He'd just reminded her that he drank tea. Real men didn't drink tea. Not in public. Not in America. Certainly not in Harmony. She still couldn't utter a sound.

He started back the way he'd come. "I have an appointment in ten minutes." He turned at the door. "And in case you're wondering. The answer to your earlier question is no. It seems that I can't."

He didn't smile. And she still didn't move. Nor did she ask him what he was talking about, at least not out loud. But inside, she thought, *What question?*

The answer came to her the instant the door closed behind him. When she'd thought it was Nick returning, she'd said, "You just can't resist me, can you?"

The nondescript accountant had answered, "No. It seems that I can't."

She could feel her face growing hot. Surely, she was having an embolism. Or perhaps it was a tumor.

It was worse. She was blushing.

Placing both hands on her cheeks, she ran to the back room for a broom.

Nick parked at the curb under an oak tree in front of the school. He could hear kids playing on the playground. He didn't know why he'd driven over here, or why he'd stopped. He wasn't going inside. He hated schools. He'd always hated them. He certainly had no reason to go inside this one.

He got out of the Land Rover anyway. That alone should have set alarm bells ringing in his brain. He entered through the front door, just as he had last week. The corridor was in plain view of the main office. This time he didn't ignore the sign instructing all visitors to check in.

He could play by the rules.

He signed the visitor ledger, charmed the school secretary, and generally stalled. When he couldn't put it off any longer, he sauntered out into the hall and started toward Jenna's classroom. He didn't have a clue what he planned to say to her. He didn't even know why he'd come.

Pizza was still on the air from lunch, mingling with the scent of paste and paint and chalk. Art projects lined the walls. Art. Now there was a subject he'd liked.

He passed three empty classrooms. He strode past a fourth, only to backtrack. Benji sat forlornly at a desk, at an angle to the door. His shoulders were hunched, his chin in his hand, his face six inches from an open book. Nick recognized the defeat in that posture. This wasn't a boy who was being punished for bad behavior. This was a child who was spending his recess doing schoolwork.

Nick stormed toward the kindergarten room with renewed purpose. Jenna's door was open today. But not for long.

"What the hell are you letting them do to that poor kid?"

Jenna startled. Recovering, she said, "What kid?"

"The only thing that makes school bearable for some kids is recess."

"Nick, what . . ."

"They can't do this, Jenna. It's inhumane."

"What is?"

Oh, no, she didn't. Nick wasn't falling for innocence. He needed to pace. He wanted to throw something. He stayed where he was, his back to the closed door. "They find a weak spot. It's what they do. It has to be something the kid hates. Otherwise, what good would it be? It's like Chinese water torture in old war movies. Imagine being forced to do something you hate, something monotonous and dreaded, something that feels like fingernails on the chalkboard."

Jenna took a step toward Nick, listening, watching.

"And then," he said, "force that person to do it ten times more and to work at it a hundred times harder. It's no wonder so many adults need their heads examined."

She stared at him. He stood across the room, tall and angry. There wasn't so much as a trace of the passion and heat she'd felt in him last night. His voice was quiet, yet it held an undertone of ice-cold steel and anger.

"Nick, what are you talking about?"

"Benji. I'm talking about Benji."

"You saw Benji?"

He nodded.

"On the playground?"

He made a derisive sound. "At his desk in his classroom. His teacher has him spending his recess doing schoolwork. He doesn't need to spend his recess doing schoolwork."

"I agree. I'll talk to Marla . . ."

"He needs to be assessed, Jenna, before it's too late. Before he believes what the everyday test scores say about him."

"Assess him for what?"

"For a learning disability. For dyslexia, ADD or ADHD, or whatever the hell other catchphrase they've come up with this year."

Jenna's mind floundered. Benji? Dyslexic?

She reminded herself that Nick's anger wasn't really directed at her. He wasn't a man of delicate scruples, but she knew he would never hurt her. This was a man who photographed wild animals and rescued turtles. Still, it required effort to hold his look.

It was as if he knew.

His eyes narrowed. Two lines formed between them, a muscle working in his jaw. Just like that, the vehemence went out of him, along with the bluster. His face had closed, as if guarding a secret.

"He needs to be tested, Jenna." Even his voice was flatter. "If you don't believe me, go see for yourself."

He'd entered quietly. He left the same way.

Jenna didn't know how many seconds passed before she moved. She hadn't expected to see Nick here today. She certainly hadn't expected this.

Leaving the end-of-the-year art projects on her desk, she tiptoed down the hall to Benji's classroom. She stopped outside the door, watching her son through the window. His shoulders were hunched pathetically, his head resting on one hand, his face close to his paper.

She opened the door and went in. "Hi, Benj."

He jerked around. "Mom. I'm doing it. I'm trying. I am."

Goosebumps prickled the back of her neck. She rubbed at them, and smiled. "I can see that. Go on outside and play now, okay?"

He looked to his teacher for the final say. Jenna would never forget the expression on that sweet, uncertain, sad face. Tears stung her eyes as her son closed his book, and slunk quietly from the room.

"What's going on, Jenna?" Marla Mason asked when she and Jenna were alone.

"Have you kept Benji inside during recess often?"

"No, but I don't want him to fall any further behind."

"I think I know what Benji's problem might be." Jenna picked up the paper he'd been working on. Why hadn't she seen this before? But of course! She'd been blind to what had been right under her nose.

* * *

It was almost five o'clock by the time Jenna pulled into her own driveway. It wasn't easy to keep Benji buckled in his seat belt until after she brought the van to a stop. "Whoa, tiger," she said, turning off the engine. "Okay, now you can get out."

Benji pushed open the door and unfastened his seat belt at the same time. Hitting the ground on a run, he dashed to the tree swing where Brandon and Kenzie were playing and Twyla Mae was fanning herself in the shade.

"Guess what?" Benji quipped.

"What?" Brandon asked.

"I said guess."

Kenzie and Brandon exchanged a look. "You got an *A*," Kenzie said.

"Better."

"An *A*-plus?" Twyla Mae asked.

"Better."

"What's better than an *A*-plus?" Brandon asked.

Jenna was nearly upon the kids, her arms full of her school bag, literature, receipts, as well as Benji's backpack, when Nick emerged from the carriage house. Benji saw him, too.

"Uncle Nick," he said on a run. "I'm not dumb. Or stupid. Or slow."

"I could'a told you that, kiddo . . ."

"I'm far-sighted!"

Nick did a double-take. "You're what?"

"I'm far-sighted. It means I can see far away but not up close. Me and Mom just came from Dr. Thomas's office."

"You need glasses?" Brandon asked.

"Yup."

"For real?"

Benji nodded importantly.

"You're going to look like a brain," Kenzie declared.

"I know."

Tears filled Jenna's eyes again. Benji was going to

look like one of the smart kids, and he was thrilled.
How could she have missed this? The clues had been
there. The drop in grades, the decreasing interest and
growing dislike of school, the underlying shame.

Twyla Mae patted Benji's head before ambling stiffly
to the house. Faith and her daughter drove up. The moment they were out of the car, Benji ran to them. "Hi.
I'm Benji. And I'm getting glasses."

Jenna couldn't hear Faith and Rachel's reply. She
didn't need to. Benji, being Benji, was busting with
pride all by himself. Kenzie and Brandon followed him
to the verandah. Rachel hung back, waiting for them.

Jenna and Nick looked at each other. She was beginning to understand a few things about Nicholas Proffit.
There was so much she wanted to say to him. She didn't
have all the answers yet, but she knew he'd been hurt
by his childhood. Inadvertently, she'd been part of that
hurt. How far would simple human kindness go toward
healing both old and new wounds to the heart?

"You're not saying anything." His voice had been
stern.

"I'm sorry, Nick."

"For not talking?" When she didn't answer immediately, he said, "I'll tell you what. When I want your
pity, I'll ask for it."

She fixed him with a wide-eyed stare he didn't stay
long enough to see. When his door slammed, she came
out of her stupor.

She was alone in her own backyard. So much for
being nice. Evidently, it was going to take a lot more
than kindness to heal whatever was bothering Nick. A
sharp kick in the shins came to mind.

She spun around. Arms full of school bags, she
stomped into her house. Bother the man!

It was 9:45 that evening before Jenna faced the fact
that she'd read the same page four times and still had

no idea what the book was about. It had won a Pulitzer Prize. Therefore, there was a good chance that it wasn't the author's fault she couldn't concentrate. She wandered through the house, jotted a note to herself for morning, and checked on the boys. Finding them sound asleep, she decided to go upstairs and visit with Suzanne. The steps creaked in all the usual places. Strangely, her knock at the door at the top of the stairs went unanswered. She decided to go across the hall and say hello to Faith. Her new neighbor didn't answer her door, either.

Twyla Mae always went to sleep with the sun, so it wouldn't do any good to ring her doorbell. For lack of a better plan, Jenna went back downstairs. Eventually, she wandered out to the verandah. Compared to the house, the backyard was bursting with sound. For once, the songs of the night peepers and crickets had to compete with the laughter coming from the carriage house.

She would recognize Suzanne's bawdy laugh anywhere. Nick's deep, rusty chuckle wasn't hard to identify, either. She didn't know who belonged to the third voice until she followed the path to the carriage house and looked through Nick's screen door. The place was crowded with furniture. The bed and dresser and two night stands filled one end of the room. The rest of the furniture had been arranged in a close huddle on this side of the room.

Suzanne lounged on the sofa, a tankard of what could only be mint julep in her hand. Nick sat ahead in a straight-backed chair, elbows on his knees, a long-neck brown bottle dangling from the fingers of his right hand. Another tankard sat on a low table next to Faith. At least this explained why Faith and Suzanne hadn't answered her rap on their doors.

Jenna was trying to decide whether to knock, simply enter or leave. Just then, Nick noticed her, and it became a matter of pride. Chin up, shoulders back, she strode inside.

Suzanne raised her tankard to Jenna. "Care for a taste?"

Jenna was still angry with Nick. She was rarely angry, and she didn't much care for the emotion. Lowering to the cushion next to her dark-haired friend, Jenna took a sip from Suzanne's glass.

"It looks as if the party"—she was terribly pleased with herself for refraining from saying "pity party"—"started without me."

"It was impromptu," Suzanne said. "I made up some mint julep for Pinkie to try. Nick happened along, and invited us out here, and one thing led to another. It's been an informative night."

Jenna glanced around the room. Faith was nodding. Nick was looking at his bottle of beer. "Informative in what way?" Jenna asked.

Suzanne grinned. Obviously, she didn't mind carrying the conversation. "Did you know that humans and dolphins are the only species that have sex for pleasure?"

They were talking about sex? Jenna wondered how long this party had been going on. "No," she said, "I can't say I knew that."

"It's true. I read it in a magazine."

"Suzanne has the best magazines," Nick said.

Suzanne stuck her tongue out at Nick then continued. "The male praying mantis can't procreate while its head is attached to its body."

"Then how . . ." Faith asked in that quiet, cultured voice of hers.

Suzanne grinned knowingly. "The female praying mantis initiates sex by ripping the male's head off."

"That," Nick said, "would definitely take most of the fun out of it."

Everyone except Jenna laughed. Even Faith.

"Are you'all drunk?" Jenna asked.

Nick held up his nearly full bottle of imported beer. Suzanne and Faith giggled. Evidently, two out of three of them were getting sloshed.

"Did you know," Faith asked, "that an ostrich's eye is larger than its brain?"

"Hell, Pinkie," Suzanne said. "I know some people like that."

Faith turned her head slowly and leveled a calculated look at Suzanne. "My late husband called me Pinkie."

Jenna didn't remember the last time Suzanne had been rendered speechless. No one knew what to say.

"His name was Grant," Faith said. In the ensuing silence, she rose to her feet, as regal as a queen. Well, as regal as a slightly tipsy queen. Slurring the tiniest bit, she thanked Suzanne for her first taste of mint julep, then quietly left.

Suzanne finally broke the ringing silence. "She *tasted* two glasses full. You were right, Jenna. Faith isn't half bad once you get to know her. She sure does know how to sober up a party, though."

Teetering slightly, Suzanne stood and gathered up the tankards. "I have to open Marcel's in the morning. Would you take Kenzie to school tomorrow, Jenna?"

"Of course."

"I owe you one. By the way, I've decided I'm going to find a man."

Jenna glanced at Nick. He shrugged. "You've decided that, have you?" she asked.

Suzanne's face was flushed, her short hair sticking out adorably as she nodded. "This Friday."

She'd even chosen the day?

"I told her Wednesday would be more appropriate," Nick said. "It being—"

"And I told you to shut up—"

"Hump day and all."

"I mean it, Nick."

Jenna waited to make sure they were finished before asking, "How are you going to accomplish such a feat, Suzanne?"

"Tell her, Nick."

Jenna looked at Nick again. He made no move to add to the conversation. "Why Friday?" she asked Suzanne.

"Because Kenzie's spending Friday night at Aleesha Borden's house."

"So, of course, Friday is the day."

"Don't scoff." Suzanne sashayed to the door. "I'm going in search of a man who's rugged, unshaved, uncivilized. No pasty-skinned, pencil-pushing accountant for me, thank you very much."

"Where will you find such a man?"

Suzanne pondered that. "I'll have to get back to you about that. But I'm telling you, Jenna. Come hell or high water, I'm getting back in the saddle."

She left without saying good-bye or good night. Jenna stood, too, but instead of following Suzanne out the door, she moved closer to Nick and took a seat. It wasn't difficult to do. The room was wall-to-wall furniture.

She looked all around. "I love what you've done with the place."

"If you're nice, I'll give you the name of my decorator."

"Nice, Nick? And here I've been thinking about kicking you in the shins." She had his undivided attention. She'd surprised him. And it felt good. She placed her hand on his forearm. "All that aside, thank you."

"For what?" he asked.

She wondered how a man could be so suspicious, so untrusting of simple gratitude. "For pointing out Benji's problem."

He would have gotten up, she was sure of it, if it hadn't been for her hand on his arm. "I didn't point out anything."

"Yes," she said, "you did."

"I thought . . ."

She looked into his moss-green eyes. "You thought what? That he had a learning disability?"

Nick didn't move, not even to nod. One of the owls chose that moment to call out, three short *whos* and one long one.

Jenna slid her hand along Nick's arm, across his wrist, to his fingers. Still holding his gaze, she took his fingers in hers and said, "Like you, Nick?"

Chapter Eleven

"Look, Jenna, I don't . . ."

"Please. I believe it would be best if I went first."

Nick could see her getting agitated. She was perched on the edge of a chair at a right angle to him. Her fingers remained gentle around his, but her eyes flashed and her color was heightened above the neckline of a simple black T-shirt.

"None of this is necessary," he said.

"I'll be the judge of that, thank you very much. I would have said this earlier. Which reminds me. In the future, I would appreciate it if you would let me explain before slamming the door in my face."

"I didn't slam the door in your face."

"Not in my face perhaps, but a slammed door is a slammed door, is it not?"

Nick put his nearly full bottle of beer on a nearby table.

"Well?" she prodded.

He ended up ducking his head slightly in order to hide a small smile. "Yes, ma'am."

"There. Isn't that better?"

"If I disagree, will you make me write *I will not talk back* a hundred times on the chalkboard?"

She shook her head and closed her eyes. "You're going to be the end of me. You know that, don't you?"

Nick thought she had it backward. *She* was going to be the end of *him*. She was right about one thing, though. Anyone who'd ever psychoanalyzed him over the years was right. He was worn-out, scuffed up and, worst of all, he had issues.

And Jenna, ever a lady, from her beige chinos to her pearl earrings, was killing him with kindness. He was too tired to ignore her scent and her softness, but not tired enough not to want more than the fleeting touch of her fingertips on his.

"Tell me about this learning disability," she said.

Nick didn't move. After all these years, she and his bed were finally in the same room, and all she wanted to do was talk—and about learning disabilities, of all things. "What's to tell?"

She looked at him expectantly. "You had trouble with reading?"

Jenna felt the tension in Nick's fingers. Even beneath the warm glow of the lamp nearby, everything about him looked stark, as if cut from stone. His face was all hard angles and sharp planes. The whisker stubble didn't help. Neither did the piercing stare.

"You don't want to talk about this." He looked relieved, until she said, "I think we need to talk about it, Nick. I want to understand."

Jenna already understood a few things about the child he'd been and the man he'd become. It was no wonder he'd acted tough growing up. It was one thing for a Proffit boy, any boy, but a Proffit boy in particular, to be mouthy and belligerent and openly defiant, to get in playground fights and pool room brawls and to drop out of high school and leave town, rarely to return. It would have been unthinkable, unbearable and degrading beyond belief if word had gotten out that he couldn't read.

He took an audible breath. Finally, he said, "Trouble didn't begin to describe it."

"But you can read now. I mean, you read Craig's letters."

"Yes. I can read when I have to. It's still a slow process. Sometimes only a few letters act up. Most of the time entire words slide over onto their sides or float off the page."

"Dyslexia. How did you discover it?"

"I didn't."

"But, you said . . ."

He cast her a haughty look. "Do you want to hear this or don't you?"

She leaned away slightly, rebuffed.

"As I was trying to say." He paused, making his point. "I always knew I was different than the other kids in school. I just didn't know why. Early on, my memory got me through. By the third or fourth grade, the directions got more complicated and my papers started coming back with big fat *F*'s in bright red ink. So, I quit doing assignments. I got good at ditching tests. I got by. I'd never heard of dyslexia until a few years after I left Harmony."

"Then how . . ."

"A woman pointed it out to me during my second trip to Central America. Lolita taught me more than any other woman in the world."

"I thought we were talking about reading."

He sat up a little straighter, as if surprised, but Jenna saw the ghost of an unholy grin lurking around the edges of his mouth. Rubbing his chin, he said, "Now that I think about it, maybe Sabin taught me more. Or perhaps it was Madisha."

"You've known a lot of women."

His expression stilled and grew serious again. "We've gotten off the subject."

"Do you keep in touch with any of them?"

He shook his head.

"Somehow I doubt that was their idea."

Nick didn't want to talk about other women, and hadn't expected her to, either. He'd assumed she would lead him down the garden path, figuratively at least. Surprisingly, she didn't turn around at the end and lead him straight back again. Instead, she studied him unhurriedly, and asked him about the places he'd lived and the people he'd known. Their conversation was neither here nor there, this or that. She talked, and listened, sometimes smiling, sometimes laughing, sometimes doing neither, and it occurred to him that she was lonely. It was all he could do not to pull her to him, and bring her into his arms. And kiss her. God, yes, although kissing her would never be enough.

She seemed perfectly content to talk. She wanted to know about his life, his work, the friends he'd made and the women he'd known. He didn't ask about her past loves. He already knew who she'd loved. She'd loved Craig, first and foremost. There was no undoing it. He knew she wouldn't if she could. She'd loved Craig Proffit, would probably always love Craig Proffit. And damn it all to hell, he respected her, admired her for it.

Perhaps that was why Nick kept the conversation light and playful. When she asked him to describe a woman he'd met in southern France, he answered, "You know what they say. Beauty is only skin deep, but ugliness goes clear to the bone."

"Who?"

"Who-who?" he asked.

She looked at him, her eyes dilated in the semidarkness, so that only a circle of blue surrounded them. "Are you taking lessons from the owls?"

"Maybe I should. I think the male got lucky last night."

She rolled her eyes. "You are one contrary man, do you know that?" Her gaze settled on his mouth. Her eyes took on a new depth, as if her thoughts were slowing, her body warming. Like his. "I should be going. In case the boys wake up."

She got up. And he let her. She walked to the door. And he followed her. At the door, she said, "I'm glad we're friends again. It means a lot to me."

Nick knew that what she'd said a few days ago was true. She was going to be fine. She was already fine. She was strong. She certainly didn't need him to stick around. He was free to go. If he left, they would part friends. He had a decision to make. He either had to make his move, or move on.

She opened the door, this woman who was content to be just friends. Any minute now she would be out of his reach, and he would be left wandering around until all hours in the cluttered apartment where he hung his hat these days.

"Jenna, wait."

Jenna's hand fell away from the door. She didn't intend to meet Nick's gaze. Once she did, she couldn't seem to look away. The entire room had grown silent. The air had darkened. He'd done it all with two words and one long, searing look.

"What is it?" she whispered.

"Don't go in yet."

"But the boys . . ."

"Do Brandon and Benji wake up once they're asleep?"

She felt herself faltering.

He must have noticed, too, because he said, "Go check on them if it would make you feel better. And then come back."

"I have to be up early tomorrow."

He looked at the watch on his wrist. "It's ten-fifteen."

She shook her head and hugged her arms close to her body. He was right. It wasn't late. "I'm turning into Twyla Mae." It was a sobering thought. She wasn't ready to be old. She glanced around the room, her gaze straying to the bed. Forcing herself to look elsewhere, she said, "What would we do?"

He grinned that cocky, bad-boy grin that could make all but the most determined, focused woman forget her own name. Jenna swatted him on the shoulder. And he said, "I developed the film we used yesterday. Would you like to see the photographs?"

She thought about that, and said, "I'd like that." She glanced toward the big house. Neither Brandon nor Benji were prone to nightmares. They'd both been known to sleep through storms and sirens alike. She couldn't remember the last time either of them had awakened in the night. She ran inside to check on them just the same. The house was silent, the boys sound asleep in their beds.

Nick wasn't in the living room when she returned. She called his name as she entered, and again from the center of the room.

"I'm back here, Jenna."

She followed the sound of his voice into what had been the apartment's only bedroom before Nick had moved the furniture out. She stepped over the threshold, her eyes adjusting to the dim bulb of the safelight. He'd turned the space into a rather primitive darkroom. The window was completely covered so that no light filtered through. There was a shelving unit on one wall, tables containing trays and crates on another. She noticed a box of photographer's printing paper and jugs of developer and other solutions, as well as cameras and lenses, a tripod and other paraphernalia.

Nick was unclipping photographs from a wire strung in the far corner. "They're dry. We could see them better in the living room."

He led the way to the outer room. There, he turned on another lamp and handed the photographs to her. Jenna looked at the first one, and the second, and so on. He stood behind her, peering over her shoulder, her elbow a hairsbreadth away from his waist.

He was a genius with a camera, with composition and space and shape. All the photographs were in black and white, and yet she could sense the colors and emotion in each and every one.

"Now this is attractive," she said of the picture he'd taken of her sticking her tongue out at him down by the river.

He took the photograph from her, his fingers brushing the palm of her hand. "And here I was thinking I captured the real you."

His humor assuaged her nerves. Until that instant, she hadn't realized she'd been nervous. But of course she'd been nervous. She was standing in a room lit by two small lamps, with a man whose mouth was made for rakish grins, a man who'd been with exotic women in foreign lands. He was terribly attractive, his lips wide, the bottom slightly fuller than the top, the corners raised ever so slightly right now, a little insolent, undeniably masculine. She let her gaze travel higher, and found him looking back at her. Her mind spun, and her nerves returned, skittering across her shoulders and into the pit of her stomach.

He appeared completely at ease. His breathing was steady, as was the hand he brought to her hair. Heat filled her, and strangely, tears stung her eyes. She'd been starving for something as basic as a human touch. And she hadn't even known it.

"What is it?" he asked. "What's going through that mind of yours?"

She wet her dry lips, took a shaky breath, and said, "When I was a child, people always touched my hair. My mother said people had a fascination with the curl, thickness and texture."

His laugh surprised her. She'd expected more of the rusty laughter she'd heard before, not this slow, rising rumble that floated from deep inside his chest.

He took a thicker section of her hair into his hand, rubbing it between his fingers. "Here's a news flash for you, Jenna. I don't have a fascination with your hair. I have a fascination with you."

She backed out of his grasp without looking away. It had been a knee-jerk reaction. She stood, rooted. She rarely found herself at a loss for words. Her mind was blank. Neither of them, it seemed, knew what to say.

Nick let his hand fall to his side before releasing the breath he'd been holding. It was too soon. He saw it in Jenna's eyes. He'd never been one to rush a woman, but he was rushing her plenty. He wanted to hurry her some more. A lot more. He reeled in his impatience and pointed out the next photo, lest she get it in her head to leave. She didn't run. He took that as a good sign.

She turned her attention to the photographs. "Your talent is amazing."

"It's not too bad for a kid who had to repeat the fourth grade."

"Your teachers should have caught it, Nick."

"Yeah, well, I made it easy for them by living down to their expectations." He paused. "I think they're all secretly relieved that I didn't become an ax murderer."

"Yet."

She'd answered without looking up. And he laughed. He actually laughed. He didn't know who was more surprised, her or him.

He handed her the photograph she'd taken in the rain. In the picture, Brandon held the umbrella, Benji was bent at the waist, and Nick was hunkered down, reaching for the turtle. "It's hard to tell that's me, and not Craig."

She stared at the photograph. "He was always proud of you, Nick. Always. Do you think he would have tried to help, if he'd known about the dyslexia?"

"St. Craig? But of course."

Nick didn't know where his viciousness came from. But he'd done it this time. He'd shown his true colors, and they weren't pretty. He thought she might reprimand him, or retaliate, or do or say something to let him know he'd blown it.

He endured a long, brittle silence. She got herself under control, and did none of the things he'd expected. She flipped through the remaining photographs. Earlier, her desire for him had been tangible. It was but a memory now, nearly as distant as the easy camaraderie had been. Nick had gone too far. He didn't apologize. It would do no good.

When she finished looking at the photographs, she prepared to leave. This time he didn't ask her to stay. Although she insisted it wasn't necessary, he walked her to her back door. When she slipped inside, pulling the screen door closed after her, Craig was between them again, as surely as if he were there.

Jenna closed the solid oak door, then stood leaning against it, her heart racing. Sometimes, she swore she knew Nick backward and forward, inside and out. He didn't let many people close. He'd let her. Once upon a time, he'd probably fancied himself in love with her.

Taking a deep, calming breath, she knew that back then, Craig had been in the way. It wasn't Craig's fault. It wasn't anybody's fault. She'd loved Craig, and vice versa. No matter what Nick thought now, Craig wasn't between them anymore. It was Nick's lack of faith in her late husband, in the father of her two children, and in the brother who'd never spoken a disparaging word about him, in the brother that had never stopped hoping that Nick would return to Harmony some day.

Nick, himself, was between them.

Fifteen minutes ago, she'd been worried about her burgeoning feelings for him. Nicholas Proffit was a difficult man to say no to. He would probably always be a difficult man, even in love.

In a sense, his lack of faith in Craig made this easier for Jenna. It made resisting him not only possible, but necessary and in some perverse way, natural. It insulated her from his charm, from the empty places inside him that called out to the empty places inside her. As long as Nick didn't believe in Craig, she didn't have to worry about falling in love with him.

With a mild sense of relief, and a persistent, lingering loneliness, Jenna got ready for bed, and eventually fell asleep.

Nick sat in the dark, staring out the window, his ankles crossed, his feet propped on the windowsill. The sky was dark. His apartment was dark. Jenna's windows were all dark, too. Between them, the owls occupied the same branch now. One or the other of them had made its move. Now, the night birds would go about the business of the rest of their lives.

Nick had made his move, too, but with far less satisfactory results. With the deepest of sighs, he lowered his feet to the floor and stood. Kneading a knot in the back of his neck, he wandered to the center of the room. He undressed, then lay on top of the covers on the bed. A fan stirred the warm, late night air. Hands behind his head, he stared at the ceiling. He was a world-renowned photojournalist. In his hometown, he might as well have been gum on the bottom of his shoe. It was no wonder Jenna had loved Craig better. Craig had been better. He fell asleep, bitterness, like bile, thick in his throat.

He woke up hours later, his heart beating an ominous rhythm. It took a few minutes to get his bearings and figure out what had awakened him.

He'd dreamed.

He never dreamed, but he'd dreamed tonight. In his dream, he'd been an eight-year-old kid again, planning his afternoon with his eleven-year-old brother. He and Craig had both had haircuts that morning, so that a narrow ring of white skin not yet exposed to the sun encircled each of their heads. Rosita packed them a lunch, exclaiming that they looked dapper. Craig and Nick agreed they looked like dorks.

For that afternoon while their parents were gone, they were just like any other brothers in Harmony. They played, they teased, they talked, their laughter ringing through the quiet summer day. It was the day they'd both been waiting for, working toward. It was the day they would launch their raft.

"We're the best!" they both said, laughing as they hopped onto the wooden raft. But as water seeped first into and then over their shoes, their laughter stopped and their hopes plummeted. The gentle current carried them down river, and the raft continued to sink. Nick panicked when it went under, him with it. He thrashed, resurfacing. Craig was beside him suddenly, water running off his hair, into his steady brown eyes. "It's okay, Nicky. I'm right here. I've got you."

Nick stopped flailing and started treading water.

"Grab my shirt," Craig said.

Craig Proffit had towed his brother to safety.

The night breeze billowed the curtain in the carriage house apartment as Nick brought his hand close to his face. His fingers were still curled into a fist, as if clutching the sleeve of Craig's wet T-shirt.

He didn't sleep anymore that night.

Nick discovered Dixie's piano bar by accident after lunch the next day. He'd been driving around Harmony most of the morning. He'd gone back to the cemetery first thing. Simon hadn't been around; Nick had pretty much had the place to himself. He didn't know why people visited cemeteries. To find peace? There was nothing there for Nick. There was certainly no peace. He didn't begin to understand life and death, but he knew, without knowing how, that Craig's spirit wasn't there.

Next, Nick drove out to the old roller rink. The place was boarded up, the property surrounded by a chain-link fence. He hopped the fence and poked around his old stomping grounds. It was where he'd had his first French kiss and more than one fistfight. Other than a few out-of-focus memories, he found nothing, no answers or revelations there, either. Feeling as though he had to keep moving, he went to the park, and since it was near the elementary school, he drove past the playground. Brandon and Benji were both outside today. Maybe he'd accomplished one good thing by coming back to town.

The sun shone overhead. Birds and squirrels and people seemed to be in high spirits. Not Nick. A shadow followed him wherever he went. He figured it was Craig's shadow. Nothing new about that. No matter how many times he'd tried to step out of it growing up, it was always where he'd ended up. Nick had needed his own day in the sun.

He parked his Land Rover on Center Avenue and got out, making certain to walk on the north side of the street in full sun. He'd done a lot of walking in the sun today. He wasn't certain what he'd been looking for. He was pretty sure it wasn't a piano bar named Dixie's.

Balloons bobbed atop a two-sided sign sitting in the middle of the sidewalk. He read the sign announcing the grand opening, but it was the full-toned notes from the theme of an old Rocky movie wafting through the open door that drew Nick inside. Good old Rocky. Now there was one washed-up, beat-up underdog who knew what he wanted and fought for it. They didn't make movies like that anymore. They didn't make real life like that, either.

Dixie's was buzzing with more than piano music. A construction worker wielded an electric drill. Somebody was vacuuming. Two women were arranging stools around the small, high tables filling most of the room. The place had a thirties feel. A bar dominated one wall. A player piano sat on the far end, a baby grand in the window. The man playing it had his eyes closed and didn't notice that Nick was watching. The musician opened them as he swung into a short rendition of another movie theme.

"Nick Proffit!" Brian Jefferson grinned as he played.

Several people looked up from their tasks. Nick recognized most of them. Brian Jefferson had been on the football team with Craig. Even then, his heart had been more into music. It seemed to Nick that Craig and Jenna had gone to Brian and Dixie's wedding.

Chip Gunther, the electrician, was another of Craig's former classmates. He'd put on a few pounds since high school. He certainly seemed to know his way around power tools.

Dixie turned off the vacuum cleaner and exclaimed, "Hello, Nick! We heard you were in town." Her hair was still red, but her freckles had faded. She'd grown pretty with age. "I'm glad you stopped in," she said, her smile revealing dimples.

She hauled out several cans of cola from a cooler behind the bar. After handing one to everyone who wanted one, she popped the top on her own and took a long swig.

"Nice place," Nick said.

"It's getting there," Dixie agreed. "Who knows. It might even be ready by the time we open Friday night."

"It'll be ready," Brian said. "Are you coming to the grand opening?" he asked Nick.

This was the first Nick had heard anything about a grand opening. Maybe he would attend. It wasn't as if he had anything else to do.

Simon Smith shuffled into the room hauling a step ladder and several strands of white lights. "Where do you want these?" he asked Brian.

"Dix," Brian called to his wife, who had disappeared behind the bar.

"Yeah?"

"Simple Simon wants to know where you want these lights strung."

"Put them on the bar for now." Dixie popped up and got Simon a cola.

"Where are you staying?" she asked Nick. Before he could answer, she added, "I see they turned your father's old house into a museum, so I doubt you're staying there."

Nick almost managed a smile. "I'm staying in the carriage house at Jenna's new place."

Simon's cola top popped noisily in the otherwise quiet room. As if in his own world, he strolled to the player piano, and inserted a coin. When it started to play, he scratched his head and grinned.

Now that the quiet had been covered, Dixie said, "How are Jenna and the boys doing?"

Nick took careful note of the way nearly everyone's attention was suddenly trained on his answer. "Jenna, Brandon and Benji are good, thanks."

"That's nice. Really, I'm glad. Most people are." Chip tucked a carpenter's pencil above his ear. As if unable to sit still when there was work to do, he started putting screws in the light switch covers, talking as he worked. "Such a shame."

"Craig's death, you mean?" Nick asked quietly.

Nick couldn't help noticing all the gazes darting back and forth. "That, too, of course." It was Brian who'd spoken this time.

And Nick said, "You're referring to the scandal."

"It's hard to believe Craig could have done such a thing," Chip said.

"Everyone was in shock for weeks after," Brian declared.

Nick felt as if he were watching a tennis match. "Then you think Craig did it?"

Their silence spoke volumes.

Nick didn't know why the hell it rankled so much. "If Craig took the money, where is it?"

"That hundred grand in his savings account had to come from somewhere, Nick." There was compassion in Dixie's voice.

Big deal. "So all of you believe Craig Proffit stole four hundred thousand dollars?"

They stopped shuffling.

When they made no move to reply, Nick said, "And you were his friends?"

"He was *your* brother."

Everyone turned to look at the man who'd spoken. Simon peered back at them from the back of the room. The man who was considered simple-minded had nailed the truth with one blow. Why should Nick expect anybody else to believe in Craig's integrity when Nick questioned it?

He didn't have much to say for himself.

Brian and Dixie issued another invitation for him to attend the grand opening Friday evening. Nick left the piano bar without committing one way or the other.

Jenna and the boys were just getting home from Little League practice as Nick came jogging into the yard. Brandon and Benji emerged from the van, disgruntled.

"You went running without us?" Brandon sputtered, his ball glove still on his left hand.

Nick nodded. "I made it a mile."

"But we're your trainers!" Benji pushed his glasses back up on his nose.

"So put your stuff away and train me!"

The boys hopped to it, scampering toward the house. Jenna handed each of them a backpack on their way by. "Put these on the pegs. And you'd better get something to drink first. It's hot out here in the sun."

A car turned at the corner, a teenager's bass *ba-bum-ba-bum-ba-bumping*. The scent of Twyla Mae's roses wafted on the afternoon air. As happened so often lately, Nick and Jenna found themselves alone in the backyard.

"Hey," he said. "How was school?"

What? she thought. *He's making small talk now?* "It was fine, thank you."

Silence stretched between them.

"And how was my day, you ask?" he said. "I've had better." He started toward her. "I've had worse, too."

Who hadn't? Oh, no, she wasn't going to feel sorry for him.

He continued toward her, his stride long, his gaze steady. "Aren't you going to ask me what I did today?"

"I hadn't planned to, no."

If he noticed the cool tones in her voice, he didn't let on. "I drove around, saw some people, did some walking and a lot of thinking." He stopped a few paces from her. "What did I think about, you ask?"

She shook her head, released a pent-up breath, and gave up. "What did you think about, Nick?"

"Craig."

She stared at him. "You thought about Craig?"

"He didn't take that money."

Jenna didn't know what to say.

"He was my brother. He couldn't have done it, anymore than I could have."

Jenna closed her eyes for a moment, letting Nick's belief in Craig filter through the tiny fissures and cracks all those rumors had made around her heart. Nick believed in Craig. She'd always considered herself a reasonable woman, but this relief was dredged from a place beyond logic or reason, a place where there were only shimmery emotions and dusky yearnings. "Oh, Nick. What changed your mind?"

"Craig did. He wouldn't steal *four* dollars, let alone *four hundred thousand*."

She smiled. She couldn't help it. "Yes, I know."

"But somebody did."

Nodding once, she blinked back tears. Nobody could

make an understatement like him. Nick Proffit rarely let a person know what he was thinking and feeling. When he did speak, it was the gospel truth. And once he said it, there was no going back. Jenna didn't know what had happened to Nick today, what he'd thought about, who'd he'd seen, what he'd remembered that had made a believer out of him. She probably never would. That was okay. It was enough that he believed. It was so much more than she'd thought she would ever have.

"I'm going to find out who took that money and pinned it on Craig." He began walking backward, toward his apartment.

"How are you going to do that?" she called.

"I don't know yet." He stopped walking and said, "But I have a few ideas. You said you tried to prove Craig's innocence two years ago."

"Yes."

"I'll need to know what you did, who you spoke to, what they said, and so on. Whoever put that money in your bank account had to have access to a hundred grand and your account numbers."

Jenna nodded again. A lot of people in Harmony had money, and in this day and age, God only knew who might know how to break into computer codes and access confidential information.

He turned, and began to run. His feet were light on the ground. Nevertheless, she felt a vibration under her skin. It carried her into her house. He was the one with the learning disability, which he'd so admirably overcome, and yet she couldn't put two thoughts together.

Nick was having no such trouble. Going straight to the sink in the tiny bathroom, his thoughts came fast and furious, piling up in his mind like a logjam on a river. He downed a glass of water, splashed more cool water on his face. Leaving a wet imprint on a towel, he stared in the wavy mirror over the old sink.

Green eyes looked back at him from a face that was losing its gaunt lines and hollows. "What kind of idiot am I?" he said aloud.

His reflection stared back at him, mute.

For once the people in Harmony didn't think of Craig as the better man. They thought he was a liar and a cheat and God only knew what else.

Nick was about to set out to prove them wrong.

An idiot, perhaps the biggest idiot in all of Harmony, flung the towel over the bar and headed back outside where Craig's sons were waiting.

Chapter Twelve

Jenna moved a stack of boxes aside and squeezed between the wall and a long rod that held old clothes. The air in the back of the deep narrow closet was stuffy and smelled of cardboard and old things. She lifted her hair away from her damp neck and held it there, surveying the items on high shelves. Before the house had been divided into apartments, the space had been a passageway connecting this room and the room that had once been the parlor. She and Craig had planned to restore the house to the way it used to be. Plans had a way of changing.

Moving deeper into the closet, she brushed past evening gowns and matching shoes and handbags she no longer had any use for. Her hand went still for a moment when she came to Craig's things. When she could breathe again, she touched the lapel of one of his suits, glided her hand across the shoulder, and over the tie draped around the hanger. Sorrow seeped inside her chest, aching, aching.

She'd gotten rid of much of Craig's things in a rare fit of temper two years ago. She'd cried for hours afterward. Finally, she'd hung those items she hadn't been able to part with back here: his high school football jersey, his favorite sweatshirt, his college cap and gown, a few of his suits, the flannel, monogrammed bathrobe she'd given him their first Christmas together. Surrounded by his things, she'd been comforted by the scent of his aftershave and the bracing scent of the soap he'd used that had permeated his things. Tonight, she rubbed the worn fabric of his old robe between both hands, the flannel smooth and soft. Closing her eyes, she brought one sleeve to her nose. It smelled like the closet. His scent was gone forever now, too.

She stood, bereft and silent, fighting tears. She hadn't cried in months. Perhaps it was what she needed. Or perhaps it was time to stop crying once and for all. She wasn't certain how people did that, but she knew it had something to do with breathing, and with living, with looking forward, not back. To that end, she took a shuddering breath, then stood on tiptoe. Reaching to a high shelf, she brought down Craig's briefcase. At least this looked and smelled exactly as she remembered. The leather was soft and supple, the handles conformed to the shape of Craig's large hand. Clutching the satchel-style case to her chest, she made her way out of the dimly lit, dank closet, and into her bedroom.

Switching on a lamp, she lowered to the edge of her bed, and perched there, looking at the case. Finally, she reached for the zipper. It rasped as it opened. She remembered the sound well. She couldn't count how many nights her young husband had brought work home with him. Instead of the files and briefs that had once filled the compartments, the leather case now held mementos of Craig Proffit's life and death. His gold watch, the plastic hospital bracelet he'd worn the last hours of his life, his day planner, the months after March forever empty. There was a copy of his death certificate, the newspaper containing his obituary, copies of receipts and the damning evidence of their bank statement that had mysteriously shown a total that was a hundred thousand dollars more than it should have been. There was a leather-bound journal that contained notes of conversations she'd had with people concerning his supposed faux pas, the dates she'd spoken to them, some of the questions she'd asked, and the answers they'd given.

She remembered assembling everything and placing the items inside the briefcase, and storing them with his other things in the back of her closet shortly after she'd had to sell the other house and move here. It was as if she'd known she would be taking the briefcase out again, and opening it when the time was right.

Nick believed in Craig's innocence, and wanted to help her prove that he hadn't stolen that money. Poking around in the past would surely open up old wounds, and would stir up the scandal. She had the boys to consider, therefore, she and Nick would have to do this quietly. And yet the boys were the ones who would benefit most when their father's name was cleared.

She stood. Grasping the case by its handles, she marched past the room where her sons were sleeping, not stopping until she reached the kitchen. There, she took another deep breath for courage and headed for the door.

She and Nick arrived at the screen at the same moment, from opposite directions. It wasn't the first time it had happened. The sky was dark behind him as their gazes met. They shared an awkward moment. It wasn't the first time that had happened, either.

He cleared his throat. She swallowed a lump in hers.

"We have to stop meeting like this," he said.

She smiled, and shook her head, because nobody could make an understatement like Nick Proffit. Stepping back, she said, "I was going to bring this out to you. Come on in."

He entered quietly, then stood across the room, leveling that gentling gaze of his on her. Jenna felt herself reacting to it, and to him. It had been less than twenty-four hours since she'd come to the realization that his lack of faith in Craig made resisting him not only natural, but necessary. Nick's suspicions had insulated her from whatever it was inside him that called out to her. Those suspicions were gone now. She felt shaky, vulnerable, and on the brink of something unknown and dangerous. Which was silly. Nick posed no threat to her. He wouldn't hurt her anymore than he would hurt a turtle trying to make its way across a busy highway.

"Perhaps we should sit down." She carried Craig's briefcase to the table and pulled out a chair. After Nick took a seat, too, she opened the case and drew out its contents.

The air-conditioning came on and eventually went off again. Somewhere, a faucet dripped. Other than asking an occasional question, Nick took each item from her without comment, listening to every word she said. He leafed through Craig's day planner, and stared at the grainy picture that accompanied his obituary in the newspaper. Jenna's fingers shook slightly as she pushed the incriminating bank statement toward him. He studied it but again made no comment.

One by one, he looked every item over, then stacked everything to one side. Finally, he said, "About this trust fund that Craig supposedly skimmed. You said it belonged to Nathaniel Sherman. Is the old man still alive?"

She looked Nick in the eye and answered, "Yes. He's eighty-five and can barely walk with a cane, but he would still sooner cross the street than come face-to-face with me."

"Somebody did a good job convincing him of Craig's guilt."

She nodded.

He strummed his fingers on the table and said, "Who? That's the four-hundred-thousand-dollar question we have to answer."

"What do you think our chances are?"

"A grieving widow and a severely dyslexic international photographer with a bad reputation back home are about to try to uncover a truth that somebody went to a lot of trouble to hide. The trail is more than two years old and stone cold. There are more questions than answers, and damned little speculation to go on."

"When you'all put it that way, it sounds so easy."

They exchanged a subtle look of amusement.

Reaching across the table for the items he'd looked over, she said, "Thank you, Nick."

"For what?"

"For believing."

Their gazes met, blue eyes delving green. Nick knew what she was saying, but he didn't know what to say in return. She was thanking him for believing in Craig's innocence, when by rights, he should have believed in it all along. He felt guilty about that, and damn it, there wasn't a thing he could do about it.

What's done was done. No one could change the past. But the future was a wide-lens camera, the view fuzzy and in need of the right focus. Proving Craig's innocence wasn't going to be easy. Nick felt energized and ready for the challenge.

There was more going on here than a challenge. There was Jenna. There was always Jenna.

She looked beautiful, ethereal, even beneath the old fluorescent light overhead. She hadn't changed her clothes after school. Her dark blue shirt was open at the neck, allowing him a glimpse of the hollow at the base of her throat and a few inches of creamy skin below it. Her hair was in its customary total disarray, and yet there was simple dignity in the way she stacked the papers and slid them into that briefcase, closed it, and handed it to him.

"Despite all the things you mentioned," she said, "I believe you'll uncover the truth."

Her faith in his abilities amazed him. He took the briefcase from her and stood. "At least there's no pressure."

A smile stole across her features. It must have been contagious, because it stole across his, too.

"I'll help. We'll get to the bottom of it," she said. "Cohorts in crime."

"Please don't say crime."

He chuckled, surprised she could joke about that. Smiling too, she held out her hand. "Partners?"

He nodded, and they shook on it, her fingers slender and slightly cooler than his. Something intense flared through him. This time, she didn't back away.

He did.

He grasped the handle of Craig's old briefcase, leaving via the door he'd entered. He'd taken five steps before something made him stop. Lowering the briefcase to the flagstone patio floor, he turned on his heel and retraced his footsteps.

He entered without knocking. Jenna looked up from the chair she was pushing in. He walked directly to her. Without saying a word, he held her face still with one hand, and kissed her.

Her eyes closed, her breathing hitched, her lips parted beneath his. It was over as quickly as it began.

He lifted his mouth from hers. "There. That needed doing."

"I see."

"Just so you know, that wasn't your brother-in-law kissing you."

"I know who you are, Nicholas Proffit."

"Nick Proffit, just an ordinary man."

Jenna stared at Nick. She saw more than he knew. But ordinary? There was nothing ordinary about him. Forget the wiry build and virility. She looked beyond that, and what she saw was a generous man who thought he was somehow second rate, a kind man who was too stubborn to admit it, a good man, no matter what the people in Harmony said. He was also a man who'd known exotic women with exotic names in exotic places. She'd lived with one man in the most ordinary place in the world. Her experience was no match for Nick's. That scared her, but not enough to keep her from saying, "You realize this could get complicated."

"It so happens I like complications."

Oh, that attitude, that bad-boy, barely there smile. "In that case." She eased toward him slightly. "I think we should do that again."

"Do what again?"

"Shh." Steadying herself with a hand placed gently on his shoulder, she breathed in the scent of man and soap and late-night breezes. "Only this time," she whispered, "like this."

She went up on tiptoe, and touched her mouth to his. Beneath her closed eyes, everything was silvery-blue and white. Beneath her hand, the muscles in Nick's shoulder flexed. His skin was warm, his heartbeat strong, his lips a heady sensation. He gave her free reign for a few more seconds, and then, as if he couldn't help himself, he took the kiss over, moving his lips against hers, his arms going around her back, drawing her against the entire length of his body. This close she could feel every inch of him, and yet his ardor was surprisingly restrained. It was that restraint that caused her heart to continue to hammer long after the kiss ended.

They both took a moment to catch their breath. He was the first to find his voice. "I'll go over all those papers—it'll take me a while to read them. We can touch base tomorrow, and maybe come up with a plan. By the way, I like a woman who knows her own mind. Any time you want to tutor me some more, feel free."

He had the audacity to smile.

He left then, and Jenna was left standing in her kitchen, thinking, of course, the papers. That was why she'd rummaged through her closet.

This entire situation was complicated. And confusing. Despite what he'd said, she didn't know her own mind. In fact, it was entirely possible that she'd lost it completely. As she prepared for bed later, her body still sensitized from that kiss, she didn't have it in her to care.

"Hey, Faith!" Suzanne called, leaning back in her chair. "Come on back and join the party."

Faith closed her car door. Looking hesitant at first, she made her way toward the other three women who lived at 317 Beulah Street. It was Thursday evening. The sun would be setting soon. Jenna, Suzanne and Twyla Mae had gathered on the back patio half an hour ago to watch the kids play. Suzanne had kicked off her shoes, exclaiming that the flagstones were warm beneath her feet. Lemon slices and a few remaining slivers of ice floated inside a crystal pitcher in the center of the table.

Jenna and Twyla Mae looked at each other. "What's going on with Suzanne?" Jenna whispered.

"She must have taken a nice pill," Twyla Mae replied.

Suzanne smiled all around and bit into one of the chocolate chunk macadamia nut cookies she'd brought home from Marcel's. She was up to something. Jenna just wasn't certain what.

"So," Suzanne said, washing her cookie down with lukewarm lemonade. "What's wrong with Brandon?"

Faith was nearly upon them when Jenna glanced into the backyard. Brandon sat pitifully alone, twirling himself on the tire swing.

Twyla Mae placed her glass of lemonade on the table, and in a whisper that could penetrate steel, said, "He's got his tail in a knot because Kenzie's more interested in talking to Rachel than in playing with him."

"Oh, dear," Faith said, coming to a stop near the table. "I'll talk to Rachel."

"Don't you dare!" Suzanne said. "I mean, I hope you don't. Brandon's a great kid, but think about it. He's nine years old. Rachel's thirteen. That alone makes her totally intriguing and superior to any younger boy. This is the most normal thing my kid's done in a while. Have a seat."

Faith lowered into one of the two empty chairs on the other side of the table. Instantly, a disgusting noise erupted. She jumped up again, bumping the table, color creeping up her neck, clashing with the pale pink satin trim at the neck of her sleeveless shell.

With her liver-spotted hands, Twyla Mae drew a whoopee cushion from the seat of Faith's chair. "Suzanne, really!" the old woman admonished.

Faith straightened, all stiff dignity, and, without a word, prepared to leave.

"Pinkie, I mean Faith. I'm sorry. I mean it."

Faith took another step.

"The joke was meant for Nick, all right?"

Turning slowly, Faith tucked a length of blond hair behind her ear. "Of course it was."

"I'll take a lie detector test if you want me to," Suzanne grumbled. "Come on, have a seat. You're just in time to get the scoop about what's going on between Jenna and Nick."

Jenna gasped. Suzanne grinned. Obviously, the ploy worked, because Faith put her animosity aside enough to sit down, cautiously, of course. Twyla Mae wasn't the only one who was suddenly all ears, but she was definitely the most obvious about it. All eyes were turned to Jenna.

Jenna didn't know where to begin. Deep in the back-yard, Benji threw the ball to Nick. Nick caught it on the run, scooping it out of the air mere inches before it hit the ground. He chose that moment to look her way. He'd been here less than two weeks. Already he appeared relaxed and more robust. He wore frayed jeans he'd obviously cut off himself and a white T-shirt that molded to his shoulders and chest. Earlier, he'd told her he'd spoken to some people in town, some of Craig's old friends and such. So far, neither of them had a clear idea who to talk to next. They had decided that they needed to be seen together in public, so that whatever they did next didn't seem strange to anybody.

"To tell you the truth," Jenna said when he finally turned his attention back to Benji. "I'm not sure what's going on between us. He's decided, we've decided, to find out who took that money from the Sherman trust fund. We're trying to keep this as low key as possible." She turned to Faith. "You see, rumor has it that my late husband stole . . ."

"It's all right, dear," Twyla Mae cut in. "I've already explained all that to Faith."

Jenna shouldn't have been surprised. Twyla Mae loved to gossip. Still, Jenna appreciated the apology in Faith's blue eyes. "If it makes you feel any better," Faith said, "I know about Suzanne's quest for tomorrow night, too."

Suzanne snatched the whoopee cushion out of Twyla Mae's hand. "Some people just can't keep a secret."

"It serves you right for playing all those practical jokes," the old lady said, adjusting her straw hat. "One of these days, somebody's going to get even. Mark my words."

"Yeah, right. You'all know I'm too careful for that." Suzanne popped the last bite of her cookie into her mouth.

"How, exactly, are you planning to pick up a man tomorrow evening?" Faith asked quietly.

Suzanne tilted her head slightly. "Good question. I could use some moral support. Care to come along?"

An inexplicable look of withdrawal came over Faith's features.

"Is it too soon, dear?" Twyla Mae asked.

"Yes."

"How long's it been?" Suzanne asked. "Less than a year?"

Faith rose to her feet. "No. If you'll excuse me." She called to her daughter, then went inside.

Jenna and Twyla Mae turned on Suzanne the moment Faith disappeared around the front of the house. "Have you ever heard of subtlety?" Twyla Mae sputtered.

"Or subjects that are too painful and personal to talk about?" Jenna said at the same time.

"I was just being neighborly, all right?" Suzanne grumbled. "There's something she isn't telling us. Don't tell me you're not dying to know what it is." As if she had every right to be indignant, she called to Kenzie, then marched inside, too.

"Hurry, Mom!"

Suzanne closed her car door and practically ran after her daughter. "In case you haven't noticed, I am hurrying!"

Kenzie was not appeased.

It was Friday. The day had started out bad. They'd overslept. Consequently, Kenzie had been late for school and Suzanne had been late for work. To top it all off, Cherie had given notice today, which meant that beginning on Monday, Suzanne would be short of help. Suzanne didn't blame her for taking a job at an insurance office downtown. The hours were better. The pay was better. And it actually had benefits like health insurance and vacation and sick pay. Suzanne was happy for Cherie. It didn't make Suzanne's day any easier, though. As if that wasn't enough, Kenzie had forgotten to pack her pajamas. Somehow, that was Suzanne's fault, too.

"We'll just run upstairs, grab your pajamas, and run back down again."

"But Jessica is already at Aleesha's."

"I know, kiddo." The reason Suzanne knew was because Kenzie had told her twenty-three times.

"None of this would have happened if you wouldn't have forgotten to set your alarm," Kenzie sputtered at her mother as she stomped up the last step.

Everybody was sputtering at Suzanne lately.

No matter what Kenzie thought, Suzanne distinctly remembered turning on the alarm last night. She must have turned it off in her sleep. She'd been doing strange things in her sleep lately. Which was precisely why she was going to go through with tonight no matter how bad the day was going.

"Look," she said to her daughter at the top of the stairs. "Your sleep-over is still salvageable." She reached for the doorknob with one hand, her key with the other. "All you have to do is throw your pj's in a bag, and we'll be on our way again."

She grasped the knob. Something wet and slippery squished beneath her hand. "What the . . ."

She lifted her hand and stared at it, palm side up, fingers spread apart like a claw. Her palm was covered in white goo. She sniffed her fingers. "Shortening?"

Kenzie shoved her way closer, testing the goo with the tip of one finger. "It is shortening!" For the first time all day, her darling daughter grinned. "Somebody played a joke on you!"

Suzanne peered around the empty hallway. "If you laugh, you're grounded."

While Kenzie was busy holding in her laughter, Suzanne fished a tissue out of her bag and used it to grasp the doorknob. "Did you know about this, Kenzie?"

"Like I'd help somebody mess with my own door-knob when I'm already late for Aleesha's." She walked into her room with a grandeur that far surpassed her eleven years.

Suzanne headed for the kitchen and a paper towel. She stopped in the middle of the room. She stared at her apartment, a strange feeling coming over her.

"What are you doing?" Kenzie asked, the pajamas she'd worn all winter clutched in one hand.

"Does something look different to you?" Suzanne asked.

"What do you mean different?"

"Weird," Suzanne decided.

Kenzie gave what she could see of the apartment a sweeping glance. "Of course it looks weird. You cleaned, remember?"

Suzanne supposed Kenzie had a point. She'd put the umbrella, long since dried after Sunday's rain, in the hall closet where it belonged. For once, there were no shoes littering the living room. She'd thrown away potato chip wrappers and shoved a week's worth of mail into a drawer in the hall table. She'd vaccumed, hell, she'd even dusted. The place looked neat and tidy. No wonder it felt strange.

She was being paranoid, she told herself as she wiped off her hand and then the doorknob. She had the jitters. That explained why she hadn't been paying attention when she'd reached for her doorknob. She hadn't picked up a man in a long, long time. She wasn't sure what to say, what to wear, how to act. Casting one last look around her apartment, she followed Kenzie out the door.

"Wow!" Suzanne said after Jenna slid onto a high stool on the other side of the counter at Marcel's.

Jenna had twisted her long, dark hair and secured it on the back of her head with pearl-studded hairpins. She looked like a million bucks. If Suzanne could get her hair to do that, she would wear it long, too. "I see you've broken out the Givenchy pantsuit."

Jenna wrinkled her nose, the mannerism at odds with her air of calm and sophistication. "I thought it was the right touch to make a statement to all the doubting Thomases in Harmony."

In other words, Suzanne thought, tossing coffee grounds into the trash, they could knock Jenna down, but they couldn't keep her there. It didn't explain what she was doing at Marcel's. The door opened again before Suzanne could ask. Nick sauntered in. Dressed to the hilt, too, he was a handsome devil, his movements deliberate, his gaze steady. He waved to Suzanne, but came no closer, Suzanne's first clue that there was a reason for Jenna's impromptu visit to Marcel's.

To Suzanne's utter amazement, Nick introduced himself to the accountant, and took a seat opposite him. The two men struck up a conversation, and Jenna said, "Are you ready for tonight?"

Suzanne figured she was as ready as she would ever be. "You know what they say. Ready or not . . ."

Nick glanced at Jenna then. Instantly, his expression heated about ten degrees. If Suzanne had been a betting woman, she would have laid odds that Jenna had a better chance of getting lucky tonight than she did. Which reminded Suzanne. "Did you go upstairs to my apartment today?"

"No, why?"

"Did you see anyone else lurking around?"

"You're the only one who lurks, Suze."

"Then you didn't see anyone who might have been preparing to play a practical joke on me?"

Jenna stopped studying her fingernails and studied Suzanne. "Somebody played a practical joke on you?"

Suzanne pulled a face. "Getting an answer out of you is almost as difficult as getting an answer out of Kenzie."

Jenna turned her head, the light catching on the diamond earrings Craig had given her the Christmas before he died. "What did they do?"

"Somebody smeared shortening on my doorknob."

"And you fell for it?"

"I was preoccupied. I'm having a bad day, all right?"

Jenna, always a lady, did her best not to smile. Suzanne appreciated that.

"Who do you think is responsible for the prank?" Jenna asked.

Suzanne shrugged. "Twyla Mae?"

"It's hard for her to manage stairs with her knees."

Who, then? Not Brandon or Benji. Nick? Suzanne stared at his back. He laughed at something the accountant said. What on earth could a man like Nick have in common with a man like that?

"Maybe you're having a bad day because you're nervous about tonight. You don't have to go through with this, Suzanne."

Suzanne eyed her one and only customer. He was staring back at her over the rim of his teacup. The man drank tea. In a French café. He was five-ten, at the most. Eddie was six-two, okay, most of that was ego. This guy was thin, almost skinny. Eddie probably outweighed him by fifty pounds.

She was comparing every man she met to her shithead ex-husband. She needed her head examined. All that aside, this man was an accountant! He wore a pocket protector. Well, not right now, but most of the time he did. And he was looking at her again, his gray eyes steady. Something strange was happening in the pit of her stomach. Her skin felt extra-sensitive, her lips, her breasts, her thighs.

"Suzanne?"

The accountant lowered his cup. He didn't quite smile, his gaze suggestive and knowing, as if he could read her mind. Her stomach heated a little more. *"Hmm?"*

"I said, you don't have to go through with this."

"Oh," Suzanne replied, her gaze straying to the accountant's hands. She gave herself a mental shake. "Yes, I do."

Suzanne stared at her reflection in the mirror. Butterflies, about a million of them, had taken over her insides. Marcel's had closed at seven. It had taken her fifteen minutes to clean up, and half an hour to shower and finish getting ready here at home.

What exactly did a woman wear to pick up a man for

a one-night stand? Pretty underwear was a must. The butterflies in her stomach took a nose dive.

She flipped through the hangers in her closet, considering her choices. In the end, she opted for a wraparound green dress that buttoned at her waist and tied in the back. She skipped pantyhose entirely, and sprayed perfume in places she hadn't sprayed perfume since she'd divorced Eddie.

This was all Eddie's fault.

"Damn you, Eddie," she said, smoothing lip gloss over the undercoat of red lipstick. If he hadn't screwed around on her with anything in a skirt, she would still be married to him and she wouldn't be having to prove that she was still female.

She damned Eddie as she fluffed her hair and applied another coat of mascara to her lashes. She damned him as she tucked tissues, a hairbrush, breath mints and a packet of protection into her purse. She damned him as she locked her door. She was still damning Eddie when she parked her car along Center Avenue.

She'd heard about a new piano bar opening in Harmony, and figured it was as good a place as any to find a man. It wasn't as if Harmony was crawling with eligible men or good places to find them. Her choices included a couple of bars, the truck stop, and Dixie's. She'd considered going into Savannah, but she had to be up early in the morning, and she didn't want to drive that far. Besides, she'd cleaned her apartment. That was where she would feel the most comfortable, therefore that was where the seduction should take place. She gulped and clamped her mouth shut so fast she almost bit her tongue.

Clearing her throat, she practiced a demure smile and one or two lines. "Hello . . . why thank you . . . Yes, that sounds lovely. Your place or mine?"

Her voice rasped.

She tried again. "Your place? If it's all the same to

you, I would prefer mine." That was much better, not perfect, but better.

When she was younger, she'd been told her voice contained a tinge of sultriness and the kind of warmth that called to mind moonlit nights and rumpled sheets. Back then, most of the boys who said it were more interested in rumpling sheets than in moonlight.

It was amazing the way things had a way of coming full circle, for rumpling sheets was all she was interested in tonight. She gulped all over again, nerves fluttering in the pit of her stomach. Touching a hand to her hair, she wet her lips, smoothed her dress over her hips, and entered the piano bar.

The appreciative, speculative glances she received as she meandered inside buoyed her self-confidence. Dixie's was nice, a little smoky perhaps, and a little loud, but crowded enough to give her a few options. Most of the people were here in pairs and couples. No surprise there, but there were some unattached men scattered throughout the room in groups of two or three. She glanced at a table of college boys nearby. Too young. Warding off more butterflies, she sidled up to the bar, and eased onto a high stool. A man wearing a black cowboy hat smiled approvingly. Doing her best to appear casual, she looked the man up and down. Men in Harmony didn't wear cowboy hats, which meant he wasn't from here, a real plus in her book. He had broad shoulders, a strong chin and an interesting mouth. More pluses.

She happened to glance behind him. John and Emma Cameron, the parents of a friend of Kenzie's, were sitting at a table nearby. Three of Suzanne's regular customers at Marcel's were two tables away. Great. Since the last thing she needed was for Kenzie to find out about this, Suzanne eased right back off that stool.

"You're not going to run off already, are you, sugar?" the cowboy asked.

She swallowed her nerves and practiced her smile.

"I forgot to put money in the meter." Of all times for her voice to sound like the wind after midnight.

"You're coming back, right, sugar?" The cowboy had a rodeo smile, and an indentation on the ring finger of his left hand.

"You're just going to have to wait and see, aren't you, *sugar?*"

Her wink was all he would be getting from her tonight. Turning on her three-inch heels, she sashayed toward the door. She looked back once, peering through the smoke-filled room. The cowboy was watching her. So was Emma Cameron, who waved.

Waving back, Suzanne walked out the door, grumbling under her breath. "Damn you, Eddie."

She considered her other options. There was Chelsea's Café. But Nick and Jenna had gone there, and she really didn't want an audience. She supposed she could go to the truck stop. But she preferred to find an unmarried man who'd taken a shower recently. Was that too much to ask?

It seemed her only hope was Sully's Bar and Grill, two blocks away.

Chapter Thirteen

As far as Nick could tell, not much had changed at Chelsea's Café. The interior was posh, the décor antique, the food expensive, the portions adequate. Their waiter, a college student named Dustin, was knowledgeable, attentive and well trained.

"How is your swordfish, ma'am?"

Jenna cast the young waiter a kind smile. "It's delicious, thank you."

"And your meal, sir?"

As he placed his knife on the edge of his plate, Nick was mildly aware of all the covert glances being cast his way. Nonetheless, he let his gaze travel over Jenna before turning his attention to the waiter. "It's as good as any meal I had in India last summer."

"India, huh?" A little too good looking for his own good, and just cocky enough to know it, Dustin sidled closer and quietly said, "Is it true monkey brains are considered a delicacy there?"

Nick's reply was very blasé. "They're highly overrated."

Dustin did a double-take, as if unsure whether to laugh or cringe. Even after Nick winked, he seemed uncertain. In the end, he smiled tentatively, then hurried away.

When he was out of hearing range, Jenna whispered, "He doesn't know you're kidding, Nick. He's going to run straight to the kitchen and tell everyone that you've eaten monkey brains."

"I'm just giving the fine folks in this fine southern restaurant in this fine southern town what they're expecting."

"And you're enjoying it, too." She shook her head, the light catching on the diamond stud earrings. "I suppose you deserve some compensation for putting on that tie."

"In case you haven't noticed, I'm having a good time."

She leaned ahead, elbows resting lightly on the table, her chin resting lightly on her laced fingers. "Nick Proffit is having a good time in Chelsea's Café. Will wonders never cease."

He picked up his knife and fork again. "I'm as surprised as anyone, not to mention concerned. You don't suppose I'm growing." When she smiled, he added, "Perhaps it's the company."

Jenna unlaced her fingers and lowered her hands to the table. Nick was flirting with her. Their date had a hidden agenda, but he wasn't hiding anything with that expression. He cared about her. He wanted her. And that wasn't for the benefit of the fine people of Harmony. It was real. And it did crazy things to her thought process, not to mention to her pulse rate.

She studied his lean face. The Proffits had never been pretty-boy handsome. Dressed up or dressed down, they'd all turned heads, but none more than Nick. There was a vein of the uncivilized in him, something the white shirt and navy tie covered but didn't conceal. The Tiffany lamp hanging overhead gave the illusion of privacy and intimacy. A table would have made them more visible. Visible or not, everyone in the room knew they were here. Jenna had expected to feel uneasy about that. What she felt was a subliminal energy, like the vibration of a guitar sting being strummed with one finger.

Many of the businesses in Harmony had been given a first name. Chelsea's, Dixie's, Sully's, Marcel's. It put them and their customers on a first-name basis. And yet the wealthy people who frequented Chelsea's Café preferred to be addressed more formally, such as Miss Lily and Miss Violet, as if hoop skirts were still in fashion. Most of the men answered to Mr. High-and-Mighty.

Of course, Nick called them all by their first names.

"Didn't your mother ever teach you it isn't polite to stare, Jenna?" His voice was low and deep, and brought out her smile.

With a mild shake of her head, she picked up her fork and said, "They could take the bad boy out of Harmony, but no one could take the last traces of bad boy out of Nick Proffit."

"You make that sound like a good thing."

Jenna didn't know what was happening to her. Well, she knew, but she didn't know what to do about it. She knew what she wanted to do, and the idea was . . . invigorating.

"Hello, Jenna."

She jumped a fraction, and found Wendy Schumaker and Dawn Miller standing a few feet from the table.

"We haven't seen you in ages," Wendy said, loud enough to be heard by those seated at nearby booths and tables.

Jenna didn't believe for a second that it had been unintentional. She'd sat on committees with both of these women. They'd attended the same luncheons, had been in the same clubs, shopped in the same stores. Their children had been in the same play groups. She and Craig had considered them and their husbands their friends. She wouldn't make the same mistake twice.

"Have you been to Dixie's yet?" Dawn asked, as if it

hadn't been nearly two years since she'd bothered to speak a word to Jenna.

Jenna didn't so much as shrug.

After eyeing Jenna in that warm, curious way he had that made a woman feel understood, Nick finally glanced at Dawn and Wendy and said, "I stopped in a few days ago while Brian and Dixie were still putting the finishing touches on the place."

"Yes, well," Wendy said, "Of course an adventurer like yourself would go. Still, I would think you would be bored to tears back in quiet old Harmony."

Nick didn't quite smile. He didn't quite reply, either.

"Dixie's isn't our normal cup of tea," Dawn confessed. "Honestly, David and I don't know what Brian and Dixie are thinking!"

"But we'll go, of course," Wendy insisted. "Anything to support our friends and all."

A ringing silence ensued. As if trying to fill it, Wendy finally said, "It's amazing, Nick. Clean shaven, you're the spitting image of your brother, especially under this lighting. Don't you think it's positively amazing, Jenna?"

Jenna studied Nick somberly for a moment before speaking for the first time. "I suppose you could say the Proffit brothers shared a similar bone structure."

It wasn't the kind of response that lent itself to further conversation. "Yes, well, er, that is," Dawn stammered.

"It's nice to see you, Jenna," Wendy said, coming to her friend's rescue.

Again, Jenna made no reply. Dawn and Wendy stared at her, eyes narrowed, lips thinned. Looking at each other, they finally returned to their husbands who were waiting back at their table.

Nick leaned toward Jenna over the table. "A similar bone structure?"

She picked up her fork. "I can't believe I ever considered them my friends. They act more like Abigail and Lenore every day. Perhaps now people will give that whole *you're the spitting image of your brother* line a rest."

Nick hadn't expected to laugh. It probably rankled the hell out of good old Wendy and Dawn, but it felt good to Nick. He noticed that Jenna's grim expression softened, too. She looked at once elegant and casual. Her hair was twisted into an intricate knot and secured high on the back of her head. He didn't know how women did that. It was only one of their many mysteries. He liked women, liked the way they looked, the way they smelled, the way they could do four things at once and still remember to thaw something for supper. Mostly, he liked the way they felt, and the way they made him feel in return.

There was something different about Jenna, always had been. Oh, he liked all the usual things about her, but Jenna was more than simply a woman with pretty hair, a nice body, and a good mind. In her heels, she was taller than a lot of the women in the room. She would have outclassed them if she'd been barefoot. Her jewelry consisted of a slender gold watch, diamond earrings, and her wedding ring. That ring had a lot of people speculating. She had to know it. And yet she appeared completely unaffected. It was as if she had her own agenda, and everyone, including Nick, was going to have to wait until she was ready for the unveiling.

Lucky for Nick, he was a patient man.

He looked around, viewing his surroundings as if through the lens of his camera. He doubted there was a man in the room who hadn't noticed Jenna. The women, either, for that matter, although the women looked at her with a different form of speculation.

Dawn and Wendy were the only two who had spoken to her, if you called their little drama speaking. No matter what they'd said about being supportive of the new piano bar, Dixie and Brian Jefferson's latest venture, Nick knew damn well that the people they were *supporting* were Brian's parents, who were influential in local politics.

Given a choice between a snake pit and people influential in local politics, Nick would take the snake pit every time. He swirled his wine, and said, "I don't know how the hell you kept from telling them off."

She turned her head slowly, her eyes contemplative and ringed by dark lashes. "That's probably what they wanted me to do. It would have fed the gossip mills, and I've had enough of that to last a lifetime."

"You put them in their place. In their place isn't where they want to be."

She swirled her wine. "Thanks for the recap."

He took another sip of wine, his regard for Jenna's intelligence and wit growing a little more every day. He couldn't be sure what Jenna was thinking, or feeling for that matter. There was warm affection in her eyes, but there was also that wedding ring to deal with, not to mention Craig's shadow. They'd put their heads together last night, and reviewed everything in Craig's briefcase a second time. They would have to be careful how they approached this situation. They wanted to discover the truth, but they had to do it without hurting Brandon and Benji, for another wave of gossip could harm the boys.

Nick and Jenna had gone over Craig's day planner word for word, appointment by appointment. There was a clue there. They knew it. They just couldn't put their fingers on what it was, what it implied, or who it implicated. The fact remained that somebody had stolen four hundred thousand dollars, then deposited one-fourth of it into Craig and Jenna's account. Nick hoped that more than one person knew about it. It would be next to impossible to get a confession out of the thief. An eyewitness or an accomplice was another matter.

They talked as they finished their wine. And when they were ready, the waiter appeared, as if by magic.

Jenna was assuring Dustin that the meal was delicious when Nick noticed the woman with auburn hair and small glasses who was sitting at a table across the room. It was the same woman that had run the stop sign the first time he'd gone running. Shaye Townsend was in the middle of laughing at something her friend said when she happened to glance at Nick. Her eyes widened, her gaze locking on him much the way it had that other time when she'd been driving. She turned her attention back to her friends before he could identify the emotion in her eyes.

Was it sorrow? Disappointment? Or yearning?

Dawn Miller had said it earlier. Clean shaven, and with the lights turned low, Nick was the spitting image of Craig.

"Here you go, sir." Dustin had returned with Nick's credit card and a copy of the check.

Nick pocketed both items then dealt with the tip. The next time he looked, Shaye Townsend's chair was empty. He turned in his chair in time to catch sight of her heading for the Exit.

He strummed his fingers on the table after she'd gone, wondering what she had to do with Craig. He didn't like what he was thinking.

"Nick?"

He started.

"Is something wrong?" Jenna asked.

He raked a hand through his hair and eventually shook his head. "It's stuffy in here."

"In that case, what do you say we get out of here?"

Nick wondered if Jenna had seen Shaye, too. "After you," he said quietly.

The evening was warm and scented by the musk roses growing along the sidewalk outside Chelsea's Café. He and Jenna strode to the Land Rover in silence. He held her door, then walked around and climbed in on his side.

Even after he was inside, they were both quiet for

interminable moments. Jenna finally broke the silence. "Walker, Whitman and Sinclair."

Nick's hand stilled in midair, keys and all. "What about them?"

Jenna was looking straight ahead. "Somebody at that law firm has the answer to this puzzle."

He looked at her as he started the car. Walker, Whitman and Sinclair was where Craig had worked, and where he'd collapsed hours before he'd died. The firm had handled Nathaniel Sherman's trust. They'd also employed Shaye Townsend.

"Can I ask you a personal question, Jenna?"

The streetlight slanted across her face as she turned her head and looked at him. "What do you want to know?"

"What happened to the hundred grand that mysteriously turned up in your bank account?"

He heard the deep breath of air she released. If he'd been a betting man, he'd have laid odds that she was relieved that he'd asked that particular question, and not another, more personal one.

"The partners seemed to think I should turn it over to Sherman's trust. It was as I told them. I don't know how that money ended up in our account. And they hadn't been able to prove it came from Nathaniel Sherman's trust fund. Because it didn't. If I had turned it over to them, it would have looked as if I believed Craig was guilty."

"I doubt they took that kindly."

There was no humor in her sudden laughter. She looked out her window. "The rumors got even uglier after that."

Good old Harmony. Checking for traffic, Nick pulled away from the curb. "Then where is the money?" It sure as hell didn't appear as if she'd used it on the house or vacations or a new wardrobe.

"I moved it to a bank in Savannah."

"It's just sitting there drawing interest?"

"I let the interest accrue six months at a time."

"And then what happens to it?" He pulled to a stop at a traffic light.

"It's donated to the library in Craig's name, anonymously, mind you, once at Christmas, and once at the peak of the fund-raiser every summer."

"Isn't the library the society's—"

"Biggest charity? Yes, it is." The streetlight on the corner couldn't hold a candle to the sheen of purpose in her eyes as she added, "It was your father's, too."

Nick tipped his head back and laughed. "Damn, Jenna, I like your style."

"Not everyone in Harmony shares your opinion." But there was satisfaction in the way she said it.

Nick wished he could get the image of Shaye Townsend out of his mind. He wished he could get rid of the thoughts that came with it even more. "Look," he said, pointing. "That's Suzanne's car." He couldn't tell if anyone was in the ten-year-old sedan parked in front of Sully's Bar and Grill. "Do you think she'll go through with it?"

"Knowing Suzanne? She'll give it the old college try."

All hunkered down in the front seat of her car, Suzanne stared at the neon sign in the window of Sully's Bar and Grill. Three of the letters were burned out. It didn't appear as if it was hurting their business. She'd come here a couple of times with Cherie. It wasn't the classiest place in town, far from it.

She sighed, and smoothed a wrinkle from the skirt of her dress. Other than her waitress uniform, it had been a long time since she'd put on a dress. All that effort, wasted. Tight jeans would have worked at Sully's. According to Cherie, hello worked at Sully's.

Suzanne had been holed up in her parked car for ten minutes, alternately cussing Eddie out and picturing the bar's interior. She had a decision to make, her courage to get up.

She recognized most of the vehicles parked around her. Old Willard Pringle and his cronies were undoubtedly playing poker and puffing on their smelly cigars in the back room. It looked as if Roy Gleason had driven his new Jeep. He'd come into the coffee shop a few days ago. And everyone knew that Roy didn't drink coffee. He was on the prowl, and had made it clear to both women that he was theirs for the asking. Roy was married. Cherie hadn't seemed concerned about that. Far be it from Suzanne to judge anyone, but she wasn't going to be responsible for contributing to the breakup of even a bad marriage.

Finally, she skewed up her courage, fixed her hair, and headed inside. The low din died down as, one by one, a dozen or so men noticed her enter the smoky room. Lenny Pratt was holding up one end of the bar. He slanted her a gap-toothed grin and motioned for her to join him. Hiding a shudder, she locked her gaze on the pay phone like a lifeline and said, "I just came in to make a phone call."

She'd lied. It was either that or explain to Lenny that although she wanted to have sex tonight, it had to be with someone who hadn't neglected his teeth. Okay, maybe she was being picky. She wanted a man who'd showered recently, was single, and had most of his teeth. She had standards. What could she say?

Taking a calming breath, she dialed up her own phone number. Pretending to speak with a friend, she glanced around the bar. The O'Leary brothers, one a plumber, the other a house painter, both sloppy drunk tonight, watched her openly. Lenny Pratt winked and grinned again. Revulsion reared inside her. She hung up the phone, hitched her purse higher on her shoulder, and fled.

Her hand was shaking as she unlocked her car door. "Damn you, Eddie." Her voice shook, too.

Once inside her car, she faced the fact that she couldn't do this. She couldn't sleep with a man she found repulsive. What would she say? "Excuse me, but would you mind putting this paper bag over your head?"

She didn't even have any paper bags. She took her groceries home in plastic, which was a strange thing to think about at a time like this. Perhaps she was a strange woman. Or maybe she just plain wasn't ready. Maybe she would never be ready. Maybe she would end up like Tywla Mae, old and brittle, with creaky knees and a different hat for every day of the week.

Suzanne pulled out of the parking space and stopped at the light. Strumming her fingers on the steering wheel, she tried to decide what to do now. It was nine-thirty on a Friday night. Kenzie wouldn't be home until tomorrow afternoon. Jenna and Nick were out, Twyla Mae was baby-sitting, Cherie was probably someplace she shouldn't be with some man or other, and Faith wasn't exactly a laugh a minute. The night stretched into monotonous infinity, much like the rest of Suzanne's life.

She was feeling sorry for herself. Telling herself to knock it off, she counted her blessings. She had her beautiful child, her health, a few close friends, her mother and sisters, Marcel's, a roof over her head. She had a good mind, a strong will, a smart mouth, and a few far-reaching dreams. She wasn't going to have sex tonight. So what? There were other pleasurable things she could do.

Like what?

Suzanne stared at the red light, and then into space, thinking. There was chocolate. Not just chocolate. There was triple chocolate fudge ice cream, by the cup, by the pint, by the gallon.

A horn blared. Suzanne jumped. Wondering how long the light had been green, she wet her lips, put her foot on the accelerator and headed for the new A & P on the east side of town.

*   *   *

The lines on the parking lot of the new grocery store were straight, the lights overhead almost as bright as daylight. She didn't recognize any of the cars parked near the building. She took that as a good sign.

She strode inside, a little overdressed, perhaps, for buying groceries. At least now she had a plan. Without bothering with a basket, she headed straight for the freezer section, her heels clicking as she traversed the tile floor. A bagger watched her sashay past. She winked. He blushed. She grinned, feeling more like her old self.

A frazzled woman pushing a cart containing smashed bread, kids cereal, and three small children nearly crashed into her. More amicable than usual, Suzanne said something kind and then marched the remaining distance to the ice-cream freezer.

Starting at one end, she moved slowly, studying the bounty behind the glass doors: shelf after shelf, brand after brand, flavor after flavor of rich, decadent frozen desserts. She was so engrossed in her selection she didn't notice the man reading the back of a half-gallon of ice cream until she bumped into him.

"Oh," she exclaimed. "Excuse me."

"No problem." He glanced at her, and then looked more closely. "Don't I know you?"

She found herself peering up at a man with a deep voice and broad shoulders. He had a square chin, most of his hair. And he was tall. Now that she thought about it, he did look a little familiar.

"You played football," she said. "A few grades ahead of me. Reed Carlson, right?"

He nodded, and held up the carton of fudge praline delight ice cream. His ring finger bore no indentation. A good sign.

"Suzanne Hartman, isn't it?"

"It's Suzanne Nash, now. I kept my ex-husband's name."

He nodded, as if storing the information. He seemed to have good concentration, another good trait in her book.

"So you're out for a night on the town, too," he said.

And had a sense of humor. The pluses just didn't end. "My daughter's spending the night with a friend, and I thought, well, never mind what I thought."

He smiled. He really had a very nice mouth, and all his teeth. He looked at her closely. With just the right inflection, he said, "We could both choose a flavor, and sample some of each."

Oh, my, she thought. "Ice cream?" she asked.

"I'll leave that entirely up to you."

She was pretty sure she remembered that he'd been married once, a long time ago. He'd left Harmony before she did, and had come back alone. Like she had. She couldn't remember if she'd heard he was divorced, or if his wife had died. Either way, he was single. He didn't appear to be a player, but he obviously knew his way around a woman.

Suzanne opened the glass door and reached blindly for a container, any container, of ice cream. "My car's outside."

"So is mine."

Well all-righty-then. She took a deep breath. "Follow me."

She paid for her ice cream, and when the bagger asked if she wanted paper or plastic, she cast a surreptitious glance at Reed Carlson and said, "Plastic, thank you."

She wouldn't be needing a paper bag tonight.

Chapter Fourteen

Suzanne felt a little dizzy when she reached the top of the stairs leading to her apartment. Reed Carlson wasn't the slightest bit winded.

"Do you work out?" she asked.

"I take the stairs at the school. It builds stamina."

Sometimes, she took the stairs a dozen times a day, so her breathlessness couldn't have been from exertion. She swallowed tightly. "What do you do?"

"I'm a guidance counselor at the high school."

His list of attributes was growing. He had a good job, good teeth, broad shoulders, a sense of humor, and stamina.

"What about you?" he asked. "What do you do?"

"I own a coffee shop downtown." Hoping he didn't notice her hand shake, she drew her key from her purse, and reached for the doorknob, only to stop suddenly. Not about to fall for the prank twice, she examined the antique knob more closely. Finding it dry, she unlocked her door. "You're not married, are you?" she asked.

"No." He followed her inside. "Tried it once."

She turned on a lamp and put her purse in the closet, talking as she went. "Ah. Another of the walking wound-ed. Isn't it strange the way marriage is grossly over-rated, and yet divorce is exactly how you expect it to be?"

He didn't reply, not with words, anyway. He shrugged one of those broad shoulders of his. Starting at the top of her head, he let his gaze travel slowly down, and back up again, coming to rest on her eyes. She could tell from his expression that he liked what he saw. And all she could think was *Let's hurry up and get this over with*.

What was wrong with her?

She took the ice cream from him and placed both containers on the counter in her small kitchen. Giving her some room, he leaned a hip against the stove a few feet away.

Suzanne wished she could think of something to say. Taking two bowls from the cupboard, she tried to remember how to make small talk. She opened her mouth to say something about the weather, and out slipped, "My feet are killing me."

She froze.

"Kissing me might shut me up."

Reed Carlson eased closer, tall and confident and obligingly male. Tipping her face up with two fingers, he covered her mouth with his. His lips were firm and just moist enough to make the kiss interesting. He tasted good. When she finally breathed, she realized he smelled pretty good, too, a little like soap and after-shave and a lot like man.

Not bad, she thought after it was over. The kiss hadn't curled her toes, but it had potential. Feeling less shaky, she returned to the ice cream. "I guess you can tell I haven't done this in a while."

"How long have you been divorced?" he asked.

"Six years." She didn't tell him she'd carried a torch for Eddie for a long time after. Instead, she said, "My husband had affairs while we were married, and then came home to me."

"What a guy."

"He's legendary. Just ask him. I wanted to make sure I didn't have anything, you know, communicable. I don't."

"I'm clean, too. Suzanne?"

She looked up at him. For the first time, she noticed he had blue eyes. "Yes?"

"What do you say we save the ice cream for later?"

His arms went around her back. Drawing her closer, he kissed her again, right there in her newly cleaned little kitchen. He knew exactly what he was doing, and took charge with quiet assurance. It just felt so darn good to be held, to be on the receiving end of all that animal grace and masculine energy. She could feel herself relaxing, responding. He touched her breast, massaging, cupping, taking the weight of it in his hand. That felt good, too. She wasn't a mass of pulsating nerve endings, but her nipples hardened beneath his hand, and her hips seemed to have found a rhythm she'd thought she'd forgotten.

He rubbed against her with just the right amount of pressure. Oh, yes, the man definitely had potential.

He kissed her again, and finally reached for her hand, quietly waiting. Realizing what he wanted, she led the way out of the kitchen, across her living room, and into her bedroom. She'd left a lamp on earlier. The dim bulb cast just enough light throughout the room to give it ambiance. The curtains were drawn, the room straightened. She'd never done much with the furnishings. Reed wasn't interested in décor. He tugged his shirt from his jeans, then unfastened the three buttons at the neck.

She watched the way he dragged the shirt over his head, tossing it to an old French–style chair. The move couldn't have been sexier if it had been choreographed by a pro.

"I bought that chair at an estate sale for a dollar," she said, gliding the zipper down the back of her dress.

"I've been meaning to refinish it and use it at Marcel's." She didn't know why she was telling him this, especially while she was toeing out of her shoes and he was unzipping his pants. "I don't usually babble."

"Who says you're babbling?"

She swallowed tightly again. "Does this feel a little like stripping for surgery to you?"

Reed was down to his briefs, his socks, and a smile. "And they say romance is dead. The first time back in the saddle is the toughest. Why don't I help you?"

With his help, her dress landed on the floor with a quiet swish. Back in the saddle? She shook her head, but couldn't help grinning. He really was a very nice man. She could do this. She still wasn't a mass of pulsating nerve endings, but she—

He pulled her to him. "Oh!" Gradually, that *oh* turned into "Oh, my." Sometime later, she whispered, "Oh, yes."

Somewhere between her first and last murmur, her bra had ended up on the floor. Reed held her close, so that her breasts skimmed the thick mat of hair on his chest. She moved against him, sinuous and joyful—okay, and grateful for this opportunity. She was neither old nor brittle. She was responsive, and maybe this really wasn't going to be all that difficult.

She placed her hand boldly over the part of him straining the fabric of his briefs. His eyes closed, a deep groan starting in the back of his throat, which started something warm and languid in her belly. Keeping her right hand where it was, more or less, she reached behind her with her other hand, fumbling with the coverlet on her bed. The lightweight quilt lifted away. She tugged at the sheet next.

It tugged back.

The air-conditioning burst on, raising goose bumps on her arms. Reed kissed her again, his hands gliding over her shoulders, along the outer swell of her breasts, warming her all over, inching toward her waist, lightly skimming her hip, her belly. Her breath caught in her throat, and she tugged a little harder at the sheet.

He nuzzled her neck, caressed her buttocks through the see-through lace panties, and explored the sensitive skin on the inside of her thigh. Her stomach muscles contracted and her back arched. As if it was all the invitation he needed, he grasped her hips and pressed himself against her. Her knees were weakening and that delicious tingling sensation was but a heartbeat and a few more touches away.

She tugged on the sheet again. It held fast.

Turning around, she bent over slightly, reaching for the sheet with both hands. Finally, she was getting someplace. He nuzzled her neck again. Before her knees gave out completely, she sank to the bed and scooted toward the center. Reed was in the process of following when her foot got stuck in a fold in the top sheet. She pushed harder.

She might have been out of practice when it came to making love, but she knew how to get into her bed. What was going on? What the hell was wrong with her sheets?

She tried again, but the sheet wouldn't budge. Now both her feet were stuck in a fold a few feet from the top, and Reed was trying to help her, getting stuck, too.

It occurred to her in a blinding flash. "My bed is short-sheeted."

"You're kidding."

"I wouldn't kid about this." Somebody had played another practical joke on her. That made two in one day.

Suzanne and Reed were both down to their last scraps of clothing. Their knees were bent, their feet stuck. They looked like two flies trapped on fly paper.

How could this have happened? Who could have done it? Her door had been locked. She distinctly remembered unlocking it with her key fifteen minutes ago. Her mind darted back to that afternoon when she'd brought Kenzie home to get her pajamas. Suzanne remembered thinking that something had "felt" different in the apartment. Now that she thought about it, she hadn't needed her key then. The shortening on the doorknob had sidetracked her. She'd taken a tissue from her purse and opened the door without unlocking it. Whoever had been responsible for the first prank must have jimmied the lock, and short-sheeted her bed, too.

"I can't do this."

"We don't need to get under the covers." Reed placed his hand on her knee.

She jumped, no easy feat, stuck as she was in the blasted fold in her sheet.

"Easy," he murmured, gliding his hand along her thigh.

"Hold it right there."

The man followed orders extremely well. Unfortunately, it made her yelp, which only added to her embarrassment. Finally getting her feet unstuck, she scuttled off the other side of the bed.

"Where are you going?" he asked.

"I don't know." She looked at him. He really was a fine specimen of a man.

"It was just somebody's idea of a joke, Suzanne. Come back to bed."

Giving herself a mental shake, she presented him with her back. "Do you believe in omens, Reed?" she said over her shoulder.

"That depends." He said it as if he knew he wasn't going to like what was coming next.

"You have to leave."

"Now?" he asked incredulously.

"Now. I've been the butt of one too many practical jokes today. Pardon the pun." Arms folded to cover her breasts, she practically ran to the bathroom, where she closed the door and turned the lock.

Breathing deeply, she stared at her reflection. Her brown eyes were round and blank. Her short dark hair stuck out on one side. Except for a splotch of pink on each cheek, her face was pale. There was a scrape of pink on her neck and right breast, too where Reed's whisker stubble had rubbed against her flesh. She'd been a hairsbreadth away from making love for the first time in six years.

"Suzanne?" Reed's voice carried through the closed door.

Six cold, lonely, celibate years. "Yes?"

"Are you okay?"

No. "Yes."

"Are you coming out?"

"No." Maybe in a hundred years.

"Come on, Suzanne."

"Just leave, Reed, okay?"

"You're serious?"

"Yes. Please. Just go." She stared at her reflection. "And don't forget your ice cream." He was going to need it after all.

She listened intently. He mumbled something she couldn't make out. Footsteps faded. A few minutes later, the front door creaked open and then clicked shut.

Suzanne counted to twenty and then peeked out. The apartment was quiet; Reed was gone.

Donning her oldest bathrobe, she padded out to the kitchen. He'd left his ice cream on the counter next to hers. He probably thought she was certifiable. He might be right, but at least he'd been gentleman enough to leave when she'd asked him to go.

So much for getting back in the saddle.

She stomped around her apartment, seething. She'd been had. Twice. Somebody was undoubtedly rolling on the floor laughing right now. The question was, Who?

She eyed the melting ice cream. Carefully considering each person on her list of potential culprits, she pried off the carton's lid and took a spoon from the drawer.

Who had access to her apartment? Pretty much everyone in the building did, not to mention her mom, her sisters, Cherie. She thought for a moment. Who had she played jokes on most recently?

Everyone.

Okay, who wanted to get even?

Nick? Jenna? Twyla Mae, Kenzie, Brandon and Benji? Her sister Amanda had been spitting mad about that female impersonator, but Amanda was out of town this weekend. The kids could have put that shortening on her doorknob, but they wouldn't know how to short-sheet a bed. That left the other adults.

Suzanne sampled the ice cream with the tip of her tongue. It was called Chocolate Decadence, and had chunks of brownie and swirls of fudge. The taste lived up to its name. She closed her eyes in rapture and groaned. This wasn't the first time that sound had erupted from her throat tonight. Her face and neck felt hot. Christ, was she blushing?

Oh, for crying out loud! She would find out who was responsible for that prank, and when she did, there would be hell to pay. In the meantime, she carried the carton to the sofa, and dug in.

Lights were on in three of the apartments at 317 Beulah Street when Nick pulled into the grassy parking area and cut the Land Rover's engine. Sitting in the bucket seat, Jenna thought that perhaps now he would tell her what was wrong.

She felt his eyes on her, but instead of talking, he opened his door and got out. Sighing, she did the same. They met at the back bumper. Although she looked up at him, she didn't invite him to accompany her to Twyla Mae's to pick up the boys. He fell into step beside her anyway.

Jenna had no idea what was going on in that head of his. They'd gone for a drive after dinner. The radio had been turned low, their windows down, the heavy air streaming in carrying the lingering traces of somebody's barbecue, exhaust fumes, and the red Georgia clay. He'd driven past the old water tower on Center Avenue, the old law office where Craig had worked, the house on Magnolia Street where Jenna and Craig had once lived. She'd half-expected him to say something off-color about the girls he'd kissed behind the bleachers as he'd driven past the football field. He hadn't uttered a word, lost, it seemed, in his thoughts. He drove past the elementary school last. By then, Jenna couldn't even guess what he was thinking, although she was certain there was meaning behind the streets he'd chosen and the buildings he'd passed. Her attempts at conversation had been thwarted by one-syllable replies. He'd closed himself off from her. She couldn't fathom why.

He stood behind her as she raised her hand to knock on Twyla Mae's door. Looking less eccentric without her hat, Twyla Mae stepped back stiffly and motioned Nick and Jenna in. "You two are back already, too?"

"Too?" Jenna asked. The front apartment was over-furnished and fussy. Straight-back chairs were lined up between worn, overstuffed furniture, doilies and knick-knacks on every flat surface. The frilly clutter didn't bother Brandon and Benji in the least. Her older son was sprawled on the sofa, Benji on his stomach on the floor, his chin resting on his hands, his new glasses perched securely on the bridge of his little nose. They were both so engrossed in their favorite video they didn't look up. Fleetingly, she wondered if they would one day retreat inside themselves, too. It *was* a strong Proffit trait. It was also one of her least favorite.

"Suzanne's home?" Nick asked.

Twyla Mae nodded. Jenna strolled farther into the room.

"Is she alone?" Nick asked.

Twyla Mae must have nodded again, because Nick

said, "She didn't find anybody suitable for her little plan?"

"I didn't say that."

Nick and Jenna both looked at Twyla Mae in surprise. "Are you saying she did?" Nick asked. "Is he still here?"

"He left," Twyla Mae said, her whisper loud enough to penetrate steel.

"How long did he stay?"

Twyla Mae sniffed and stuck her nose in the air. "Now how on earth would a God-fearing old lady like me know that?"

Jenna saw the way Nick glanced at the rocking chair pushed close to the window overlooking the street. For once, his thoughts were crystal clear. It occurred to her that he let her see what he wanted her to see, and nothing more. Agitated, she ejected the movie and coaxed the boys to their feet. After giving Twyla Mae a quick hug, they ran ahead to the common foyer. Nick and Jenna followed in single file.

"Twelve minutes," Twyla Mae said. "That's how long he stayed." Lips pursed, she closed her door.

Nick thought it was too bad Twyla Mae hadn't worked in Craig's law office. She would have known exactly what had gone on in that practice.

He and Jenna were alone in the foyer. The antique light fixture cast shadows into the corners and beneath Jenna's eyes. Her lipstick was long-gone, her hair windblown, her eyes less serene than they'd been at the start of the evening. He knew she didn't appreciate the silent treatment, but he had to hand it to her. She didn't pry. She didn't stay in the foyer, either. She was miffed at him. Miffed, hell, she was royally pissed.

Nick ran a hand through his hair and loosened his tie. Did a man owe his brother's widow an explanation? What about his brother's sons? What did Nick owe them? That was the four-hundred-thousand-dollar question.

Following the course Jenna had taken into her apartment, Nick heard the boys talking as he neared the bathroom. Arms folded at his chest, he leaned against the door jam. Brandon's back was to Nick, but Benji noticed his uncle right away. "Hey," he said after spitting into the sink.

"Hey."

Brandon spit, too, then rinsed off his toothbrush. These two boys did everything together. It had never been like that between Nick and Craig. And it never would be.

"Are you coming to our baseball game tomorrow?" Brandon asked.

A fist squeezed Nick's airway for a moment. Somehow, he managed to ask the pertinent questions about the time and the place.

"Bring your camera," Benji bossed.

Nick was smiling when the boys scurried past him and tried to talk their mother into letting them stay up a while. Perhaps just being in the same house with two Proffit urchins who insisted they weren't tired despite their yawns was reason enough to smile. Seeing Jenna with the kids was certainly reason enough to yearn.

She sent the boys to their room with strict instructions to get ready for bed. And then she looked at him. The drive through Harmony had tied him up in knots. Her gaze was undoing him, one knot at a time.

"What do you think we should do next?" she asked quietly.

That *we* nearly undid him completely. "I think I'll call it a night."

They were standing in the kitchen, Jenna, a table and five chairs between him and the door. He could tell she wasn't satisfied with his answer.

"I was talking about Craig."

He knew that, dammit. "I think we should give it a rest."

A lady would have moved aside so he could pass

without having to give her a wide berth, thereby making it obvious that he didn't trust himself to be close to her right now. She held her ground.

"Good night, Jenna."

Jenna's mind spun. A few short hours ago, she and Nick had been in total agreement regarding the issue of proving Craig's innocence. "What's going on, Nick?"

"Nothing." He answered without turning, his hand on the doorknob. "I realized something tonight, that's all."

She waited for him to continue.

"Maybe we haven't thought this completely through. Sometimes it's best to let a sleeping dog lie." He opened the door and strode through.

That was it? Jenna thought, her feet rooted to the floor. That was the explanation she'd waited nearly an hour to hear?

She told the boys she would be right back, then rushed out the back door and down the steps after Nick. "Best?" she called, her voice more shrill than she would have liked. "Is that what this is about? Better and best?"

He'd stopped in the darkest area of the backyard, between the flagstone patio and the tree where the owls looked on from a high branch, where the moonlight didn't penetrate and the porch light barely reached. "Maybe you haven't thought this through completely, Nick, but I've had two years to think about it."

"The grieving widow. Yes, you drove home that fact every time you flashed your wedding ring tonight." He turned again, heading for the carriage house.

Jenna felt as if she were reeling backward. In reality, she hadn't moved. The evening played through her mind in fast forward. Nick had been relaxed and attentive most of the evening. She tried to pinpoint when that had changed.

It was after they'd left Chelsea's. Or was it before? He was the one who'd come back to Harmony. He was the one who'd stirred everything up. And now he thought they should just forget everything?

She shook with emotion. "So once again Nicholas Proffit is going to walk away. How convenient for you." She took a shuddering breath, so that her voice was steadier when she said, "You can do whatever you want. Heaven knows you always do." She could tell by the way his shoulders squared that she'd hit a nerve. That, at least, was some consolation. "I'm not going to let this sleeping dog lie."

She walked inside with quiet dignity, then stood shivering, waiting. A car started outside. She knew without looking that it was Nick's Land Rover.

She'd fancied herself falling in love with him. She'd let her guard down, something she'd known better than to do. Wondering if Nick was leaving for the remainder of the evening, or for good, she took another shuddering breath and went to tell her sons good night.

Chapter Fifteen

Suzanne was lifting the lid on the washer when Jenna entered the service porch the following morning. Neither of them spoke, Suzanne's first indication that something unusual was going on. It wasn't uncustomary for Suzanne to wake up on the wrong side of the bed, but Jenna had been known to be cheerful when she was running a fever of a hundred and two.

Leaning down to yank open the dryer as she always did, Suzanne paused suddenly, then opened the door very slowly. When nothing came shooting out at her, she glanced behind her.

Jenna wasn't even looking.

Suzanne tossed in her towels, telling herself she was being paranoid. She had good reason, two to be exact. "If I'd just pulled off two successful practical jokes of such magnitude, I'd be gloating."

Not only was Jenna not gloating, she wasn't even listening. Her basket of unfolded clothes evidently forgotten, she stood staring out the window. It wasn't like her to be idle.

"This is even less fun without mint juleps."

Jenna didn't reply one way or the other, which prompted Suzanne to venture away from the fan and take a closer look. Her beige Capri pants and royal blue shell appeared freshly ironed, but there were dark circles under those blue eyes.

"Is everything all right?"

More silence.

Suzanne looked out the window, too. Twyla Mae was fussing with her roses. Suzanne had drilled her eldest neighbor earlier, and was pretty sure she hadn't been responsible for the pranks. Brandon and Benji were warming up for their softball game. Jenna seemed to be looking beyond them, all the way to the carriage house.

"Any idea what Nick was doing between three o'clock yesterday afternoon and seven last night?" Suzanne asked.

Suzanne thought the fact that Jenna finally looked at her when she mentioned Nick's name was extremely telling. "He picked Brandon and Benji up from school and took them to the dentist," Jenna said. "After that he showed them how to develop film."

"Does he have witnesses?"

Jenna blinked, refocused, then stared straight into Suzanne's eyes. "I saw the pictures they developed, and Brandon has one cavity. Why?"

Suzanne ran her fingers over her face and on up into her hair. She was having a bad hair day, and messing it up probably wasn't helping. So be it. "Somebody played another practical joke on me. It brought the evening to a less-than-satisfactory conclusion."

"Twyla Mae said your date didn't stay long."

Suzanne glared at Twyla Mae through the window. Who needed a security camera when they had Twyla Mae? "It wasn't exactly a date. I met a single man at the freezer section in the grocery store." The dryer hummed, the fan whirred. And Suzanne thought out loud. "If Nick has an alibi, who could have done it?"

Some of Jenna's old spunk was back in her eyes as

she said, "What did this person do, besides putting shortening on your doorknob, I mean?"

"Somebody short-sheeted my bed. It was a real mood buster."

Jenna had to cover her mouth to hide her grin. "Oh, dear. Then you didn't . . ."

Suzanne rolled her eyes, because it had been a lady-like way of asking an unladylike question. "No, I didn't. I'll spare you my sordid details. What happened with you and Nick?"

Outside, Benji threw a wild pitch, and Brandon sputtered about having to chase after it. Twyla Mae was sputtering to no one in particular. Everybody was sputtering today. Even Jenna came close as she said, "I haven't the faintest idea."

Just then, Faith entered the service porch, humming. Her smile fell slightly as she eyed the other two women. "Am I interrupting something?"

Jenna shook her head, and Suzanne said, "There are darn few secrets around here. Come on in. I'm using the dryer, but the washer's all yours."

Pink, Suzanne mouthed to Jenna when Faith's back was turned. *She's wearing pink.*

Jenna nudged her friend, then looked out the window again. Twyla Mae was ambling toward the front door. The boys had forfeited their ball gloves in favor of the climbing tree. She hadn't seen Nick. His Land Rover had been parked next to her van when she got up this morning. He hadn't left Harmony. She wasn't certain how she felt about that.

She'd sat next to him during that drive last night, but he'd already been miles away by then. Moments ago Suzanne had said there were few secrets here. There were secrets inside Nick, distant, far-off places he went to, and he took no one with him.

"If you're going to sigh like that," Suzanne said, "you might as well tell me what happened."

For the first time, Jenna noticed that Suzanne was wearing her French maid uniform. Of course. It was Saturday morning. Suzanne always went to work around ten on Saturdays. Jenna had plenty to do. So far, she'd done next to nothing. "I don't know what happened. The evening started fine. Nick and I dined. We talked; we came face-to-face with some of Harmony's finest, exactly as we'd planned. It had been Nick's idea. He thought that if we got people talking about seeing us together, they would be too busy speculating to notice when we start searching for the truth. And then, out of the blue, he said we haven't thought this through. He's decided to let a sleeping dog lie."

"That was his explanation?"

Jenna nodded. "I guess nobody ever died from disappointment."

"Yeah, well, nobody ever died from embarrassment, either, but last night I came close. This has not been a good week. My one and only waitress gave notice, my kid's acting strange, I haven't had sex in six years, I'm having weird dreams, and I'm pretty sure I gained five pounds last night."

"Kenzie's still acting strange?" Jenna asked.

"Your waitress quit?" Faith said at the same time. Jenna had forgotten Faith was there.

"You know Kenzie," Suzanne said to Jenna. And to Faith, she said, "Cherie found a job with benefits and better hours."

"Are you going to hire a replacement?"

Duh. If nothing else, the sharp look Jenna cast Suzanne kept her sarcasm to a low din as she said, "Why, are you'all interested?"

"I might be."

"You're kidding."

"What Suzanne means," Jenna said hurriedly.

"I know what Suzanne means," Faith said levelly. Suzanne appeared to make a conscious effort to be nice. "I wouldn't have pegged you as a waitress, that's all."

Faith shrugged. "I've never actually been employed as a waitress, but I've poured a lot of coffee." She peeked inside the washer, then made her way toward the door, as if she assumed the conversation was over.

"What sort of experience do you have?" Suzanne asked.

Faith glanced behind her. Giving the room a sweeping glance, she let her gaze settle on Suzanne. "I was a Christmas tree decorator in Boston."

"You're kidding."

"Do I look like a kidder, Suzanne?"

It was Suzanne's turn to be speechless. Recovering, she said, "Is there much call for Christmas tree decorators out East?"

Jenna thought she detected a smile along the outer edges of Faith's mouth. She tucked her straight, blond hair behind both ears and answered quietly. "It's seasonal work."

"Are you seriously looking for a job?" Suzanne asked.

Faith nodded guardedly.

And Suzanne said, "Stop by Marcel's first thing Monday morning and we'll give it a whirl."

Faith's blue eyes went round, and her mouth dropped open. Jenna imagined that her face bore a similar expression.

"Don't look so happy. It's grueling work," Suzanne said. "Besides pouring coffee and making change, I'll expect you to wash dishes and sweep the floor and fold towels."

Faith opened the door and went down to the first step. "I can wash and sweep. Oh, and I can fold anything."

"Anything?" Suzanne asked.

Faith nodded, a flicker as elusive as fireflies in her

eyes. "Part of interior design involves folding everything from napkins, to linens and window fashions, to bedding."

"Bedding?" Suzanne's voice rose an octave. "Like sheets?"

The screen door closed quietly. "Perfect hospital corners every time." Faith got the last smile, and the last word, before walking away.

It was a long time before Suzanne blinked. "Did I just hire the one person in all the world, besides Eddie, who managed to pull one over on me?"

Jenna knew a rhetorical question when she heard one. The strange thing was, she was pretty sure there had been a hint of admiration in Suzanne's voice.

"Where are you going?" Suzanne asked.

Propping the door open with one foot, Jenna smoothed a wrinkle from her pants. "I'm going to talk to Nick. I think it's high time he realizes that I'm not a woman who is satisfied with riddles."

"Please," she heard Suzanne mutter, "Don't say *satisfied.*"

It was hot in the sun, and so bright Jenna's eyes watered as she crossed her backyard. Rather than retrieve her sunglasses from the house, she stopped under the climbing tree long enough to locate the boys in the lush foliage and remind them that they had to leave for the ball field in fifteen minutes. Moving with purpose, not haste, she used the time it took her to reach Nick's door to formulate what she would say.

The windows and doors were open in the front of the carriage house. The glare of the bright morning sun made it impossible to see into the shadowy interior.

"It's open, Jenna."

The fact that Nick could see her, and she couldn't see him was disconcerting. Forcing a sense of calm she didn't necessarily feel, she opened the door and went in.

The clank and gurgle of a glass being filled with tap water gave Nick's location away. Keeping her back to him, she took her time strolling farther into the room, letting her eyes adjust to the light. An oscillating fan fluttered papers and stirred the edge of the sheet hanging to the floor. His bed was unmade, and likely still warm.

"Care for a glass of water?" His voice was a little gruff, furthering the notion that he hadn't been up long.

She finally faced him. The apartment's kitchen had a sink, about a foot of counter space, a small refrigerator, and a two-burner stove. Nick was looking at her from the narrow expanse of cabinetry that divided the alcove, his hair mussed, his jaw covered in dark stubble. His chest was bare. An imprint, probably from sleeping on a wrinkled sheet, hadn't yet faded on his side. She couldn't see the rest of him, but she remembered when he said he slept in the nude.

He guzzled the water, lowered the glass to the counter, then stepped around the cabinet. A fine line of dark hair drew the eye down his washboard stomach, disappearing beneath the low-slung waistband of a pair of sweats that had seen better days. They were torn, but not wrinkled, which caused her to assume he'd pulled them on after getting up, probably just before telling her the door was open.

He was almost civilized.

He leveled that gentling gaze of his on her. It was the softest thing about him, perhaps the only soft thing about him. She folded her arms at her chest and gave his gaze right back to him. "About last night."

As one second followed another, his expression changed in the most subtle of ways. "There's no need to apologize, Jenna."

She did a double-take. "At least we agree on one thing."

He held perfectly still, as only he could. Perhaps no one else would have guessed that he was surprised by her sarcasm. Perhaps no one else knew him the way Jenna knew him. That wasn't saying a lot, because right now she swore she didn't know him at all.

"I'll bet we agree on more than one thing," he said.

"Oh really." They were getting off the subject. "What else, pray tell, would you say we agree upon?"

"I think we both agree that you came here looking for a fight."

The fact that he was right took some of the wind from her sails. "Did it ever occur to you that I might just want answers, Nick?"

"What kind of answers?"

"Oh, I don't know. Maybe something a little more substantial than a ringing silence or a hackneyed cliché. When the evening began, we were a team out to champion an investigation regarding Nathanial Sherman's missing money. By the evening's end, you'd decided it would be best to let a sleeping dog lie."

Nick had rarely seen Jenna angry. Her eyes flashed, her color was heightened, and a vein pulsed in the side of her neck. He would have loved to press his lips to that vein, to assuage her anger and incite her passion. He was so sick of wanting something he couldn't have.

All right. She didn't appreciate his terminology. Maybe he should have come up with something better than a cliché. He didn't pretend to understand women, but he knew when one of them had something to hide, and Shaye Townsend's face had secrets written all over it. He couldn't tell Jenna. He couldn't tell her that, if they continued to search, they could very well discover who had really taken that four hundred grand. In the process, they might just discover that Craig had cheated in another way. Maybe there had been extenuating circumstances. Maybe there was some other explanation for Shaye Townsend's behavior. What if there wasn't?

Jenna loved Craig. She'd always loved Craig. As it was, she could go to sleep every night secure in the knowledge that he'd loved her, too. It wouldn't even occur to her that he might have betrayed her with another woman. Brandon and Benji believed in a father who rescued turtles and kept them safe. The current rumor couldn't hurt them any more than it already had because there was a decided lack of evidence regarding that missing money. It was enough to allow them reasonable doubt.

"What do you want me to say, Jenna?"

She walked closer, and closer, staring into his eyes, searching for God only knew what. "Why don't you tell me whatever it was you were just thinking."

He raked a hand through his hair. "Too much thinking can drive a man crazy." That was why he liked taking pictures. Photography was visual. He'd thought about that last night after he'd looked up Shaye Townsend in the phone book. An S. L. Townsend lived on Oak Street.

"Is that what you did last night?" she asked. "Thought?"

Nick rubbed his forehead. Actually, Jenna's guess was very close to the truth. He'd driven to the apartment complex on Oak Street, then sat in the parking lot, thinking about Craig, and what it all might mean. "There isn't much else to do in this town. I think I know why God created fleas."

Jenna paused two feet away. Arms folded, she stood looking at him, waiting for him continue.

"It was to give the dogs in Harmony something to do."

"Then that's what this is about?" she asked. "You're bored with everyday life? Is that why you want to discontinue this?"

A few moments ago Jenna had felt on the brink of

discovery. Now, she could tell by the way Nick shrugged that he wasn't going to tell her what had changed his mind. She turned away from him. "Have it your way, Nick. I'll be needing Craig's briefcase."

"Why?"

She spied the case next to the sofa.

"Jenna, what are you doing?"

She retrieved the briefcase. Clutching it close to her chest, she strode to the door. "I appreciate everything you've done. It was because of you that I discovered Benji needed glasses. The boys have loved spending time with you. No one would fault you for leaving. *I* won't fault you for leaving. Drop us a postcard. If you include a forwarding address, I'll let you know what I discover."

The door closed just short of a slam.

Brandon's and Benji's team was behind when the women sitting with Jenna noticed Nick sauntering toward the fence. He walked as if he were in no particular hurry, his camera held loosely by its strap in his right hand.

Suzanne fanned her face with her hand. "As if it isn't hot enough out here already."

Jenna forced her attention back to the ball game. The other team was up to bat, and their best hitter took a wild swing at the pitch.

"Uh-oh," Marla Mason said in Jenna's left ear. "Look who else has noticed Nick's here."

Delilah Prentice sashayed to the fence, too. Delilah, who had streaked hair and her father's money, wiggled her hips provocatively.

"Could she be any more obvious?" Marla whispered. "Her daughter is in my class, and is watching, for God's sakes."

"Delilah's probably in heat," Suzanne said from Jenna's other side.

"She's fawning over him," Marla said.

"Watch her hand," Suzanne whispered.

Delilah Prentice's rings glittered as her inch-long, blood-red fingernails scraped along Nick's back, the destination obvious. "Here she goes, folks," Suzanne emceed. "Lower, lower. Any second now, there's going to be definite cupping."

The batter hit the ball. While most of the fans were jumping up, Nick eased out of Delilah's reach in a motion so smooth she was hardly put off. He glanced into the bleachers, and caught Jenna looking. Flustered, she nodded at something Marla said. With no idea what she'd just agreed to, she forced her attention back to the game once again.

The ball sailed directly at the pitcher, who ducked instead of holding out his glove. It hit the ground in front of the shortstop, who misjudged the bounce. From there it took an almost comical roll between an outfielder's feet. It was Brandon who finally got hold of it, running all the way from the other side of the field. He made a good throw, but it was too late. The runner was already safe on third.

"Well," Suzanne said, hopping to the ground. "I hate to leave when the score is tied, but I have to pick up Kenzie then get back to Marcel's. Do you still want a ride back to town, Marla? Hey, Nick. Way to dodge Delilah's advance."

Jenna was aware of all the jostling as Marla squeezed past her and joined Suzanne on the ground. Of course Nick assumed the spot Suzanne had vacated. Jenna moved over, giving him plenty of room.

The next batter hit a pop-up fly. This time the pitcher not only caught it, but he made a good throw, and the runner was tagged at home plate. Jenna left the cheering to the other parents. The teams exchanged places, and Benji was up to bat. He swung and missed the first two pitches, then hit the third over the fence for an automatic home run. Jenna and Nick both jumped up to cheer. When they sat down again, their arms brushed. She looked up at him. Her sunglasses were tinted a shade of blue that enabled people to see her eyes. Nick's were as impenetrable as he was.

Jenna eased away, but not before Nick saw her chin wobble slightly. He felt like something he'd stepped in. He'd hurt her. And angered her. And disappointed her. At least he hadn't lost his touch.

The bleachers weren't crowded. Consequently, the nearest fellow spectators were six feet away. "For your information," he said, keeping his voice very, very quiet, "I have no intention of leaving Harmony any time soon."

With a cool stare straight ahead, she said, "I thought you said you were bored."

He'd never said he was bored. And he'd never said he intended to stop his investigation. He'd just planned to proceed alone. That way, if he discovered something unpleasant about Craig, he could keep it to himself. But no, she wasn't going to let him do that. "If you're hell-bent on continuing, there's no sense you doing it alone."

"Are you saying you're going to jostle that sleeping dog?"

He would have liked to jostle her.

She was still staring straight ahead, watching the game, a look of victory on her face. "We need a good reason to make an appointment with one of the partners," she said quietly.

We? How could one little word have such an effect on him? "I've been thinking about that," he said.

"You have an idea."

Keeping his voice low, he outlined his plan. When he was finished, she reached over tentatively and squeezed his hand.

A fist seemed to have lodged around his windpipe. A lot of women had tried to wrap him around their little fingers. Jenna was the only woman to succeed. And she made it look so easy.

Thunder rumbled as Jenna opened the door to Suzanne's coffee shop. Brandon and Benji rushed in ahead of her.

"Hey, Suzanne," Brandon called. "Where's Kenzie?"

Suzanne looked all around. "She's here somewhere."

It was Faith who took their order, and Faith who whispered, "I believe she's in the restroom."

In almost no time, the boys were situated in the booth of their choice and were busily polishing off an oversized muffin and a latte that actually contained no coffee at all. Thunder rumbled again. Sliding a tall glass of lemonade across the counter to Jenna, Suzanne said, "I wish it would just rain and get it over with."

Jenna agreed. The air had been dank and lifeless for two days, building to an almost unbearable heaviness that made everyone irritable. Finally, this afternoon, a slight breeze had blown in, bringing with it the promise of rain. It had been a long afternoon, a long week. On Monday, Nick had put his idea into action, making an appointment to see Oliver Sinclair, of Walker, Whitman and Sinclair. The first available appointment was for 3:45 today. He was probably there right now.

Jiggling one foot, Jenna looked all around her. The stained-glass artwork in the window appeared darker with the absence of the sun. A handful of high school girls were talking on the sofas, four women were seated at one table, a man and woman at another. The semester was over at the college, and most of the students had moved on to trips to Europe or summer jobs.

Suzanne was wiping off the counter, and Faith was gathering dishes scattered throughout the room. Jenna wondered if Nick had played the ace he had up his sleeve regarding his father's will. She couldn't remember when time had gone so slowly. "Has your accountant been here lately?" she asked conversationally.

Suzanne shot her a prickly look. "Keith isn't my accountant, all right?"

"You know his name?"

"Thanks to Pinkie."

Faith traipsed over with a tray full of dirty dishes. "I believe Suzanne's jealous," she said, unloading coffee mugs and saucers into the sink.

"If I'm jealous, it's because the man *I* picked up for a one-night-stand has the hots for you."

"Reed does not have the hots for me."

Suzanne winked at Jenna. "He hasn't stopped by Marcel's three times this week to see me."

Jenna looked from one woman to the other.

"He's a guidance counselor," Faith said. "Rachel's starting high school in the fall, and he's helping her choose her classes." She started running water in the sink.

"Then why are you blushing?" Suzanne asked.

Just then, Brandon called, "Hey, Kenzie, come on back."

Jenna, Faith and Suzanne all glanced across the room. They all gasped. "Kenzie," Suzanne said, "What happened to your hair?"

"I cut it."

Suzanne could see that. "With what, hedge clippers?" She didn't remember crossing the room. Taking Kenzie's chin in her hand, she turned her head this way and that. "Why?"

"Because."

She stared, dumbfounded, at her child. Short for her age, Kenzie wore red canvas shoes, blue jeans and a red T-shirt. With her new hairstyle, she looked even younger than she was. Suzanne had always preferred Kenzie in short hair, but not like this, as if the tresses had been frozen and broken off.

She untied her apron and tossed it to a nearby chair. "Faith? Eddie's due to arrive any minute to pick up Kenzie. Tell him we'll be back soon. Come on, Kenzie."

"Where are we going?"

"To the hair salon. I'm sure Becky can even up the edges a little. Don't worry. She'll fix it right up."

"I don't want it fixed." Kenzie's tone was belligerent, and yet she didn't meet her mother's eyes.

Suzanne was still trying to make sense of that when the door opened and a teenage girl with red hair walked in. "That woman wearing pink will take your order up at the counter," Suzanne said.

"I didn't come for coffee," The girl smiled. "Eddie sent me to pick up Kenzie."

Suzanne studied the girl more closely. She had freckles and braces, and looked about fourteen. "You have a driver's license?"

The girl nodded importantly.

Who said girls nowadays all looked older? "How long have you been driving?"

"A month."

"I'm not letting my daughter ride all the way to Savannah with anybody who's only been driving for a month."

"I don't have to go?" Kenzie asked.

"Don't you want to go?" Suzanne asked.

Kenzie looked directly into Suzanne's eyes for the first time. "Do you want me to go?"

Suzanne hesitated, baffled. Jenna had come closer, probably for moral support. Brandon and Benji ambled over, too, both sporting latte mustaches.

"Kenz," Suzanne said, "we really have to stop answering each other's questions with more questions. What I want doesn't matter. I won't let you ride with an inexperienced driver."

"What am I supposed to tell Eddie?" the redhead asked.

Suzanne and Kenzie both looked at her.

"Tell him the truth," Suzanne said. "What's your name?"

"Tina, but most people call me Teenie because . . ."

"Yeah, I get it. How do you know Eddie?"

"I work for him. I started out bussing tables. Eddie just promoted me to waitress."

That was the third time she'd spoken Eddie's name dreamily. *Jesus,* Suzanne thought, *the girl has a crush on a man old enough to be her father.* Kenzie rolled her eyes, the first normal thing she'd done all afternoon.

"Why don't you go ask Faith to fix you a latte, Tina?" Suzanne said. "On the house. But drink it here. I want both of those hands on the steering wheel when you drive back to Savannah."

Suzanne's mind raced ahead. Marcel's was open until ten on Fridays. She hadn't made arrangements for Kenzie. And what in the world was going on with her daughter? Didn't she like going to her father's?

The door opened again, and another young girl, this one Faith's daughter, Rachel, strolled in. "What's everybody doing?" she asked.

That was when it occurred to Suzanne that Faith's shift was over. Jenna said, "Kenzie can stay with the boys and me."

"I thought you were meeting Nick," Suzanne said.

Before Jenna could reply, Faith said, "Why doesn't Kenzie come home with us?"

Brandon complained. Faith saved the day again by suggesting that the boys ride with her, too. She left soon after with all the kids and a promise to keep both hands on the wheel at all times.

Watching them out the window, Suzanne said, "That Faith is a laugh a minute. *Hardy-har-har.*"

Jenna liked her new neighbor. Underneath the sarcasm, she knew Suzanne did, too.

"Did you see Kenzie's hair? Did you see it?"

"It'll grow back, Suzanne."

"Do you think she did it to prove that her father loves her no matter what she does or how she looks? Or to prove I do?"

"She knows you love her," Jenna said.

"Life would be a hell of a lot easier if kids didn't need a father."

Jenna sighed. Her children didn't have a father. All they had left of Craig was a distant memory, and the notion that he'd loved them very, very much. She wanted them to have more than that. She wanted to clear his name, so that as Brandon and Benji grew up, people wouldn't whisper behind their backs and wonder. They deserved better than that. And so did Craig.

She looked at her watch. It was nearly four o'clock. Nick was most certainly in his meeting with Oliver Sinclair by now. He'd told her he would meet her at home as soon as it was over.

Suzanne went to wait on another customer. Jenna left. The first raindrop landed on her head before she'd made it three steps. Thunder rumbled again, and the sky opened up. Finally.

She was soaked by the time she reached the van. Shivering, she stared through the deluge of water sluicing down the windshield. She didn't believe in omens. She didn't. By the time she reached 317 Beulah Street, she'd said it a dozen times.

Chapter Sixteen

"Mr. Sinclair will see you now, Nicholas."

Not many people called him Nicholas. Teachers. Principals. And Margaret Barclay.

When Nick had first arrived at the offices of Walker, Whitman and Sinclair, he'd tried charming the matronly woman who had been Maxwell Walker's executive assistant for thirty-five years. A former friend of his mother's, she'd offered him a cup of coffee and a magazine, and then politely returned to her desk. Although she'd been pleasant, it was obvious that her loyalties were with the firm. Nick's charm worked about as good on her as it did on Jenna. He wondered if he was losing his touch.

He rose from the uncomfortable antique club chair and followed Margaret into a wide hallway flanked by closed doors. The walls were lined with color portraits and black-and-white photographs of the founding fathers of Harmony. Nick was familiar with the photographs. Copies had hung in his father's study when he'd been growing up, and depicted unsmiling men with loose jowls and an air of overinflated self-importance.

Margaret Barclay opened the second to the last door.

Proper, demure and efficient right down to her buffed fingernails and sensible shoes, she announced Nick, then backed out inconspicuously.

Oliver Sinclair stood and extended his hand. The hardest thing Nick had done in a while was to accept that handshake. Sinclair's eyes narrowed slightly, as if he knew. The attorney was sixty if he was a day. He was wealthy, and looked younger than his actual years. He was well dressed. He'd never been nice. "I'm surprised to see you here, Nick."

Nick played dumb. "I have an appointment."

The man motioned for Nick to have a seat. "I meant that in a broader sense. When you failed to return following the sad set of circumstances a few years ago, I assumed you were done with Harmony for good."

The fact that Sinclair had felt the need to clarify wasn't lost on Nick. Neither was the fact that he'd said it in a blasé fashion. If voices had a color, Oliver Sinclair's was donkey-dung brown, the same color as condescension. Nick drew a deep breath. Without allowing his aversion to show on his face or in his voice, he said, "I would have come back for Craig's funeral, if I'd known."

Nick's failure to so much as mention remorse because he hadn't returned for his father's funeral hit its mark. Sinclair appeared to have a sudden bout of indigestion, proof that sometimes it was what a man didn't say that spoke the loudest. Nick kept his expression bland, but he was smiling inside.

"What can we here at Walker, Whitman and Sinclair do for you, Nick?"

A few things came to mind. Nick would have enjoyed yanking the guy's chain a little, but he wasn't here for his own enjoyment. "I understand this firm handled my father's will."

"Yes."

"I'd like to see it."

"Your father's last will and testament contains privileged information. I'm under no obligation to disclose its contents. Legally, you would need a court order in order to see it."

Outside, thunder rumbled and rain pelted the windows. Nick had to rely on his sense of hearing, for the windows in Sinclair's office were covered by plantation shutters and draperies, all part of the client confidentiality bullshit Sinclair was shoveling.

"He left the bulk of his estate to charity?"

Sinclair seemed to enjoy nodding. If the guy ever wrote a book, Nick knew what he would call it. Condescension For Dummies.

"I was surprised my father didn't leave more to Craig's widow and sons."

"Under the circumstances, do you blame him?" Sinclair leaned back in his chair and steepled his fingers under his chin. "This firm handled the legalities. Please realize they were your father's wishes."

"So I've heard."

Oliver Sinclair leveled his gaze on Nick. "Are you considering contesting the will, is that what this is all about?"

Nick stared at the other man, thinking it was amazing. He hadn't even had to plant the seed of doubt. It had been firmly in place for a long, long time. "Maybe."

"It's too late."

"Why do you say that?" Nick asked.

"You would have had to begin those proceedings during the first year, while your father's estate was in probate."

"I'm a legal heir. I didn't know he had died."

"That would be difficult for you to prove. A letter was sent. It was never returned."

Nick had no interest in the mumbo-jumbo workings of the law or in his father's money. "Are you saying the only thing left for me to do is sue?"

There remained a certain tension in Sinclair's expression as he said, "Do you really want to drag the Proffit name through more dirt?"

Nick didn't point out the fact that any dirt the Proffit name had been dragged through had been orchestrated by someone else. The question was Who?

Sinclair rose, signaling that the meeting was over.

Nick rose, too. "I've always heard a will could be contested at any time by a legal heir as long as the heir had been left out of the will completely."

Nick deserved an Oscar for this.

Sinclair opened a drawer and withdrew an official-looking document and a manila envelope. For a man who was surprised to see Nick, he was very prepared. Nick opened the envelope first. It contained his old report cards. For a moment, his stomach roiled the way it had when he'd been a kid every time it was report card time again. How fitting that it was all his father had left him.

Sinclair was watching him, so he kept all expression off his face as he replaced the old records and leafed through his father's will. It would have taken him hours to read it word for word. He wasn't interested in the terminology, and yet he stared for a long time at his father's signature.

His father was dead. He'd been a legend in his own mind, but he'd been neither the making nor the breaking of Nick Proffit. Other than contempt and some emotional scars left over from childhood, Nick felt very little. He certainly felt no loss, no love, no respect. It didn't make him happy, either. Hell, who could be happy in this place?

How had Craig stood it?

"It would be a waste of your time and money to contest this will," Sinclair said. "And with your reputation, I doubt suing would be a good idea, either."

If they gave out awards to condescending bastards, Sinclair would have had a shelf full. Nick didn't bother telling Sinclair that in every place except Harmony, his reputation was sterling. He didn't waste his breath, because he didn't care what Sinclair thought of him. He was here to find clues regarding the scandal. "I see."

"At least you're able to see reason."

Sinclair might have been surprised by what Nick could see about the man behind the desk. Oliver Sinclair wasn't a self-made man. He wasn't even a decent one. Telling him might make Nick feel better, but it wouldn't serve the greater purpose, and that was to clear Craig's name.

He tossed the document to the desk. "I'll be in touch."

Clutching the manila envelope, he turned on his heel and left, passing the closed doors and somber portraits. Not a decent landscape or animal print in the bunch. Again, Nick wondered how Craig had stood it.

Although he hadn't planned to, he stopped suddenly when he reached the outer office. Watching him intently, Margaret Barclay said, "Was there something else?"

"Which office was Craig's?"

Her expression softened. "The second door on the right."

"Whose office is it now?"

"Mr. Walker didn't have the heart to assign it to anyone else. The partners and clerks use it for research and storage. Would you like to see it?"

Nick appreciated the offer but shook his head. He'd had his fill of this place. He tossed the manila envelope into the waste basket, then continued toward the exit, lost in thought. Prepared to make a run for his Land Rover, he threw open the door. And nearly ran headlong into a woman with auburn hair and wire-rimmed glasses.

"Oh!" she exclaimed as her umbrella popped out of her hand and clattered to the sidewalk. She bent down to retrieve it.

Nick beat her to it. "I'm sorry."

She smiled at him as he handed it back to her.

"You're getting soaked," she said.

He held out his hand. "I won't melt. I'm Nick Proffit. I've seen you before."

She fit her hand in his. "I'm Shaye Townsend."

He knew that, of course, but she didn't know he knew. She was petite, her auburn hair thick and soft-looking where it fell across her cheek. Rain poured off her umbrella and splattered on the sidewalk. Young and pretty, she wore a short jacket and skirt the color of ripe plums, the fabric woven with a tiny thread that sparkled even in the rain. Her eyes sparkled, too.

"We didn't have weather like this in Madison."

Her voice contained a certain lilt Nick liked. "Do you work here?" He motioned to the office building at his back.

"I'm a clerk part of the time, a law student at heart."

She had changeable, hazel eyes, gray one minute, gray-blue the next. She laughed, and Nick imagined that she must brighten all that mahogany paneling and gray carpet. Had she made that colorless, lifeless office endurable for Craig?

He hated what he was thinking.

"I have to get to work," she said. "And you're still getting soaked. It was nice meeting you. I mean that."

Did he detect something else in her voice? And if so, what?

She eased around him, and entered the brick building that housed the offices of Walker, Whitman and Sinclair, Attorneys at Law. Nick finally came out of his stupor.

Things had been strained between him and Jenna all week, because somehow she knew he was keeping something from her. He couldn't very well tell her this.

One thing was certain. The visit to the firm hadn't been for nothing after all. He wouldn't get anything out of Sinclair. At least now he knew who he needed to talk to next.

"Jenna's mad at Nick."

Kenzie and Rachel were propped on pillows on the

matching beds in Rachel's room. Kenzie hadn't heard any yelling. In fact, Nick and Jenna had been playing a card game with Brandon and Benji when she and Rachel had come upstairs to the Silverses' apartment.

Kenzie looked up from the lame movie Rachel's mother had rented, and studied Rachel Silvers. She wore jeans with something embroidered on the bottoms and a ycllow T-shirt with something embroidered on the sleeves. "How can you tell Jenna's mad?" she asked.

"I sensed it." Rachel tossed her silky blond hair behind her shoulder then stretched out on the other twin bed in a room that was way too frilly, if you asked Kenzie.

She raked her fingers through her own chopped-off hair. What had she done? The kids at school were going to tease her for sure. Why couldn't she have shimmery yellow hair like Rachel?

"It'll grow back."

Holy shit, Kenzie thought. Rachel really did sense things. "Who says I want it to?" She pretended to watch the movie. Now that she thought about it, she was glad her hair wasn't long and pretty like Rachel's. That would make things even worse.

Kenzie could hear Faith moving around out in the living room. Her mom called Faith Pinkie. Although she preferred her own mom and her own apartment, Faith was pretty nice and the apartment was comfortable even if it was a girlie-girl's place. "Does your mom like pink, or what?"

Even the sound Rachel made in the back of her throat sounded cultured and grownup and sort of feminine. Kenzie cringed. She'd seen Rachel at school. Nobody teased her about anything, not even for wearing pink. In fact, everybody liked her, and not just the boys, either.

Kenzie tugged at a chunk of hair sticking straight out.

"Why didn't you let your mom take you to the beauty shop to get it fixed?"

"I dunno." Kenzie was getting sleepy. She always tried to stay up late on Fridays, but she hadn't slept much last night. She never slept well when she knew she had to go to her dad's.

"Why'd you cut it, anyway?"

"It's a secret."

Rachel fluffed a pillow and lay down, facing Kenzie. "Know why my mom wears pink all the time?"

"Why?"

"Because when my dad was alive, he made us wear gray."

"How could he make you wear gray?"

"Well, not just gray. Gray and black and brown. He was sick."

"Like he had cancer?"

Rachel shook her head. "You promise not to tell anybody?"

Feeling very important, Kenzie whispered, "I promise."

"He kept dead flowers and swore that anything that wasn't brown or gray or black was evil. Everything in our house was ugly and depressing and gray or black or brown."

Kenzie yawned, thinking about that. "Was he crazy or what?"

Rachel stared at the television. "He was sick. In the head. That's what he died of."

After a while, Kenzie said, "I thought he died in a car accident."

"He committed suicide. He just used the car to do it. After that, my mom threw away everything that was black or brown or gray and bought everything brand-new. Guess she kind of got carried away."

Wow. That was some secret. Poor Rachel. Kenzie snuggled deeper into the pillows on the other twin bed with its matching pink and yellow comforter.

"Your turn. So why did you cut your hair?" Rachel asked.

Kenzie sighed. "You swear you won't tell and hope to die?"

Rachel crossed her heart.

"I did it so he wouldn't touch it." She was proud of herself, now that she thought about it. Cutting her hair had been pretty smart.

"Who? Some boy at school?" Rachel asked.

"No."

"An older boy on the bus?"

The bed and the pillows were the softest Kenzie had ever felt. They curled up around her. It felt almost like floating. She was so comfortable, and she was so tired. "No," she said, her voice almost a whisper.

The noises on the television seemed to be coming from far away. So did Rachel's voice as she said, "Where, then? At Marcel's?"

Kenzie could still hear Rachel, but her eyes were so heavy she couldn't open them. "In the shower."

"What shower?"

"At my . . . dad's."

Rachel didn't move for a long time. Her heart beat so hard it hurt. She stared at Kenzie. Rachel's father had been in and out of the hospital the last couple of years. He'd cried a lot. But he'd never . . .

Her throat felt funny. Bad. Her stomach, too. She sat up. "Kenzie?" she whispered.

The dark-haired girl didn't move. Rachel studied her for a few minutes to see if she was faking it. Her hair was sticking up, but her eyes didn't twitch. The only thing moving was the rise and fall of her chest. She was kind of a strange kid. Rachel's friends at her old private school back East would have called her trailer trash. Now that Rachel lived here, she realized how mean some of her friends had been. Kenzie wasn't trashy. She was smart, and kind of funny a lot of the time. What she'd just told Rachel wasn't funny.

Rachel swung her feet over the side of the bed and sat up. She glanced at the movie, and then back at Kenzie. She didn't know what to do.

She took a deep breath, and smelled acrylic paints. Her mom often painted this time of night. Tucking her hair behind her ears, she padded barefoot to the door. Kenzie didn't so much as stir.

Out in the living room, her mom looked up, and smiled at her. "Is the movie over?"

Rachel shook her head.

"Where's Kenzie?"

"She fell asleep."

Her mom went back to the vase of flowers she was painting. "At nine o'clock? She must have been tired."

"I guess." Watching the fluid movements of her mother's slender hand, Rachel thought about how mad she'd been at her mom for making her leave her old school and her friends and move down here. So what if their old house had seemed morbid after her dad died? They could have fixed it up or sold it and moved someplace in the same neighborhood. But no, her mom had wanted a change of scenery. She'd insisted they would be all right as long as they were together. Now, Rachel knew her mom had been right.

That sick feeling was still in the pit of her stomach. "Mom?"

"Yes, honey?"

Her silence drew her mother's attention. Rachel found that she couldn't hold her mom's gaze.

"What is it?" her mom asked in that quiet way she had.

Hiding behind a curtain of hair, Rachel stared at her toes. "Is it ever okay to tell someone's secret, even if you swore not to and hoped to die?"

Her mom put the paintbrush down and turned in her chair. Rachel was thirteen. For about a heartbeat, she wished she was little again so she could fit on her mom's lap. Everybody said she looked like her mom, but Rachel knew she looked like her dad, too. Her mom said that was a good thing. Her mom was usually right. Although lately that had started to annoy Rachel, right now she was glad about that.

Her mother looked up at her, her eyes brimming with care and concern. "Sometimes," she said, *"not* telling can hurt someone more than telling. Do you know a secret like that?"

Rachel swallowed. And nodded.

"Why don't you tell me what this is about, and together we'll decide if this is one of those times."

Her mom scooted over and pulled Rachel onto the chair next to her. It was the next best thing to being little again.

In a small voice, Rachel whispered what Kenzie had told her.

Suzanne took her shoes off at the bottom of the stairs. It had been a long day, and her feet were killing her. Since Twyla Mae was probably already asleep, she avoided the noisiest creaks in the steps, and trudged quietly to Faith's door.

Faith opened it before Suzanne could knock.

"Hey," Suzanne said. "It quit raining. Is Kenzie still up?" Something about the way Faith shook her head made the hair on the back of Suzanne's neck stand up. "Is she all right?"

"She's sleeping. Let's talk at your place."

Okay. Suzanne was sweating now. She traipsed to her door, only to stop suddenly. "If you played another practical joke, I swear I'll . . ."

"No jokes."

Suzanne felt herself going pale. She unlocked her door with shaking fingers. Faith followed her into the apartment and closed the door. Leaning against it, she didn't make Suzanne wait a second longer before repeating what Kenzie had told Rachel and Rachel had told her.

At first Suzanne could only shake her head. Then she asked a few questions. It wasn't easy to talk at all. Something was wrong with her throat. "My little girl," she whispered.

Faith laid a hand on Suzanne's arm. "Kenzie is sleeping peacefully right now. She's safe. The important thing is that you know. Now you can help her."

Suzanne rubbed her eyes with the heels of her hands, and then she rubbed her ears, because it sounded like a freight train was rumbling through her living room. *Oh, Kenzie. What am I going to do?*

She cut around Faith and ran to the apartment across the hall. She had to see her little girl. Rachel looked up from that mauve sofa in the living room. Suzanne didn't slow down until she had Kenzie in her sights. She sank to the edge of the bed where her daughter was sleeping. A lamp was on in the corner. The television was on, too. With a gentle hand, Suzanne touched Kenzie's shoulder. "Kenz?" she whispered.

Kenzie didn't stir. Suzanne tried again, a little louder. A movement in the doorway drew her gaze. Faith and Rachel stood together, two peas in a pod. And Suzanne said, "Unless she has a nightmare, I can never rouse this kid once she's asleep."

Suzanne's hand went to her mouth. Oh, God, the nightmares. She tried to remember when they'd started. It hadn't been long after Eddie started showing an interest in Kenzie again.

Clutching her stomach, Suzanne made a mad dash for the bathroom. She made it just before her stomach turned itself inside out. With a groan, she flushed the toilet and tried to get her bearings. Faith handed her a warm washcloth, and then a glass of cool water.

When she was able to speak again, Suzanne asked Rachel to repeat everything Kenzie had said, word-for-word. Hearing it from Rachel was even worse. Suzanne wished it was a lie. She would give up Marcel's if it could be a lie. But Rachel wasn't lying. Kenzie didn't lie, either. Oh, she got belligerent and stubborn and refused to answer sometimes, but she didn't lie.

Suzanne placed the glass on the counter. She couldn't stand still. She had to do something. "Can Kenzie sleep here for a while?"

"Of course. Where are you going?"

Filled with a sudden and irrepressible energy, she brushed past Faith and her daughter. Faith called to her when she reached the stairs. "Suzanne, what are you going to do?"

Suzanne hopped, first on one foot and then on the other, putting on her shoes. And then she dashed down the stairs. "I'm going to kill that no good son of a bitch."

Chapter Seventeen

Jenna dropped Benji's and Brandon's soggy shoes on the braided rug by the back door. Their backpacks hung on their designated pegs. Already, Benji's papers and worksheets boasted stickers and stars instead of check marks and "See me" notations. Soon, school would be out for the summer. Brandon and Benji were planning their adventures.

The boys were finally asleep. They'd fought it right up until the moment their eyes finally closed. They'd been rambunctious all evening. Not even splashing in puddles and climbing trees had held their attention for long.

Nick had been as antsy as Brandon and Benji, but he'd been quieter about it. He'd been this way all week. Earlier, she'd tried to blame it on the approaching storm. The rain had passed. Nick's stony silences hadn't. Judging from what he'd told her, his unease hadn't resulted from his meeting with Sinclair. What, then? What wasn't he telling her?

She brushed the unruly strands of hair off her forehead and tried to tuck them into the clip holding the rest of her hair off her neck. There was plenty to do, papers to check, bills to pay. She couldn't even think coherently tonight. That was how tied up Nick had her.

She straightened the kitchen, wondering what she'd expected. Nick Proffit had never been an open book. Until lately, that hadn't bothered her. She really didn't want to think about the reason it bothered her now.

She returned to the living room where Nick was going through Craig's day planner again. His chin was down, his neck and arms tan above his white T-shirt. He'd gotten his strength back this past month. Now she understood why he'd been pale, just as she understood why he concentrated so hard when he read. There were still plenty of things she didn't understand about him. Perhaps she never would.

Now why on earth should that make her sad? She took a deep breath. "What are you looking for?"

He sat at Craig's old desk, and answered without looking up. "A clue."

She'd looked over that day planner several times. All Craig's appointments checked out. If Craig had suspected that something was going on at the firm, it wasn't apparent in his planner. "What kind of clue?"

"I don't know. Maybe to his frame of mind."

"Why don't you ask me about his frame of mind?"

He met her gaze. "All right. Can you think of anything he might have said? Was he acting strange?"

"Strange, how?"

"Was he more quiet? Did he seem worried? Preoccupied?"

"With work, you mean?"

"With anything!" He jumped up and paced to the wall and back.

He reminded Jenna of a caged tiger. She didn't believe it was Harmony that was causing his agitation. Since trying to understand Nick was getting her nowhere, she considered the question. "Craig wasn't preoccupied. I've wracked my brain about this, too. I've gone over and over and over what he said and who he mentioned in the months, weeks, even the evening before that fateful day."

"And?"

"He told me he'd seen Nathaniel Sherman. And he'd spoken with Maxwell Walker. Craig had a great deal of respect for Max. There was the usual office politics, of course, but he got along fine with Stuart Whitman, too. Craig didn't like Oliver Sinclair anymore than you do. He was handling the usual divorce cases and wills. He mentioned representing a man who'd been charged with drunk driving. Nothing out of the ordinary."

"Are you saying he seemed bored?"

She looked at Nick, perplexed. "You knew Craig. He was interested in everything. If he could have done ten things at once, he would have, but he never seemed to get bored. The night before he collapsed, the four of us went out for supper. Benji ordered corn on the cob, and we all laughed until our stomachs hurt because he'd lost all his front teeth and couldn't eat it. Craig showed Benji how to cut it off the cob."

Smiling at the memory, she turned slowly. Nick was still holding Craig's day planner. He wasn't smiling. "What about this entry in the margin? Chattanooga."

"What about it?"

Nick's eyes narrowed slightly. "Had he taken a trip recently?"

She shook her head.

"Maybe he was planning one."

"We were saving for a family trip to England. He never mentioned Chattanooga."

"Maybe he wanted a weekend away, just the two of you. Maybe he wanted to—"

The way his voice trailed away prompted her to prod a little. "Maybe he wanted to what, Nick?"

He raked a hand through his hair. "Why do couples plan getaway weekends? To rekindle, or maybe to jump-start . . ."

"Are you referring to our sex life?"

If she hadn't been looking closely, she would have missed his nod.

"That didn't need jump-starting."

"Then he was—the two of you were—"

Jenna tried making light of this. "And Suzanne says I have a hard time talking about sex."

He didn't even crack a smile.

"Craig and I were fine in that department, Nick. Your brother had a strong sex drive. From what I've heard, it was a Proffit trait. Now why don't you'all tell me what this is all about."

Nick couldn't remember how many nights he'd tried conjuring up the soft, southern lilt in Jenna's voice. His memories hadn't done it justice. He loved the way she said *suppah* for supper, *you'all,* when it was only the two of them in the room. She'd probably tried to be patient with him this week, but even she was losing her patience with his secrecy. He couldn't tell her that there was a remote chance that Craig might have had a fling with the young clerk in the law office. The very idea would hurt her. It didn't matter that everyone from presidents to priests had been tempted in similar situations. Maybe Craig had been above that sort of thing. What if he hadn't been?

What if, what if, what if?

If Craig had never mentioned going to Chattanooga to Jenna, why had he penciled it in in the margin of his day planner? Somebody had to know something, just as somebody had to know how that money had ended up in Craig and Jenna's bank account. That was another thing that didn't make sense. Why had this person only used the money to ruin Craig's good name? Why not go for the jugular?

Perhaps there had been no affair.

Then what the hell was Shaye Townsend hiding?

"Nick?"

Nick finally looked at Jenna. Gravity and humidity had had its way with her hair. She looked tired, at her wit's end. There was nothing overtly sexy about her sandals, baggy beige shorts or lavender T-shirt. And yet Nick's blood thickened, which proved she was right about that Proffit trait.

Just how strong a sex drive had Craig had? Strong enough to cause him to stray? Even when he had Jenna waiting for him at home?

He'd said it before. It didn't make sense. None of this made sense.

"What is it?" she whispered. "What's wrong?"

She held perfectly still. She was waiting for him to say something. Not telling her was giving him ulcers. Telling her would be worse.

She stared at him. Finally, she said, "You're not going to tell me, are you?"

She would never know what it cost him to say, "Tell you what?"

She turned her back on him just as a commotion arose out in the foyer. Footsteps thundered down the stairs. And somebody yelled, "Let go of me, damn it!"

That sounded like Suzanne. Nick raced to the door and threw it open, Jenna right behind him.

"I mean it!"

It was Suzanne. She was straining toward the door. Faith was doing everything in her power to drag her back.

"Faith, let go of me." Suzanne turned beseeching eyes to Nick and Jenna. "Get her away from me!"

Faith yelled, "Don't let her leave."

"Why?" Jenna asked.

"Because she says she's going to kill him!"

Just then, Twyla Mae's door opened. Suzanne stopped flailing and looked at her neighbor.

"Kill who?" Twyla Mae asked, blinking owlishly, her long, thin gray braid hanging over her shoulder. When Suzanne didn't reply, the old lady turned to Faith and asked again.

Now that Suzanne was no longer trying to make a

run for it, Faith relaxed her hold and said, "She says she's going to kill her ex-husband."

"Why?" Twyla Mae asked.

Suzanne peered at each of her neighbors. She'd always considered herself a reasonable woman. She tried to speak but couldn't. She felt sick and light-headed. Her skin was crawling. It felt too tight, as if she needed to climb out of it.

"Do you want me to tell them?" Faith asked quietly.

Suzanne nodded.

The moment Faith turned to the others, Suzanne made a run for it. She didn't bother closing the door. She didn't watch where she stepped. The fact that water splashed around her barely registered.

She was almost to her car when Nick caught up with her. Faith must have given him the short version. Suzanne's stomach roiled again. This time, she didn't give into it.

With a hand firmly at her elbow, Nick steered her toward his Land Rover.

"What are you doing?" Suzanne asked.

"Nick's going to drive you," Jenna said.

They'd all followed her outside. Even Twyla Mae. Jenna said, "And Twyla Mae, Faith, Rachel and I will take care of Kenzie while you're gone."

Tears burned the backs of Suzanne's eyes. She didn't give in to them, either.

Nick opened the passenger door.

Suzanne said, "You don't have to do this, Nick. I'm not really going to kill Eddie. That would be too good for him."

"I agree," he said. "If you try to drive, you'll kill yourself. Get in."

Faith gasped.

Suzanne didn't understand why Faith would gasp, but she did as Nick said, and got in.

* * *

Nick and Suzanne didn't say anything for a long time. The radio was on. Suzanne heard noise in the background, nothing more. Strangely, her mind was blank.

She started to come out of her stupor as Nick merged onto Highway 280. Staring at the approaching headlights, she said, "I meant what I said earlier. I'm not really going to kill Eddie."

He waited until he was up to speed to ask, "What are you going to do?"

"I'm going to castrate him with a dull knife. And don't you dare cringe! I know how you men operate. When it comes to your Johnsons, you all empathize."

"Tell you what. I'll hold him while you get the knife. Do you want the heater on?"

It hurt to smile. It hurt to breathe. It hurt to think. He must have noticed her shiver. She'd seen him shudder, too. Since he was willing to turn on the heat even though it was eighty degrees outside, she decided to forgive him for being a man.

Eddie wasn't going to get off nearly that easily.

Nick didn't let her out at the curb in front of Eddie's sports bar and restaurant, and since the doors wouldn't unlock until he put the car in park, and she couldn't find the stinking lock release, Suzanne had to wait to storm into the place. By the time she finally opened the stinking door, she was ready to scream. She held on to her temper, saving it all for that son of a bitch she'd once married.

She'd lived in Savannah for five years. There were places in the city where the scent of the ocean carried on the slightest breeze. Here, the earth smelled damp and wormy. It was fitting.

She knew where the back entrance was. She marched through the front door. Nick followed, there for moral support, and more if she needed it.

A tired-looking hostess appeared. "May I help you?"

Suzanne gave the room a sweeping glance. It smelled

like beer, smoke and hamburgers. Class with a capital *C*. It was late. Only a handful of stragglers were still dining. A handful more sat at the bar. Televisions droned from strategic locations. Several people, men mostly, looked across the room from an area that housed three pool tables. Suzanne homed in on the man whose attention was trained on the shot he was trying to make.

She strode closer, and in a voice loud enough to penetrate steel, said, "Can anybody spell pervert?"

A murmur went through the restaurant. And Eddie missed his shot. "Suzanne, what the hell?"

"What about incest?"

He handed his cue stick to somebody.

"Can you spell that, Eddie?"

Eyes narrowed, he started toward her. Edward Nash was over six feet tall. He had a membership at the gym, and the physique to prove it. Looking at him turned Suzanne's stomach.

"I'm talking about our daughter. Or are there others?"

"What are you smoking, Suzanne?" He had the nerve to chuckle to his friends.

"Oh, that's a good one. You think that up all by yourself?" She could hear the hysteria in her own voice. Rather than risk going off the deep end and behaving like a raving lunatic, she reigned in her fury and said, "Do you know what happens to pedophiles in prison, Eddie?"

"You don't know what you're talking about!"

"I'm talking about your filthy secret."

"I'm warning you." He propelled her toward a private room.

Nick was there suddenly, his foot blocking the slam of the door. "I'd leave this open if I were you. For your own protection." The derision in Nick's voice made it clear he didn't believe Eddie deserved protection.

Suzanne nodded at Nick. Straightening her dress, she drew herself up to her full height. "Now," she said, her voice menacing, "get your hands off me. And don't ever touch me again."

Eddie held up both hands. "You think I . . ."

"All those pretty muscles of yours?" she said, looking around the room that had been used for a party earlier. Finally, she looked up at him again. "You're going to be popular in prison."

For the first time she saw real fear in his eyes. "I'm not a pervert, for Christ's sake."

"You're going to have to tell that to the judge." She started to leave.

"Wait. Suzanne. Would you just wait a goddamn minute? It wasn't me."

Suzanne stopped in the doorway. She turned slowly.

"I didn't." Eddie looked worried. "I wouldn't." He sounded sincere. "A kid? My own kid?"

"Oh, yeah, you're real father-of-the-year material."

He held up both hands again. "All right. Maybe I'm not the greatest father, but I didn't do what you think I did. I've fallen on some hard times financially. And I had to take on a business partner. He was a decent enough guy. I thought. Anyway, he took an interest in Kenzie. No big deal, right? He came over to the house one Sunday. The three of us hung out. I went out for takeout. While I was gone, he tried to talk Kenzie into taking a shower."

Suzanne's hand flew to her mouth, but it couldn't muffle her whimper. Now that she thought about it, Rachel hadn't said Kenzie had told her it had been her father who had touched her. She'd said it had happened at her father's. Maybe Eddie was telling the truth. It was hard to say because with Eddie, the truth wasn't an everyday occurrence.

"It wasn't as bad as what you're thinking. She managed to lock herself in the bathroom. Alone. She screamed so loud the neighbors came over. Is she your kid or what?"

Suzanne tried to think. It wasn't easy. She wanted to

believe Eddie. How many times had she fallen for his lies? She shook her head. "She wouldn't be having nightmares for nothing. And she chopped off her hair."

"Really?" Eddie's surprise seemed real. "He touched her hair. I swear that was all he touched. I would have killed him myself otherwise. I handled it, all right?" Eddie kneaded a muscle at the back of his neck, the action sending a ripple effect across his shoulders and chest. "It won't happen again. Jesus, this is why I told Kenzie not to tell you. I knew you'd overreact."

"I want the man's name."

He shook his head.

"His name, Eddie."

"I said I handled it."

"Do you still do business with him?" she asked.

"Not at the house, at least not when Kenzie's over, if that's what you mean."

He called that handling it? Her poor baby! Suzanne literally shook. That was how badly she wanted to take a swing at him. "If there's so much as a hint of a lie in any of this, I'll go to the police. Whether I go to the police or not, and I'm not saying I'm not, I'm getting an attorney. You can kiss your visitation rights good-bye. You don't have a daughter anymore. No matter how inconvenient it would have been for you and your little business venture, you should have told me. I can't believe Kenzie didn't come to me, no matter what you said." She paused suddenly and looked at him. "What did you do to convince her not to tell me?"

Eddie's eyes glittered with anger. "I told her that you and I might get back together, and that would never happen if you knew."

A second later, Suzanne was cradling her hand and Eddie was cradling his chin. He took a step toward her, fist raised.

Nick appeared in the doorway suddenly. "I wouldn't if I were you," Nick said.

Eddie backed down.

Taking a shuddering breath, Suzanne cast a long look at her ex-husband. He made her sick. She couldn't believe she'd ever thought she'd loved him.

Nick stood near the door, poised and ready. It reminded her of what he'd told her he would help her do. "Forget it, Nick. He isn't worth it. He never was. I'm ready to go home."

Nick waited for her. When she reached him, he looped his arm around her shoulders. Outside, he said, "That was some right hook. You'd better have somebody take a look at your hand."

"Tomorrow." Tonight, she needed to go home to her daughter.

Nick didn't say much during the drive back to Harmony. He wouldn't have gotten a word in edgewise even if he'd wanted to. He was perfectly content to let Suzanne ramble. She talked about counselors and attorneys and how blind she'd been. Mostly, she talked about her child, regaling him with stories of Kenzie's antics through the years. Nick was glad she didn't seem to expect him to participate in the conversation, because he wasn't good at it. This was why women turned to their friends in times like these.

The women at 317 Beulah Street descended upon Suzanne the moment she set foot in the door. She wanted to be near Kenzie, so they all moved en masse up to Faith's apartment.

Jenna didn't blame Suzanne for checking on Kenzie every five minutes. Brandon and Benji were asleep downstairs. Jenna checked on them periodically, too. In between, she and Faith fluffed pillows for Suzanne's back and brought her slippers and fed her crackers and sweetened tea. Rachel had fallen asleep, too. Leaving the door open a crack, they'd talked in low murmurs in

Faith's living room. Twyla Mae and Faith wanted to know everything Suzanne had said and done. Suzanne seemed to need to talk about it.

Nick fidgeted.

Jenna wasn't the only one who noticed. Sipping the last of her sweet tea, Suzanne made a face and said, "You don't have to stick around for me, Nick."

It was with a look of relief that he smiled all around, if a person could call the slight lift of one corner of his mouth a smile. His gaze lingered on Jenna a few seconds longer than it did on the others, his eyes like moonbeams on a darkened river. For some reason, she felt sad when he looked away. He was withdrawing again.

Suzanne said, "I know you don't think you need to hear it, but thank you. For everything."

He nodded. Swallowed. "Any time."

Everyone else called good-bye when he left. Jenna didn't utter a sound. She found herself standing at the window. It was nearing the bewitching hour, and most of Harmony was asleep. She sighed for no particular reason. Honestly, she didn't know what was wrong with her.

Behind her, Faith, Suzanne and Twyla Mae were still talking. Jenna listened with one ear. She supposed the situation would have warranted male bashing, only Suzanne wasn't bashing all men. None of them were.

"In a way," Faith said, "it would be a lot easier if all men were creeps."

"Yeah," Suzanne agreed. "In fact, if Nick wasn't already in love with Jenna, I'd snap him up for myself."

Jenna spun around so fast she nearly upset a vase of Twyla Mae's roses. "What makes you think Nick is in love with me?"

Suzanne said something smart-alecky.

Twyla Mae made a *tut-tut* sound on the roof of her mouth. Fingering a button on her faded flowered bathrobe, circa 1960, she said, "Why, it's as plain as the nose on his face, dear."

The other two women nodded.

Jenna had to force her mouth closed. When she could speak again, she said, "I know there's a certain attraction. And I know he likes me, and cares about me, and about Brandon and Benji, but . . ."

"What do you think love is?" Faith asked.

Jenna turned back to the window. A man was walking through the shadows down below. It was too dark to see him clearly, but she would recognize Nick's long stride and easy gait anyplace. Was he in love with her? She thought back to that one kiss all those years ago, and the others they'd shared more recently.

Kissing either moved a relationship forward or ended it. Nick's kisses had done neither. In fact, they were followed by brooding silences.

Her hands flew to her cheeks. "How could I not have seen this?"

"Why didn't I see Kenzie's problem?" Suzanne asked.

And Faith said, "Sometimes it's difficult to see what's right in front of our eyes."

Nick disappeared around the corner down the street. And Jenna wondered what else she hadn't seen that was right in front of her eyes.

Nick hadn't had a clear destination in mind when he'd left that frilly upstairs apartment. All he knew was that he had to keep moving.

He headed east, alone.

He'd faced the world alone most of his life, at the mercy of fate and the powers that be. His childhood had hurt him, but Nick had survived. He'd survived that fever in Central America, too, and everything in between. Somehow, he would endure the long night ahead of him.

He wasn't even winded when he reached Center Avenue. He would have to remember to tell his trainers. Brandon and Benji would love taking all the credit. The thought almost made him smile.

The clock above the old water tower struck midnight just as Nick passed beneath it. He cut across the street, drawn to the far-off clink of piano music coming from Dixie's.

The interior was dim. The piano bar wasn't crowded. Still, there were enough people and enough noise to give a deep significance to the way his eyes went immediately to Shaye Townsend. The fact that she was here, and was looking at him, too, might have even been fate.

She excused herself from her friends. As if this encounter were inevitable, she walked to the bar where Nick had taken a seat. She wore heels, the requisite tight black pants, bar pants, Nick called them, and a stretchy gray top that bared an inch of her midriff when she moved just right.

She eased onto the stool next to him. Suddenly, she didn't seem to know what to say.

She wet her lips. Swallowing, she swirled the drink she'd brought with her. Nick leaned a little closer. Keeping his voice quiet, so only she could hear, he said, "So, you were in love with my brother."

Chapter Eighteen

The drink Shaye Townsend had been holding an inch off the counter slipped out of her hand. The amber-colored liquid sloshed to the rim but didn't spill. A lot of women probably would have come up with a quick rejoinder to Nick's little bombshell. Shaye's mouth dropped open and her face flamed. Nick couldn't help wondering what kind of attorney she would make.

"How?" she whispered.

"How what?" he asked.

"H-how d-did you know?"

Nick gritted his teeth, irritated and annoyed and, damn it all, disappointed. Dixie was singing and her husband was harmonizing from the baby grand in the alcove at the front of the room. They weren't going to win any awards, but at least it covered the quiet. The bartender placed a soft drink in front of Nick. Nick left the can where it was. He saw no reason to tell Shaye that he made his living by reading creatures' expressions. She must have been adept at reading expressions, too, because she stopped stammering. Regaining her composure, she studied him. And he thought that perhaps she would make a decent attorney after all. Not that he cared.

"It wasn't what you're thinking," she said.

"What was it then?" He sounded snide. Being non-judgmental had never been his strong suit.

Her eyes were nearly the same pewter gray as the frames of her glasses. They weren't shooting daggers, nor were they brimming with warmth and friendliness. Nick would have been willing to bet she was trying to decide whether he deserved an answer.

"Look," he said. "Jenna doesn't know, and I would just as soon keep it that way."

"That's just it." She stared up at him. "There's nothing for her to know."

"What are you talking about?"

"It was completely one-sided."

"Are you telling me Craig didn't know?" Yeah, right.

She glanced at her hands. "He figured it out about as quickly as you did. He tried to let me down gently. He said I was young, and what I felt was infatuation." Her ironic tone didn't conceal her disappointment.

"Then the two of you never . . ."

She could have taken the Fifth. Instead, she sighed. "He never looked at me with anything other than friendliness. Of course, that made me love him more. No matter what he said, it was more than infatuation. I *did* love him, but it was unrequited love. You probably have no idea what that's like."

Nick's sudden bark of laughter contained no humor.

"I was devastated when he died," she said, waving away the smoke heading her way from an ashtray at the end of the bar. "The first time I saw you in Harmony, I thought I was seeing a ghost."

Other people had told Nick the same thing. Perhaps Jenna was the only person who'd ever looked closely enough to know the difference.

Shaye's hand shook slightly as she raised her drink to her lips. Lowering the glass to the counter again, she said, "I've only recently started dating again. Not that

Craig and I ever dated. We never even had a cup of coffee alone together. He only had eyes for one woman."

That was his brother, all right.

Nick wasn't prone to smiling, and yet he felt the
strangest urge to grin. "The legend of St. Craig lives
on. Unless you count the major consensus among the
fine citizens of Harmony who believe he stole four
hundred thousand dollars from right beneath the partners' noses."

"You don't believe he took that money, either, do
you?" she asked.

She smiled at him, and he realized just what Craig
had passed up. Nick was proud of Craig. He was proud
of Shaye. And when he shook his head and meant it, he
was proud of himself.

Someone who'd had too much to drink jostled Nick.
After the other man tottered away, Shaye placed her
hand on Nick's arm to steady herself as she slid off the
bar stool. Her fingers were cool where they'd touched
her glass, but the tone of her voice was warm as she
said, "I'm glad we had this little talk."

"Me, too."

As she sashayed back to her date, Nick turned his attention forward, and then inward. Something he'd said
bothered the back of his mind. He'd insinuated that
somebody had stolen that money right under the partners' noses. It was the partners who had accused Craig.
Oh, someone had transferred that money out of the
Sherman account, all right, but it hadn't been Craig.

Nick popped the top and took a long swig of soda
straight from the can. It didn't quench his thirst like
water or warm his stomach like whiskey. But it was wet
and it didn't muddy up his thoughts. He needed to
think clearly, for this wasn't a question of whether or
not one of the partners had done it. The question was
Which one of them had done it?

That was what Nick was going to find out.

* * *

"Do you think Uncle Nick will be home before supper?" Benji asked from the backseat of the van. "Where'd he go again?" he asked before Jenna could answer the first question.

"He went to Macon to see a friend." She didn't tell the boys that the friend he'd gone to see was a former policeman turned private investigator he'd met on his travels, or that Nick and the PI were going to do some digging into the backgrounds of Walker, Whitman and Sinclair. She hoped Craig's good name would be restored before summer's end.

"Uncle Nick has friends everywhere." The hero worship in Brandon's voice came through loud and clear.

"But he doesn't have a house," Benji quipped. "Or kids. Or a dog."

Jenna smiled to herself, because lately the boys had been relentless in their quest to convince her they needed a puppy.

"That's how it works," Brandon said matter-of-fact. "You either live in a gazillion places and get a ton of friends or you stay in one place and get a house and kids and maybe even a dog. Can we get a puppy after Uncle Nick leaves?"

She drew to a stop at an intersection, jarred by the thought of Nick leaving. "Did he say he was leaving soon, Brandon?"

"I guess not."

Jenna's relief was cause for concern. She reminded herself that he hadn't said he would stay, either, and she couldn't expect him to. But he was here for now.

School would let out for the summer in a little more than a week. Her kindergartners had grown so much since the beginning of the school year. They would spend the remaining days finishing workbooks and taking field trips and compiling a booklet of some of the funniest things they'd said and the progress they'd made since September. Filled with airy hopes, the children were already talking about vacations they would take and grandparents they would visit. It wasn't easy to corral all that giddy excitement and convince them to concentrate on reading and addition. It was always this way at the end of May. This year, Jenna was experiencing airy hopes, too. The way her heart took turns speeding up and slowing down during the drive to the ball field made her feel like a girl on the brink of womanhood.

"Have a good warmup," she told the boys. "I'll be back before your game begins."

Watching the boys race toward their coach, Jenna came to her senses. She wasn't a girl on the brink of womanhood. She was a thirty-four-year-old mother who taught kindergarten and owned a half-painted apartment building with a leak in the roof and a sizable mortgage. It was Saturday, and she had stops to make, errands to run. She reached for her stack of dry cleaning, and wound up staring at her left hand.

She was a mother, teacher, property owner, daughter, friend. Touching a finger to her wedding ring, she wondered when she'd stopped thinking of herself as a wife.

She'd anticipated the guilt that flooded her. She loved Craig. She missed him. If he hadn't died . . . She sighed. But he had died, and for two years it had seemed as if she'd died with him. And then Nick had come back, and suddenly, she was coming alive again. It was as if the summer stretched languidly before her, and with it endless days of discovery.

She hummed to herself as she drove to the little dry-cleaning store around the corner from Marcel's. She parked at the curb, fed the meter a quarter, then carted her stack of winter coats and blazers inside. She stood at the back of the line, waiting as the first two women in front of her picked up their clothing. Jenna didn't pay much attention to the other woman ahead of her.

Evidently, an item the customer had brought in was missing from her bundle. It wasn't until the younger woman pointed to her receipt and asked about her brown suit that Jenna recognized Shaye Townsend's mild midwestern accent.

While the attendant shuffled off to search for the missing article of clothing, Jenna sidled closer. "Would you mind if I put these on the counter?"

Shaye glanced at Jenna, then quickly away. She'd always seemed shy to Jenna. She stepped aside, though, and said, "How are you, Mrs. Proffit?"

"I'm fine, thank you. Please, after everything, well, I think Craig would want you to call me Jenna, don't you?"

Shaye's eyes went round, her lips parting. "Then you're not angry?"

Mind racing, Jenna shook her head.

Shaye blushed slightly. "Nick probably explained everything to you, but I want you to know that I was young and stupid and new in Georgia, and I guess I was lonely. I know that's no excuse. Craig never even looked at me. Not like that. I think Nick believed me. He should. It's the honest to God truth."

Shaye had had a crush on Craig? And Nick knew it? Suddenly, a few things began to make sense.

"Thank goodness I had the fortitude to pine after an honorable man. Belle wasn't nearly that lucky."

"Belle?" Jenna asked.

"Belle Watson. It's really water under the bridge."

Jenna didn't know anyone named Belle.

"She didn't live here long," Shaye said. "She used to come into the law office to see Mr. Sinclair."

The attendant returned with Shaye's missing suit. After Shaye walked away, the heavyset clerk started going through Jenna's stack of clothing. Jenna looked over her shoulder. "Shaye?"

Shaye paused, one hand on the door.

And Jenna said, "I take it Belle wasn't seeking legal counsel?"

Shaye didn't appear to know how to reply.

Since Jenna knew better than to compromise client-attorney confidentiality, she tried a different question. "Where is Belle now?"

"The last I knew she was talking about moving to Tennessee. That was a few years ago. We lost touch. Have a good day, Mrs., er, Jenna." She left with a small smile.

Shaye Townsend was petite and pretty, kind and smart. And young. Craig had worked with her on a daily basis. She'd fancied herself in love with him. He could have easily had an affair. But he hadn't. *Her husband had been a good man.* Not that she'd ever doubted it. Nick had doubted it.

He'd had his suspicions, but he'd kept them to himself. Why?

He kept so much inside. What on earth was a woman to do with a man like that? Jenna's mother used to say she never knew whether to throttle that boy or love him. Jenna understood the sentiment. She couldn't throttle him. That left loving him.

Did she dare?

Nick pulled into the driveway at shortly after five. He recognized everybody lazing on the verandah. Seeing Jenna, the boys and Twyla Mae sipping ice-cold beverages was a common occurrence. Nick hadn't seen the man sitting with them in more than three months.

"Uncle Nick, Uncle Nick!" Benji called racing to meet him halfway. "You missed the excitement!"

Stopping with a foot on the first step, Nick glanced up at everyone, in turn. Although his gaze lingered on Jenna the longest, it settled on the man with a three-day beard and two-day hangover. Rocky Gallagher lifted his drink in a mock toast and took a sip.

Everyone, including Jenna, looked as if they'd been doing a lot of laughing. That Rocky was a barrel of laughs. For once, Brandon and Benji weren't competing to talk. However, Twyla Mae looked as if she was going to burst right out of her ridiculous straw hat if he didn't hurry up and ask.

"What excitement, Twyla Mae?"

"Well." She smoothed a wrinkle from her faded flowered dress with arthritic fingers. "I just happened to be looking out my window, and I saw a man I didn't know nosing around the carriage house. How was I to know he was a friend of yours? He is a friend of yours, isn't he?"

It had been a long drive, a long day. Nick could have dragged it out a little more by insisting he'd never seen the guy before. Rocky Gallagher was watching him lazily, because Nick had done it before. They both had. It was good to see him. "Rocky and I go way back."

They'd started out at another magazine together, eventually working their way to bigger and better things. They'd helped each other out of scrapes over the years. Once, Nick diverted a charging rhinoceros, saving Rocky's life. It had been Rocky who'd hand-delivered that letter from Jenna earlier this year.

"In that case," Twyla Mae exclaimed. "I can't apologize enough for calling the police."

The police? Nick was momentarily speechless.

"That's what she did!" Benji exclaimed, as if he couldn't stand being still another instant. "Twyla Mae sicced the cops on him."

"They came, too, sirens blaring!" Brandon added.

Nick lifted Rocky's glass to his nose and took a whiff. With one eyebrow raised, he put the glass back where he'd found it. "I guess I did miss all the excitement." He'd certainly never known Rocky to drink iced tea.

"You didn't find anything exciting in Macon?" Jenna asked.

Nick turned his attention to Jenna. Subliminally, he was always aware of her. She sat next to Brandon on the wicker settee, her legs crossed, one sandal dangling from her toes as she moved her foot in lazy half circles. She'd probably been working in the yard before Rocky had arrived. There was a sheen of perspiration along her hairline, and a curious intensity in her blue eyes.

Nick thought about the computer check Pete Reynolds had run on Max Walker, Stuart Whitman and Oliver Sinclair. For a few hours, they'd thought they had a good lead. Maxwell Walker and Oliver Sinclair had sterling credit histories. Stuart Whitman had serious health issues, and had run up some costly medical bills over the years. Upon closer scrutiny, Pete had discovered that the majority of the expenses had been covered by two separate insurance policies.

Nick gave his head a small shake. "Back to square one. Has this character been here long?"

Jenna glanced at her watch, but Rocky answered. "I've been enjoying this fine southern hospitality for about an hour now."

"He's been regaling us with stories," Jenna said. "I didn't know you stayed with his family when you first left Harmony."

A month ago, Nick would have said something flip, something like, "He's the brother I never had." Such a comment would have been dripping with sarcasm and resentment. And it would have been untrue. He'd had a brother. It had just been complicated, that's all. Nick had changed, and the new Nick didn't know what to say.

He found himself looking at Rocky. A year older than Nick, Rocky had been christened Dwight Lee Gallagher. He would give Nick a kidney, if all his drinking didn't pickle them, but he'd flatten a monk's nose if he called him Dwight. Right now, he was staring back at Nick. He didn't look so good, largely due to the fact that he'd rarely gone a day without a drink these past ten years. Only a handful of people knew why. His hair was the color of lake sand and was shaggy around the edges, his clothes wrinkled, his eyes red-rimmed. No matter how much he'd had to drink, nothing got past him.

"Did you know Rocky had a dog when he was a kid?" Benji asked.

"He named him Bullwinkle," Brandon said. "Get it? Rocky and Bullwinkle."

Nick cast the other man a sardonic look.

Rocky ducked his head all around. And Nick said, "I'm afraid the Gallaghers sometimes lean the tiniest bit toward Irish bull."

Twyla Mae sat up straighter. "Are you saying some of the things he told us this afternoon might not be true?"

Nick nodded.

Rocky shrugged, and Twyla Mae made that *tut-tut* sound on the roof of her mouth. Jenna smiled when Twyla Mae rattled off a few of the facts she'd insisted she'd questioned in the first place.

Benji said, "Then your dog's name wasn't Bullwinkle?"

Brandon exclaimed, "I don't think he even had a dog."

Despite the tall tales, Jenna had enjoyed the past hour. She'd wondered about the kind of friends Nick had and the company he kept. Rocky Gallagher might have embellished the truth a little, but she'd learned more about Nick's life away from Harmony than she'd ever learned from Nick, himself.

As if he could read her thoughts, Rocky looked at Jenna and said, "Now I know why nobody's heard from Nick in months. I was hoping to enlist your help in convincing him to take a little trip to the Orient to do a photo shoot with me next month."

"Is that why you're here?"

She'd spoken quickly, and it drew Nick's gaze.

Rocky ran a hand through his hair, then slowly stood. "It was my father's idea. Don't shoot the messenger."

"I thought Nick free-lanced."

Rocky said, "When you're the best, they come to you."

An unwelcome tension settled to the pit of Jenna's stomach. She tried to keep it out of her expression, though. Years of practice and design enabled her to smile at Rocky and mean it when she said, "If you know Nick as well as I think you do, you know he comes and goes as he pleases. You two probably want to catch up. Brandon, Benji, what do you say we go find something to do?"

Brandon looked at his younger brother. "Let's go see if the owls have laid any eggs."

The kids raced off the verandah. Excusing herself, Jenna walked regally inside. Twyla Mae returned to her post near the window. When the two men were completely alone on the verandah, Rocky gestured to the nearly empty porch then looked at Nick. "Was it something I said?"

Nick was still adjusting to the fact that Rocky Gallagher was here in Harmony. They'd both traveled around the world and were adept at finding their way. Rocky had probably memorized the return address on the letter from Jenna.

The men started down the steps side by side. "You look in the mirror lately?" Nick asked.

"I'm going for a rugged look."

"Your rugged look gives all beards a bad name."

"You can't tame a wild rose."

"No, but you could give it a bath." They went through a similar exchange every time they saw each other. The boys were already climbing up the tree when Rocky and Nick passed. Rocky didn't speak again until his eyes had adjusted to the dim interior of Nick's cluttered apartment. "Why'd you tell those boys I didn't have a dog?"

Nick hadn't told them in so many words. They'd figured it out for themselves. "They don't need any more lies."

"You saying I'm not trustworthy?"

Nick looked at his shaggy-haired friend. "I'd trust you with my life, Rocky, but not with my sister."

"How about with your sister-in-law?"

Nick took a deep breath before replying. "Jenna's not your type."

Rocky dropped onto the couch. "I see. Then she's yours."

"It isn't what you think."

"He who denies the quickest has the best secrets. I'm not leaving until you've spilled a few of yours."

"Come on back to my darkroom. There are some photographs I'd like you to see. And then I'd be interested in your take on this situation involving my brother."

Rocky didn't say much about the pictures Nick showed him. He listened intently as Nick told him about the brick wall they'd run up against trying to disprove those rumors about Craig.

When he was finished, Nick said, "Well? You must have an opinion about all of this."

Rocky stared at him. "In my opinion, your idea of a vacation could use a little work. I also think somebody has to know something. It's like getting the perfect picture. You have to set the camera up-wind. And then you wait. It's all in the timing."

Nick thought about that.

Rocky stood. With an agility that caused Nick to question the likelihood of that two-day hangover, Rocky headed for the door.

"Where are you going?"

"I'm on a mission. This was just a layover." Rocky ambled to his Jag.

Nick followed a few steps behind. "Hey, Rocky? Tell your father . . ."

"He already knows you're planning to have him canonized after he's gone." He opened the door and slid into the low seat of his sports car. "I'll tell him you said hello. You might as well know. I haven't had a drink in three weeks."

Nick stood, statue-still.

Rocky said, "If you tell me you're proud of me, I'll have to climb back out of the car, walk over there, and hit you."

Nick laughed. Inside, he was proud.

Brandon and Benji sidled up to Nick, one on the right, one on the left. With a wink, Rocky called, "Keep working on your mom about that dog."

"We will!"

He drove away with a wave out the window and a honk of his horn.

Jenna was watching out the window much the way Twyla Mae did. The thought was a little disconcerting. Nick stood, unmoving, his back to the house. She wondered if Brandon and Benji's presence gave him comfort, or if he was wishing he were in that car, heading toward his next adventure.

Earlier that very day, she'd been sure the airy hopes filling her would lead to long summer days of discovery. She'd imagined that she was a butterfly slowly emerging from its cocoon. Nick had been at the heart of her evolution. Oh, she knew better than to ask for promises and forever. She'd fallen for forever once. Now, she knew forever was an illusion. All anyone ever really had was this moment. Sometimes, if you were lucky, the moments added up to a series of days, weeks, years. She'd hoped hers would last the season. Those idyllic days of endless summer were dwindling with every passing moment, and technically, it wasn't even summer yet.

Jenna had to decide what to do. And she didn't have much time.

"Hey, Uncle Nick. Can we come in?"

Nick left his makeshift darkroom, closing the door behind him. Taking a short cut between the bed and the sitting area, he ambled closer to Brandon and Benji. "You're already in."

The boys, dressed in baggy athletic shorts and muscle shirts, failed to see the humor. "Mom wants you to come over for a snack," Brandon said.

"And she told us not to take no for an answer." Benji pushed his glasses up on his nose. "She ordered pizza. Me 'n Brand don't know what we're celebrating, but hurry, Uncle Nick. It's pizza."

It was eight-thirty. An hour ago he'd been dressed much like Brandon and Benji. They'd ridden their bikes and he'd gone for a long run. He'd needed the exercise almost as much as he'd needed the shower he took afterward.

"Are you coming?" Brandon prodded.

"Of course he's coming," Benji said. "Mom said. Plus, it's pizza."

Unable to argue with that kind of logic, Nick followed his nephews out the door.

They ate their pizza on the back patio. A soft evening breeze kept all but the hungriest mosquitoes at bay. Tree frogs serenaded them and the low drone of a lawnmower competed with the hum of a small airplane that was nearly invisible in the pink-streaked sky. Had it really been a month since Nick had sat at this very table with Jenna and these boys, drinking grape Kool-Aid out of Waterford crystal?

"Mom says your friend Rocky is a character, Uncle Nick."

"Benji, there are some things a woman doesn't want repeated."

Nick gave Jenna a sidelong glance. There was something different about her tonight. Either he was a textbook case of arrested development, or everything she said contained a soft drawl that somehow wound up sounding suggestive.

She'd changed out of her jeans, and had donned a casual, pale blue dress, softly gathered at the waist, a row of small buttons down the front. She looked cool, refreshed, and very, very southern. The boys were working on their second slices of pizza, Nick on his third. Jenna had stopped with one.

"Not hungry?" he asked.

With the come-hither smile of a woman who knew exactly what she was doing, she said, "I'm saving my appetite for other things."

Nick choked on his iced tea.

In the background, the boys were talking about the eggs they'd discovered in the owl's nest in the hollowed-out portion of the oak tree. Brandon had a book opened, and was reading pertinent facts about barn owls. "It says here that after they hatch, the babies won't fly until they're nine or ten weeks old. And guess what they eat?"

"What?" Benji said, his mouth full.

"Mice and bugs and frogs."

"Tree frogs?" Benji quipped.

Brandon nodded importantly. "And sometimes snakes."

That launched the conversation into the snakes Benji had seen on his last field trip to the zoo. "Have you ever been bitten by a snake, Uncle Nick?" Brandon asked.

He shook his head. "I've come close to boa constrictors, and once I got a great series of shots of an anaconda, the shiest of all the snakes. They have teeth, but they're not poisonous."

"Boas and anacondas are constrictors, I believe," Jenna said, looking from Brandon, to Benji, to Nick. "They wrap their bodies around a warm-blooded creature of their choosing, rolling on the ground like a coil, slowly, surely, around and around, tighter and tighter."

A vibration started in the pit of his stomach. Anyone who hadn't heard the entire conversation would never know she was talking about snakes. It was that voice, those eyes, that intoxicating tilt of her head.

Nick had always thought of her as softly southern, fragile almost. That come-hither smile was back. It was provocative. It wasn't fragile. It made him want to kiss her. There was nothing unusual about that. What was different was that he was almost positive she wanted the same thing.

Oblivious to the private message taking place between the adults, Benji and Brandon washed down the last of their pizza with red Kool-Aid. They swatted mosquitoes and tried to pinpoint the exact location of the night peeper singing from deep in the backyard. When an argument broke out, Jenna said, "It's time for you two to hit the showers."

Wiping their mouths on the backs of their hands, they complained. Knowing it was inevitable, they plodded off to do as she said.

Jenna started gathering up plates and the cardboard pizza box. Nick reached over, stilling her hand with his. "Are you going to tell me what's going on?"

She stared at their entwined fingers. "To coin a phrase, who says anything's going on?"

Touché. She seemed to have enjoyed that.

She drew her hand out of his, placing hers on top, so that her fingertips rested gently on his knuckles. "Quite a coincidence. Today you saw somebody you hadn't seen in a long time, and I ran into someone I haven't seen in a long time. I don't know if you and Rocky talked about anything interesting, but Shaye and I certainly had an interesting chat."

"Shaye?" He sat up straighter. "Shaye Townsend?"

"She's really quite shy, but after you get her talking, she opens up. Of course, you'all know that." She finished stacking all their plates, then looked directly into Nick's eyes. "Why didn't you tell me about your suspicions?"

He shrugged.

For once, she wasn't letting him get away that easily. "Oh no, you don't. I want to hear you say it."

"What good would it have done, and whose purpose would it have served to tell you?"

"Then you *were* trying to protect us."

He would have shrugged again, had it not been for her stern expression. He relaxed, because this was more like the Jenna he'd always known.

"Do you have any idea what it does to a woman when an honorable man tries to protect her and her children?"

"Who are you calling an honorable man?"

Jenna wished she had more experience at this sort of thing, because suddenly, she was having a hard time meeting Nick's eyes. She glanced at her hands. She believed she and Nick had been leading to this since the moment he'd arrived back in Harmony. It had been a bit like a dance, two steps forward and one step back. She'd been asking herself what he was waiting for. And it occurred to her that maybe he was waiting for a sign from her.

"Mom, Benji's hogging the shower."

She glanced over her shoulder and then stood up. "I'll be right in, Brandon."

"You, Nick. You're an honorable man." She reached to take his empty glass out of his hand. He didn't readily release it, and she said, "Are you finished with that?"

She tugged, the action drawing his gaze to her hand. Nick released the glass, and all of his breath along with it.

He couldn't look away. The ruby ring she wore on her right hand had belonged to her grandmother. Her left hand was bare.

Head held high, she said, "Are you coming back later, after the boys are asleep?"

"I'd be careful what you're offering if I were you."

She didn't quite smile. "I like your terminology. I wasn't certain I would be able to bring myself to beg."

He stood up with enough force to send his chair clattering backward. She slipped inside the house before the chair hit the ground.

Chapter Nineteen

Jenna heard the back door open, and close, and had to clasp her hands together in order to stop the trembling. Footsteps sounded in the kitchen, and then in the short hall.

"You're taking a chance, leaving the door unlocked the way you did." Nick's voice was barely more than a hoarse whisper, but it drew Jenna around. He stood in her bedroom doorway, feet planted, eyes hooded. The next time he spoke, it was a little more gruffly. "Anybody could have gotten in."

"I didn't leave it unlocked for just anyone, Nick."

She could hear the deep breath he took from ten feet away. She'd turned on the lamp earlier, and turned down the bed. She could see him taking it all in in one all-encompassing glance.

"Don't expect me to ask if you're sure." He let his gaze linger on every inch of her before speaking again. "And for the record, a woman like you should never have to beg."

It was obvious what was on his mind. It was in his movements as he closed the door and locked it, in his stride as he met her in the middle of her room, in the way he breathed between parted lips. He reminded her of the animals he photographed in the wild, sure-footed, determined, and stealthily aggressive. And yet he'd waited for a sign from her.

She melted a little inside, so, so relieved. "When you didn't come right over, I thought I was no good at this."

"I beg to differ."

"Now who's begging?"

Nick had always known Jenna was witty and bright. Her conversational skills had always far surpassed his. He could have told her that. She probably would have disagreed. He didn't want an argument, not when every prayer he'd ever said was about to come true.

"Nick, do you think you could say something?" she whispered.

He could have asked her why tonight, why now, why, period. He wasn't certain he wanted to hear the answer.

"Okay," she whispered. "Then do you think you could kiss me?"

He hauled her into his arms and lowered his mouth to hers. He'd kissed her before, but this was different. Now, he wasn't satisfied with just a kiss. She made a sound deep in her throat, and kissed him back. And he knew she wasn't going to be satisfied with just a kiss, either.

His breath rasped as he dragged it in. "Are you sure the boys are asleep?"

She nodded, her lips parted slightly, swollen from that kiss. "Your run must have tired them out. Did it tire you out, too?"

"I seem to have gotten my second wind."

A few weeks ago, Nick would have grimaced at his choice of words. First and second. Better and best. She took his face in her hands, as if she knew. And then nature took over, a man's need for a woman, and a woman's need for a man. Their clothes were discarded, one at a time, their murmurs and sighs blending with the creak of the bed as the mattress shifted and accepted their weight.

He'd never seen her naked. Although he'd imagined the texture of her skin, and pale plumpness of her breasts, the soft suppleness of her thighs, he couldn't believe her beauty, the tan of her arms and shoulders, the paleness of her belly, the exquisite length of her thigh, so narrow at the knee. She was a woman, with a woman's curves. And he was a man who appreciated everything about her. He kissed her, and touched her, taking great pleasure in discovering the things she liked, and the things she loved.

An owl called through the evening quiet. The wind sighed, and Jenna moaned. The curtains were drawn, the sheet blessedly soft. "Ah, Jenna?" he said, when she sprawled on top of him, moving her body languidly down his, her legs straddling his hips, her breasts white in the semidarkness, deliciously puckered, her eyes half closed. "Do you think you could do that again?"

She got a knowing smile, and did as he asked, with a few improvisations. "I was afraid I wouldn't know how to please a man like you."

"You're kidding."

She wrapped her fingers around him. "You've been with exotic women, and I'm far from exotic."

He groaned, loud. It was a good thing the boys were deep sleepers. It was inconceivable that a woman like Jenna could be insecure about anything. Just in case there was a chance she didn't know how badly he wanted her, had always wanted her, he eased her onto her side and kissed her, long and deep, first her mouth, then her jaw, her neck, each breast in turn. She responded to his touch, every touch. When he discovered the sensitive little spot along the front edge of her hip, her breath caught. He trailed his lips from there to her thigh, over and over, until she writhed. And then he found a place even more sensitive.

"Nick!"

"I know."

Her eyes were closed. Somehow, they'd wound up

with their heads at the foot of the bed. He kissed her all over.

She wasn't exotic. She was exquisite. She was wild. And that was so much better. Best of all, she didn't take sex lying down. That fever had nearly killed him last spring. He'd never been more glad to be alive, if for no other reason than to experience this. It was sex. Brand-new, first-time, mind-blowing sex. Pure. Raw. Hypnotic.

Jenna didn't know which way was up. But she knew she had to have Nick. And soon. She needed air. And she needed sex. With Nick. She wasn't surprised he was an incredible lover. What surprised her was how free she felt, how wanton and passionate. And she knew it didn't matter that he'd been with exotic women. What mattered was that she'd come back to life.

She didn't know what his plans were. The way he felt about Harmony, she didn't expect him to stay here. In case it made him feel trapped, she didn't tell him she loved him. Instead, she showed him with every kiss, every sigh, every touch and murmur and groan and lusty cry for more, for release, for everything he could give her, and everything she could give him. He wasn't all give and no take, that was for sure. He told her she was wild, whispered it, muttered it, ground it between clenched teeth. And with him, she was.

He was thin, strong, the muscles in his arms and chest and legs well defined. He was sparsely haired, lightly tanned, and long limbed. She wasn't content to take her time. In that respect, he was much more patient than she was.

She found she liked that in a man.

The sheets became tangled. They kicked them away, and took up where they'd left off, kissing, touching, savoring, until neither of them knew where one of them ended and the other began. She used her hands, and her mouth, and every inch of her body to show him how she felt. And when she couldn't wait another second, she clung to him, blind, wild, ravenous.

He saw to protection. It was a good thing, because by then she was beyond conscious thought. And then he filled her, and she cried out, her heart thundering, his body heavy, heavenly on hers.

It was a long time before Jenna moved.

Nick eased to his side. "Wow." It was all she could think to say.

He chuckled. He actually chuckled.

Her heart felt full, and she thought it was true what they said. There was pleasure after sorrow, joy after sadness.

The mattress shifted as he got up.

"Where are you going?"

"To get a drink of water, and maybe some vitamins, so we can do that again."

She went up on one elbow. "Don't let me keep you here talking."

He was back within moments. She was waiting for him at the door. This time, they didn't make it to the bed. He took her standing up, her back against the wall, her legs wrapped around his waist. It was amazing, the way passion cleared his mind of old hurts, old wrongs, old resentments.

It was pure, raw, earthy. A few months ago, Nick would have insisted he was on an intimate basis with all three. Intimacy with Jenna redefined what sex was.

She clung to him. Eventually, she became aware of the cool wall at her back. She opened her eyes, sighed. "Well."

He kissed her, his hand moving down her spine. "I thought you didn't give out grades."

She swatted him on the shoulder, then pressed her lips to the same spot. Faith, Suzanne and Twyla Mae all seemed to think Nick loved her. Now, Jenna believed they were right. She wasn't certain it was the kind of love that led to marriage. She wasn't even certain Nick was the marrying kind. For all she knew, he could be preparing to leave Harmony tomorrow, or the day after, or another day soon.

Nick Proffit had never been an easy man to know. It was because he didn't talk.

He was an easy man to love.

Somehow, she wound up standing, facing him. She smiled, and said, "Maybe we both need to lie down."

She led him to the bed. They lay down together beneath the sheet. "Nick," she said, ten minutes, or perhaps twenty minutes, later. "I understand why you didn't tell me about your suspicions regarding Craig and Shaye." Making circle-eight patterns on his chest with the tip of one finger, she continued. "But why didn't you tell me about Sinclair's torrid little affair?"

He covered her hand with his, stilling it before it could inch any lower. "What torrid little affair?"

She rose up on one elbow so she could see his face. She'd never seen him so relaxed. He looked years younger. It was amazing what great sex could do for a person. "Shaye didn't tell you?"

He shook his head. "She told you Sinclair had an affair?"

She drew her hand out of his, and took up where she'd left off with those figure-eights. "Her name was Belle Watson. She and Shaye were friends of sorts. Shaye insinuated that Belle and Oliver Sinclair had an affair, and he broke her heart."

"When?" Nick's breath caught at what Jenna was doing.

"Apparently, the affair ended a few years ago when Belle moved up to Tennessee."

They both held still for a moment. When they finally moved, it was to look at each other. "Chattanooga is in Tennessee," Nick whispered.

"And Craig wrote Chattanooga in the margin in his day planner."

"I think we should pay this Belle Watson a little visit," Nick said.

"Tonight?" she asked coyly, her hand finding its target.

"Jenna, I'm trying to think. Maybe Belle knows something about that missing money."

"I think I might have discovered the secret to making you talkative."

His breathing hitched. "I'm serious, Jenna. What time is it?"

"It's early. You don't really want to talk, do you?"

"I suppose you have a better idea."

"If you play your cards right, it could be a long night." She slanted him a smile that went straight to his senses.

"If you don't stop that, I won't be able to stop, either."

She reached up and nipped his bottom lip playfully. He had her on her back before she could gasp.

It was late. It had been one more long day, in a series of long days. Suzanne had locked the doors at nine. All the chairs were up, the floors mopped, magazines straightened, dishes almost done. The portable radio was playing an old Bob Seager song about that old-fashioned rock and roll. Tonight, she couldn't bring herself to sing along.

She was wiping off the counter when a knock sounded on the front door. "It's late!" she called. "I'm closed."

In no mood for this, she trudged around the counter and stomped to the door. Keith Emerson, formerly known as Pocket Protector, stood on the other side. "I left my wallet," he called.

She'd found the wallet earlier. The driver's license inside belonged to a Keith D. Emerson. Height: Five feet nine and one-half inches. As if that half inch made all the difference. Weight: One-hundred sixty-five. She would have guessed less. But men didn't lie about their weight. Eyes: Gray. Hair: Brown. She'd thumbed through the money compartment. He carried a credit card, no receipts, a twenty-dollar bill, a five and two ones, all faceup and in the correct order. It figured.

He was looking at her the way he'd looked at her over his teacup too many times to count. She turned the lock and opened the door.

"Look," she said. "I'm tired, and you're trouble. Your wallet's on the counter up front."

She didn't know he'd followed her until she glanced over her shoulder and saw him pause several feet away. "You're troubled?" he asked.

She rolled her eyes. "I said you're troubled. Trouble. I said you're trouble. Is this going to be anything like who's on second?" It wasn't until she handed him the wallet, and he took it, that she noticed that he had something in his other hand.

He held it toward her. When she took it automatically, he stepped back, giving her some room. It seemed very old-fashioned, gentlemanly.

"What's this?"

"A gift."

Her eyes narrowed suspiciously. "For me?"

"For Marcel's. Open it up."

She untied a simple purple string. Underneath a thin layer of tissue paper was a book. It was heavy, hard-covered, and measured at least twelve by fifteen. She leafed through it and discovered it wasn't just a book. It was a coffee-table book. About France.

He smiled, and for a second or two, Suzanne forgot what she was doing. "I hear they're the rage in France," he said. "Here, too. I was going to try to find something written in French. I know you're fascinated with France's history and culture, but I wasn't sure you spoke the language."

"How did you know I like the history and culture of France?"

He held out one hand, gesturing to the coffee shop's interior. "Look at the name, Marcel's, the stained-glass artwork featuring the Eiffel Tower, the menu, your outfit."

It occurred to her that this was the first time she'd heard his voice. It was deep, smooth, pleasant. He must have been thinking along similar lines, because he held out his hand and said, "I'm Keith Emerson."

"Suzanne Nash." She placed her hand in his without thinking. And winced.

He reached for her hand again, taking it gently by the wrist. "That's some bruise."

"You should see the other guy."

He didn't release her hand, but continued to hold it gently. She hadn't gone to the doctor. The swelling was already going down, but the bruise was ugly. She noticed his hands were broad but average size, the tips of his fingers slightly square, the nails neatly clipped, the cuticles pushed back. A saying about hands filtered through her head.

"Until last night," she said, "I'd never laid a hand on anyone in my life."

"Who did you hit last night?"

"My ex-husband."

He tucked his wallet into his back pocket. She noticed he was wearing khakis and a simple white shirt, no tie, no pocket protector. He probably thought he was going casual.

"Did he have it coming?" he asked.

"Oh." She nodded. "He deserved a lot worse."

Suzanne wasn't a fanciful woman, or a particularly romantic one. She knew her strengths and her weaknesses. She was a modern-day woman with a smart mouth and an honest soul. And she honestly didn't know how she came to be sitting across from a too-nice accountant with no tan and only a hint of a five o'clock shadow. And if that wasn't cause enough for alarm, they were sitting in his favorite booth, and she was telling him every last bit of the sordid tale, right down to how she'd threatened to neuter her ex-husband. Keith shuddered.

It figured.

Men.

When she was finished, he said, "Feel better?"

And strangely, she did.

He motioned to the sign over the cash register, and read out loud. "Work like you don't need the money. Love like you've never been hurt. Dance like no one's watching."

Suzanne didn't know what to say.

He was looking into her eyes, and for a moment, she forgot that he was a nerd. "Dance?"

"What?" she asked.

"Would you care to dance?"

The radio was still on, but it was mostly static now. The signal always faded in and out this time of night. "There's no music," she said.

"Use your imagination."

She was just tired enough and just intrigued enough to let him take her hand and draw her to her feet and lead her to the center of the room. He left her there for a moment, and continued on to the counter, where he flipped off the radio.

"That was my favorite song." Oh, why was she always so argumentative?

He strode to her. There were lights on at either end of the room, but this center area was shadowy. Even in the shadows, she saw enough challenge in his eyes to take the starch out of her knees. Swallowing a sudden case of nerves, she said, "You should probably tell me what song we'll be dancing to so I don't step on your toes."

He took her hand. "Don't worry about that. I'll lead. You follow."

Following had never been her strong suit.

He fit her hand on his shoulder, his chin at the top of her head. And whispered, "If you must know, it's called 'Save the Last Dance for Me.' "

She sighed. "By the Drifters. It's my favorite song."

"I thought you said that old Bob Seager song was your favorite."

"Do you want to dance or do you want to talk?"

"Suzanne?"

"Hmm?"

"We're already dancing."

Her eyes opened, and then closed. Keith was right. They were moving dreamily around the floor. And he was singing, and it was a pretty good rendition, too. "So darlin', save the last dance for me."

When it was over, Suzanne's heartbeat was deep and her breathing was shallow. Soft-touched thoughts shaped her smile. Everything inside her had started to swirl together in a slow, smooth spiral, all her thoughts turned to oblivion, all her needs became one. Their faces were an inch apart, their bodies closer than that. A lot closer. Heat emanated from him, from every hard inch of him. Every hard inch . . .

She backed out of his arms. Eyes wide, she couldn't think of anything to say.

"I'm sorry. Give me a minute." He still hadn't moved. "This doesn't usually happen without, that is, I can usually think of something to . . ."

"Keep it down?" She knew she should be ashamed of herself for being vulgar, and then for grinning about it. She couldn't help it. His embarrassment was easier to focus on than hers. Plus, it was kind of cute.

She'd always heard big hands meant big . . .

So much for the reliability of that saying.

Somewhat back in control, he said, "Would you like to go out sometime?"

"Out?"

"I guess grabbing a cup of coffee somewhere is out of the question."

He had a nice smile. No he didn't. Okay, he did, but everyone knew that nice guys finished last. "You don't drink coffee."

This time, he was the one who had the audacity to smile. "So, you noticed."

She got lost in that smile, and in the heat and depth in his gray, gray eyes.

"I like what you're thinking, Suzanne, but we're not going to."

How the hell did he know what she was thinking? And why the hell not?

"Believe me," he said, "I'd like to. You have no idea how much. On second thought, maybe you do. When the time is right, we will. But we're going to take this very, very slow. And then, if we still like each other, after say, a month or two, or three, maybe then we'll see if we're as good in bed as we are in my dreams."

"You've been dreaming, too?" She clamped a hand over her mouth.

His smile broadened. "Unless you decide it would be best to set an example for your daughter, and think it would be better to wait until after the wedding."

Suzanne gasped. There were so many reasons. "There isn't going to be any wedding!"

He was walking away from her, toward the front door. "The justice of the peace would work, too. As long as it's legal, I don't care. Lock this after me."

"Go to hell."

He looked at her with a lift of his eyebrows that as good as called her a brat. "Do it, or I'll take you over my knee."

"That must be one of your fantasies again. I would tell you some of mine, but you're just not going to get that lucky."

Completely nonplused, he said, "I think luck has a lot to do with it. Don't you agree?"

"Look. I don't even agree with myself half the time.

I appreciate the fact that you listened to my problems, but you've gotten the wrong idea."

"It's as clear as sunshine, Suzanne."

She rolled her eyes. "In case you haven't noticed, the sun hasn't poked through the gray haze in the sky in four days."

He pointed out the window. Suzanne found herself staring at the sky where a full moon was in plain view through a gap in the crape myrtle trees lining the street. It took her breath away.

If you asked her, Keith walked just a little too knowingly out the door. If that wasn't bad enough, he waited on the other side as if he fully expected her to do as he said. She gave her head a shake but turned the lock. She happened to look down. Now she knew why he wore pleated pants. She sneaked a glance at his face.

His jaw was set, his lips parted, as if he was breathing between them. He was looking back at her on the other side of the window. And this time, he wasn't apologizing.

Suzanne backed away from the door. Heart beating in her throat, she looked around Marcel's, trying to understand what was happening to her. She'd closed all the windows earlier. That must have been why it suddenly felt a hundred degrees in here. It simply wasn't possible for her to be blushing.

She made short work of wiping off the remaining counters. Finally, she turned out the lights. Locking the back door, she headed for her car. Keith was parked nearby, his engine running. He drove a Volvo. Surprise, surprise. He had probably waited for her to make sure the big bad boogeyman didn't get her.

He followed her from the parking lot, turning right where she turned left. She didn't know where he lived, but she knew he liked French history, and could dance without music. He'd been coming into Marcel's for months. And tonight, when she'd needed a friend the most, he'd offered her his friendship. He'd hinted at a lot more.

She remembered well the imprint his *hint* had left on her belly. She shook her head, thinking that was one thing that even Jenna hadn't called it.

All the lights were on at 317 Beulah Street when Suzanne got home. Jenna and the boys, Nick and Twyla Mae and Faith and Rachel were in that big old house. And somewhere out there in the moonlit night was a man who wasn't quite what he seemed.

He was more.

Chapter Twenty

The single-engine airplane shimmied slightly when it hit a patch of rough air. Jenna held onto her stomach; Nick eased up on the control, leveling the plane out. He made flying look easy.

The engine was noisy, the cockpit drafty, the view incredible. Cotton fields stretched for miles, eventually giving way to orchards, that eventually gave way to more cotton fields. And then Atlanta sprawled as far as the eye could see.

They'd been in the air for an hour, and were more than halfway there. Church bells had been ringing when they'd taxied down the grassy runway at a private airstrip just outside of Vidalia. The plane belonged to a friend of Nick's. Brandon and Benji had said it best yesterday when they'd speculated that Nick must have a lot of friends. His friends weren't ordinary people, either. They owned airplanes, which they were willing to loan out at a moment's notice.

Nick had done some checking first thing this morning. Belle Watson had an unlisted phone number. He'd put in a short call to the same friend he'd visited yesterday. Within minutes, Pete Reynolds had tracked Belle's address via a parking violation. It would have taken five and a half hours to drive up to Chattanooga, and only two to fly. Of course both boys had automatically assumed they could go along.

"The plane's only a two-seater, guys," Nick had said, dashing their hopes.

Perhaps Jenna was more emotional this morning, for the sight of the silent tears coursing down Benji's face had made her eyes water. Nick had gone down on his haunches, talking quietly to the boys. In the end, Suzanne had agreed to come to the airstrip so Kenzie, Brandon and Benji could see Nick and Jenna off. It was small consolation to two boys who pretended the climbing tree was an airplane, and their little backyard a magic door to the rest of the world.

Nick's face had been grim as he'd flipped switches and checked dials. "Think they'll understand that we had to do this in order to clear Craig's name?" he'd asked.

Jenna had nodded. Brandon and Benji were resilient. They would forgive and forget and go on to their next adventure. One thing Jenna had noticed, and wouldn't forget: Nick hadn't promised them a ride some other day.

Nick Proffit made no promises he didn't plan to keep. She would be wise to keep that in mind, for he'd made no promises to her, either. Living for the moment was going to take some getting used to.

She still hadn't adjusted to the reality of what she'd done, and how she'd felt. Scientists believed that love-making released endorphins in the brain. That might explain the feeling of euphoria she'd felt last night, but she was convinced it took more than the release of endorphins to make her feel this way. It took Nick.

It seemed he *could* do anything. She smiled to herself as she thought about some of the things he'd done, some of the things they'd done, last night. And she'd had no idea he knew how to fly an airplane. "Where did you learn to fly?" she called over the engine and air noise.

He shrugged. "I picked it up here and there in my early twenties."

Jenna shook her head. "Just like people pick up the Japanese language and quantum physics."

He looked at her, and before her eyes, his eyes darkened.

"You're the king of understatement, do you know that, Nick?"

"Everybody's gotta be good at something." There was something lazily seductive in his expression.

"Flying isn't all you're good at. You pretty much proved that last night."

Nick turned his attention back to the sky for a moment. Nothing about the conversation should have been lust arousing. Okay, maybe they were talking about sex, without actually saying so. And maybe there was a good reason for the desire pulsing through him, hot and heavy.

"You're not the kind of woman I expected to bring that up."

The coy lift of her eyebrows only appeared ladylike. His thoughts heated further.

"That's probably what you tell all the women you're with."

"I haven't been with all that many women, Jenna."

"And you don't have all that many friends."

He wasn't quite sure what she was after here. It wasn't as if he'd been keeping track of how many women he'd been with. Sex had always been pleasurable. But it had always been just that. Sex. Last night was the first time he'd made love. It had shaken him, the powerful emotion, the awe, the culmination of twenty years of yearning. He hadn't completely recovered.

"If you must know," he said, in case she could possibly be feeling insecure, "last night will go down in history."

For a long moment she looked back at him, her face flushed with heat that told him that she was remembering, too. And as if to forever remind him that she didn't belong on some narrow, confining pedestal where only proper southern ladies perched, she wet her lips, lowered her voice, and said, "Which time?"

His heart took turns speeding up and slowing down. "All of them."

"What about this morning? What would you call that?"

He called that amazing. She had to know that.

Nick enjoyed flying. There was something invigorating about being in control of something that wasn't connected to the ground. It was nothing compared to being on the receiving end of Jenna's knowing smile. They'd both agreed that it would be best if Brandon and Benji didn't find Nick in their mother's bed this morning. Sometime after midnight, Nick had pulled on his jeans, and kissed Jenna good-bye, long and lingering and deep. He'd tiptoed out of the house carrying his shoes and the rest of his clothes, then crawled into his own bed, satisfied and spent. He should have slept for a week. He'd awakened at four-thirty, aroused all over again. On a whim, he'd crept outside again. He'd considered knocking on her door. In the end, he'd decided to try her window. She'd awakened to the soft brush of the pebble on her window, and had opened it sleepily. Climbing through the window had seemed like a good idea at that particular moment because right then, his ego had him convinced he could scale Mount Everest. Not quite as agile and nimble-footed as he'd thought he would be, he'd eventually made it up and in. After that, he'd gone to great lengths to turn Jenna's fit of giggles into sighs and groans.

The engine noise and air leaks in the cabin had made conversation difficult. Jenna was looking at him. And he said, "There are no words to describe this morning. Amazing, beautiful, exhausting don't come close."

She smiled, and turned her attention to the view out

her window. They would be arriving at the Chattanooga airstrip in half an hour. There, they would rent a car and drive to the address Pete had given him. Unless there were two Belle Watsons living in Tennessee, he and Jenna would come face-to-face with the woman who could very well point them to the partner who had stolen four hundred thousand dollars and ruined Craig's name.

Nick was looking forward to getting to the bottom of this. He was doing it for Brandon, and Benji, for Jenna, and for himself. And he was doing it for Craig.

"There it is." Jenna pointed, and Nick pulled to a stop at the curb in front of a two-story house in a pretty neighborhood on Chattanooga's west side. She stared out the rental car's window. If this indeed was Belle Watson's house, she was living extremely comfortably these days.

Chattanooga was a historic city near the southern boundary of Tennessee. From the air, it had been easy to see that it spanned both banks of the Tennessee River. It was surrounded by ridges and plateaus. The parts of the city that hadn't been industrialized were picturesque.

"Are you ready?" Nick asked.

They'd driven from the landing strip with the windows down. Jenna was glad she'd worn her hair up.

"We know nothing about her," she said. "She might not want to talk to us."

"She'll talk to you. You have one of those faces."

His vote of confidence came out of the blue, settling around her like an arm draped across her shoulders. She opened her door and got out. She used the time it took Nick to join her on the sidewalk to smooth a wrinkle from her beige chinos and simple silk shirt.

The covered entry was flanked by pillars; the doorbell was answered after the first ring. Until that moment, Jenna hadn't known what to expect.

"Can I help you?"

The woman was in her mid to late twenties, and pretty in her own way. Her flowered sundress and matching jacket complemented her hairstyle. The cigarette she held between two fingers explained the raspy voice.

She looked at Nick. "I know you."

Jenna took over. "I believe you were acquainted with my late husband, Craig. This is Nick Proffit, Craig's brother. I'm Jenna."

"What do you want?"

"Are you Belle Watson?" Jenna asked.

Just then a toddler came bounding into the foyer. Adorable, he was a walking advertisement for Baby Gap. His resemblance to Oliver Sinclair was uncanny. Sinclair was a nasty man. Until recently, Jenna had had no idea just how nasty. But he was incredibly handsome, and this child was, too.

"Your son is precious. I have two boys of my own. Benji and Brandon are eight and nine. They're the reason Nick and I are here."

Lifting her son to her hip, Belle took a long draw on her cigarette. She studied Jenna through the curtain of smoke, which she blew away from her child.

"I'm trying to quit. Second-hand smoke is bad for my boy. I don't know how I can help you with your kids."

"Please," Jenna said, "We've come all the way from Harmony. May we come in?"

Belle sighed loudly. She stepped back, letting them find their own way in. Jenna and Nick exchanged a quick look. Nick opened the door.

Belle was crushing her cigarette in an ashtray in the room next to the foyer. She motioned for Nick and Jenna to be seated on the couch. The furnishings looked expensive and were arranged just so, as if the placement had been drawn out on a decorator's graph. The toys scattered throughout the room were all that made it feel homey. Belle sat in a chair adjacent to the couch. Her little boy immediately squirmed to get down. The instant she set him on his feet, he scurried off to bang two toys together.

"How old is your baby?" Jenna asked.

"He'll be two in September."

"What's his name?"

Now that she'd put out her cigarette, Belle didn't seem to know what to do with her hands. She wound up folding them in her lap. "I named him Harlan, after my grandfather. I call him Harley. I hope he doesn't hate me for it some day. I'm raising him on my own. Once you become a mother, you second-guess every decision you make, you know?"

It was the perfect opening for Nick to say, "Jenna's boys don't have a father anymore, either."

Jenna said, "He died of an aneurysm in his brain. It happened a little over two years ago."

"I hadn't heard. That's too bad. I mean that," Belle said. "I still don't see what that has to do with me."

"His death had nothing to do with you. I ran into an old friend of yours. Shaye Townsend."

Nick watched Belle Watson closely. She was one of those women most men gave a second look. Stacked, she wore strappy sandals with three-inch heels. Her face was a little too angular to be classical, her makeup a little too heavy for his taste. She wore colored contacts. Nobody had eyes that shade of green. She'd probably spent a hundred bucks on her hair cut, a hundred more on the dye job, and who knew if the breasts were really hers. Obviously, she wasn't a Wal-Mart shopper. No matter how she arranged herself in that dress, she wasn't hiding the fact that she was no princess. How did a single mother afford all this?

"I know Shaye," she said. "Or I used to."

"It's all right," Jenna said. "I know she was in love with Craig. She mentioned that the two of you used to talk about that. You had a lot in common."

Belle's son chose that moment to toddle over to Jenna, a toy in his hand. "Baw," he said, handing it to her.

Jenna touched a baby-fine curl above his ear. "That's right. This is a ball. You are so smart!" She looked at Belle and quietly said, "He looks a lot like the man you loved, doesn't he?"

Belle drew her son away from Jenna. "What is this really about?"

Nick said, "We don't want to cause you or your son any trouble."

"We just want . . ." Jenna said. "I don't know how to ask you this. You see, Craig collapsed at the office, and died in the hospital hours later on a dreary day in March. He'd been handling a trust fund for the firm's wealthiest client. After the funeral, it was brought to my attention that four hundred thousand dollars was missing from the account."

"I don't see what that has to do with me. I know nothing about trust funds. Your husband died in March? I was already living up here then."

"We don't think you had anything to do with it. We're not accusing you. We don't even so much as suspect you of any wrongdoing."

Belle visibly relaxed.

"I believe that someone in the firm transferred a hundred thousand dollars from Nathaniel Sherman's trust fund into our savings account," Jenna said.

"And we believe Oliver Sinclair did it." Nick sat ahead, wrists crossed, fingers dangling loosely between his knees. Anyone who didn't know him would assume he was relaxed. "I think he planted the hundred grand in Jenna's account and used the rest to pay somebody off."

Belle jumped up. "I'd like you to leave."

"Look," Jenna said. "I know this is difficult. I know you didn't do anything illegal. If we take this to the police, it will become a legal issue. If that happens, you'll probably have to testify. As it stands, this is a moral issue. I'm giving you the opportunity to do the right thing, for your son, and for mine."

Belle tottered over to a bookshelf and got herself a cigarette. Her hand shook as she lit it. Her child looked up from the blocks he was stacking. The chubby-cheek smile he gave his mother was pure adoration.

Belle's lips quivered as she smiled back, and her voice shook as she said, "I met Oliver at a convention. I'm a paralegal, and well, let's just say we hit it off. I fell for him and his lines, hook, line and sinker. I loved him. Guess there's no accounting for taste, huh? And he loved . . . well, never mind what he loved."

"And then you discovered you were pregnant," Jenna said.

Belle nodded, her eyes closing, as if her memories weren't pleasant. "I wasn't even worried. I mean, he couldn't get enough of me. That changed the instant I told him about the baby. The next day, he called me from his office. He wanted to meet me someplace. I figured the shock had worn off, and he was going to tell me that he would divorce his wife, and we'd be together. Was I naïve or what?"

"What happened when the two of you met the second time?" Jenna asked.

Nick said, "He told you to get rid of it, didn't he?"

Belle nodded, her eyes on her son. "Those were his exact words. Like we were talking about an old pair of shoes or something that had gone bad in the refrigerator. He took out his checkbook, and proceeded to write me a check for a thousand dollars to take care of things."

"Only a thousand dollars?" Nick asked.

Belle made an unbecoming sound. "I was beside myself as I watched him write my name. Belle T. Watson. Something happened inside when I heard him mutter Belle Twatson under his breath. That was when I realized that that was exactly what I was to him. I told him I wasn't born in a barn, and our child wasn't going to be, either."

"You told him you were going to need a little more," Nick said.

Belle looked from Nick to Jenna. "He asked me how much more. Five thousand? I told him to add two zeroes to that. And if he didn't come up with the money, I would go to his wife and daughters, and to Maxwell Walker."

"Then he came through with the money?" Nick asked.

"No."

Jenna's heart fell.

Belle said, "He gave me three hundred thousand. I took it, too. I probably could have gotten a lot more if I'd gone for monthly child support for the next eighteen years. He's a full partner at the firm. To someone like him, three hundred grand was pocket change, right? I agreed that I would never see him again, but I figured he owed our child something."

Jenna and Nick shared a long look. The three hundred thousand dollars Sinclair gave to Belle and the hundred thousand that had turned up in her bank account totaled four hundred thousand, the exact amount missing from the Sherman trust fund.

"I didn't know he stole the money. He was rich. I figured he just took it out of some investment plan. He wasn't going to help raise our child, at least he could help me get on my feet. I can't go to jail. Who would raise my baby?"

Jenna said, "You've done the right thing by telling us, Belle. You won't go to jail for something Oliver Sinclair did without your knowledge."

"I hope you're right."

Half an hour later, Belle saw Nick and Jenna to the door. She reached for another cigarette on her way by, then put it back. "I really am going to quit this time."

Jenna said, "Good luck, Belle. And thank you. For everything."

Nick held out his hand. "Oliver Sinclair's tidy little life is about to blow up in his face."

Placing her hand in his, Belle said, "I guess what goes around always comes around eventually." She turned to Jenna. "Would you call me and let me know after you've met with the partners?"

Jenna promised.

She and Nick left Chattanooga. Two hours later they were back home at 317 Beulah Street.

Nick came to her bed again that night. This time, he used the back door, not the window. Afterward, they lay in the dark, listening to the *who-who-who* of the owls and outlining what would happen tomorrow. Jenna would call the law firm first thing in the morning, requesting a meeting with all three senior partners. They would attend the meeting together; two heads were better than one. In a matter of hours, Craig's name would be cleared, his good reputation restored.

Nick left her in the wee hours of the morning. She fell asleep thinking how ironic it was that she'd fallen in love with both Proffit brothers. And in the back of her mind, she wondered how long Nick would stay after tomorrow.

The outer office was as quiet as a tomb when Jenna and Nick entered it the following afternoon. Just as she'd planned, Jenna had spoken to Margaret Barclay first thing that morning. Of course, Margaret had wanted to know why she was requesting a meeting with the partners. Jenna had told her, in all truthfulness, that it had been more than two years, and she wanted to speak with them about what had happened and Craig's involvement so that she and her sons could move on.

Mrs. Barclay was loyal to the firm, but she wasn't cold. "This must be very difficult for you, Jenna."

Jenna had taken a deep breath. "Yes. I have one more request. I would like Nathaniel Sherman to be present, too."

"I'll see what I can do."

At ten o'clock that morning, Jenna had made another call to the law office. Margaret had informed her that the meeting was scheduled for four o'clock that very afternoon. Jenna and Nick arrived right on time.

Unlike the last time Nick had been here, he didn't have to cool his heels while pretending an interest in drab artwork and old photos. Mrs. Barclay ushered them directly to Maxwell Walker's private office at the end of the long dark hall. She opened an extra-high, extra-thick raised-panel door. Four men were seated around the polished conference table. Maxwell Walker and Oliver Sinclair rose to their feet immediately. Stuart Whitman did so more slowly, then leaned heavily on his cane. Nathaniel Sherman remained seated near his walker, chewing morosely on an unlit cigar.

Nick felt like he had as a child when his father had forced him to stand in a similar office, facing down the school principal, his teacher, and the parent of some boy he'd probably punched. Jenna touched his arm lightly, the action reminding him that he wasn't standing here with his father's heavy hand flattened along his back. He was a man, here of his own free will. He was at least equal to three of them, and far better than the one remaining. These men didn't intimidate him.

"Would either of you like a cup of coffee?" Margaret Barclay asked.

Jenna and Nick declined. And Margaret backed unobtrusively from the room. The instant the door was closed, Nathaniel Sherman removed the fat cigar from his mouth and waggled it at Jenna. "So you've finally decided to admit what that husband of yours did!"

Chapter Twenty-One

Jenna could literally feel Nick's tension as he followed her into the room. She didn't appreciate the elderly man's attitude anymore than he did. For now, she nodded at each of the three senior partners.

There hadn't been time to change her clothes after school. Her only concession to vanity had been tucking in her blouse and putting on lipstick. That was fine. She wasn't here to restore her reputation. She was here to restore Craig's. That in mind, she approached Nathaniel Sherman. "I *have* come to talk about the money that came up missing in your trust fund, Mr. Sherman, and Craig's involvement in it."

"Please," Maxwell Walker said, indicating that Jenna and Nick should take a seat.

They did so. When everyone was seated, Jenna placed Craig's leather satchel-style briefcase on the table in front of her and folded her hands over it.

Tan and robust, Oliver Sinclair smoothed a hand down his tie and said, "I'm a little surprised you wanted Nathaniel to be here for this, Jenna."

Jenna stared at Oliver and answered without smiling. "That was Nick's idea."

It was obvious to Jenna that Sinclair didn't think

Nick had any business being present for this. Craig had never cared for Oliver Sinclair. The man had always been too smooth and grossly arrogant. A chauvinist, he was one of those men whose voice changed when he spoke to a woman.

She turned her attention to Maxwell Walker. "I'd like to begin by saying that when you called me to this very office and told me about the money that had been stolen from Mr. Sherman's trust fund, I believed with my whole heart that Craig was innocent."

"It was a difficult time," Maxwell said. "For all of us."

Nick sized up everyone in the room with one sweeping glance. Maxwell Walker's expression was guarded but tolerant, as if he were waiting to hear everything before making up his mind. Stuart Whitman had lost most of his hair since the last time Nick had seen him. His illness had aged him beyond his sixty-two years. There was intelligence in his gaze, though. He, too, appeared to be waiting to hear what Jenna had to say.

It was Nathaniel Sherman's money that had been stolen, and while he wasn't a partner in the firm, his and Max Walker's families went way back. For as long as Nick had known him, Nathaniel had worn the pinched expression of a man who could have used an enema. He and his wife hadn't had any children. Twenty years older than the other three, the rich old codger had spent the better part of the last thirty years since she'd died counting his moldy money.

Nick studied Oliver Sinclair last. Although he was nearly the same age as Whitman, he looked fifteen years younger, at least. He knew it. He flaunted it. He made Nick sick.

Nick reeled in his derision lest he ruin Jenna's little surprise. Other than the ticking of the antique grandfather clock in the corner, the room was quiet.

Finally, Max Walker said, "And what do you believe now, Jenna?"

"Now I know the truth."

There hadn't been a doubt in Nick's mind that Sinclair would take the floor next. "Look, Jenna dear, we here at Walker, Whitman and Sinclair understand how difficult this has been for you. Nathaniel agreed not to go to the police two years ago, so there is really no need to put yourself—"

"And the truth is—" Jenna interrupted the man beautifully. "Craig didn't take Mr. Sherman's money."

Walker and Whitman looked perplexed. Nathaniel Sherman looked disappointed. Oliver Sinclair was angry. He stood. "You're wasting our time!"

Nick stood, too. "Sit down, Sinclair. Unless one of us has an aneurysm in the next few seconds, you're not going to have anyone to pin it on this time."

"What?" Nathaniel Sherman nearly bit off the end of his cigar.

Ever the southern gentleman, Max Walker restored order to the meeting by saying, "I assume you've brought proof, Jenna?" But he pushed his chair out, blocking the path between Oliver's chair and the door.

Jenna unzipped Craig's briefcase, and drew out several items. The top paper fluttered slightly as she slid it across the table toward Maxwell Walker. She didn't take her hand off it until it was safely out of Oliver's reach.

Max skimmed the statement signed by Belle Watson. He studied the copy of the canceled check signed by Oliver Sinclair. But it was the glossy color photograph of Belle's smiling toddler that caused him to make a fist, and slam it on the table. "For God's sake, Oliver."

Sinclair's eyes seemed riveted on the damning photo. "Where did you get that?"

Nick looked at the other man in that still way he had. "Belle loaned it to us. You remember Belle."

Jenna drew out another photograph. "Your daughter loaned me this one." It was an old black-and-white photograph of Oliver Sinclair at two years of age. "A remarkable resemblance, don't you think?"

Sinclair had turned green underneath his tan.

Nathaniel Sherman groused. "Let me see those." He stared at the evidence, and then at Oliver Sinclair. "You knocked some young girl up, used my money to pay her off, then blamed it on a dying man?"

Nick couldn't have put it better himself. Since this had been Jenna's battle, and this was Jenna's moment of glory, he waited for her to speak.

She did so, softly. "Now that I know who was responsible, I'll return the hundred thousand dollars Oliver planted in our account, Mr. Sherman."

Max Walker said, "Now would you like to press charges, Nathaniel?"

"Wait." Sinclair's eyes darted nervously and his manicured hands shook. "We all know what it's like, a woman like that rubs up against men like us. We think with the wrong head. Jenna just said she'll return that hundred grand. I'm good for the rest, with interest. Nobody else has to know."

"Nathaniel?" Stuart Whitman spoke for the first time.

Nathaniel was looking at the picture of Belle's baby. He looked at Jenna next, and then at Nick. Finally, he turned his attention to Oliver. Eyes glittering, he said, "As much as I'd enjoy sending you to prison, I have a better idea."

By the time Nathaniel Sherman had outlined his better idea, Oliver looked like a man facing a firing squad. "Taking this public is ludicrous. It'll ruin me and my name."

"The way you ruined my brother's name?"

All eyes turned to Nick. Tears swam in Jenna's eyes as she slowly released a deep breath.

"Dolores will divorce me, and take half of everything I own. And you want the other half? Our daughters will side with their mother. I'll be disbarred. Destitute."

Nick simply couldn't refrain from saying, "Maybe

Simon Smith could use an apprentice over at Deep Dell Cemetery."

Sinclair glowered. But Nathaniel Sherman cracked the first smile his face had seen in perhaps a decade. "I like your style, young man. You remind me of me at your age."

The only man in the room who failed to see any humor whispered, "Nathaniel, please. I'm begging you to reconsider. You're rich. You don't need the money."

"Need. Now that's an interesting thing." Nathaniel held up his cigar. "Anybody care if I light this, because I could really use a smoke."

Max Walker offered Nathaniel a match.

The old codger had it under control. He took his lighter from his pocket, and with shaking arthritic fingers, held it to the tip of his cigar. After taking a few puffs, he held the lighter up for everyone to see. "This belonged to my father. He made his first dime honestly and eventually went into local politics back when the corner store was the real seat of legislative decisions here in the South. I've tripled what he left me three times over. Maybe I don't need your money, Oliver. I'm going to have it, though. And instead of watching it accumulate on some fancy printout, I'm going to do some good with it, all of it. You're right about one thing. You'll be ruined. Nobody in this town will give you the time of day, certainly not any pretty young women. Your membership at the club will be revoked. You won't even be able to order a sandwich at Chelsea's without worrying that somebody used it to wipe their nose or their ass or both."

"He can't do this!" Sinclair looked to his partners.

"Sure he can," Stuart Whitman said. "Or would you prefer twelve to fifteen?"

Nick would have bet his favorite camera that Whitman had enjoyed asking that question. Nick and Jenna prepared to leave. "I'll have the hundred thousand dollars wired from my account in Savannah first thing in the morning. I don't have the interest it accrued, because I donated it."

"To the society's library fund. Yes, I know," Nathaniel Sherman said. "You've got spunk. Keep the hundred grand. It's like Oliver said. I don't need it. Oliver will pay back everything he took. It's the least he can do after the damage he caused."

Margaret was summoned. Max and Stuart dictated letters and documents, which she hurried off to type. Once they were signed, not even suicide would get Sinclair out of paying for what he'd done.

Everything was in place when Nick and Jenna left Max's private office and walked past the room where Craig had so loved working right up until the day he had collapsed. Jenna opened the door and looked in. Slowly, she closed it again. Justice had been served.

Oliver Sinclair would be free to leave Harmony, but he would do it penniless and with his tail between his legs. Perhaps it wasn't as horrible as spending twelve to fifteen years in prison, but at least this way, some good would come out of it. The money he was being forced to pay back would be used to help those in need.

Jenna and Nick were both silent as they left the office building. Nick held the passenger door for her, then walked slowly around the front of his car. He slid behind the wheel, and stared out the window. Finally, he looked at her. "Good job, Jenna. You did it. Craig would be proud."

She nodded and wiped away a tear. "We did it."

"It's over. All of it is over. Now you can get your life back." Nick started the engine. "What do you say we go tell the boys the good news?"

Thoughts of Brandon and Benji made Jenna smile. She could practically hear all their questions, could picture their grins.

The sky was muted by a haze of soft clouds, rays of yellow sunlight poking through every place they could. It would be evening soon. And then it would be tomorrow. Jenna didn't want to think about tomorrow yet. She told herself to be happy that she had today.

She *was* happy. And she was proud.

And Nick was right. It was time to go home.

Chapter Twenty-Two

It was Friday.

Jenna was alone in her apartment. It had been quite a week. School was officially out. And although it wouldn't officially be summer for a few more weeks, summer vacation had begun.

She'd been a bit of a celebrity this past week. Cards and phone calls and letters and people had been pouring to 317 Beulah Street. Brandon and Benji had eaten up all the attention. Jenna's mind was still spinning from it all.

The kitchen table contained all sorts of memorabilia. There was a letter from Max Walker and Stuart Whitman naming Craig an honorary senior partner in the firm. There was another letter from Abigail Prichart and Lenore Jones, inviting Jenna back into the folds of the Harmony Hills Historical Society. Jenna didn't plan to answer it. Wendy Schumaker and Dawn Miller had shown up on her doorstep in person, gushing all over themselves about how sorry they were and how they'd known all along that Craig couldn't have done such a thing, and now that they thought about it, Oliver Sinclair always had had shifty eyes.

Jenna had cut their little act short by saying, "Excuse me. My friends are waiting for me."

Suzanne had had a field day with that one.

Actually, Jenna had never seen Suzanne like this. Although she wouldn't admit that she was falling in love with Keith Emerson, she and Kenzie were out with him tonight. Earlier, Faith had gone for a long walk with Reed Carlson. Twyla Mae was as happy as a clam keeping track of all the comings and goings of the residents at 317 Beulah Street.

Jenna should have been happy, too. And relieved, and proud. She *was* happy and relieved and proud.

"It's over," Nick had said. She couldn't get it out of her mind.

Nick had stayed in the background this past week. He'd taken pictures. He'd gone for long runs. He'd played with Brandon and Benji. He hadn't knocked on her window in the middle of the night.

He hadn't even said much when a reporter from the *Harmony Herald* had stuck a microphone in his face and asked him what part he'd played in clearing his brother's name. The paper had used Nick's quote, "It's a shame my brother's gone. You'll never meet a better man." The headline had read, "Craig Proffit. The Better Man."

The newspaper was on the table, too. Jenna got choked up every time she read the article. It was a beautiful tribute to Craig's life. It made her miss him terribly. Nick was in her own backyard. And she missed him, too.

And it was really starting to get on her nerves.

"It's over," he'd said.

Why did it have to be over? She would have liked to know the answer to that. But of course she didn't know, because Nick wasn't talking. And that was getting on her nerves most of all.

Maybe she should ask him about his plans.

Before she let herself talk herself out of it, she marched through her kitchen, out her back door, and across her grass. It was time to put an end to all this restless yearning and tossing and turning. She passed beneath the tree where the owls were busy these days, and nights, keeping their babies fed.

Her knock on his screen door went unanswered. She let herself in.

He'd cleaned the place up a little. There were no shirts hanging from chairs or dishes in the sink. His bed was made, too. And noises were coming from his makeshift darkroom.

She turned out every light in the room, then felt her way toward that closed door, no easy feat. She arrived there with minimal bruising to her shins. Opting not to knock, she let herself into that room, too. There, she paused.

Nick was working beneath a safelight. He looked at her over his shoulder, his surprise at seeing her slowly giving way to what she'd come to know as his smile. "Wait'll you see these pictures I got of those newly hatched owls."

He started toward her, the photographs he'd just developed in his hand. His easy stride and masculine swagger no longer fooled her into believing he had all the time in the world.

"The thing is, Nick, I can't have my old life back."

The safelight bleached all the colors from the room, except shades of gray and black and white. Everything about Nick looked stark, his shirt, his pants, his face and hair and the deep emotions in his eyes. Jenna averted her face, her brief flirtation with shyness. But then her resolve took over, and she said, "Craig died. He was part of my old life. And I can't get it back. I appreciate everything you've done, all your help, in clearing his name. In a sense, you brought me back to life, Nick, and I just want you to know—" She swallowed, uncertain how to proceed.

Nick held perfectly still, trying to prepare himself for what was coming next. The old *I'll never forget you, have a good life* routine followed closely by *there's no hurry but here's your hat.*

"Death is one thing," Jenna said. "How on God's green earth am I going to find any joy in a sunset or an owl's call after you leave?"

Nick was stunned. "I'm not leaving Harmony."

"You're not?"

"You don't want me to?"

She shook her head, her eyes round and brimming with unshed tears. "No, I don't. I thought you knew that."

"I figured. Until a few minutes ago, that is."

"You did?"

He nodded. "I think you love me."

"Oh, you do, do you?"

She crossed her arms, and Nick had to hold in a grin. "Do you want to know why I think you love me?"

"By all means enlighten me."

"Because a woman like you wouldn't have let me grace her sheets unless I'd graced her heart."

"Oh, Nick."

"Of course, you realize that now you're going to have to marry me. Will you, Jenna?"

Would she . . . "Then you love me, Nick?"

He made a sound only men could make. Suzanne had tried. She and Jenna never had figured out how men got their breath out through their noses while they were groaning so deep in their throats.

"I have for a while now. A long while. Since the fourth grade."

"If you love me, why have you stayed away this week?"

"I've been figuring some things out."

"What things?" she asked.

Nick looked around him. His darkroom was stuffy and cluttered and smelled of developer. Jenna Brannigan Proffit deserved wine and roses and candlelight. If she would have given him one more day, he would have presented her with all three. But she was here now, and she wanted—he smiled to himself because demanded was more like it—answers. Her reached for her hand, and led her out of the darkroom. The rest of his apartment was dark, too.

He was sure he'd left the lights on earlier. He banged his knee getting to the lamp.

"Have I told you how glad I am that I came back to Harmony?"

"I thought you hated Harmony."

He shook his head.

"What changed your mind?"

"It was something Nathaniel Sherman said that did it. He said I remind him of him when he was my age. I don't want to wait until I'm eighty to make a difference in someone's life. Besides, Harmony's just a town. And like every other town in the world, there are good people here. And there are bad people here. I should know. I've been everywhere. It isn't the town people come back to, Jenna. It's the people. And I came back to you."

He took a deliberate step in her direction. He'd left her near his bed. It hadn't been intentional, but it was fortuitous. "I'll watch sunsets and sunrises, fly in Benji's make-believe airplane and marvel at how much Brandon is like Craig. Where are the boys, anyway?"

"They're camping out in pup tents in Toby Miller's backyard. Pups. That's all they talk about."

"Maybe we can get them a dog this summer." He placed a hand on her shoulder, slowly bringing it to her neck, gliding his palm up to her face, threading his fingers through her unruly dark hair. "Right now I'd like to roll you underneath me and improve on that last time."

"Improve on perfection?" She looked directly into his eyes. "I suppose we could try."

"For a prim-and-proper schoolmarm, you're awfully capricious."

"Capricious, huh?"

He lowered his face, his eyes on her lips. "I learned a new word. I've been doing that since I learned to read, really read, after I left Harmony."

He kissed her. And it sang through his veins. And when they both needed air, he lowered the zipper down the back of her loose-fitting summer dress. "Besides perfecting this over the next fifty or sixty years, God willing, I'd like to learn how to build boats, the way Craig and I talked about doing when we were kids. I'm looking at some property on the river."

Jenna shuddered when her dress swished to the floor. "I never knew you and Craig wanted to build boats. There are so many things about you I don't know."

"What do you want to know, Jenna?"

Her mind filled with possibilities. She wanted to know everything. "I'd like to know how you met Rocky Gallagher, and how you learned to take pictures, and if you think Brandon and Benji and I might help you build those boats." She placed her finger on the top button. "I'd like to know if you want some help getting out of this shirt."

His shirt was inside-out in an instant, and flung somewhere in the room. He kissed her again. And a moment before he lowered to the bed, taking her with him, he stopped, and flung his coverlet back.

"What are you doing?"

"I didn't make this bed. And I saw Brandon and Benji hanging around earlier. And a person never knows what's going to come shooting out at him around here."

He folded down the sheet. Sure enough, a real-looking fake garter snake was curled up at the foot of the bed. The real-looking *real* garter snake moved.

Jenna screamed. She was on top of the dresser in one bound. The snake uncoiled and slid off the back of the bed. Nick crawled around on his knees, Jenna asking if he'd found it every few seconds, and him swearing that these practical jokes were going to be the end of him one of these days. Eventually, he found the ten-inch-long garter snake curled up next to the laces of his shoes. Holding the reptile gently in one hand, he started toward the door. "Wouldn't the owls love a midnight snack?"

"Are you going to give it to them?"

He let the snake go on the ground outside the door. "If they find it, so be it. Now it's up to nature to see who gets fed or goes hungry."

He looked back at Jenna. She was sitting on top of his dresser in a lace bra and panties. Her hair was a mass of waves around her shoulders; her eyes were round and so, so blue. His favorite color. She didn't appear to be in any hurry to take up where they'd left off.

She stared at him. He stared back at her. And they started to laugh. They laughed until their stomachs hurt and they were out of breath.

Nick helped her down, a newspaper fluttering to the floor along with her. Still breathless, she bent to retrieve it. She had an identical copy on her kitchen table. The headline read, "Craig Proffit: The Better Man."

She put the paper back on the dresser. Rising up, she took Nick's face in both of her hands. And in case he had any doubts, she said, "There is no better or best. But there is right and wrong. And you're the right man, the perfect man for me. Do you believe me?"

He started to lower her to the bed a second time.

"Wait," she said. "I'm not getting between sheets that a snake was between."

"Do you want to continue this back at your apartment?"

She turned her head toward the door. "That snake could be in the grass between here and the big house."

Nick groaned again, sputtering that he should have fed the blasted thing to the owls when he had the chance. He watched her slip into her dress. Accepting the inevitable, he said, "I planned to bring you wine and roses anyway." He reached for her hand, and drew her with him to the couch. Settling her close to him, he draped an arm around her shoulders, and began. "I met Rocky Gallagher at a pool hall in upstate New York. He's from an affluent family who had their own share of problems. I was hungry and he was angry. I beat him at pool, and he took me home and let his mother feed me. He drank too much, even then. It was a year before I discovered the reason. We both loved to take pictures. Rocky hates to fly. Ever heard of a slow boat to China? That first summer, Rocky and I took a slow boat to France."

Nick talked for a long time. Jenna pictured the places he described, the people he mentioned. And when he was finished, she had a better idea of how he'd become the man he was today. She didn't know if there was such a thing as destiny. If there was, it would explain the reason she'd fallen in love with Craig, and now with Nick. Just as the brothers were different, her love for them was different. Her heart felt so, so full, her body warming with need.

She eased off the sofa, and stood, skirting a chair on her way to the screen door. Standing there, she said, "How far would you say it is to the back steps?"

"How far?"

"How many feet? Sixty? Eighty?"

"Closer to ninety, I'd say."

"How adventurous are you?" she asked.

"How adventurous am *I?*"

"There's a good chance that snake is long gone. Even if it isn't, I'm thinking that we could make it to my back step in less than thirty steps, as long as we take giant ones."

Nick strolled closer. "You want to go to your place?"

"We can't make love here."

"You want to make love?"

"Oh, yes. I want to a lot."

Suddenly it didn't matter that he'd faced down rhinos and grizzly bears and tribesmen and a raging fever.

She was braver, not because she was willing to chance coming upon a harmless snake. Because she dared to love again.

"I think we can make it, Jenna."

Into her house, and into their future.

They were laughing by the time they reached her kitchen. Holding her stomach, Jenna said, "I've never laughed so much in my life, as I've laughed with you."

She held out her hand, and he took it. The time for laughter had ended.

But only for a while.

Please turn the page for
an exciting sneak peek of
Sandra Steffen's next novel,
COME SUMMER,
coming in April 2004 from Zebra Books!

Chapter One

Other than Millie Prescott's three cats watching from the windowsill next door, nothing stirred on the cul-de-sac at the end of Desert Moon Drive. It was too early in the morning to be stirring. It was too early in the morning to be *up*. The sun was already blinding though, the sky clear, but then it seemed the sky was always clear in Nevada. It was the reason people moved here.

Liza Cassidy was leaving, this time for good.

"I'm not sure this was a good idea, Liza." Denise Bailey, of Bailey Brokerage & Associates, gestured feebly with her right hand. "Technically, it isn't your house anymore."

Denise had been Liza's friend since childhood, and more recently, her real estate agent. Liza wasn't ignoring her out of rudeness. It was just that her thoughts had turned inward, her attention on the tiny yard surrounding the house where she and Laurel had grown up.

Plus, Denise was wrong. Liza needed to be here today. She needed to leave from here, because this was where it had all started. Laurel had known it, and had put it in words in one of her letters.

Sometimes, Liza, she'd written, *what we think is the end is really just the end of the beginning.*

The house on Desert Moon Drive was the beginning of the beginning for the Cassidys. Built in the fifties, it was a modest, single story. Like the others on this block, the exterior was stucco. Most of the neighbors' little yards were stone and gravel. Liza's mother had insisted on grass. Never mind the fact that Nola Cassidy forgot to mow it half the time, and the other half of it burned up in the scorching heat of the Nevada summer. Kids needed grass, she'd said. And this yard had grass. It also had a fountain, which Liza's mother had called a bubbler, like the one Nola had growing up in Madison, Wisconsin. The plastic pink flamingo next to it was as tacky as always. Liza was of the opinion that her mother had stuck it near the front steps to serve as a warning of the bright colors visitors would inevitably encounter inside.

They'd had a lot of visitors. Nola had had a lot of friends, and every one of them was as non-traditional and unconventional as the interior of her house. And as her daughters.

Shading her eyes against the glare of the June sun, Liza glanced all around. The Cadillac parked in the driveway looked as out of place here in this neighborhood as the four-karat rock on Denise's ring finger. How many times had she become exasperated with Liza throughout this process? How many times had she said, "But it's a good offer, Liza. You can't allow the buyers' personality to enter into your decision."

As far as Liza was concerned, that was the only thing that should enter into her decision. This house needed a new family. Only someone who understood the personality of the house, itself, would live here. She'd refused to sell to the highest bidder, a woman who'd looked at it with dollar signs in her eyes, as if all she saw was how a few upgrades would add to the market value when she turned around and sold it for a tidy profit.

This house was a home, not a tidy business deal. The Bullards, a young couple who worked on the strip to support their rambunctious brood were moving in later today. Their three urchins would surely mar every last inch of the newly buffed hardwood floors. Those little boys with their adorable dimples and cowlicks were going to be so happy here, just as Nola and her precocious daughters had been happy there.

They *had* been happy here.

No matter how right the Bullards were going to be for this house, everything would change with their arrival. Of course, everything had already changed. Liza stared at the house, her feet rooted to the sidewalk, her gaze glued to the place over the front door where her mother's sign had hung.

Nola Red's.

"You have a burning need to go through it one more time, don't you?" Denise asked.

Denise was very astute. She'd graduated from high school with Liza fifteen years ago. Denise had married well. She and her stuffy husband and their two well-behaved children lived in a big house with high ceilings and not much personality, if you asked Liza, in one of the new gated communities that were springing up around Las Vegas. Not that Liza would ever say it out loud. To each his own. Besides, Denise had earned her commission on this house, and then some.

Liza took a deep breath. "I'll only be a few minutes."

She let herself in through the front door. Pocketing the key, she was suddenly uncertain which direction to go first. She'd left some of the furniture for the new owners. The belongings that didn't fit in the back of Laurel's old car had either been stored or sold. The house smelled of floor polish and pine cleanser, foreign scents in a house that once carried the aroma of her mother's perfume, acrylic paints and whatever casserole happened to be bubbling in the oven. All of Nola Cassidy's casseroles had tasted the same, due largely to the fact that condensed cream of mushroom soup was the main ingredient in each of them. Liza and Laurel had taken over the cooking as soon as they were old enough to work the stove. Still, to this day, Liza's favorite comfort food was tuna noodle casserole made from her mother's simple recipe.

That was the first thing she would cook when she reached the Atlantic coast and found a place to stay. For now, she strolled through the living room with its purple walls and stenciled ceiling, and on into a short hall. Her mother's room had been at the far end, Liza's on the right, Laurel's on the left.

She paused in the middle. The girls had never had a canopy bed, nor had they wanted one, and nothing in either room, or in the entire house, had ever been pale pink or pale yellow or pale anything. Nola Cassidy had been a self-taught, wonderfully gifted artist, and it was like she'd often said, artists simply didn't do pastel. At least not the red-haired, flamboyant artist who had, at barely eighteen years of age, fled the lush greenery of one of the prettiest towns in the Midwest to fulfill her passion to become a dancer. She'd ended up a showgirl in Vegas.

Oh, and pregnant.

The father—even thirty-three years later, Liza still thought of the man who'd sired her as *the* father, not her father—had been a dashing Frenchman. To hear Nola tell it, he'd spoken barely a lick of English, but evidently was fluent in the language of love. His name had been Pierre, and he'd moved on long before Nola had started her daily morning tête-à-tête with the toilet.

The pregnancy had forced a temporary hiatus from Nola's dancing career, but it had been the stretch marks and ruined stomach muscles, the result of carrying identical twin daughters with a combined birth weight of almost twelve pounds that had made her leave permanent. Nola Cassidy may have been a little ditsy at times—she *had* stepped off a curb and had gotten run over by a bus, something many woman thought might happen to them one day, but few actually experienced—but my, how she'd loved. One thing she'd never been was bitter. So, when her dancing career ended, she'd started helping with make-up and costumes. Before long, she was designing and creating costumes that were works of art. She'd been carrying one of her creations with her the day she'd died. The bus driver thought he'd hit a woman and some sort of live exotic bird. Liza had laughed about that. It had been a welcome respite to the tears.

It hadn't been uncommon for Nola to bring the headdresses home. In the early days, she'd put them on the console table outside Laurel and Liza's bedrooms to work on them. Until the time Laurel let loose a blood-curdling scream in the middle of the night about monsters in the hall, that is. After that, Nola kept her creations in her own room. Laurel hadn't been any more afraid of that costume than Liza was. She'd simply been experimenting. Oh, Laurel had been a stinker. They'd both been. They were Nola's girls, after all.

No, Laurel hadn't been afraid of that headdress. Until she'd gotten the diagnosis, she hadn't been afraid of much of anything. She'd rarely cried, either, not even when the headaches that had been plaguing her had gotten bad enough to send her to the doctor. She'd cried when the diagnosis had come in. All three of them had, for Nola and Liza had been with Laurel when the neurologist delivered the news. The empathy in his deep voice hadn't made his words any easier to grasp. A slow-growing tumor was putting pressure deep inside Laurel's brain. Without surgery, she would die. With surgery, she would most likely die. There had been other options, trials, studies, treatments that offered a slight extension of life, along with horrible, grotesque side-effects that would have robbed her of her independence in the months she had left.

There had been no question in Laurel's mind which option she would choose. She would live until she died. Period. That had been almost six years ago. Laurel had been gone nearly five.

Finding herself standing in the middle of her old room, Liza knew she would have done the same thing. Through the window she saw Denise head for her Cadillac and air conditioning. She wasn't rushing Liza. That Denise was all right.

Liza turned in a complete circle. The walls in her old room were painted the colors of the ocean. Dark blues and vivid greens and the murkier shades of deeper water. There were schools of fish and even an old shipwreck, and on her ceiling a mermaid seemed to float in translucent water. Leaving her bedroom behind, she strolled into Laurel's.

Every wall in this room was covered with murals in the lush greens that made up the tropical rain forest. There were fronds and vines and birds and monkeys. The ceiling was a canopy of trees. Liza stood in the middle of it all, peering at the distance between the two rooms. How many times had hairbrushes and hangers and the occasional shoe gone sailing between rooms during those heated, volatile moments of anger and angst? The house had been noisy. How could it have been anything else with three hormonal red-haired artists living and breathing and growing strong under its slate roof?

It had been Nola who had insisted the girls have their own rooms, Nola who had insisted that her identical daughters have their own identities. No look-alike outfits for them; they'd grown up happy and close. They'd started out at UNLV together, but had ended up transferring to colleges in different states. Born first, and according to Nola, squalling, Laurel had begun to make a name for herself in the fast-paced world of newspaper journalism in Chicago. Liza had been quieter and for a long time, weaker. "Not weaker," Nola would often say. "Sickly." As if that was better.

Liza had outgrown that, though, and had settled in wine country along the California coast where she sold her pottery and artwork from her tiny studio that doubled as her apartment.

No matter where she and Laurel lived, this house had always been home. No more.

The Cassidys were down to one. And Liza was moving on. Life without Laurel had been inconceivable. At times it still was. They'd all cried a lot those first months after the diagnosis. They'd gotten a second opinion. And then they'd cried some more. A lot more. One day, Laurel's tears stopped. She'd looked at Liza and said, "I'm dying. But I'm not dead yet." She'd said it again, louder. By the fourth time, Liza had joined in. Nola had rushed in to see what the commotion was about. Soon, all three of them were laughing and singing as they danced around the room. It was amazing the way the saddest times had a way of transforming themselves into the most vibrant and vivid and poignantly beautiful memories.

That day was a turning point for Laurel. She'd taken stock of her life, and had set off to be the curator of her own contentment. Those were her exact words. Laurel had always had a way with words, which was why she'd insisted upon going out east to write the novel that was inside her. Out east. She couldn't have come to California with Liza. Oh, no. Laurel had to seek her inspiration on the rocky Atlantic coast, with its unsullied landscapes and the constantly heaving ocean. It was like Liza had said: The Pacific ocean heaved, too, all the time, in fact. But Laurel had made up her mind, and when that happened, there was no changing it. She was going east alone, and had used every feminine wile she possessed to extract a promise from Liza and Nola not to visit unless she invited them. She needed to do this her way, and no amount of argument or pleading or bribing had budged her decision.

She'd come home, once at Thanksgiving, and again for Christmas. She'd looked good, so good in fact that there had been something almost ethereal about her. Although she slept a lot, she swore the headaches were no worse. After that, they spoke on the phone. And Laurel wrote letters, one nearly every week. As far as Liza knew, that novel never did get written, but those letters were works of art unto themselves, the words lyrical. Week after week Nola and Liza read about the spray of the ocean, the howl of the wind, the ever-changing salt marshes, and the people Laurel met. Liza felt as if she knew Addie and Rose Lawson, two elderly sisters everyone in the small town of Alcott, New Hampshire called "The Aunts," and Skip Hoxie, a former sea captain, and Matilda Kemper, an old woman who'd buried three husbands. Laurel hadn't befriended many young people. Perhaps because she was dying, she'd felt a greater connection with the other old souls. She wrote about one young person, though. His name was Jack McCall. From nearly three thousand miles away, Liza and Nola saw Laurel falling in love with Alcott, and with Jack. Late at night, Liza reread those letters, putting them to memory.

One week, no letter arrived. Fear and dread-filled days passed, one, and then another, and another. Laurel didn't answer her phone. Nola and Liza waited. And then, after nearly three excruciating weeks, the final letters found their way to Nola's and Liza's mailboxes. Liza had known it was the final letter before she'd opened hers. It had been postmarked in Boston, not the tiny town of Alcott, but it was more than that. Maybe there was something to the research about identical twins and a kind of telepathy that existed between them. Regardless of how she'd known, her fingers had shaken as she'd opened the envelope and unfolded the crisp stationary, and stared at her sister's loopy scrawl. *My dearest Liza.* She'd crossed off the My dearest, so it read simply:

Liza. No sense getting maudlin, right? Aw, hell, if I don't have a right to be a little maudlin, who does?

She'd started again.

My dearest Liza,

Well. This is it. The end of my beginning. What do I say to the sister who has understood me (most of the time), encouraged me, cheered me, angered me, and loved me?

Bless you.

And thank you for being in the other half of that egg. And for letting me rant and dream. And thank you for loaning me that little black dress before you'd even worn it, the one I never returned. Thank you for lying to Mom for me. And you're welcome for all the times I returned the favor. Thank you for granting my wish these past months. Lord knows I probably wouldn't have been able to keep such a promise if the situation were reversed.

It's been a truly amazing final year. Do you know what I've learned, Lize? No one, and I mean no one, stops exploring until they're dead. Maybe not even then. I'll have to get back to you on that. Sorry. It's not funny, I know. But I'm not sad. Not like I thought I would be. Back to what I discovered.

I came here to explore my life. And at the end of my quest, I find myself back where I started. Somehow, I think it must be the same for everybody. Everything I thought I knew is false, and it's as if I've reached this place inside me for the first time only to discover that I've been here before. I just didn't know it. Now, I know. And what I know, what I recognize, what I am, is the very thing I've always been searching for, what we're all searching for. What I am, Liza, what we all are, is love.

I know, I know. I could have left you anything, money, jewelry, a winning lottery ticket, and I leave you my puzzling philosophy about life.

I'm sorry for shutting you out. I don't know why, but I had to take this journey alone. Or maybe I'm selfish, and wanted to hoard this blessing I call life to myself as long as possible. I'll leave you to your own conclusions after you sort everything out. God knows you wouldn't take my word for it anyway.

I need you to do me one last favor. I need you to meet Jack. Go to the lighthouse on the Isle of Shoals next Wednesday at noon. You should be awake by then. He'll be waiting. You'll recognize him. Tall, dark and brooding. He'll be angry. That's his MO. Give him a kiss for me. (Gracious, no one can kiss like Jack McCall.) There are blanks he'll fill in for you. Once you've met him, you'll understand why I love him so. Even I don't know why I couldn't explain everything to him. Do that for me, okay?

Oh, and my car? It's yours. And Gran's ruby ring. I can't give you back that little black dress, because I lost it. But you already know the story, just like you know the story of how I lost my first tooth and my virginity. You know all my stories, except for the ones I've left out these past eight months. Jack will fill you in on those.

You're going to love Alcott. And I love you.

Take care of Nola. Tell Jack I tried. And don't forget, give him that kiss from me.

She'd signed it with a flourish of loops and curves that spelled, simply, *Laurel.*

That letter, along with all the others, were in a tin in the back of Laurel's old car. Liza was taking them to Alcott with her. She had a long drive ahead of her, and probably should get started pretty soon.

Dazedly, she strolled out to the hall. She peeked inside her mother's old room, but didn't go any farther. Instead, she opened the door to the attic and climbed the steep steps. It was stuffy and sweltering at the top. She strolled around an old trunk she was leaving for the Bullards, her thoughts turning inward again.

She'd gone to the island on that Wednesday at noon just as Laurel had instructed. She'd waited at the lighthouse all afternoon. The love of Laurel's life hadn't bothered to show up. That evening, Liza had found his number in a phone book, and dialed it up from her hotel room. A woman with a soft, sultry voice had answered. "Hello?" she'd said, and then, "It's okay, Jack-honey. I've got it."

Liza had frozen.

The woman prodded her with another soft, sultry "hello" before Liza lowered the phone. Well, well, well. Laurel's ashes hadn't even settled, and Jack-honey had already moved on.

That had been the end of it for more than four and a half years, and would have been for longer if her mother hadn't been thinking about something else instead of looking out for approaching buses. After the shock of losing Nola had dulled slightly, Liza had come back here to sort things out and decide what to do with the house on Desert Moon Drive.

She hadn't been sleeping well. The therapist she saw in Santa Rosa said it was perfectly understandable. Neither of them knew what to make of the dreams she'd been having for six months, more particularly the fact that a red-haired little boy had been the star in each one. The psychologist had suggested that perhaps subconsciously Liza wanted a baby because she was yearning for a strong physical and emotional bond,

now that Laurel and Nola had died. The explanation
had made sense, until Liza had discovered Laurel's autopsy report along with every important document,
every letter of recognition and artistry award, every receipt, and every birthday card Nola had ever received.
It had taken Liza two weeks to go through everything
in the attic. It had taken only a matter of minutes to
read the autopsy report the neurosurgeon evidently had
sent after Laurel died. Liza had no idea how it had
ended up here in the attic, unopened. Nola had probably had her reasons. Perhaps it had been sadness, or
forgetfulness. The reasons weren't important, not anymore.

The autopsy report was.

Once again, Liza's hands had shaken as she'd
opened it. According to the official report, Laurel had
opted to have the surgery. That was surprising, shocking, because she'd been adamant about NOT having it.
Twenty-eight-year-old Laurel Cassidy had died during
surgery. All her organs were donated per her wishes,
her body cremated. Other than the brain tumor, she'd
been extremely healthy. In fact, the only other scar had
been the result of her recent cesarean section.

Those last three words had staggered Liza.

Laurel had given birth?

When?

How?

And she hadn't bothered to tell Liza? Why the hell
not?

Liza had fumed. She'd ranted. She'd implored the
heavens. And every night, for two more months, she'd
dreamed of a little boy with dark auburn hair, the exact
color hers and Laurel's had been when they were small.

Two months ago, the dreams stopped as abruptly as
they'd started. Liza had to find out why they'd started,
why they'd stopped, and what it all meant.

She would have had her answers a long time ago if

Jack McCall had bothered to show up that day. Thinking about that, she descended the attic stairs and swept out of the house.

Denise met her on the sidewalk. Taking the key from Liza's outstretched hand, Denise said, "Now are you ready?"

Liza looked back toward the house. Was she ready?

She had a sudden memory of the day Laurel left. The hot Nevada sun had pummeled the burnt up grass in the yard much the way it was this morning. Liza had known what Laurel was doing when she'd looked all around at the sidewalk where the two of them had played jump rope, and tattled on the Walsh boys for burning ants with their grandmother's magnifying glass. That last morning, Laurel had taken it all in, putting it to memory, the house, the yard, the sign over the door. She'd looked at Liza and their mother last, and with a hug, a wink, and an all encompassing grin—Laurel always had hated good-byes, she got in her car and drove away. She hadn't looked back.

On a similar morning nearly six years later, Liza, too, looked all around one last time. There was the front walk, the inviting little house, the brown grass, the bubbler and pink flamingo.

Liza's gaze returned to the front stoop. Without stopping to analyze her actions, she rushed up the sidewalk and plucked the gaudy pink flamingo from its perch. After stowing it in the back of Laurel's old car, she rubbed the dust from her hands and climbed behind the wheel. Now, she was ready.

Waving to Denise, the last Cassidy drove away. She didn't look back, either. She looked forward. She was going to Alcott, New Hampshire with its heaving oceans and unsullied landscapes.

Give Jack a kiss for me, Laurel had written.

Liza didn't know with whom she was more angry, her darling, daring, deviant sister, or Jack-honey McCall.

"Give him a kiss?" she muttered to the dash. No way in hell. A punch in the nose, now that was a distinct possibility.

It would take at least four days to drive to the East Coast. That should give her plenty of time to decide just how much she hated Jack McCall.

More by Best-selling Author
Fern Michaels

Discover the Thrill of
Romance with
Lisa Plumley

__Making Over Mike
0-8217-7110-8 $5.99US/$7.99CAN
Amanda Connor is a life coach—not a magician! Granted, as a
publicity stunt for her new business, the savvy entrepreneur has
promised to transform some poor slob into a perfectly balanced
example of modern manhood. But Mike Cavaco gives "raw material"
new meaning.

__Falling for April
0-8217-7111-6 $5.99US/$7.99CAN
Her hometown gourmet catering company may be in a slump, but
April Finnegan isn't about to begin again. Determined to save her
business, she sets out to win some local sponsors, unaware she's not
the only one with that idea. Turns out wealthy department store mogul
Ryan Forrester is one step—and thousands of dollars—ahead of her.

__Reconsidering Riley
0-8217-7340-2 $5.99US/$7.99CAN
Jayne Murphy's best-selling relationship manual *Heartbreak 101* was
inspired by her all-too-personal experience with gorgeous, capable . . .
outdoorsy . . . Riley Davis, who stole her heart—and promptly skipped
town with it. Now, Jayne's organized a workshop for dumpees. But it
becomes hell on her heart when the leader for her group's week-long
nature jaunt turns out to be none other than a certain . . .